WOUNDS IN THE SKY I

THE DRAGON HUNTER AND THE MAGE

V. R. CARDOSO

Tittle: The Dragon Hunter and the Mage
Author: V. R. Cardoso
ISBN: 978-15-4239-720-9

Editors: Cate Courtright, Jack Lartin, Richard Shealy
Cover Illustrator: Yin Yumming
Map Illustrator: Tad Davis
Cover Graphic Design: Alexandre Rito
Graphic Design: O Alfredo é Fixe – Design Studio

www.vrcardoso.com

To my parents, for all the support.

N

20 10

A R R

Nosta

70

C A N D I A

Aparanta

60

T h e P i a

Ragara

W

40

Arkhemia

30

0 200

SCALE IN MILES

S

10
20
30
Fausta
Augusta
SAMEhRIA
Capra
Samehr
Niveh
E
Sandahar
Saggad
Awam
Engadi
Belleragar
AKhAM
Ashan
CYRINIA
Nish
Mahari
Desert
2015

PROLOGUE

The Purge

Three knocks at the gate.

"Pherlam, open the gates!"

Three more knocks: quick, dry, demanding.

"Pherlam, this is madness. Open the gates."

From a neighborhood not very far away came screams, first of surprise, then of fear and pain.

"Pherlam, if you surrender yourselves now, you will be treated fairly."

"Fairly? Like they treated the mages of Augusta? Of Victory?"

Inside the courtyard, Pherlam stormed from one side to the other as if he were trying to carve a path on the cobblestone. Outside the school's walls, three smoke columns rose up from the city.

"How they treated everyone in the school of Saggad?" he continued. "Uh, Tigern? Every member of the school. Even apprentices, Tigern. Children!"

"That was in the beginning. The emperor was nervous, fearful. Things are much calmer now."

"Calmer?!" Pherlam exploded. "Look around you, Tigern. The whole city is in a riot."

"Yes, it is. And it is about to turn against you, you old fool! Open the gates. I can't promise you everyone will be saved, but at least the youngest, the uninitiated, will be."

Pherlam slowed down to a halt and took a deep breath as he looked around. The courtyard was peaceful. There were no nervous stares glaring out the window, no movement besides that of the curtains shaken by the wind, no sounds except those that came from outside, from the city.

Tersia stepped forward and placed a hand on Pherlam's shoulder. She had the hood of her gray robe over her head as if it could somehow protect her from what was coming.

"We should prepare," she said.

Pherlam felt the hairs on the back of his neck stand up. Tersia was a vain woman and the enchantments covering her were easily felt.

There were three more knocks at the gate.

"Pherlam, open the gates. Pherlam…are you there?"

"I'm here, old friend…." He paused. "And here I will remain."

There was a moment of silence.

"I see… I'm sorry."

"So am I."

This time, there was no silence, because somewhere in the city a crowd broke into screaming. Tigern turned around and looked over his shoulder at those stubborn gates, but could not bring himself to say goodbye.

From her window at the top of the student's tower, the city looked almost beautiful. Eliran knew that everything she saw was the fruit of violence, that there were pain and suffering in every street. But still, it was like looking at a moving version of the paintings of the main hall. The fires made columns of black smoke dance upward until they dissolved into the sky. Destruction had splashed the empty squares with colors that didn't belong there. On the riot-clogged streets, the mounted guards and the crowd danced back and forth in hypnotizing movements while, outside the city walls, the emperor's legionaries marched in a tight formation, like blocks of iron self-assembling bit by bit. Behind them, catapults hurled fireballs that left arching trails of smoke until they crashed down, splashing somewhere in the city like buckets of red and orange paint. Eliran wondered if that was also what it looked like when a dragon spat fire.

Inside her dormitory, none of the other students made a single sound or movement. They were all nestled in their beds, just as they had been told, their eyes wide and their arms tightly around themselves. Eliran wasn't any less scared or anxious, but she couldn't just lie on her bed, not with a window only a few feet away, because after two weeks locked inside the school, it had become the only way to go outside.

The dormitory door swung open and every girl turned toward it as a Grand Wizardess's dark green tunic glided in.

"You are all to report immediately to the courtyard. Dress in your own clothes. Leave school tunics and accessories here."

The Grand Wizardess disappeared back through the door. For a moment, all the apprentices could do was exchange nervous glances, until Eliran dove into her personal chest. She opened it and rummaged inside, looking for clothes. Her colleagues did the same. There were a few sighs and a couple of sobs, but no one said a word. Eliran saw several hands shaking and even a tear sliding down the pale cheek of a novice girl.

When the floor was covered in white and light blue tunics, Eliran headed toward the door, the other girls following her out to the corridor. They turned the first corner and a group of ten Initiates came through the male corridor. The dormitory delegate leading them looked so pale, Eliran was sure he would faint before reaching the stairwell.

He didn't. Instead, he trotted down with the quick, apathetic, and consistent step of someone who had done it thousands of times.

The apprentices from the twenty dormitories – novices and initiates – arrived at the courtyard almost at the same time, arranging themselves into formation just like they did every week for evaluation. Eliran, however, did not remember them ever doing it so efficiently.

At the center of the courtyard, Arch-Mage Tersia faced them, arms crossed, as tall as one of the pillars holding the school building up. One other wizard stood beside her. Behind the two of them, as if it were perfectly normal, Arch-Mages and Grand Wizards carried barrels, chairs, and cupboard, placing them against the school's main gate. Eliran was sure she had never seen them carry anything heavier than a fork.

"What is happening is no secret to any of you." Tersia's voice thundered all over the yard as she spoke. "You've heard the news, heard the rumors. They are all true. There is no point in pretending...."

Somewhere among the apprentices, a cry burst out.

"Guira, stop that!" Tersia commanded. "I will not listen to one single sob." She waited for the girl to swallow her weeping. "It has been decided that until sunrise, all apprentices will abandon the school. Hide. Don't show yourselves. Don't even try to mingle with the crowd. The Legions should leave the camp around the city within days. Only after that should you try to escape Niveh."

Tersia stopped for a moment, examining her audience. Over two hundred young wizards, frightened and confused. What would happen to them? How many would survive, and of those who did, what sort of life could they hope to have?

"Each dormitory must stay together and follow their delegate's instructions. However, if you see another dormitory, leave them. Don't band together. They will be looking for large groups of young boys and girls."

The wizard beside Tersia unfolded his arms and spoke.

"Delegates, step forward to collect some equipment and receive your final instructions."

Eliran and the other nineteen dormitory delegates advanced. Behind Tersia was a pile of satchels, and they gathered around it, each taking one at random.

"Pay attention. You can search the satchels after this. Obviously, we can't remove you from the school through any of the gates. However, there is a tunnel that goes under the school. A sanitation tunnel..."

"You mean a sewer?" Eliran asked.

"A sewer," the wizard confirmed. "The tunnel flows out to the river, between Fruit Square and Iron Street. Each dormitory will depart in half-hour intervals. You must pay special attention when leaving the tunnel. If any of you is detected, everyone coming behind you is doomed. Find a place to spend the night quickly, and whatever happens, do not leave until the sun rises. Understood?"

The wizard waited for a collective nod and wished them all good luck. Each delegate returned to their group. Eliran stuck an arm into her satchel and tried to make a mental list of its contents. She was happy to find a flask of runium. There were also some cookies, coins, and a dagger. Eliran removed it and inspected its blade.

"What is that?"

Rissa was a novice and wasn't even ten years of age yet. She had been surprisingly calm up until this moment, but now she was staring at the dagger with her eyes so wide open, they seemed about to pop out.

"We may need it to unlock a door."

The little girl seemed happy with the answer, and even though Eliran knew that was a lie, the truth was that she couldn't picture herself using it in any other way.

⌒⌒

Tigern walked down the cobbled street, ignoring the wreckage around his feet. What little sunlight still peered over the walls of Niveh was disappearing, making the alleyways even darker. He could still hear the occasional screams, and at least two fires were close enough that he could smell the smoke.

The figure waiting for him was standing beside a horse, holding it by the reins. Behind him were a smashed barricade and half a dozen stinking corpses, two of them wearing city guard uniforms.

"I did what I could," Tigern said. "The school's gates will remain closed."

"No. No, they won't."

"No, they won't," Tigern agreed. "There are a dozen Arch-Mages in that school. Plus thirty Grand Wizards and a hundred and something initiated wizards. A lot of blood will flow before this is over."

"Intila has more soldiers than he can waste. All he needs is to get into the city."

"Intila is here?"

"He arrived this afternoon."

"The emperor must be truly confident that it is all over, if he is letting his guard dog come play this far from the capital," Tigern said. He looked back at the spy and tried not to stare at the hideous scar that disfigured the corner of his mouth. He removed a rolled piece of parchment from his jacket and handed it to him. "When the temple strikes midnight, every banner along the city wall will be removed. At that moment, the city guard will leave the walls and open the gates."

"And the duke?"

"No one knows."

The spy grabbed the rolled parchment Tigern handed him, mounting his horse as a satisfied smile twisted his scar even further.

"Have a good night, treasurer. After an incident such as this, it's safe to assume the emperor will declare the end of the Niveh Duchy. After all, the entire ducal family is missing…." He trailed off as the horse danced beneath the spy impatiently. "If I had to bet, I would say he will transform Niveh into an Imperial province. These hereditary lands have no place in a modern empire." Then, as if he suddenly remembered something, he added, "Is there any prominent citizen in Niveh you can think of for the position of governor?"

Tigern did not answer.

"No? Well…in my opinion, it should be someone experienced, who knows the city's issues."

"Hamur…" Tigern said, "men like me pay men like you to *not have an opinion.*"

The moon was so full and bright that no one had remembered to light up the torches in the courtyard. Eliran was happy for that, at least. She had no idea what she would do, or where to go, but at least they wouldn't have to feel their way across the alleys. Dormitory number eighteen was sitting in a circle, singing softly. She looked at her own dormitory girls and wondered if they should do the same, if maybe singing could distract them. They were looking around, eyes lost as if they were waiting for someone to arrive.

Maybe they still believed someone would come and tell them that it had all been a big mistake, that everything was going back to normal.

A wizard in a dark blue tunic came through the door that led to the kitchens, baths, and latrines.

"Dormitory number eighteen, come with me."

The chant of the twelve boys died awkwardly and they stood up. Allard, their delegate, glanced at Eliran. There was fear in his big blue eyes, but still the boy found the courage to smile at her.

"IN THE NAME OF TARSUS V, OPEN THE GATES!"

Tersia pushed the boys from dormitory eighteen into the corridor, and a dozen wizards hurried to the main gate. They heard the crash of a battering ram pounding against the wood, and Eliran watched Pherlam approach the apprentices who were left. She had always thought that he looked too young for a headmaster, but the school of Niveh was famous for its illusion spells, and she suspected that his looks were probably not entirely his.

The voice from outside spoke with the authority of someone reading instructions. "Open the gates, surrender, and you will be treated in accordance with the law!"

"What are these apprentices still doing here?" Pherlam asked.

"We can't make them leave all at once," Tersia replied.

"Well, we can't have them in here for much longer, so get them out. Now."

Once again, the thundering sound of the battering ram echoed across the courtyard and Pherlam returned to his post. Tersia called the remaining two dormitories, glancing anxiously at the wizards gathering in front of the main gate and the apprentices surrounded her.

"We can't wait another half-hour," she said.

Eliran's heart suddenly became much heavier.

"We will have to get you all out at the same time. Try to separate as soon as you reach the river. Dormitory nineteen goes one way, dormitory twenty goes another."

As she finished her sentence, a burning projectile crashed in the courtyard, breaking and spreading its fuel everywhere. Some wizards put the small fires out with a hand wave as if dismissing them, and while they did, the furniture blocking the gate jumped with another blast from the battering ram.

Tersia put a soft hand on Eliran's face and every hair on her body stood up. "Now go."

The wizard with the blue tunic signaled them to follow him, and Eliran felt Tersia's hand pull her back. The Arch-Mage dropped a scroll of parchment in her hand.

"This is for you, and only you," Tersia told her.

Eliran didn't even have time to ask a question before Tersia turned her around and pushed her after the rest of her dormitory girls. At that moment, she was sure her heart forgot to beat, but she stepped forward nonetheless.

The dark corridor swallowed them, and suddenly several tiny blue lights flickered into existence. Low-ranking wizards were lining the walls, each holding a sphere of light. Eliran knew that spell.

"Go on, little ones," encouraged one of the wizards.

They went through two hallways, past the access to the cantina, and once they arrived at the latrines, the corridor officially became a sewer. They stepped down a ladder and landed in a tunnel whose floor was a knee-deep river, the noxious smell rising around them. There was one last wizard down there, and he pointed in one direction.

"Go that way," he said. "The exit to the river is right beneath a bridge, so you will have to dive in and swim to the other side. There you will find a small dock."

The delegate of dormitory twenty stepped forward determinedly and his boys followed him, but Eliran hesitated. She looked back at the wizard and realized that he couldn't be much older than she. Two, three years at maximum. Eliran herself should graduate within a year.

"I should stay and fight beside you."

The wizard took a little while to reply. There was no despair in his eyes, but there was no hope either.

"You can't help us...but you can help them."

Flara, a nine-year-old novice, grabbed Eliran's sleeve and pulled, somewhat brutishly.

"Eli, please..."

"Eli, come with us," Rissa sobbed.

Eliran sighed. She smiled at them and told them not to worry. She took Flara and Rissa by the hand and took them away, looking back over her shoulder to see the wizard climb the ladder back to the school. There was no one up there to force him to come back. No one to stop him from following her, from saving himself.

⟋

The duke's palace had been looted. Almost everything worth anything was gone. Tapestries and paintings had been ripped, broken, or somehow deformed. The few doors still standing had had their locks broken, and most of the furniture was either cracked or missing. Tigern walked through several corridors beneath the inexpressive eyes of Legionaries until he found the door to the duke's study. Inside, he saw the Imperial Marshal rolling a chair over with a kick, revealing a forgotten silver jar.

"Ah, Tigern, at last."

Marshal Intila was a tall and powerful man. His golden armor had the Imperial lion sculpted in his chest, and the cape flowing down his back had the light blue of Augusta's Legion's.

"I need names, Tigern."

"Names? Of what?"

Intila sighed and walked over to the duke's secretary – a bloc of ebony too robust and heavy to suffer at the hands of the mob that had pillaged the palace.

"The emperor's orders were refused. Then Imperial agents were arrested, just for trying to uphold those orders. And finally, when my Legions arrived, the city was closed. I had to mount a siege."

"And the lord of the city, the duke, is nowhere to be found," Tigern replied. "The city is yours again. What other names do you require?"

"I cannot return to Augusta empty-handed. Someone has to pay," Intila said. "You are not going to convince me that the duke was alone in all this."

"Of course he wasn't. Even the people supported him until the Legionaries arrived." Tigern aimed a finger at Intila. "I was guaranteed you would be reasonable if the problem was taken care of."

"You're not behind bars," Intila said matter-of-factly. "Even though you are a member of the city's government. I would say that part of the agreement is being kept."

Tigern paused. He couldn't believe what he was hearing. "How am I supposed to take over the city if I don't have the trust of the noble families?"

"Listen to me," Intila said. "The emperor cannot afford to not punish the families who openly affronted him. I am here, Tigern. Me and not others. You know there are others far less reasonable than me."

Openly affronted him? Tigern wanted to scream. Those families had done only what any decent human would have done. Tarsus was a tyrant, and his Purge was an unforgivable crime. If Tigern were a brave man, he would have said so.

"How many names?" he asked instead. "Is two enough? I want you to assure me their families will be spared."

Intila said no with a shake of his head. There was no irony or malice in his expression, just the pragmatism of a soldier.

"Tigern, rebels are like dragons. The problems they don't cause today will become twice as bad tomorrow. That's why we hunt dragons, and that's why you will tell me all the names. All of them."

⌒

They had been hiding in that shack for three hours and their clothes were still wet. It had taken them too long to find a place to hide, and twice they had almost crossed paths with Legionary patrols. On a square that Eliran thought was the fruit market, she had seen the body of Allard lying over a pool of dark blood, his blue eyes staring at infinity. She was the only one who had seen him, because as soon as she recognized him, she turned the girls around and fled though an alleyway, where they crouched in the shadow until the clanking sounds of a patrol drove them off.

She didn't really know what the place was, but it looked abandoned, and at least it protected them from the skin-slicing wind. To warm themselves, they nested against each other, but Eliran made sure she was the only one with a view to the hill where the school rose. It was visible through a slit in a closed window, but the scenery was terrifying. Red fire, black smoke, green lights, blue explosions, and the most sinister noises Eliran had ever heard. It had been going on for hours.

Flara had cried uninterruptedly for a whole hour, as had Sarina, Lassira, and Tajiha. Now they slept deeply, claimed by exhaustion. Eliran herself was making an effort to stay awake, as if that macabre spectacle was a vigil she was bound by duty to attend.

Suddenly, a noise distracted her. It was just a small crackle, but it was close enough to make her stomach tighten. Then the door spun open, and a man with a messy grey beard entered the shack. Confusion took over the stranger's face for a moment.

"What's this? What are you doing here?"

Eliran jumped up and the other girls did the same.

"I am so sorry. We thought this was abandoned."

"Abandoned? My house?"

"M-my apologies," Eliran mumbled. "That's not what I meant."

The man grabbed the girl closest to him, Rissa, by her arm, making her scream.

"Who are you?" he asked.

Eliran felt alarm flash through her, but going back to the Legionary-filled streets wasn't something she looked forward to.

"We just need to spend the night. We won't cause you any trouble...."

"Won't cause any trouble?" The man pulled Rissa closer to him and she squirmed. "Who are you hiding from? The soldiers?"

"From no one." Eliran had her eyes fixed on Rissa. The man was clearly hurting her. "Please let her go."

"It's the soldiers, isn't it?" The man smiled. "Yes... You're little wizard-esses, aren't you? And if the Legionaries catch you, they'll snap your little necks." To demonstrate, he took Rissa's neck and squeezed it.

"Let her go now!" Eliran stuck her hand in her satchel and fumbled inside, looking for the flask of runium. She would need it to cast a spell, put him to sleep, whatever.

"Shush, little wizardess. Do you want the soldiers to hear you?"

Eliran's arm fiddled inside the satchel. She caught coins, cookies, more coins.

"You are all going to be very quiet if you don't want to end up like your teachers." Once again, he squeezed Rissa's neck until she turned blue. Then he pointed at Lassira. "You, take off your shirt."

Like a flock of birds, every girl took a step back.

Eliran was about to give up and throw a bunch of coins in the man's face – *where was the damn flask?* – until she touched something cold. She wrapped her fingers around the object and felt the blade's metal. Desperate, she pulled it out and held it awkwardly in front of herself.

The man's eyes became wide, and in that moment, she realized he was drunk. He let Rissa go and stepped toward Eliran. She aimed the knife at him defiantly.

"What do you think you're going to do with that?"

He was a big man, and his nose bore the marks of many tavern brawls. He advanced toward her, his hand ready to grab her wrist. At first, Eliran stepped back out of fear, then out of her own will. The man chased her until she was cornered against a wall. At the last moment, Eliran stepped forward instead of backward.

Caught off balance, the man didn't even see Eliran grab the knife with both hands and swing it up, clumsily, until the blade drove itself through the man's chin into his mouth. He howled in pain, grabbed the knife's handle, and pulled it off. A jet of blood gushed from it.

The wizard apprentices panicked and screamed hysterically. Not even Eliran managed not to.

Scared from the pain and the streaming blood, confused by the screams, the man dashed off in a random direction, bumped into a window, and fell from it.

Eliran grabbed her satchel firmly, took Rissa by the hand, and rushed out the door. The other girls didn't require her to tell them to do the same.

⌒

It wasn't hard to understand why the mages had told them they could only step out from their hideouts when the sun came up. The streets quickly filled with people and life. With the exception of the physical signs of violence from the previous days, everything seemed to have gone back to normal. A group of children strolling down the street looked completely commonplace. Still, though, the city was covered with Legionaries and Eliran thought it best to leave the girls behind a fish stall that, apparently, had lost its owner during the riots.

Accompanied by Flara alone, Eliran looked for ways to leave the city. She talked to merchants planning to restock somewhere south and asked the price of hiding in the potato carts of a couple of farmers from a neighboring village. She discovered there were spice caravans headed for Saggad within two days, and eventually arrived at Fyrian Square, from where people could climb Mage Street, the one that led to the school of magic. Flara was scared out of her mind and stayed by the entrance to an inn, but Eliran walked right up to the center of the square.

At first, she pretended to examine the statue at its center, where five dragon hunters defeated a colossal Eastern Short-tail. Then she found the courage to approach the exit to Mage Street. Even at that distance, it was very obvious that not much of the majestic building was left. Only one of its five towers was still standing, and even that one was missing a third of its original height. From the ruin, columns of smoke still rose, and what had once been the main gate was now dust beneath the boots of a dozen Legionaries. They were formed up rigidly, blocking the access to the smoldering building.

Eliran wanted to see it, to search the building for survivors. What if there were people trapped in the basement or the underground tunnels? She could go around the back, use some distraction spell, or maybe wait for night to fall....

Her planning was interrupted by a panicking Flara.

"Please, let's get out of here," the little girl begged.

Sighing, Eliran did as she asked. The two of them talked with a couple of other potential rides out of Niveh and finally decided to join the other girls. They were exactly as Eliran had left them, and it was as if they were even more scared than the night before. Eliran wondered if that wasn't her case as well. After all, what was she was going to do? Where could she go? Was it safe to return to her family in Ragara? What if the emperor had arrested them for being the parents of a girl with the Talent? What would she live off if she really was alone? How was she going to hide the fact that she was a mage for the rest of her life?

"Where are we going?" Eliran asked the girls.

By the looks on their faces, the question hadn't occurred to them yet. They had been all too happy to let Eliran make all the decisions for them. Shouldn't she decide that as well?

"I can't decide where each of us goes," she explained.

"But...aren't we going to stay together?" asked Rissa.

"We can't," said Flara. "I want to go home, to my parents. We should all find our families."

Sarina agreed.

"My family was arrested," said Tajiha, staring at the ground.

"We should head west," said Lassira. "They say the school in Awam is still functioning."

"That's a lie," Flara replied. "No school survived."

The twelve apprentices broke into a discussion over whether there were any schools left or not until Eliran silenced them with a yell.

"We're going north. To avoid the Legions, the best way out of the city is through the river, and the river goes either to the north or to the Shamissai

Mountains, so we're going north. After that, anyone who wants to go a different way can go. Anyone who wants to finds their parents can look for them. Anyone who wants to find the school in Awam can do that as well."

Everyone agreed, and shortly after, they were headed for the docks. There was a boatman who intended to transport wine barrels to Augusta, and whose barge had more than enough room for all of them.

"Twenty-five golden crowns, here you are."

The boatman took the coins and felt their weight.

"Yes, but now it's fifty."

"Fifty?" Eliran couldn't believe it. "We agreed twenty-four, two for each person, and I'm offering you an extra coin."

"Yes, but that was before I knew you were all children."

Eliran felt her stomach turn and her face became as red as a pepper. "What difference does that make?"

"It makes all the difference," the boatman replied. "I don't know if, for some reason, you're running from the authorities." As if to prove his point, he stared ostensibly at two Legionaries leaning against a nearby wall.

Eliran wanted to shove the idiot in the water and watch him drown. Instead, she turned around and stuck a hand in her satchel.

"Let me see what money I still have," she said with her back to him.

The boatman smiled.

Eliran searched for a little while and finally found the runium flask she so desperately had wished for the night before. She opened it and took a generous sip from it. Confused, Rissa opened her mouth, but Flara covered it before she had time to blurt out anything.

Eliran turned back around to face the boatman.

"I have exactly what you need."

She held out her hand and the boatman looked curiously at it. When Eliran opened her hand, all the man saw was a flash of light, quicker than a blink of an eye. The boatman was ecstatic.

"Oh, my lady! For that money, I'll take you to south Aletia, if I have to." With a smile the size of the world, he indicated the way to his barge.

"This way, please. Go right ahead, little mistresses. Careful with that step. That's right. Feel right at home."

They all embarked and sat down on the deck. All except Eliran, who remained on the dock.

"Eli?" Flara was confused.

"Good luck, girls. Hope to see you all one day."

The boatman jumped to the barge, still smiling, and placed himself aft of the ship.

Rissa looked about to cry. "Eli, where are you going? What's wrong?"

"Take care of them, Flara," Eliran said, then she snapped her fingers and the boatman untied the ship and propelled it away from the dock.

"Eli, please!" Rissa begged. Flara had to hold her.

Eliran waved as the boat sailed away, but she was unable to hold the girls' sad stares for very long.

She turned around and left.

CHAPTER I

The Half-Prince

Aric could see the inner courtyard five stories below him. Two men circled each other with swords held high, their bodies tense, ready to spring into action. Without warning, the shortest one struck directly at the other's head. The rest was a mess of wooden swords smacking against each other until the fake blade of one of them hit the other's wrist. Aric heard another series of smacks, but this time, they were right next to him.

"Your class is up here, my prince." Old Macael was probably the only person who called him that.

The professor pointed at a parchment filled with geometrical shapes and numbers. Aric followed his twig-like fingers and examined the values before him, adding some numbers in his head, moved a few pieces in his abacus, then ended up sighing, defeated. Macael gave him a look that demanded more than that, but Aric paid him no attention. Down below, the inner courtyard witnessed a pirouette that finished with a sword smashing uselessly against a shield. What did he care about the height of that triangle? And if it was so important, why couldn't he just measure it with a ruler?

"You can stand there sighing all afternoon, but I'll still have to give you this lesson and my prince will still have to hear it. Might as well pay attention and learn something."

"Why can't I learn how to fight instead?" Aric asked.

"I'm afraid that's not something I can teach you," Macael replied.

Aric sank in his chair, hugging his abacus.

"That's not what I meant," Aric said, staring down at the combat in the courtyard.

"I know..." Macael replied. "The goddess gives us all a different role to play. It's up to us to enjoy it as best we can. There's no point in envying what other people do."

At that moment, a sword smacked squarely on the head of one of the warriors in the courtyard, knocking him down and making his helmet fly. Aric laughed.

"The goddess should have given Fadan faster legs."

This time, it was Macael who gave up, rolling the parchment with his circles, triangles, and hexagons.

"Well, I think I've had enough of trying to compete for your attention today. You may go."

Aric's face lit up. He threw his abacus onto the table and jumped toward the door.

"My prince!" Macael called. Aric stopped halfway through the door. "It might be better if you don't get too close to the courtyard."

Aric's face darkened again. He gave a dull nod and disappeared.

⌒

Intila, High Marshal of the emperor's Legions, watched the light pouring in through the stained-glass window behind the massive oak table where the council met. The glasswork consisted of a very colorful depiction of the siege of Victory. Intila was sure that whoever had lived through the event would have witnessed no other color beside arid brown and blood red. Yet, on that three-story window, the last great battle of the unification of the Empire looked more like a tribute to spring than a faithful representation of the historical siege.

As usual, Chancellor Vigild read an unending list of reports, missives, and related documents, so the marshal took the opportunity to examine the fragments that made the stained glass, each one meticulously cut to achieve its particular form. He calculated that it was the millionth time he had done so.

Beside the emperor, there were five other people attending the meeting. Fressia, the emperor's secretary, was furiously scribbling down everything that happened. Scava, the treasurer, slept in silence. Seneschal Daria was organizing several piles of documents in preparation for her own briefing of the council. And finally, there were Admiral Cassena and Constable Fervus, two creatures Intila considered most useful exactly as they were right now – blankly staring at nothing with their mouths open.

"Apparently, our agents in Imuria haven't gone mad. There truly is a king, or chieftain, or whatever they call him, who has gathered over fifteen tribes under his banner." Vigild threw the piece of parchment onto the table as if he was about to yawn. "Naturally, the Aletines are in a panic." He grabbed another document but was suddenly interrupted.

"Well, that sounds important…" Cassena said, unsurely. "Maybe I should put the Eastern Fleet on alert?" The admiral faced Intila, looking for help, but didn't get as much as a glance in return, so he found himself facing the piercing eyes of the emperor instead.

Tarsus was a tall man whose flesh had been consumed by worries, leaving nothing but bone beneath his pale skin. His long hair, slightly below his shoulders, was no longer black, but streaked with grey, just like his beard.

"Alert?" Tarsus asked. "Because of half a dozen barbarians?"

The Admiral trembled and tried to mumble out, "Well… it is known that, I mean, historically speaking, these unifications… In fact, during your great-great grandfather's… No, before that…."

It was Intila who put him out of his misery, placing a hand on his shoulder to quiet him down. The poor man simply let himself wilt.

"Moving on…" Vigild said. "We have the issue of the tax collection in South Ake."

"Issue?" the emperor asked.

"There have been problems with tax collection among the farmers in South Ake," Vigild explained. "It's nothing unusual. These situations tend to happen after a tax hike."

"We increased taxes? When?"

"Two months ago, Your Majesty," Vigild replied.

"Where does that report come from?" Intila asked.

"It's not a report. It's a letter from the Duke of Ashan." Vigild returned to the document and read out loud, "Upheavals across the plateau, yada yada yada… was forced to mobilize my guard, etc., etc. Marching on the revolting farmers –"

"The Duke of Ashan with an army? Marching?" The emperor suddenly lost his color.

"To pacify a revolt, Your Majesty," Intila said.

"Excuses!" Tarsus slammed his fist against the table so hard, Intila was sure the emperor would have blood on his knuckles. "Duke Amrul is a traitor. He supported and protected mages openly during the Purge. This is a display of strength." He stopped for a moment, his eyes obsessing over the horizon. "The tax hike is nothing but an excuse. He probably intends to turn the population against me."

The council members exchanged a few looks. Unsure about what to write on the minute, Fressia asked, "Majesty… what… how should I register that?"

Tarsus V, Emperor of Arrel, paused and studied the face of each of his councilors.

"It is unacceptable!" he said at last. "I cannot allow the lord of some half a dozen acres of land the right to command his own military forces."

The table was silent. Intila felt his spine freeze and saw Vigild raising his eyebrows.

"Majesty…it's the distribution of powers. It has always been like this –" Intila said.

"Fire take the distribution of powers!" Tarsus exploded. "There can be only one power in the Empire. *The emperor's.* Distribution" – he sneered – "what do the dukes and counts want with an army? Are they planning to invade a foreign country?" Intila was going to explain but Tarsus didn't allow it. "They want to challenge their emperor! That's the distribution they seek."

No one was brave enough to reply, and Vigild didn't even seem interested in doing so, but Intila could not hold himself back.

"Majesty…we've had this discussion dozens of times. They want to protect themselves. They want a guarantee that the emperor won't just take everything for himself."

"They will have my personal guarantee it won't happen," Tarsus argued.

"With respect, *my* lord, but after the Purge –" Intila suddenly felt an urge to choose his words carefully. "After the prohibition of magic…they won't understand."

Tarsus punched the table once again. "It has been ten years! The Purge is nothing but a memory."

"A memory of rebellion and insurrection, Your Majesty. Thousands of dead. Dozens of noble houses annihilated. Not to mention…" Intila paused a moment, but he was no coward. "Not to mention the hundreds of wizards that were executed."

"Traitors, all of them!" Tarsus turned to Vigild with a burning stare. "I want a law drafted within the month."

The chancellor nodded respectfully.

"I'm afraid I must protest, Your Majesty." Intila took a deep breath and prepared himself to elaborate, but Vigild cut him off.

"Worst-case scenario, every count and duke raises his army against the emperor." Tarsus froze at the sound of that as Vigild continued. "Would the Legions not be able to contain them?"

If he weren't such a proud man, the marshal would have been offended by that question.

"If the Legions march, no army will stop them," the Marshal declared. "We will scale the Phermian Mountains with our bare hands, cross them on foot, destroy the combined might of the Imurites and Aletines, and occupy the whole of Arkhemia if the emperor so wishes. But this is…"

"Then we are fully prepared for the worst possible outcome." Vigild smiled. He gave the emperor a pleasant bow. "I shall have the law drafted as you ordered, Your Majesty."

Tarsus looked relieved and Intila slumped in his chair with a sigh. He turned around to the stained-glass window beside him, where the battle for

Victory still raged colorfully. His mind was flooded with countless corpses hanging from the emperor's gallows, oceans of flames swallowing entire cities, and rivers of blood covering the streets.

Aric ran down the spiral staircase of the Green Tower. The emperor's wizards had called the tower home for centuries, but only a dozen tutors lived there now, all of them non-magic. Once at the base of the tower, he ran toward the courtyard of the Core Palace, sneaking in through one of the corridors that fed the hundreds of rooms of the building. He climbed two stories and reached the outermost corridor of the west wing. The sun was so low, it was almost impossible to stare directly at it through the windows.

The walls were lined with stone statues the size of real men. Aric walked through them. He passed a general with the Imperial lion roaring on his chest, a chancellor reading from a scroll, a Dragon Hunter with a spear over his shoulder, and finally, he stopped in front of a peasant armed with a fork in one hand and the flag of Arrel in the other. He didn't even bother checking to see if someone was watching him before he removed the flag from the peasant's hand, untied the cloth with the Arreline arms, and ran back to the staircase with the flagpole in his hands.

He lunged down the stairs with impetuous pirouettes, swinging the pole from one side to the other. He slashed, parried, and thrust through the air, knocking down a dozen enemies, until he landed back in the great hall. At that moment, the gate creaked and Fadan, all dressed for war, stepped in, followed by his combat instructor. His head was wrapped up in bloody bandages.

"Aric!" he called with a smile. "I took a real beating today."

Aric smiled back. "Nah, you were great."

"You saw?"

"I was having a class with old Macael."

Fadan's instructor moved uncomfortably but didn't have the courage to interrupt them.

"Oh, then you must have seen my whole training." The two laughed. Fadan motioned his chin toward the flagpole. "Were you practicing?"

Aric hid the pole behind his back. "No…of course not." He blushed.

There was an uncomfortable silence when Fadan was unable to reply; a voice seized the moment of silence.

"The prince should clean himself up. Dinner will be served briefly."

Fadan rolled his eyes. Sometimes, he could swear Sagun spied his every move. He said goodbye to Aric and left, followed by his instructor, who was stopped by a piercing stare from Sagun.

"Next time, do not allow these conversations to last this long." He pointed at Aric as if he was a shelf. "Grab the boy and force him away if you must." He gave the instructor leave to go and turned to Aric. "It's not proper for you to delay the prince. The emperor is most punctual."

"It is also not proper to talk about someone as if he isn't there when he is."

The castellan's eyes narrowed. "Your dinner will be ready in the kitchens. You may go as soon as…" He looked down at Aric's flagpole. "…you finish your weapons training."

Sagun turned around, making his black braid twirl around him as he walked away.

Aric watched him leave, picturing a thousand ways to use his "weapons training" on Sagun.

The sun was still refusing to set, so Aric wandered around the castle. He roamed through corridors and stairwells, visited empty halls, and peeked through the locks of immovable doors. It was a familiar ritual; one he did with most of his free time. Sometimes, he would leave the Core Palace and visit one of the smaller palaces in the Citadel. The empty ones were his favorites.

He sat on a battlement, watching the sun disappear behind the countless towers of the city of Augusta. Then he considered visiting his mother, but she would be getting ready for dinner. The emperor demanded that she be always glamorous. Sometimes, though, she excused herself from dinner, claiming to be sick, then found a way to tell Aric, who would then sneak into her room so they could eat together.

But today wasn't one of those days. He decided to go to the library. He enjoyed reading about the Empire's expansion and the various wars that had led to the unification. His favorite book told of the second war of Akham and the conquest of Saggad, where one his ancestors, Geric Auron, had scaled the walls of the city alone and under the cover of darkness. The book ended with Geric opening the gate from the inside, with half a dozen spears sticking out of his chest. On that day, an Auron had been a hero of the Empire.

He walked along the bookshelves but none caught his attention, and he ended up sitting on the floor in front of a massive tapestry covering an entire wall of the library. In it, a dragon had been painted sleeping in a cave. On the lower left corner, hiding behind a rock, a group of Dragon Hunters prepared to spring an ambush. Something in that tapestry had always scared him. It wasn't just that the dragon was so gigantic that it covered an entire wall while the Hunters were no bigger than a book; it was that, for some reason, it gave him the feeling that the dragon was not really asleep.

He heard a rumble. The dragon still slept, but not his stomach. He got up and headed to the kitchens, pushing open a service door and nearly bumping into a maid carrying a roasted duck.

"Hey! Damn kid." The woman didn't move an inch from her trajectory.

Aric laughed, watching her leave for the main hall. In there, the emperor, his mother, and Fadan would be starting dinner as well.

He sat down at a large table in the center of the kitchen between a pile of pastry dough and a bucket of potato peels. Around him, a legion of servants and cooks stirred, washed, rolled, and cut. One of them threw a plate with a roasted turkey leg in front of Aric. It smelled of rosemary.

"Thank you," Aric said.

"Eat fast and clear my table," the cook replied as he wiped his gravy-covered fingers on his trousers.

Another cook, a middle-aged woman with bouncing breasts, brought him some rye bread and a glass of red wine, then planted a kiss on his cheek.

"Good appetite, my sweet." The woman turned around, heading back to her boiling pots, but stopped midway through. Luckily, there was nothing on her hands that she could have dropped.

"Ava Mother! Your Majesty!"

Aric's head bolted toward the door in time to see Fadan passing through it.

"My prince," the woman continued, "you can't be here. I mean… Your Majesty can do whatever he pleases. A thousand apologies, Majesty."

Aric laid a soothing hand on her shoulder, calming her down. The entire kitchen had stopped, staring at the prince in frozen silence. They would not have been more shocked if a dragon had just come in and started roasting a sardine. Fadan walked toward Aric with a smile, ignoring his audience, and sat in front of the potato peels. He looked around, seeing for the first time in his life the place where his food was prepared.

"Disappointed?" Aric asked.

"No. I actually thought your room was smaller." Aric punched him in the shoulder, laughing. "And this smell of cheese… Seriously, I was expecting much worse."

⟳

The main hall of the Imperial Palace was so large you could easily fit a Dawnmother Temple inside, and Ava's priests weren't exactly famous for their small temples. The great table where Tarsus made a point of having dinner every day was filled with roasted ducks, grilled sea basses, stewed lambs, bowls of peeled fruit, jars brimming with wine, and breads of every shape, size, and color. A dozen courtesans occupied their seats, chitchatting cheerfully. The emperor came in from the main door, his steps ever worried. He glanced across the table but did not acknowledge any of the bows he received.

"Where are the empress and the prince?" he asked as he sat down at the head of the table.

"They should arrive momentarily, Your Majesty," Vigild replied.

At that moment, the empress came in, her white dress, trimmed with green, sliding calmly through the hall. Her silhouette belonged in a tailor's studio, her hair a mantle of night that poured down to the middle of her back, and her green eyes two emeralds stolen from a great lady's necklace. Cassia was the vision of a particularly talented poet.

The bows the emperor had received were repeated for her. Tarsus laid a soft, reverent kiss on her hand. Even after fifteen years of marriage, the emperor still needed a moment to catch his breath every time he saw her.

"Where is Fadan?" Cassia asked.

"I thought he was with you, my love," Tarsus replied.

There was a brief pause while the emperor decided whether to break his rigid protocol and authorize the beginning of the meal, but Sagun interrupted him before he could make a decision. He strode in through the door that led to the kitchens, neared the emperor, and whispered something in his ear.

Tarsus's face turned blood red. "You!" he pointed at a Legionary standing against a wall. "I want the prince out of the kitchens and sitting here. Immediately!"

The Legionary slammed a fist against his heart and marched away to the sound of his armor's clanking.

"Tarsus, they're brothers," Cassia said.

"To you, maybe. Not to me."

"To them," Cassia insisted.

Tarsus decreed the end of that conversation with a stare as the Legionary returned behind Fadan. The prince sat down beside the emperor with an irritated look.

"In the kitchens…like a servant," Tarsus spat. "What are the rules on speaking to Aric?"

Fadan sighed onto his plate.

"Only hello and goodbye."

Tarsus nodded, his eyes glaring.

"It won't happen again, Fadan. Do you know how I can assure you of that?" The emperor did not wait for an answer. "Because the next time this happens will be the last time he sleeps in this castle. Understood?"

A heavy silence fell on the table as those words sank into Fadan. Across the table, Cassia saw him tightening his mouth, and after a very long, and very awkward silence, the emperor decided to order the beginning of the meal. Everyone obeyed quietly.

"The master-at-arms tells me the prince has already mastered the compound attack," Intila said, trying to break the awkwardness.

Fadan placed a hand on the bandages covering his head. "Not well enough, apparently."

That made the table laugh. Even Cassia made an effort to smile. The conversation continued on the subject of Fadan's combat lessons, and Cassia was happy to see a smile return to her son's face. Despite it, she couldn't shake the thought that she had another son somewhere in the castle, all by himself. Aric would not hear compliments on his abilities or jokes. He wouldn't feel the proud hand of his father ruffling his hair as he told how he had knocked down the master-at-arms for the first time in his life. In fact, Cassia thought, Aric would hardly even remember his father's face.

At that moment, she saw a shadow slide across the arches on the rim of the hall. Aric appeared suddenly from behind a statue. Hidden by its shadow, her son peeked, looking for her.

Cassia's heart shattered into a thousand pieces. She looked sideways to Fadan, who was now laughing at a joke Intila had told. Was it possible for a mother to love one son more than the other? No, surely not. But there were sons who needed more love than others; of that, she had no doubt.

Aric stuck two fingers up his nostrils, then pulled his nose up in an antic. Cassia was unable to restrain herself and laughed out loud. She tried hiding her face, but not well enough. Tarsus saw her, looked toward Aric, and his teeth clenched. He closed a fist so hard that the blood disappeared from his hand, skin shining white. With a gesture, he called a Legionary and whispered something in his ear. An instant later, Cassia saw a metal glove grab Aric's arm, and her son disappeared.

⁓

The Legionary dragged him through the corridors. The iron gauntlet around his arm hurt, but Aric tried his best to pretend it didn't. They got to his room and the Legionary threw him in as if he were a sack of flour, slamming the door behind him. Aric heard a padlock snap shut and realized that he was in the dark. Usually, someone lit some candles so he could get dressed, but apparently, he wasn't entitled to that this time. He opened a window, letting the moon shine in, then took a sleeping tunic out of a chest but simply threw it onto the bed. He wasn't sleepy at all.

He was rarely locked in his room. Typically, he could escape and roam around the palace, maybe visit the library. But tonight, it looked like even that wouldn't be possible.

Sitting on his bed with a sigh, he looked around, not that there was anything to see. His bedroom was kept empty by regular inspections from Sagun and his minions. In fact, the only thing adorning his walls was a dark mold stain shaped as a bearded old man, or a sinking ship if you tilted your head the right way. He sighed again and looked at the locked door, wishing he were a wizard and had the power to open the lock or simply pass through the wood. If he were a great mage, Tarsus would not be able to treat him this way, but then again, maybe it was a good thing that he wasn't a wizard.

If he had the talent and knew how to use it, Tarsus would finally have a reason to get rid of him, hang him for the crime of practicing magic. He had done it to all the mages of the Academy when they numbered in the hundreds; what would keep him from doing the same thing to a fifteen-year-old boy?

A stone the size of an egg landed right beside him with a crack. It startled him, pulling him from his thoughts, but he immediately ran to the window.

"Fadan?!"

Down below in the courtyard, Fadan shushed him. Then he gestured for Aric to climb down. Aric struck his index finger against his forehead, asking if Fadan was crazy. Fadan simply crossed his arms.

Well, it was a way out....

Holding on to parapets, window shutters, and unleveled bricks, Aric climbed down the three stories separating him from the ground, finishing with a small jump that landed him at his half-brother's feet.

"Are you insane?" he whispered. "Want him to send me away for good?"

Fadan shrugged and signaled him to follow him. They reentered the building and followed along corridors and stairways, being careful enough to choose only the ones that were in the dark.

Aric kept looking over his shoulder. It wasn't the first time the two of them had sneaked out like that. In fact, he couldn't remember spending more than brief moments with his brother unless it was at night, sneaking around, somewhere in the bowels of the Citadel.

But today was different. He had heard Tarsus's threat, and he didn't like the idea of never seeing his mother or brother again.

"Where are we going?" he asked.

"Shh!"

They were on the top floor of the north wing by now. Fadan tiptoed up a spiral staircase and Aric followed, still unable to stop looking over his shoulder. At the top of the stairs, Fadan pushed open a door that squeaked from the movement. Aric went in and his brother closed the door behind him.

It was some sort of attic. There were tables and old chairs, some paintings, rolled carpets, and books, piles of books. Everything was thoroughly covered in a thick layer of dust, however; everything had also been moved close to the walls, leaving the center of the room empty as if it were a corridor.

"What is this? A storage room?"

Instead of answering, Fadan threw him a training sword. Aric's mouth dropped as he wrapped his fingers around the handle and felt its weight. It had to have a metal core – it was too heavy to be made of just wood – and Aric figured that was exactly how a true sword should feel. He admired it as if he had just been handed a relic from the unification wars.

"You want to learn or not?"

Aric snapped out of it. Of course he wanted to. It was all he could think about.

Fadan began by explaining how to properly hold the sword, then demonstrated some guard stances, trying to impersonate his master-at-arms.

"Wait, I got lost. How was the previous one?"

"Let me finish this one. You place your right foot –"

"But I don't remember the last one! Go slower."

Fadan sighed.

"You hold the sword at waist level, like this. No, don't bend that much." He grabbed Aric's hand, placing it in the right position, but his brother got angry and pushed his hand away.

"Would you mind going slower?!" Aric yelled.

Fadan rolled his eyes.

"I'm the one who got the crap beaten out of him today, all right? You have to be patient. You don't snap your fingers and learn this. It's not a magic trick."

WHUMP!

The two brothers jumped and their hearts forgot to beat. With every hair on their bodies standing up, they stared at the center of the room, their eyes widening.

Right there, in the middle of the floor, where previously there was nothing, now stood a tall, thick book. They staggered toward it, trying to understand what had just happened. There was no shelf, table, or chair from which it could have fallen, and the nearest pile of books was a good five paces away. They looked up. The ceiling was like the hull of a ship turned upside down, but there was no beam from where it could have wobbled and fallen. How was it possible? The book was much larger than any Aric had ever seen, and he had seen just about every book in the Citadel's library.

Fadan picked it up. The cover was made of wood instead of leather, and he wiped the dust from it with a swipe of his hand. The two of them read the engraved title.

INTRODUCTION TO THE MAGICAL ARTS – TOME I

Fadan opened the book to a random page. The pages and text looked perfectly preserved, as if the book had just been written.

Aric glanced around the room again and the hairs on the back of his neck stood up. Was someone watching them?

CHAPTER 2

The Forbidden Book

"I don't understand. Where did it fall from?" Fadan looked in every direction, but they were as alone as they had been when they had walked in.

Aric stole the book from his brother's hands and flipped through its pages as if he wanted to read it all in one fell swoop. He caught a few terms here and there but understood none of them. *Singulums, Cognitive Projection, Entropic Abstraction;* Aric felt like he was in a class with Macael if the old man had decided to speak in another language.

"I wonder if one of us has the Talent," he mused. "There has to be some kind of test in here."

"What do you mean? What are you planning to do with this? We have to get rid of it. Right now! If my father so much as dreams –"

"How is he going to find out?" Aric asked.

Fadan groaned as Aric kept flipping the pages in his hand, studying them like a new puzzle.

"Test...test... There has to be a test."

"Look for a stupidity test as well," Fadan muttered. "I'm sure you'll get the highest score."

Aric gave his brother a disappointed look.

"Are you telling me you're not curious? What if one of us could do magic; wouldn't that be incredible?"

Fadan didn't answer him right away. "A little bit, maybe," he admitted, at last, shifting his weight nervously. "It would also be a great way to end up in the gallows."

Aric didn't care. All he could think about was everything he would be able to do if he were a mage. Leave the Citadel anytime he wanted, see his mother whenever he felt like it, maybe even visit his father...

Aric cascaded through the pages. "This is an introduction book. There has to be a section about discovering the talent," he said.

Fadan tore the book away from his hands. "Give me that. You're getting on my nerves," he said, then turned the book back to the beginning and stuck his finger in one of the first pages. "Check the index!"

Aric ignored his tone and quickly found what he was looking for. With the book in his brother's hands, he flipped the pages until he got to where he wanted. The two of them read in silence.

"Ah... I see..." Aric said. He didn't sound too sure about it, though. "It's not that complicated."

"Not that complicated? How is this not complicated? Where are you going to find runium? Are you going to hunt a dragon in the courtyard?!"

Aric shrugged. "We would need runium anyway. How else did you want to cast spells?"

"I don't want to cast spells! You do!"

"There is a place...." Aric said, looking through a window.

"No. Don't even think about it."

But he was thinking about it, and he even knew how he could get there.

The Paladin shifted his weight as the emperor read his report. Tarsus was sitting at a dragon bone table. The Paladin calculated it had to be worth more money than he would ever see in his entire life.

"Contraband is up. Again," the emperor murmured. "Have we ever had as many arrests as this winter?"

By his side, with a hand on the back of the emperor's chair, Vigild said no with a shake of his head. "The Paladins are becoming ever better at their job, Your Majesty," he said.

Tarsus threw the report onto his table.

"Don't pretend to be naïve, Chancellor," Tarsus said. "The more runium we catch, the more gets to the streets. It's almost as if trafficking has become normal."

"I already gave orders to double the patrols on the docks and customs offices," Vigild assured.

"And the contrabandists will find someplace else to bring the runium through," Tarsus replied.

Vigild held his chin thoughtfully. "I don't see that there's much else we can do, Your Majesty. Not with the resources we have available."

"More resources? How many more times will I have to raise taxes, Vigild?"

"Not every resource is money," the chancellor replied. "If the Paladins had more authority, they could carry out their searches without the bureaucracy to delay them. Am I right, commander?"

The Paladin shuddered. "Yes!" he blurted out. "Yes, of course." He tried to pull himself together. "In most cases, when the magistrate's authorization arrives, the smugglers have already had time to move the merchandise. Right under our noses."

"Probably tipped off by tribunal clerks on their payroll," Vigild added.

Tarsus rose, walked to a window, and contemplated his capital. The Citadel was the highest point in Augusta. From there you could see all twenty bridges that crossed the Saffya River, as well as the Docks District – the commercial heart of the Empire and the shadiest part of the Imperial city.

"And the nobility will protest, once again," Tarsus lost his gaze in the city. "When will I lose them for good, Vigild?"

The question went without an answer and the chancellor moved nervously.

"No," Tarsus said. "We are already preparing a controversial law. I will not risk another provocation."

"Maybe we can do more at the source of the problem," the Chancellor said. "After all, there is no runium without dragon blood."

Tarsus didn't move. Down there, at the docks, a ship untied itself, released a sail, and was pushed down the Saffya. Toward Capra, the emperor assumed.

"The Paladins have a mandate to control the Dragon Hunters, Chancellor. If the problem resides there, then this mandate is not being well executed." Tarsus spun to face Vigild.

"That's where all dragon blood comes from, Your Majesty," Vigild replied, "and I will be the first to admit the mistakes of my men. There are two possibilities. Either the Hunters aren't delivering everything they hunt to my Paladins, or the Paladins themselves have found…a new source of income."

Tarsus glared at the Paladin in his office. The man shifted his weight from one foot to the other while swallowing through a dry throat. "I shall begin an inquiry immediately, Your Majesty!" he said.

"Do that, commander. It would be a horrible thing if you found yourself not controlling the Hunters but keeping them company in some dragon cave in the desert."

The Paladin kept still, but color abandoned his skin. Vigild gave him permission to leave with a gesture.

"One more thing, commander." Tarsus was once again looking at his city. "From now on, it would be best if the arrests produced not just the runium, but also the Mages buying it."

The day dragged on endlessly. Aric spent the whole morning in a Samehrian literature class. When he finally finished analyzing page after page of an anthology of pre-unification poems, he headed for the kitchens to have lunch, wondering if the place they had chosen to hide the book was safe enough. He considered moving it, but it would be stupid to do so during the day.

As he walked into Macael's class in the afternoon, he bumped into Fadan, but to the great amazement of the mathematics tutor, they simply exchanged a nod. This time, Macael forced him to sit away from the window, where the courtyard would not be visible. But it wasn't the weapons training that filled Aric's mind that day. He tried his best to keep up with the lesson but was unable to take his eyes off Macael's hourglass. If only he were able to speed up time…

Unfortunately, today, the sun seemed to have decided to move slower. When Macael finally dismissed him, Aric headed for the battlements and sat there with his eyes wandering between the setting sun and a small window way up high in the north wing, his feet frantically beating against the bricks of the wall.

When the sun decided to leave at long last, Aric returned to the kitchens. A pair of grilled trout waited for him on top of two slices of corn bread. He imagined himself using only his mind to lift them through the air. He saw himself summoning a jar of wine with a flick of his fingers. In the end, though, it was a servant who brought the wine, throwing the jar in front of him on the table. It twirled and threatened to tumble, but only a couple of droplets spilled onto Aric's shirt.

He returned to the battlements once more and sat there, this time watching the moon rise in the sky. He stayed there for hours, counting every moment. It would be insane to try to leave the Citadel before everyone else was asleep. Actually, it would be insane no matter what time he did it, but he was still determined to do it anyway.

When the castle finally looked quiet enough, Aric went back inside. He went to his room and put on a dark brown cloak. Then, with silent steps, he crossed the main hall and climbed the great staircase in the castle's vestibule, being careful enough to drop to all fours as he reached the final steps. At the top, two Legionaries guarded the hallway that led to the Imperial family's rooms. He heard a soft whistle coming from the one on the left, and a heavy snore from the one on the right.

One hand and one foot after the other, he slid across the marble flagstones. When he finally left the guards behind him, he rose and resumed walking. There should be no more guards from there onward.

He turned the first corner. Torchlights made his shadow dance, and he stuck his tongue out at a series of portraits of former emperors hanging on the wall. Finally, he turned another corner and his body froze. Right there, five steps from him, was Sagun, at his mother's bedroom door. The castellan was saying something, but Aric could only hear his own heart beating in his chest. From the other side of the door, he saw his mother's gaze find his and immediately return to Sagun's.

"What was that, Castellan?" Cassia asked.

Sagun sighed and indicated Tarsus's room with a wave.

"The emperor requests your presence tonight."

Cassia nodded repeatedly, as if her head was stuck in a loop, but said nothing. Her gaze met Aric's again, very quickly. He was still frozen in the middle of the corridor.

"Very well," the empress said, but stood motionless nonetheless.

Sagun looked extremely confused.

"Uh.... Your Majesty wishes something else?"

"Something else?" Cassia asked. Aric was still in the same place, paralyzed halfway through a movement. "Something else, yes," she said.

Sagun frowned, unsure whether to say something or not. To Cassia's great relief, Aric finally decided to move. He took one step, then another as he drew nearer to Fadan's room.

"And...what will it be?" Sagun asked.

"It will be..." Cassia mumbled, "a jar of wine." She saw Aric get to his brother's door, right behind Sagun, and shrink against it.

"A jar of wine. Right away, Your Majesty." Sagun made a small bow.

Cassia held her breath as he turned to leave. On the other side, Aric pushed himself against the door so hard, he almost went through it.

"Sagun!" Cassia grabbed his arm, squeezing it.

The castellan looked at her as if it was the first time in history something like that had happened. Cassia thought it probably was. To her great relief, at that moment, Fadan's door opened and Aric disappeared into the bedroom.

"White, Sagun. A jar of white wine," Cassia said, then shut her door in his face.

The castellan nodded. The empress had definitely lost her mind.

⌒

"Are you thirsty?" the emperor asked.

Cassia was standing at the room's entrance, holding a jar of white wine and two glasses.

"Not really." The empress set the wine and glasses on a mahogany table by the door. "You look tired."

Tarsus let a sigh answer in his stead. He did not remember not feeling tired. He shrugged and got closer to her. Softly, he held her waist and smelled the hair around her neck. Cassia's body tightened.

"Help me undress," he said, turning his back to her. "Did you have a nice day?"

Cassia moved his once-black hair out of the way and opened the pin holding the blue cape around his shoulders.

"Yes," the empress replied.

How he hated when all he could get out of her was a yes or a no. He nodded affirmatively, pretending the answer pleased him.

"Fadan behaved nicely today," he said. "No nonsense in the kitchens or that sort of thing."

Cassia exhaled loudly. She grabbed Tarsus's blue cape and carried it to a corner. The emperor stood watching her folding the cape over and over before laying it down. He could not remember one single time in his life he had not thought she was the most magnificent thing he had ever seen.

"Come here," Tarsus said.

She straightened, exhaled loudly again, and turned around.

"Take off your dress."

Cassia looked through the window and recalled a time when she had believed that one day she would get used to this. Then she remembered one other time before that, when she had been in another man's room. He had had blond hair with misbehaved curls and hadn't needed to ask her the same thing.

⌒

The light from Fadan's torch burned on Aric's blond, curly hair. In front of him, the corridor stretched like a well. The crown prince had the feeling that the darkness might never end.

"Are you sure this is the way?" he asked.

"Of course I'm sure," Aric replied in a whisper. "Now be quiet."

Fadan protested inaudibly. They tiptoed across the corridor with the light of the torch trembling on the stone walls. Eventually, they arrived at a rust eaten-railing, and Aric dislodged two metal bars with a kick. On the other side, a black river flowed silently. The smell told them it was a sewer.

"You want to know something really exciting?" Aric asked. "If you go that way, you'll get to the dungeons." He stretched an arm, pointing in the same direction the river was running.

"I'm sure they're charming. We should spend an evening there one of these days."

Aric shook his head in disappointment and walked the other way. They followed the sewer until they reached a crossing. There, three rivers of dark, foul-smelling water joined in a large circle to then leave through the canal the boys had just come from. Aric pointed at a trapdoor in the center of the crossing's ceiling.

"Up there is the Paladins' headquarters. This is where they dump the confiscated runium."

"That's your plan? Wait for them to dump a shipment?"

"Of course not! They only do it every once in a while. They must store it and only dump it when storage is full. All we have to do is go in, find the storage room, and take a small vial."

"A small vial… It's as if you're talking about strawberry jam. Are you mad? That place must be crawling with Paladins."

Aric placed his torch in a sconce, climbed up an iron ladder nailed to the wall, pushed the trapdoor, and disappeared into the Paladin headquarters. One short moment later, his head popped back out.

"Do you really think they expect someone to have the nerve to walk into their main headquarters? They don't even lock this thing."

Fadan stood motionless for a moment, staring in utter disbelief at Aric's face hanging from the trapdoor. Then he shrugged, put down his torch, and climbed up as well.

The room was a dark cubicle with nothing except for the trapdoor. What little light there was inside came from its only entrance. Aric walked up to a corner and sneaked a peek, then called his brother with a gesture. Passing through the entrance, they penetrated deeper into the Paladins headquarters, then stopped at a door. Aric opened it carefully and looked inside. He saw only a few shelves covered in spider webs and an upturned bucket.

They kept going, tiptoeing along the same corridor until they heard voices. They had arrived at an intersection where one of the corridors seemed to lead to a common room or dining hall, where the voices seemed to come from. Obviously, they chose to go through the other one.

With each step they took, Fadan looked over his shoulder twice. Until Aric shoved a palm against Fadan's chest, making him stop. With a finger over his lips, Aric made a silent *shush.*

With careful steps, Aric peeked around a corner, then signaled Fadan to do the same. The prince stepped in front of his brother and leaned forward. On the other side, a Paladin was sitting on a small wooden stool with his chin on his chest. Was he sleeping? Fadan made the question with a gesture. Aric shrugged.

They peeked again, this time simultaneously. Suddenly, a noise made them jump. The two brothers shrank against the wall and heard a voice becoming louder. They looked in one direction and then the other. There wasn't much choice. They turned the corner and darted past the sleeping Paladin, slipping into the room behind him.

It looked to be a library, with bookshelves reaching as far as darkness allowed them to see. In a hurry, they sneaked in between two of them and crouched, waiting. The voices grew louder and louder. Aric felt something slapping his shoulder and looked at his brother. Fadan was staring at the shelf next to them, his eyes ready to pop out. Aric could not believe it.

Those weren't books; those were flasks. Thousands of them.

For a moment, Aric forgot fear entirely, grabbing two of them. The red liquid inside was thicker than stew but shone like a plate of armor in front of a fireplace. If that wasn't runium, nothing was. He slid the two vials into his jacket.

"HAHA! Look at him, bravely guarding the storeroom," a rough voice mocked from outside.

"Nothing gets past you, big guy," another voice said in an annoying tone.

"Huh?! Wha… Let me go, you bastard," a third, sleepy voice protested.

Aric felt the hand of his brother pulling him back. They both held their breaths. This place had only one way out, and apparently it was now crowded with Paladins.

Crouching, Aric moved toward the end of the shelf so he could take a better look at the exit. Fadan's arms protested, but Aric just signaled him to be still. At that moment, he wanted to be a mage more than ever. All it would take would be a sip from one of those flasks and with a simple gesture, he could make the Paladins go away.

"What's that?" the annoying voice asked.

The two brothers froze.

"A shelf, idiot," the rough voice replied.

"Seriously. I saw something move."

There were several laughs, followed by comments on the amount of wine the Paladin with the annoying voice had drunk. Aric looked behind him and saw Fadan dislodging a wooden box from the lower shelf and then cross through to the other side. He looked at the entrance once again and saw a shadow growing into the storeroom.

"Over there. I swear I saw something," the annoying voice said.

The one with the rough voice really didn't care, replying, "Of course you did. A rat. Good luck finding it."

"Fire take the both of you!" the sleepy one said. "Won't you shut up?!"

Aric saw the shadow grow bigger and bigger. He tried to find some place to hide, but all he could see were vials and more vials.

"It wasn't a rat," the annoying voice insisted.

"Right. If you won't let me sleep, I'm getting myself a drink."

"Good idea."

Aric heard a slap on someone's back, followed by disappearing footsteps. The two men had clearly walked away, and the third must have turned around, because Aric saw his shadow become thinner.

"Bastards!" he cursed.

Then the shadow grew thicker once more, and Aric could see the contour of his head and shoulders again. He looked everywhere for a hiding place, but the only thing he saw was the box Fadan had removed from the shelf. He ran and placed himself behind it but immediately felt ridiculous. A small dog would not have been able to hide behind it.

At that moment, he looked up and saw the Paladin. He was a tall, thin man and wore the black cuirass and red waistband of the Paladin uniform. For a moment, the Paladin did not see him and Aric stepped back instinctively, trapping himself against the wall. Then the man turned, gaze locking on him.

The Paladin's eyes bulged and his hand drew a long knife from his belt. He opened his mouth to yell something, but before he could, Fadan came out from behind another shelf case, a massive wooden board in his hands. The prince smacked the man across the head and he collapsed.

"Quick!" Fadan said, then dashed away.

Aric didn't need to hear that twice. He raced after his brother, the two of them running through the corridors. Whether someone had heard or seen them, they had no idea. How they found the right way back to the trapdoor was a similar mystery. They opened it, dove into the sewer, swam to the walkway, and then kept running. They only stopped when they reached the railing they had broken on their way in.

Panting heavily, they stood before it, collecting their breaths, hoping their hearts didn't jump out of their chests. Aric felt his jacket pockets and removed the two vials. One was broken and its contents had disappeared. The other, however, was as intact as when he had picked it up in the storeroom.

⌢

Panting, Tarsus wiped a drop of sweat from his forehead. He looked at Cassia beside him and stared at her naked chest, rising and falling with her breath. He laid a caring hand on her arm, but she rolled onto her side, turning her back to him. What he would have given for her not to do that...

"I love you," he said.

"I'm tired." Cassia pulled a blanket and covered herself. "We should sleep."

Every man suffers the same, people had told him. *It's the curse of marriage,* he had heard between laughs. Tarsus wasn't so sure.

"Everything I do for you, I do out of love," he confessed.

Cassia turned and faced him.

"Everything you do... everything you did... that's not love. That's selfishness." Cassia turned her back to him once again.

Tarsus stared at the ceiling without an answer. If only she could understand.

"Your birthday is coming," he said.

"I know. I'm sure you won't spare any expense to make sure the festivities are magnificent." There was no joy in her voice.

"You call me selfish," Tarsus said. "Very well. Ask for anything."

Cassia turned to the emperor. "What?"

"I'm going to prove to you that while you are mine, I am willing to give you anything. As your birthday gift, you can ask me anything."

Cassia looked at him suspiciously.

"Anything?" she asked.

"Anything."

There was a silence while the empress studied her husband. Was he serious?

"All right..." Cassia sat up in the bed and Tarsus did the same. "I want Aric to see his father."

⌒

Aric and Fadan washed away the sewer stench with water buckets, then ran up to the attic of the north wing. They didn't even bother drying their clothes. Fadan dragged a table to the center of the room and placed a candle, two glasses of pure crystal, a jar of water, and the precious flask on top of it. The candle flame danced, and inside the vial, red waves swirled within the silvery liquid.

Across the attic, Aric dug the book from its hideout. He felt his stomach tighten and his eyes close as he muttered a plea. Would Ava grant him his wish? It would certainly be a first.

He dropped the massive tome on the improvised table and quickly found the page he was looking for.

"One portion of runium, five portions of water," Aric read.

Fadan measured and poured the liquids in each crystal glass. He gave one to his brother and took the other one for himself.

Aric reached for his belt and removed a small kitchen knife. He looked up, searching the heavens, and closed his eyes in another plea. Then he made a small cut on the palm of his hand, dropped the knife, and squeezed some blood droplets into his glass.

Please…

He reopened his eyes. The blood drops unraveled inside the translucent liquid and he waited, watching each undulation of his blood threads as they dissolved.

Please…

The red became duller and duller until it turned white. Other than that, nothing happened. Like a puppet whose strings had been cut, his body sank, and he let a long sigh escape him. Devastated, he lifted his head slightly.

Across the table, Fadan was staring at his own glass with his mouth wide open. He lifted his cup and showed it to Aric.

The liquid inside was as bright blue as an Imperial flag waving in the sun.

CHAPTER 3

The Traitor

Ava looked at him from above. Serene, crystalline, glowing, the stained glass where she was portrayed stretching across multiple stories up to the temple ceiling. Aric wondered if the star floating above her head were not a more accurate representation of her. After all, had she ever even stepped on Arkhemia?

He heard steps from behind.

"We don't usually get visitors this early." The priest wore a white tunic with Ava's Dawn Star embroidered on his chest. By the complicated, fili-gree-like cutouts of the cloth covering his head, Aric assumed he should be an important member of the temple. "Why don't you return in an hour, when the morning celebration begins?"

"Does she ever reply?" Aric asked.

The priest pondered the question for a while.

"It depends on the answer you are looking for. Mother Ava does not grant wishes."

"Why not?"

"The city is full of fountains," the priest said. "The naïve throw gold coins into them; the wise quench their thirst in them." He stepped besides Aric, searching for his face. "You're the empress's son, Aric!"

"What's the point of praying to a goddess if she can't hear us? Or just won't?"

The priest looked at his glass-made goddess.

"Ava did not create us, yet she cared for us as if she were our mother. She risked her own life to protect us." The old man turned to Aric. "We pray to her because we are thankful. Because if it weren't for her, we wouldn't be here."

"Risked her own life?! She just gave us weapons," Aric protested.

"Dragons have their own gods, you know. By taking our side, Ava crossed them. She lost her own lover because of it."

"Now, there is a god worth praying to," Aric said. "He was a warrior. He came down to fight on our side. Ava just watched."

"I thought you saw no point in praying to a god that doesn't answer your prayers. How is a dead god going to help you?"

Aric opened his mouth but no answer came.

"At last!"

Aric and the priest turned around at the voice. At the other end of the temple, by the entrance, stood Sagun.

"Where have you been? I've been looking for you for hours," the castellan said as he walked through the temple's seating area. "My apologies, Holy Brother. I hope the boy was not disturbing you."

If there was something Aric did not want to see right now, that thing was Sagun.

"Not at all. He's just a curious boy."

The castellan returned the priest's bow, then turned to Aric.

"Your mother wishes to see you in the main hall," he said.

His mother? In the main hall? The last time he had entered the main hall, he had been removed by the steel gauntlet of a Legionary and then locked in his room. The time before that... He could not recall a time before that.

With his black braid snaking at his back, Sagun led Aric out of the temple and back through the myriad palaces of the Citadel. The castellan left a trail of perfume behind him so intense that Aric felt nauseous. On the other hand, everything about Sagun gave him nausea, from the shaven top of his head contrasting with the gigantic black braid, to the overly decorated and colorful Akhami tunics. Even the way his brown skin always glowed without a single drop of sweat was repulsive. Were all people of Akham like him? If so, it had to be a horrible place.

The gates of the main hall were open when they arrived at the Core Palace, and Aric could see the blue dais where the two thrones rose. Their backrests, covered in blue satin, climbed up to the ceiling like two veils dropped from the heavens. But what truly intrigued Aric was that, standing up there, waiting for him beside his mother, was the emperor himself.

Had Fadan said anything about the book? Or the runium?

I'm going to be thrown away! Or worse.

Tarsus had a rigid expression, his eyes piercing through Aric. Cassia, however, gave him a delightful smile that made Aric feel warm inside.

"Aric, my love," his mother said, "your father is in Augusta. Today, my dear, you will be allowed to see him."

Aric's chin dropped. He turned to the emperor, sure he would forbid it at once, but Tarsus did no such thing. He just kept his eyes locked on Aric without saying a word.

That was not possible.

"Seriously?!"

His mother nodded. The smile had not faded from her face yet, and it didn't look like it was going anywhere anytime soon.

⌒⟶

"I need to stop."

The sergeant leading the escort gave him an astonished look.

"Again?!"

Doric shrugged. "Horse riding makes me want to piss," he said.

"I imagine drinking four wineskins probably doesn't help either."

"Unfortunately, that's all I brought."

"The city gates are right up there," the sergeant told him. "You can piss when we get to the inn."

Doric did not reply. He stopped his horse, dismounted, and tied him to a branch. Then he lowered his pants and started relieving himself.

"What are you doing?!" the sergeant asked.

Doric looked down his body, then back at the sergeant.

"What do you mean, what am I doing?" he asked.

A Legionary started laughing but was quickly silenced by the sergeant's look. Doric finished, pulling his pants back up. He climbed back onto his horse and took the view in.

The Imperial Citadel rested like a crown above Mount Capitol. Its sharp towers jutted upward like swords challenging the sky, and somewhere inside were Cassia and his son.

Around the Citadel, Augusta spread like a mantle of houses, streets, and plazas. Throughout the centuries, the city had grown so much, it already had three separate, concentric walls protecting it. Doric still remembered when there were little more than a few shacks outside the outer wall, but the last couple of decades had brought so many people to the Empire's capital that soon it would be necessary to build a fourth one.

With his escort surrounding him, he passed through the city gates. They rode through cobbled streets, crowded squares, and avenues so large you could fit entire villages inside. It was incredible how so much had changed, and yet everything was exactly the same. The Saffya still flowed as wide and blue as ever. The towers of the temples, public buildings, and nobles' estates still competed among themselves for the place closest to the sky. Even the Legionaries still guarded their posts everywhere he looked. To Doric, the only changes were the Paladins. More than a dozen times, he saw columns of twenty of them, marching around with their black cuirasses and red waistbands. As if the Legionaries weren't enough.

They arrived at Maginus field, a colossal, rectangular plaza around which gathered a collection of public buildings from post offices to courts. In the center of the plaza, cutting it in half like a spine, was the largest collection of statues Doric had ever seen. In it, the Legions of Maginus II triumphed over the last army of Akham.

"It's a breathtaking monument, is it not?" Doric asked. When no one answered, he added, "If you're into ultra-realism, of course."

Once again, silence.

"I prefer Fyrian, myself." He waited for an answer again, and once more, none came. "Saggad is full of Fyrian pieces. Have you ever been to Saggad, Sergeant?"

"Yes," the sergeant replied at last.

An entire day of journeying and that was all he had gotten out of him. Yes or no. Doric hadn't even discovered his name. In fact, all he had heard from him had been orders to his men. He was too young to be an officer, which meant he was no plebeian. Besides, the clean way in which he moved gave him away. Doric had also noticed the obsessive way in which he cleaned the silver plates of his armor as if it were the most valuable thing he possessed. It was curious, considering he could obviously afford a sergeant's rank.

Doric stopped his horse again.

"What is it now?" the sergeant fumed.

"Do you have any idea how many of those Legionaries are my ancestors?" Doric asked, indicating the statues.

That clearly got the man's attention.

"No."

"Not one," Doric said.

The sergeant was about to reply with something rather unfriendly, but Doric didn't give him enough time.

"As for the high-ranking officers, however..." He pointed at a figure riding a horse, who looked like he was giving orders to those around him. "See that general over there?" Doric hoped it was, in fact, a general. "He is my great-great-grandfather's great-great-grandfather."

"Your what?"

"My great-great-grandfather's... He's my ancestor," Doric explained. "A great man."

Probably a cretin.

The sergeant was clearly impressed with that.

"General Lucena was your ancestor?" he asked.

Who?

"Precisely." If there was something Doric's family had in abundance, that thing was famous generals. What difference did it make if that particular general wasn't one of them?

The sergeant gave Doric a sullen look. "A great man, without a doubt," he declared. Then, as if waking up, he ordered his men to resume their march, except this time, he placed his horse beside Doric's.

As the Citadel got closer, the city became denser. The streets grew narrower, the buildings more compact. The column was forced to form a single-file line in order to fit through the crowd. A group of kids dashed by them and under Doric's horse. He wanted to yell at them, tell them that it was dangerous, but the boys were gone before he could decide what to say. He turned around and looked ahead, and saw a man being squashed against the wall by the horse of one of the Legionaries. Exasperated, the man pushed the horse. The gesture was useless, but the soldier did not like it. He smashed his boot right into the face of the poor man, who fell sideways into a puddle of what Doric hoped was not urine.

Suddenly, there was a thundering up ahead. Doric saw a carriage at the crossing in front of him. A wheel had broken and its cargo of green apples was spilling over the ground. The escort stopped.

"Fire take my luck!" the sergeant cursed. "Belba, go see what's the matter."

The Legionary spurred his horse with a "Yes, Sergeant" and advanced ten paces until he reached the carriage, but a curious crowd had enveloped the accident, and the Legionary found himself blocked.

Doric saw the owner of the apple cart yelling and waving his arms. Then someone pushed someone and someone else replied with another punch. Some spectators decided to intervene, and a brawl began.

"Look at these idiots," one Legionary sneered.

Doric rubbed his horse's neck to calm him down as the sergeant exhaled impatiently next to him.

"We can't leave Lord Auron waiting here all day," he said. "Clear the way."

The Legionary horsemen advanced, opening a path, but the fight was spreading and the advance lost its momentum quickly. The horses got nervous, and soon the Legionaries were part of the brawl as well.

Two men, entangled in a fight, fell over the sergeant's horse, and Doric saw him struggling not to fall off. His own ride squirmed beneath him, circling.

Then a hand hugged Doric's horse's neck and it froze. A pair of blue eyes looked up. It was a woman covered in a dark cloak. The hood did a poor job of hiding a mischievous smile.

"Welcome back to Augusta, Doric Auron."

Doric was confused.

"Hum… Do I know you?"

The woman offered him an apple.

"A welcoming gift," she said. "Just don't open it until you are alone." Her voice was as sweet as a lullaby.

Doric grabbed the apple, trying to decide if the woman was insane.

"A gift?" He studied the fruit. It was indeed just an apple. "Hum… Thank you."

The mischievous smile on the woman's face turned into a satisfied chuckle, and without another word, she disappeared into the middle of the crowd.

⌒

The carriage rattled down Mount Capitol. Through the slit between the curtain and the window, Aric saw a parade of annoyed faces. People were squeezing themselves against the houses to make room for the carriage and had no problem showing how much they were enjoying it. Some yelled insults, others spat. However, after five years without leaving the Citadel, it didn't bother Aric one bit. He laughed when a flower saleswoman slapped a man who had taken the chance to put his hand on her bottom.

"That was probably worth it," said the escort captain sitting beside Aric.

"What?" Aric asked.

"The slap. It was probably worth it."

Aric disagreed. Maybe it had been worth it for the man, but he thought the woman was too old. Not that he could brag on that count. Aric didn't even remember talking to a girl of his age. At least, not since he had started liking girls. The next chance he would have to meet one would be his mother's birthday in a few days. Every great family would bring their daughters to the empress's ball, but of course, they would all be hoping to get a dance with Fadan. After all, he was the crown prince; a single glance from him would make any girl's day. Aric, on the other hand, would be lucky if he could even get close to the main hall. In all likelihood, to him, the ball would consist of eating a cake sent by his mother in secret, and he would have to eat it alone, locked away in his room.

He shook his head. Today was not one of those days. Today, Aric was a normal boy. A boy who could go out and be with his dad. Well, most normal boys probably remembered their father's faces. But besides that, today he was a normal boy.

The carriage stopped and the cabin door opened. They were at an old inn. The rotten wood tablet hanging over the door was shaped like a barrel, and if you tried really hard, you could still read The Rusty Barrel in washed-out letters.

There were Legionaries everywhere, and several civilians were peeking, trying to figure out the reason for such a fuss. One of the soldiers opened the door to the inn and the captain shoved Aric inside. They were immediately intercepted by a rather helpful fat man, whom Aric assumed was the owner.

"It is an honor to welcome you, my lords," he said beneath a thick mustache. "If there is anything I can do to help –"

"Get back to the kitchen," the captain told him. "And don't you dare climb these stairs."

The man bowed quickly and left even quicker.

Aric climbed the stairs with the captain's hand on his back. Would he live his whole life with Legionaries following him?

No! Today was not one of those days. Today, he was going to see his father. What would he be like?

Aric had always pictured him as a big soldier. Tall, dignified, brave. Almost every Auron had been a famous warrior. Aric had read in the library about Geric, the conqueror of Saggad, about Maric, terror of the Samehrians. His own grandfather had been the late Faric Auron, high marshal and commander of the Legions during the Thepian miners' revolt, and had won that war despite being severely outnumbered. Of course, Tarsus would never allow Aric's father to serve in the Legions, but the warrior would be there, underneath all of the emperor's bans and impositions. Aric was sure of that.

They reached the top of the stairs and walked along a corridor until they got to a door guarded by three Legionaries and one sergeant.

This is it.

"He's alone?" the captain asked.

"Yes," the sergeant replied.

"You left him alone?"

"I saw no need to —"

"Open the door, you idiot!"

Aric had the feeling he forgot to breathe.

Doric poured another glass of wine, finishing another jar. Today was a happy day. He was finally going to see his own son after so many years. So, why was he feeling so damn miserable?

"I guess I'm just used to it," he said to himself as he emptied the glass in his hand.

At that moment, the door opened, revealing the sergeant who had brought him there, and a captain holding a boy by his shoulders. It was Aric; there was no doubt.

The boy's eyes opened wide and his mouth dropped. Doric felt his son examining him from head to toe and admonished himself for not having been more careful when he had dressed up that morning. His clothes were expensive, or at least they had once been, but now they were in terrible shape. Raggedy, stained, even burned in some places.

Doric ran his fingers through his hair as if that could conceal his miserable look. He knew very well that his blond curls were so long, dirty, and tangled, it was hard for anyone to believe they belonged to a nobleman.

"Son…" He stepped forward and hugged Aric, hoping he would not smell the wine. "Can you give us some privacy?" Doric asked the guards.

"Not a chance," the captain said, locking the door in its place.

"Captain, Lord Auron…" the sergeant tried to explain.

"Sergeant, report outside the inn and wait for me there."

Obediently, the sergeant tapped a closed fist to his heart and marched away. The captain took an hourglass from his jacket and placed it on a chest of drawers.

"Time is running."

Doric swallowed a protest. What else could he do?

He grabbed his son by the shoulders and studied him.

"I remembered you had your mother's eyes, but I didn't know you have my hair," he said, ruffling Aric's curls. "And apparently my nose and my mouth as well." He looked at his son from various angles. "Sorry about that."

Aric laughed. Doric was pleased with that.

"How is life in the Citadel?"

Aric shrugged. "Boring," he replied.

Doric laughed.

"I stroll around the empty halls of the outer palaces. Alone, because the emperor won't let me see Fadan. But sometimes we escape at night and do stuff together."

"So, you're friends?"

Aric nodded affirmatively.

"Why won't the emperor let you see Fadan?"

"I don't know. I mean, the emperor doesn't like me." Aric paused. "He doesn't like you, either."

Doric laughed again. The laughter of a condemned man.

"I bet your mother hates that rule."

"Yeah. We used to sleep in the same room, beside Mum's. But when I turned ten, the emperor sent me away to the servants' wing and forbade Fadan from seeing me."

"I see," Doric said with a nod.

There was an awkward silence and Aric shifted his weight uncomfortably.

Doric felt like an idiot. He couldn't waste their time together; he had to say something.

"What about lessons? Do you have lessons?"

Stupid question…

"Yes," Aric replied. "I have lessons about everything. I share Fadan's tutors. Except weapons. The emperor doesn't let me learn how to fight."

"Oh, I almost forgot!" Doric said. "I brought you something." He smiled and walked to a chest.

The captain unsheathed half of his sword.

"Easy," Doric told him. He removed a small packet and a large parcel from the chest and showed them to the captain.

"Half your time is up," the captain said after deciding the objects were harmless, then sheathed his sword again.

Doric knelt in front of his son with the two packages in his hands.

"This is for you." He untied the parcel and revealed a magnificent cuirass. "It's made of dragon scales and reinforced with glowstone. You won't find any Mage to enchant the glowstone shards anymore, but still, no sword or spear can go through armor like this. It's rarer and more valuable than a barrel of runium." He smiled, proudly. "But it's not illegal, don't worry."

Aric's eyes were glistening. The scales were dark, and each one was the size of Aric's palm. Beneath them, where they overlapped each other, shone the teal hue of the glowstone shards, as if an ice storm were brewing inside.

"It has been in the family for decades," Doric said. "Do you like it?"

"Very much," Aric replied without taking his eyes from the gift. "But I can't have any weapons training."

Doric shrugged. "It's armor. It works just the same with or without training." He indicated the captain watching them from the door. "Do you think Legionaries would carry so much of it if it was hard to use?"

Aric laughed. The captain ignored them.

"Tell me," Doric said, "do you usually see your mother?"

Aric told him yes.

"Then please give this to her." He handed the small packet to his son. "The emperor has nothing to worry about." This time, he was addressing the captain. "It's not a gift. It's something that used to belong to the empress."

Aric peeked inside. It was a small silver necklace with a very thin, oblong jewel that was almost as long as a finger.

"Tell her I still don't remember asking her to take it off. She will understand."

The captain took one step into the room. "Time is almost up. Say your goodbyes."

Doric exhaled loudly.

Already?

"Do you want to ask any questions?" he asked Aric. "Is there anything you would like to know?"

"Do we have a house?"

Doric was not expecting that.

"Ye… Yes. We have a house in Fausta. It's like a farm, but with a palace. It's big and…and we have lots of animals. Horses, for example."

The captain grabbed the hourglass. "Time is up. Let's go."

"Can I go live with you one day?" Aric asked.

Doric felt tears growing in his eyes.

"I'll be sixteen next year. Maybe the emperor will let me."

The captain's steel gauntlet closed around Aric's arm.

"Yes, maybe he will."

"Goodbye, Dad."

"Goodbye, Son."

The door slammed shut, just in time so Aric couldn't see a tear run down his father's face.

⌒

Only when the door opened did Doric realize he had heard someone knocking.

"Is everything all right, my lord?" the sergeant asked.

"He doesn't remember our home," Doric said, staring at the floor.

The sergeant had a little trouble answering. "I – It must be hard for you… I will leave one man at your door. If there is anything you need…"

Doric nodded absentmindedly.

"We leave for Fausta in the morning. Good night, Lord Auron."

"Good night, Sergeant."

The door closed and Doric looked out the window. It was getting dark. It had been many years since a day had gone by this quick. Mother Ava, how he needed a drink….

He thought about asking for some wine, but he wanted something stronger. Besides, judging from the jar he had drunk before, they only served vinegar in this place. He remembered his silver flask. He hadn't touched it on his way to Augusta. Had he even brought it?

He searched his jacket from one end to the other. No sign of the flask, but he did find something else. An apple. He had forgotten all about it.

"Just don't open it until you're alone," the woman had told him.

Probably just some lunatic. But how had she known his name?

Cassia…

This was exactly the kind of thing she would do, and she knew he was in Augusta. She surely wouldn't waste a chance to see him.

No, she wouldn't take such a risk. Aric could end up paying for it. She wouldn't dare. He looked at the apple. There was only one way to find out.

He brought the apple to his mouth and stuck his teeth on it.

What if it's poisoned?

Tarsus would love nothing better than to have him killed. Doric took the apple away from his mouth. His teeth were now imprinted on the peel.

No. If Tarsus wanted him dead, he would have killed him already. No one would stop him, but in fact, there *was* someone stopping him. Cassia would rip his heart out if he tried.

Doric went outside and asked the soldier to light the candle in his room. Then, he locked himself in again and studied the entire surface of the apple. With the exception of his teeth marks, there was no sign that the apple had ever been opened. There was no way something had been placed inside it.

He smiled cheerlessly. A crazy woman had given him an apple and look at how he had gotten. Of course, Cassia wouldn't risk Aric's life just so she could meet him in some smelly alley. Naturally, Tarsus wouldn't try to kill him either. That was the agreement the emperor had made with Cassia. The marriage in exchange for Aric's and Doric's lives. It wasn't an agreement Doric liked, but it was the agreement.

He shook his head, looked at the apple, and took a bite from it so as to close the matter for good.

He chewed twice and then stopped. Something wasn't right. He put two fingers in his mouth and pulled a strange rough and yet soft object. It was a roll of parchment half as long as his pinky. How in the mercy of Mother Ava had that gotten inside the apple?

He unrolled the parchment and read silently.

BEHIND THE CLOSET THERE IS A DOOR
WAIT FOR MIDNIGHT
OLD TEMPLE

CHAPTER 4

The Secret Meeting

He read the message three times. The second time, he spat out the pieces of apple still inside his mouth. The third time, he dropped the apple to the floor, then looked at the wardrobe.

Was it possible?

The piece of furniture looked like a gigantic brick made of wood and appeared to weigh accordingly. He tried moving it, pulling on one side, but the wardrobe did not budge. He placed a shoulder against it and pushed with as much strength as he could. It was like trying to move a wall. He stopped so he could take a breath, then resumed pushing until his face turned red and finally the wardrobe gave in. It moved only one foot, but as it dragged along the floor, it screeched.

Doric stopped, scared, and stared at the room's door, holding his breath. Had the guard heard anything? Nothing happened. The door did not open. He decided it was safe and looked at the piece of wall that had been revealed. There was a door back there, no doubt about it.

Cassia…

This time, he pushed with both his hands. Sweat broke out on his forehead and the veins in his neck looked like they were about to pop. The wardrobe moved across the floor but squealed so loud that everyone in the inn had surely heard. He looked at the room's door again and saw the doorknob spin.

Crap!

Like lightning, he grabbed the wardrobe's door and flung it wide open, hoping it was large enough to cover the secret passage that was now visible. The Legionnaire entered the room with a confused look on his face.

"Damn old furniture," Doric said, still holding the closet door. "Squeals like an Akhami pig." He bent into the closet and inhaled. "Smells like one, too."

The Legionary laughed, then wished him good night and left. Doric sighed with relief before returning to inspecting the secret door. He peeked through the lock and saw an empty room on the other side. Cautiously, he opened the door and crossed to the other room. It was just like his, except for the entrance door, which was placed perpendicularly to his own, meaning it led out to a different corridor.

Once again, very carefully, he opened it and peeked outside, trying to be as quiet as possible. It was indeed a different corridor, and it was unguarded, but the secret note did not have any further instructions. What was he supposed to do now? He figured it shouldn't be too hard to get out of the inn from there.

Tiptoeing, he walked to the end of the corridor and down a flight of stairs, where he found a dark pantry with bags full of potatoes, beans, and onions. There were muffled voices coming from nearby, which probably belonged to the Legionaries who had brought him there.

He took a look around, searching for a way out. It was clearly the back of the inn, so there should be some kind of service door around, and he soon discovered that he was right. He found it right after a row of wine barrels, and almost stopped for a cup. If he was really going to see Cassia after all these years, he sure could use one. But he was more afraid to get caught than he was thirsty, so he decided to leave the barrels alone and get the hell out of there.

Once outside, he started running like a madman, his heart jumping, and did not slow down until he had turned three corners. He stopped to catch his breath. All he had to do now was get to the old part of town. He remembered the Old Temple but could not understand why Cassia had chosen it. There were so many places in the capital that had a special meaning for them. The Moon Garden, where they had kissed for the first time, The Lost Tunnels, which they always visited on their trips to Augusta... Why the Old Temple?

Because after fifteen years, she obviously doesn't feel the same way about you, he thought. She probably just wanted to know if he was all right.

Doric disappeared into the crowd. In Augusta, the streets were never empty.

The Old Temple was stuck between a series of abandoned houses. Once upon a time, it had been the center of the city; now it was home to rats and homeless people. The streets had never been cobbled, so Doric hopped between dry portions of road, trying to avoid the mud and the puddles of water and urine.

The temple building, the oldest in Augusta, had walls covered in moss. The entrance was a stairway into the underground, where the nave was located. In fact, the visible part of the building was merely decorative, as it had been built centuries before, during the Great Dragon Scourge, when cities were still built underground. In those days, the size of the temple would have been mind-blowing. Now, though, it looked like a smelly basement. Everyone knew that every priest or priestess not aligned with the Supreme Sister could end up presiding over the celebrations in there.

Doric walked down the stairs. The steps had been polished by time and were damp from Ava knew what. Wrinkling his face in disgust, he placed a hand on the wall, afraid of losing his step. A calico cat jumped away when he stepped near.

What a dreadful place.

The nave had a reddish color thanks to the candles that had been randomly spread about. Doric saw a man nestled in a corner, his ragged clothes exposing a myriad of scars. The man showed Doric his teeth with a mad look on his face and opened one of his shirt's tears wider, displaying the mark of the Dragon Hunters: a *V*, undulating like two wings, or two blades, it was hard to tell. With his other hand, the madman pointed with a knife to where the iron had branded him. Underneath the Hunter's symbol, there were three small triangles. With the tip of the knife, he indicated each one, showing Doric how many dragons he had slain. Then he aimed the knife at Doric and snarled. Doric decided to step the other away.

It sure did not look like a place where Cassia would go. Could the message be from someone else?

"You!"

Doric jumped. He turned toward the voice and saw a man pointing an accusatory finger. He had the beard of a beggar but wore the tunic of a priest. His milky, blind eyes were looking nowhere.

Doric looked around, puzzled. "Me?"

"You will bring the fire!"

"Ah…all right…." Doric would have gladly run away, but the priest was now practically leaning on him. "Maybe later, if I have time."

"You will bring the dragons. Thousands of dragons. They will cover the world in fire."

Doric cursed his luck. Was there anyone down there who was not insane?

He tried to escape the priest. "Nice to meet you too, Holy Brother. Now, if you don't mind, I'm going to…." He looked everywhere for a distraction. "Pray. I'm going to pray a little."

"The wound in the sky will return, and the heavens will bleed."

"That is…regrettable," Doric said, walking away from the priest.

"Mother Ava will weep for her children once more," the blind man insisted. "Ashes do not pray, Blood Carrier."

"No, I don't think they do."

"Doric?!"

His head spun so fast, it nearly snapped off, but the voice did not belong to Cassia.

"Lerica?"

The woman ran to him and wrapped him in a long embrace.

"I can't believe you came."

And he didn't know why he had, he almost said.

They studied each other without letting go. Doric thought she looked the same. How many years had it been? Five? Ten?

"I don't remember ever seeing you wearing armor," Doric said.

"Times have changed." Lerica smiled. "But we should talk somewhere else."

Doric was confused. Was she taking him to Cassia? What was going on?

"Priest Frir is runium-sensitive," Lerica said, indicating the blind man, who was now putting out every candle he could find. "But he was never trained. The Academy turned him down for being blind."

"So he tried to learn on his own."

Lerica lit a torch and cleared away a tapestry hanging behind the altar, revealing a tunnel.

"Runium is a dangerous substance," she agreed, then led him through the tunnel.

The walls were dripping and Doric saw several mice running along the wall, frightened by the flame of the torch.

"Ironically, it saved his life," Lerica continued. "If he had been admitted to the Academy, he would probably have died during the Purge."

"I suppose being insane is not the worst way to spend your life."

Lerica looked at him and placed a comforting hand on his shoulder.

"No, it's not," she said. "Besides, he's a great lookout." She smiled and winked.

Lerica and Cassia had been friends, and Doric had always liked her. On the other hand, her husband hated Doric's guts.

"How is Haldan?"

Her smile went away.

"Dead. Hanged last year."

Doric felt like an imbecile.

"Lerica… I'm so sorry, I should have known, I…"

She shrugged.

"That's okay. I'm just happy you're here."

They had reached a door and she knocked. First three times, then two, then three again. The door opened and Lerica walked him in.

"Look who's here," she said.

Inside were two men and a woman sitting around a table. They were all familiar faces, but Cassia was not one of them.

"Doric?" Hagon asked. He was Cassia's cousin, and also hated him with a passion.

"It's great to see you, old man." Eirin was the daughter of a friend of Doric's father. They had spent their childhood together, and she stood on the tips of her toes to lay a kiss on his cheek.

Doric was deeply confused. What were they doing there, and more importantly, why had they brought him there?

"You finally came to join us," Tarnig said with a smile from ear to ear. He was probably the best friend Doric had had in his youth.

"It's the right decision, Doric," Lerica said with a comforting hand on his back. "Our numbers grow every day. Tarsus's days are numbered."

Rebels. They were rebels. In every hall of every noble house of the Empire, there were whispers about the growing conspiracy against Tarsus. But why in the name of Ava had they brought him here?

"Listen, easy. I'm not..." Doric did not know how to finish that sentence.

"Brave?" Hagon suggested.

"I was going to say...a warrior, but sure, as you prefer."

"Of course you are," Tarnig said. "Everyone can have a role to play. Besides, you can learn. I'll train you."

"And you have your family's resources," Eirin added. "Ava knows we need funds."

"And your name," Lerica said. "The son of the great Faric Auron."

"You're not listening to me!" Doric snapped. "I compose songs. Write poems. Drink.... I'm not a soldier. Or a conspirator." Doric saw a wave of disappointment sweep the room. "I'm not one of you."

"I don't understand," Eirin said. "Of all the people in the Empire, who would have more reasons than you for hating Tarsus?"

Doric did not reply. She was right, of course, but what was he supposed to do? Sing poorly at Tarsus's Legions?

"Then what are you doing here?" Hagon asked, suspicious.

"What do you mean, what am I doing here?"

"Hagon, relax," Tarnig said, then turned to Doric. "Who told you about us? Ondreth? Tessa?"

"What are you talking about?"

Hagon stood up. "Answer the question, Doric. What are you doing here?" He stormed toward Doric and unsheathed his sword. "How did you find us?"

"Hagon, easy," Tarnig said.

"Shush!" Hagon demanded. "How did you find us, Doric?"

"How did I find you?!" Doric yelled, almost bursting into a fit of rage. "You brought me here!"

He removed the small parchment roll and flung it in Hagon's face.

"The mad woman in the middle of the crowd. The message inside the apple. The door behind the wardrobe," he said.

The eyes of all five of them went wide.

"What?" said Lerica, sounding terrified.

Eirin took a step back. "No…"

"Ava Mother." Tarnig drew his sword.

At that moment, Doric heard thunder behind him where the door was, and Hagon cursed. He looked over his shoulder and saw the door explode into pieces. A steel gauntlet fell on him and everything became black.

⌒

Tarsus had never called her to watch a trial. In fact, it was extremely rare for *him* to waste his time with trials. It was uncommon for a judge to pass a sentence that did not please the emperor, and when it did happen, Vigild usually fixed the problem discreetly. However, it was quite obvious why he had chosen to do it this time.

In front of her, on their knees, were five men and women. Her cousin Hagon, her friends Lerica, Eirin, and Tarnig, and finally – the real motive for the show – Doric, her former husband.

A herald struck his baton twice against the marble floor and proclaimed, "His Imperial Majesty, Tarsus V. King of Augusta and Samehria, Ultrarch of Akham, and Emperor of Arrel."

Tarsus sauntered to his throne and sat. Cassia did not move and remained standing in front of her throne.

"What is the meaning of this, Tarsus?"

"Commander, you heard the empress. Please, tell us," Tarsus said calmly.

The Legionary captain tapped a closed fist against his heart, took a step forward, and began his report.

"After several months of investigations, the Information Scriptorium handed us the details that allowed us to effect the arrest of a group of conspirators. Our intelligence indicates that the suspects belong to an organized group of nobles whose goal is to topple the emperor and seize the throne."

"Rebels, you mean," Tarsus concluded. "Traitors."

The captain agreed with a nod and proceeded.

"At the location where the arrest took place, we found several documents, from maps of Augusta's underground, to ship cargo manifestos, to the emperor's own schedule. We also found several letters filled with incriminatory messages, signed or addressed to the suspects. All prisoners are members of one of the Great Houses, and some have connections to the Imperial House itself, as is the case of…" he trailed as he took a look at the document in his hand. "Hagon Sefra, cousin of the empress, and Doric Auron, former husband of the empress. It is the opinion of the agents of the Information Scriptorium that the role of these two suspects was to provide sensitive information about the emperor."

When he had finished the captain once again saluted, then took a step back.

"I think you forgot the part where one of your agents gave me –" Doric was interrupted by a punch from one of the Legionaries.

"The prisoners will only speak when authorized," the captain informed him.

"The law is clear," the emperor proclaimed, rising.

"Tarsus…" Cassia said.

"The penalty for treason is death."

"You made a promise!" Cassia's voice was shaking.

"He conspired to have me killed," Tarsus roared. "What am I to do? Make an exception because he used to be your husband?"

Cassia fell to her knees. "Please!" she begged, tears rolling down her face. "He's the father of my son."

The emperor ignored her.

"For treason against the Empire and conspiring to assassinate the emperor," Tarsus's voice echoed through the hall, "I sentence you to death by hanging."

"No!" Cassia shrieked.

"The sentence will be carried out tomorrow." Tarsus spun around and left.

The empress was left sobbing on the floor in front of her throne. She saw the five prisoners being dragged away by the Legionaries. Before he disappeared, Doric smiled at her.

⌒

"I'm sorry," Fadan said.

Aric kept his eyes on the floor. "I didn't even remember his face," he mumbled.

Fadan didn't know what else to say. "Maybe Mum can do something about it."

Aric shook his head. "He's been safe all these years, and now that he came to see me they'll kill him."

Fadan sat down beside his brother and put an arm around his shoulder as Aric cried and cried. He choked on his own sobs, blew his nose a dozen times, and wiped countless tears off his face. Fadan just stayed there, quietly, as his brother wept it all out: the father he had never seen and was about to lose, the mother who could rarely treat him like a son, the stepfather who acted like he wanted him dead.

Fadan's stomach turned. He had always known his mother had not come to the Citadel out of her own free will. He had always known that the emperor, his own father, had forced her by threatening to kill Doric if Cassia did not submit. It wasn't fair for her. It wasn't fair for Doric. It wasn't fair for Aric. It wasn't fair.

"We'll save him!"

"What?" Aric sniffled.

"We'll get him out of the dungeons. You know a way in. You showed it to me."

Aric laughed. "That's insane," he said. "Even I can see that's suicide."

It was, but they had to try something.

"We managed to break into the Paladins' headquarters and steal two flasks of runium, right under their noses," Fadan said. "The dungeon can't be that different."

Aric thought about it for a moment.

"I don't know," he said. "If we're caught… Think about what your father would do to you."

"You didn't worry about that when you wanted to be a mage," Fadan said, standing up.

"That was different. If we had been caught doing that, the emperor would have locked you in your room a few months, maybe give you a beating. But if he catches you trying to break my dad out of prison…"

"Listen to me. Your father is going to be hanged tomorrow. If you want to do this, we have to do it *now.*"

If only Fadan had had time to learn a spell or two, maybe a way to become invisible…

"Aric!" Fadan called. "We're going to save your father. I promise you."

One thing was certain. They had to at least try.

⌒⟶

Cassia stormed through the hallways toward Intila's office. She found him at the door, handing documents to some officer. Seeing her, Intila sent the officer away.

"Why did you do it?" Cassia demanded.

"I did nothing." Intila turned his back to her and walked into his office. Cassia followed him.

"How could you?" Cassia asked. "The son of your beloved Faric. He's practically your brother."

"He is no such thing," Intila said.

"Why, Intila?"

"Listen to me, Cassia." The High Marshal pierced her with his eyes.

"I'm not a coward like your former husband. If I say I didn't do it, then I didn't."

There was a moment of silence as Cassia dealt with that. As if trying to defuse the tension, Intila sat at his desk. She sat across from him.

"Then who?" she asked.

"My guess is Vigild."

"Vigild?" she echoed.

"Who else?"

"But…the investigation came from the Scriptorium. Your own Legionary said so."

"Yes, my spies have been tracking the rebels for months, but I had no intention to act now. It's too soon. Besides" – Intila opened a drawer and removed a piece of parchment – "this is a list of all those who have somehow interacted with the rebels in the past months."

Cassia studied the list. There were dozens of names.

"As you would expect," Intila said. "Your former husband never even tried to get near them."

Cassia sank in her chair. That made no sense. "So, why Vigild? And how?"

Intila frowned and his jaw twitched.

"That's what I need to find out."

The dungeon was like a cave that had been dug beneath Mount Capitol. There was some light coming from torches hanging on the cell corridor, enough for Doric to see the contours of Hagon's face. There was a leak in the ceiling that caused a ceaseless trickle right beside the haystack he would use as his bed, not that he was going to stay there for long. He was also sure they were sharing their cell with a rat.

"I don't understand. Why did they make you go there? They obviously knew about our meetings," said Hagon, sitting by the cell door.

"Because you weren't the target," Doric replied. "Tarsus finally found a way to get rid of me."

"So, we're just an excuse?"

"Which says a lot about your rebellion's chances of success," Doric said.

He got up and leaned against the cell railing as Hagon stared at the floor, contemplating his own failure.

"What about the others?" Hagon asked. "If they knew about us, they probably know a lot more."

"Don't worry. After the spectacle Tarsus is planning for tomorrow, I'm sure many of them will be smart enough to go into hiding. In the end, I might have saved your friends."

Hagon jumped up.

"At least *we* tried to do something! What about you? What did you do? Got drunk every day?"

"Shush!"

That made Hagon so furious, he was about to punch him. "Don't you –"

"Be quiet!" Doric whispered. "I heard something."

Hagon was confused, but he tried to listen. "What?" he whispered back. "It's probably a guard."

Doric shook his head. Then a shape appeared outside the bars and grabbed the lock.

"Aric?!" Doric wasn't sure if he should be ecstatic or furious. "What are you doing here?"

Aric simply told him to be quiet with a gesture and continued fiddling with the lock. At that moment, a second shape arrived with his back to the bars, not taking his eyes from the other end of the cellblock. Doric kneeled in front of Aric.

"What are you doing? This is a cell door. You can't open it."

"Not every door in the Citadel is always unlocked," said Aric. "I can do it."

"Son!" Doric grabbed Aric's arms, forcing him to stop. "The guards can show up at any moment. You have to leave!"

"Shush!" the second shape said.

"Who's this?" Doric asked.

"My name is Fadan," he whispered. "We can be introduced later."

"The prince!" Hagon almost screamed.

This time, it was Doric who asked for silence. That's when they heard a metallic crackle and the cell door snapped open. By the look on Aric's face, no one was more surprised than he.

The two prisoners left the cell. Doric wasn't sure if he wanted to kiss Aric as much as he wanted to slap him.

"We have to go. Quick," Fadan said.

The four of them got out of there, moving fast. Hagon looked everywhere, checking inside every cell, until they reached the end of the cellblock. All of the cells were empty. Hagon stopped.

"Wait. Where are the others? Eirin, Lerica, and Tarnig?" he asked.

"This was the first block we searched," Aric said. "The sewer exit is right around the corner, to the left."

There was a moment of silence. Hagon's eyes wandered, indecisive.

"We have to go," Fadan begged.

Hagon looked at Doric as if his soul was bleeding. He had to save his friends.

"I can't stay here," Doric explained, indicating Aric.

"I understand, but I can't leave my people here to die."

Doric swallowed through a dry throat, then placed a hand on his shoulder.

"Don't do it. It's not cowardice when the alternative is suicide."

"Someone's coming," Fadan whispered. "A guard."

The four of them shrank against the wall simultaneously. Around the corner, a shadow stretched, and someone coughed.

"Doric," Hagon called in a low whisper. "Good luck."

Without saying anything else, Cassia's cousin broke into a run and turned the corner. They heard the sound of Hagon tackling the guard, who immediately started screaming. Doric peeked around the corner and saw Hagon picking himself up and running away until he disappeared into another corridor. The guard chased after him, yelling an alarm.

"It's clear," Doric said.

The three of them turned the corner and Fadan led them to the sewer exit. They opened the trapdoor and jumped down. Once on the other side,

Aric removed a metal block from his pocket, placed it against the door's wood, and dragged it to the left. From the other side came the sound of the metal lock sliding back into place.

Doric was deeply impressed with that. "Wow!"

"I told you." Aric smiled. "I have lessons about everything."

They strode through the sewer tunnel until they reached a rusty railing, and once on the other side, Fadan and Aric placed two iron bars back in the railing. Then they walked a few more paces until they reached a steep, narrow ladder, on top of which was the metal cover of a manhole. Doric climbed up first and held the cover open so the two brothers could go through it.

They had done it. It was unbelievable, but they had. Around them, the empty palaces of the outer Citadel stood quietly in the shadows.

Doric let himself fall onto his back panting as Fadan dusted his jacket off.

"We have to get your father down to the river," the prince said. "It's possible they'll shut the city gates as soon as they figure he's missing."

Fadan received no answer.

"Aric?"

His brother was studying the darkness with narrowed eyes.

"What is it?" Fadan asked.

Aric spun around, grabbing Fadan's collar. He opened the manhole cover and threw him in. As he slammed the cover shut again, two dozen Legionaries emerged from the darkness, forming a circle around them, their spears at the ready.

CHAPTER 5

The Sentence

Tarsus paced along his office with his eyes on the floor.

"I can't just kill him," he said, walking by his desk for the third time. "Cassia already thinks me a monster. What would she say if I did that?"

"And Your Majesty wishes *my* advice?" Intila asked. "Why not Vigild's?"

"Vigild is an efficient man, no doubt," Tarsus said, "but, in this case, I need someone a bit more…humane."

The marshal nodded an agreement. "Lock the boy in a dungeon for a couple of months, in the dark, on bread and water. Then confine him to his bedroom for another couple of months. He will learn his lesson."

The emperor looked as if he was about to vomit. "Never! What is wrong with you, marshal? Are you getting soft?"

"He's just a child. He tried to help his father, nothing more." He paused. "If Your Majesty were caught by an enemy, Fadan would certainly not rest until you were freed."

Tarsus gave Intila an intense look. His mouth moved to say something, but nothing came out. His eyes flickered and he turned away from Intila. "Ah, of course," he finally said. "It's because he's Faric's grandson. The mighty Faric Auron. The dead can't collect debts, Marshal."

"I owe Faric nothing, Your Majesty. Nor his family."

Tarsus did not look the least bit convinced. He walked to his window. From there, Augusta always looked serene. "The boy cannot stay in the Citadel," he said. "Or Augusta."

Intila could almost see the thoughts taking shape inside the emperor's mind. He stepped closer, cautiously. "Very well," he said. "Some form of exile, then. There are loyal nobles that could take Aric as their ward. They would maintain the boy under a watchful eye."

Tarsus shook his head, his obsessive stare locked on some point down in the city. "No, that's not enough. It is a punishment, after all."

"Out of the Empire, then," Intila suggested. "We can choose an Aletine Tribune, for example. Any one of them would consider it an honor."

"I'm not sending him on a nice vacation abroad, Marshal," Tarsus replied. "But you do have one point. Some sort of exile...." He paused. "Some place far from here, but where he would be kept under close watch." Tarsus spun with a glint in his eyes. "Where he can redeem himself."

Intila felt a shill going down his spine. "What do you have in mind, Your Majesty?"

But the marshal already knew the answer.

"Lamash. I'll send him to Lamash."

⌒⁊

Intila marched across the Palace halls under a succession of salutes until he arrived at the Imperial family corridor. Cassia's door was guarded by two Legionaries standing at attention.

"Open the door."

The two soldiers exchanged a glance.

"Sir...we have orders to...not to..." Intila's glare made it impossible for the man to finish his sentence.

The Legionary stepped aside and opened the door. Without so much as a look, Intila walked past him, into the empress's room.

Cassia jumped out of bed and stormed toward Intila, her eyes blood-red. She slapped him with her right hand. The Marshal exhaled loudly as a red handprint grew on his cheek.

"There wasn't –" Intila was interrupted by another slap, this time from the left hand. He shut his eyes.

"Tarsus told me that this was your idea," Cassia said. "That you advised him against being too soft. Is this true?"

Intila didn't even blink. "The penalty for what Aric did is death. At least this way, he has a chance."

"A chance?!" Cassia screamed. "At what? What's the life expectancy of a Dragon Hunter? Five years? Ten?"

"Many Hunters live to grow old."

"Yes. The ones that are lucky enough to be mutilated. Or become mad."

Cassia let herself fall into a chair, too tired to even cry.

"Aric is a strong boy. He takes after his grandfather," Intila said. "He will pull through, you'll see."

Cassia did not reply. Giving up, the marshal sighed. There was nothing else he could tell her. He turned around and headed to the door.

"And Doric?" Cassia asked.

Intila stopped. "The execution has been postponed."

"I need you to delay it as long as possible," Cassia said. "Please, Intila. At least until my birthday."

"Very well," Intila said after an overlong pause. Then left.

⌐⌐

He had been locked in for hours. Instead of the dungeons, the soldiers had taken him to a prison car in the middle of the courtyard. It was just like any other carriage, except the wood it had been built with was much thicker, and its only window was blocked with iron bars.

In the middle of the night, the Legionaries guarding him were replaced by Paladins, and one of them was kind enough to let him know where they were taking him. Lamash, the home fortress of the Dragon Hunters Guild.

It wasn't worse than the gallows waiting for his father, but it wasn't much better, either. He was being exiled to the confines of the Empire, to spend the rest of his life in the scorching, dragon-riddled desert.

I'll be dragon lunch.

His thoughts were interrupted by voices from somewhere outside. He rose, bending so he didn't bump his head against the ceiling. When he got to the small, barred window, Fadan's face appeared on the other side.

"Are you all right?" the prince asked.

"I think so," Aric said with a shrug.

There was a brief silence.

"It was a dumb question," Fadan said. "I'm sorry."

"That's okay. Did they allow you to speak to me?"

"I didn't ask for permission."

Aric nodded, and the awkward silence returned.

"Thank you," Fadan said at last, his voice cracking. "It should have been the other way around. If they had caught me —"

"You'd be in trouble and I'd be blamed anyway," Aric concluded in his stead.

"Maybe… I don't know." Fadan couldn't take his eyes off the ground. "Maybe not."

Aric summoned a chuckle. "I'm the older brother. It was about time I took care of you instead of the other way around."

Fadan looked over his shoulder briefly, then removed something from his jacket.

"I went to your room and found this on your bed." He handed Aric a parcel through the bars. "It looked important."

Aric smiled. It was the armor Doric had gifted him. There was surely no place in the world where he would need it more than where he was going.

"I found this as well." Fadan showed a small packet.

"No," Aric said, pushing his brother's hand away from the bars. "That's for Mum. My father told me it belongs to her."

The prince nodded his understanding and put the packet back in his pocket. At that moment, they heard the rattling of horse hooves. Fadan looked behind and saw a group of Paladins turning a corner. One of them, sporting a red feather on his helm, barked a sequence of orders, and the rest of them spread across the courtyard, performing their tasks.

"Majesty." The Paladin Commander bowed. "It is time. We must take the prisoner."

"One moment, Captain."

"Certainly." The man bowed again, this time just with his head, then he turned to his men and resumed his barking. "Why is that gate still closed? Sergeant, I want six horses pulling this carriage. *Six*. This is not your father's potato cart."

Fadan drew closer to the barred window, as if he could get away from the noise. Aric started shaking, and Fadan watched his color disappear.

"Calm down. It'll be all right," Fadan said.

Aric nodded, but his face seemed to disagree. "Fadan, I'm scared," he said.

"I know," He had no idea what else to say.

"Majesty." The captain was back. "We really have to go. Your father's orders, I'm afraid."

Fadan nodded, then turned to his brother. Aric looked like he was about to vomit.

"I'll get you out," Fadan said, but his brother didn't seem to be listening. "One day, I'll get you out of there. I promise."

At that moment, the carriage drove off, and Fadan, with a tear rolling down his face, watched his brother move away. It reminded him of one other promise he had made the night before.

"We're going to save your father," Fadan had told his brother.

How many promises would he have to make before he could start keeping them?

Aric watched the gates of Augusta become smaller and smaller until they disappeared behind a hill. It was hard to believe he was headed south, never to return. He would never again sneak to his mother's room to share a secret meal. He would never scour the library again for another book about his ancestors, or cross the palace on the tips of his toes, chasing Fadan through the night.

Reality began to set in as the green, flower-covered fields of Arrel became sharp, copper-colored hills. In less than a day, they were in Samehria.

He had been locked in his room many times, but this experience was very different. The rough wooden floor transmitted every single one of the road's imperfections, which at first was merely bothersome but quickly became painful. He tried standing up, but that only managed to throw him face first against a wall twice.

When the sun finally set, the carriage stopped, and the six Paladins made a small camp by the side of the road. Soon, the only visible light was that of the fire where they roasted three hares. Aric was given two slices of bread and a gulp of wine. He stood by the window, watching as the Paladins devoured their dinner. After finishing, one of them threw the bones of his meal into Aric's cell.

"Here, you can chew on those," he said with a sneer.

The others laughed. All except one, who simply stared thoughtfully at Aric. He had a huge mole on his nose and a twisted, grumpy mouth. Aric watched him take a bite out of a roasted leg with an absent-minded look on his face.

With their bellies full, it didn't take long until four of them were snoring loudly. The remaining two stood watch – the thinker with the mole on his nose, and the sergeant who lead the escort and whom everyone simply called Urin.

Aric scanned his cell. He would have to find a way to sleep in there. The dark, naked wood wrapped him like a coffin and he shrank, holding his own legs tight for warmth. He had never felt so alone.

It should be only a few more days, but as soon as he arrived in Lamash, he would simply be trading one prison for another, except the new one would be crueler and deadlier. How many Hunters usually died for every dragon they killed?

There was no way he could go to the desert. He couldn't stay in this cell. He had to escape.

But how?

"Pssst," he called.

"What?" the sergeant asked in a whisper.

"I need to pee," Aric whispered back.

The Paladin hesitated but asked the other one for a pair of handcuffs, and opened the cell door.

"Don't get any ideas," he warned as he cuffed Aric.

Aric said yes with a nod and started to walk away.

"Hey!" the sergeant called. "Where do you think you're going?"

"Behind a bush. Or should I piss on your boots?"

The other Paladin, the one with the huge mole, grabbed Aric's arm.

"Don't worry; I'll keep an eye on him."

Holding his arm, the Paladin took Aric to a small clearing seven paces behind the fire. Aric tried going farther into the woods but the Paladin's fingers dug into his arm.

"This is far enough," the Paladin said, motioning toward a small bush.

Aric stayed where he was, wobbling from the Paladin to the bush.

"What?" the guard asked.

"It's that..." he replied, embarrassed, "I actually wanted to...do everything."

The Paladin cursed his luck and gestured for him to hurry. Aric began to drop his pants but stopped midway through the movement, staring at the Paladin.

"Do you mind?" he asked.

The Paladin groaned but turned around. With the guard looking away from him, Aric crouched and combed the ground. The moon was mostly covered by clouds, so he couldn't tell a mushroom from a tree branch. Fumbling around, he found three pebbles, a twig, and several leaves, until he finally felt the polished surface of a large rock, but it was partially buried.

"Are you going to take all night?" the Paladin asked.

Aric made a sound as if he was pushing with all his strength, making the Paladin cover his eyes and twist his face in disgust. Trying not to laugh at his own theatre, he dug his fingers into the dirt around the rock, exposing its side. Then he buried his nails as deep as he could and pulled hard until the rock gave and climbed into his hands. He pulled his arm back, taking aim.

The sergeant appeared out of nowhere. "Why is this taking so long?"

Aric hid the rock behind his back.

"He wanted to take a dump," the other one replied.

Urin looked at Aric suspiciously. In one fluid movement, Aric put the rock inside his pants and rose as he pulled them up, praying that the rock would not roll down his leg.

"All done," he said.

The Paladins took him back to the cell, and when they got to the door, Aric showed them his handcuffed hands.

"You can keep those," Urin told him.

The cell door slammed behind Aric and the lock clicked into place.

Disappointed for having lost the mobility of his hands, he watched the guards walk away from the cell window. He tried to take the stone from the back of his pants. Obviously, the cuffs didn't exactly help, and he almost dislocated his shoulder trying to reach around his back, but using the wall as a lever, he eventually managed to release the rock. It fell and he grabbed it, feeling its weight. A hit over the head with that would cause a lot of damage, even to someone wearing a helmet.

He smiled happily. The following night would be very different.

⌒⟶

As they entered the heart of Samehria, it became hotter, and the cell became a dark oven. Sweat had been dripping down his body like a waterfall for the last couple of hours.

"Can you please give me something to drink?" he asked.

There were two Paladins riding near the back of the carriage. One of them was the one with the big black mole, but it was the other one who replied.

"We can't open the cell while we're moving." As he said this, he opened a wine bag he was carrying on his belt. "You can drink when we stop." He made a motion as if he was toasting with someone and drank two long gulps, then smiled.

Aric swallowed a curse. He didn't, *wouldn't* give that jerk the satisfaction.

"Speaking of stopping," the Paladin with the mole said. "How much further until we get there?"

"I don't know," the other replied. "These Samehrian roads are always the same." He scanned the landscape. "I'll ask Urin." He spurred his horse and disappeared toward the front.

The Paladin with the black mole watched his comrade depart, then got near Aric's window and gave him his own wine bag. Aric promptly accepted and drank greedily. It was without question the worst wine he had ever tasted, but it quenched his thirst.

"My name is Corca," the man said.

Aric thanked him and returned the wine bag.

"I assume you know who I am?" Aric replied.

Corca nodded and backed away, still looking surly.

For the first time since entering Samehria, Aric saw houses appear by the road. They became more and more frequent and all looked the same, their round rooftops made of the same brown stone as the rest of the walls. It was as if their builders had wanted them to be indistinguishable from the ground. At the same time, the road became busier, with carriages coming and going both ways. Eventually, they passed the gates of an enormous city wall and then crossed a series of clogged streets until the carriage stopped.

The cell door opened and he was told to step outside, his gaze immediately drawn to a gigantic fortress commanding the whole city. It possessed only one tower, around which the rest of the building was cradled. If it weren't for its white color, it would have been hard to tell the fortress from the hill where it was standing, but Aric recognized it from the illustrations of several books in the library. He was in Victory, the capital of Samehria.

That was the perfect place to stage an escape. Victory was almost as large as Augusta. If he could manage to get away from his guards, it would be impossible for them to find him in the middle of the crowd. All he needed was a chance like the one he had had the previous night.

One of the Paladins pushed him. "Move!"

They entered the door into a stone building the size of a hut. Once inside, all Aric could see was a stairway that seemed to go down forever. The polished steps and mossy walls looked far more ancient than any structure he had ever seen.

"What is this place?" he asked as they landed at the bottom of the stairs.

"Welcome to the Bloodhouse of Victory," the sergeant told him.

Aric's eyebrows moved up, puzzled.

"You rich people call these places rune temples," Corca told him.

Aric had never been inside one, especially because no one was allowed inside, except for Paladins, of course. He had read as many books about them as he had found. The accounts of the explorers who had first found them, the tales of the alchemists who had deciphered its mysteries. He had even read the ramblings of the historians who had spent their lives studying them, each with his own wild theory about the origins of the sacred places.

It was very different from what he had imagined. He had only ever seen illustrations of the brewing chambers, where dragon blood was transformed into runium. But he had expected something wider, more spacious and dignified, not these dark, cramped tunnels that were covered in moss. After all, this was supposed to be the work of gods, not men.

This place was far more interesting than any forgotten section of the Citadel. It was a shame to be inside such a building and not be allowed to freely explore it. With his head spinning in every direction, he tried to collect as much information as he could. The torches lighting the way were sparse, but around them, where the fire made the walls golden, Aric saw the famous runes etched upon the stone. The entire structure of the Temple was supposed to be covered in them. Unfortunately, and without better lighting, there was no way he could confirm it.

After a few turns and a couple of massive wooden doors, the Paladins locked him in a dark cell and Aric cursed his luck. He had never been in such a remarkable place. It was as if he had just jumped into one of the stories of the ancient Surface Runners but was not allowed to turn the page. Not to mention it would be impossible to attempt an escape that night.

He leant against the bars, looking miserable.

Maybe tomorrow.

He studied his prison. Even the walls of his cubicle were laden with the ancient, mysterious Runes. There was another cell in front of his. He peered inside and saw a shape.

"Good night," he said. He got no answer. "Smuggler?" he insisted.

Whoever it was finally decided to reply.

"No."

"Mage, then." Aric had never met one.

The man responded in a sour voice. "What about you? You're too young to be either."

"I'm just unlucky."

The prisoner chuckled and decided to approach his bars. A thin stream of light revealed his features. He was old, a long scruffy beard hiding his face. Wrinkles crossed his dark face like scars, brightened only by liquid, blue eyes. Aric was certain he had never seen such a solemn face.

"If you had runium, there would be no way they could keep you in here," Aric said. "How did they catch you?"

"You're full of questions," the man said. "Shouldn't you be crying over *your* fate?"

Aric shrugged. "I will escape. I still have several days of travel between here and Lamash. An opportunity will come up."

"Lamash?" The man studied him. "A skinny kid like you? You won't last a month."

Aric looked down his own body. "I'm not skinny."

Was he?

"You better escape, little boy." The prisoner turned around and returned to his darkness. "The desert will finish you before you even see a dragon."

Somewhere inside his cell, the man lay down and seemed to forget about Aric, who kept analyzing his own body.

Steps echoed outside his cell, and Corca, the Paladin with the mole on his nose, appeared on the other side of the bars. He just stood there, holding a bunch of keys.

What did he want?

Corca slid one of the keys into the cell door, unlocked it, and stepped in. "Have you eaten?"

Aric said no with a shake of his head, but his stare was stuck on the now-opened door. The Paladin had not locked it behind him. It was the chance he had been waiting for.

"That stone you have behind your back," Corca said. "Hand it over."

Of course...

Fuming, Aric gave the Paladin his stone. The man felt its weight.

"You could have killed me with this." His voice was unsettling.

"I didn't want to kill anyone," Aric said, avoiding Corca's look. "The plan was to put you to sleep, at worst."

"Even if you did, there are a dozen guards between this corridor and the exit. They would slice you to bits."

Aric squeezed his mouth shut.

"Just the excuse they needed," Corca continued. "They would get to go home earlier that way."

"They wouldn't!" Aric screamed. "My mother would know. They would hang for it."

The Paladin stepped up to Aric.

"Yes, your mother," he said. "She really likes you, doesn't she?"

What kind of question is that?

Aric said yes with a nod.

"Enough to pay good money if someone helped you escape, am I right?" Corca asked.

Aric couldn't believe his ears. He said yes once again, but this time, he meant it.

The Paladin smiled. "Stay quiet. Don't try anything stupid. I'll take care of everything."

Is he serious?

"As soon as we deliver you in Nish, you'll no longer be the Paladins' responsibility. After that, I'll find you and release you; that way, no one will suspect me. Then I'll take you back to Augusta and your mother will reward me."

Aric stared at him with bulging eyes and muttered another yes.

The Paladin gave a satisfied nod, then left, locking the cell behind him. "I'll get something for you to eat," he said as he walked away.

When Aric finally remembered to thank him, Corca was already gone. On the cell across from him, the old man laughed.

"I guess you're not that unlucky after all."

The days went by, as monotonous as the red landscape around him. He tried his best to do everything as they told him, to be as discreet as possible, just as Corca had instructed him. More than once, though, he had the feeling that the Paladins were trying to provoke him. It was as if they were looking for an excuse to unload their frustrations on him. In the beginning, he had no idea why a defenseless prisoner bothered them so much, but he quickly realized he wasn't just any prisoner. He was a member of the Imperial House. What did they care if he wasn't a son of the emperor, or that Tarsus hated his guts? To the Paladins, Aric was nothing but a spoiled brat who had had the gall to throw it all away by defying the emperor.

No wonder they felt jealous. A little brat had been braver than they ever could.

Cowards.

In Samehria, cities and villages were few and far between, so they were able to sleep under a roof only a couple of nights. The remaining five nights, they camped by the side of the road, but Aric refrained from any other escape attempt. The trip would last only a week or so. Nish was far down south in the Cyrinian March, a thin strip of land stretching from the Western Sea to the Eastern Sea, which separated the Mahari Desert from the rest of Samehria.

They arrived after the sun had set on their ninth day of travel, but not even darkness could explain how empty the city felt. Through his carriage window, Aric did not see a soul, and most buildings looked abandoned, with broken windows and doors sealed with wooden boards. The carriage finally stopped in front of an enormous white building, where they were greeted by an old man wearing a Samehrian tunic. The Paladins marched inside with Aric in front and were visibly upset when the old man told them the Hunter who was supposed to pick him up hadn't arrived yet.

"What does that mean?" Urin, the escort's sergeant, asked. "He arrives tomorrow? After that?"

The old man shrugged, not looking very concerned with that matter. The Paladins cursed and complained loudly about the time it would take to get back home. Ignoring them, the old man signaled Aric to follow him to a staircase.

They were on the last step when they heard "Where do you think you're taking him?" Urin asked.

"To his room," the fragile old Samehrian said.

His skin was the color of wheat. He had lost most of his teeth, so his lips curved inward, slightly disfiguring his tender expression.

"He can't leave our side," the sergeant said.

"The boy belongs to the Guild now. He's no longer your prisoner," the old man informed them.

"He'll belong to the Guild when the Hunter picking him up arrives. Until then, he's my prisoner, so get him down here."

"This Bloodhouse belongs to the Guild." The old man motioned toward Aric. "So, if the boy is here, he's not your prisoner. He's our conscript."

He might have looked fragile, but he showed no sign of fear.

"Every Bloodhouse belongs to the emperor, old fool. Now get him down here unless you want me to get him myself!"

The old man did not even flinch. He frowned challengingly.

"Admirably brave, threatening a toothless old man. I might not hunt dragons anymore, or be young enough to teach you a lesson, but you can't leave here before my fellow Guildsman arrives and takes the boy from you." He held onto the railing and bent toward the Paladins. "I can assure you, he does not possess my limitations." He turned his back to them and continued climbing the stairs.

Aric was unable to suppress a smile. He might not have any intention of joining the Guild, but he couldn't picture anything better than those jerks being humiliated by an elderly man who could barely walk.

The Samehrian opened the door to one room and showed Aric inside. He walked in but stopped midway through.

"I don't mean to abuse your generosity, but…" Aric showed his cuffed hands.

"Don't worry," the old man said. "As soon as they fall asleep, I'll steal the key." He winked, then left.

The man kept his promise. One hour later, he showed up carrying a tray of food. There was goat cheese, slices of grilled ostrich meat, dried dates, bread, a large mug brimming with beer, and a small key. He helped Aric get rid of his cuffs, then stood watching him devour his dinner.

"Are you scared?" the old man asked as Aric licked some fat from his fingers.

He wasn't anymore. Not since Corca had promised he would help him escape. But before that he had been, a lot, so he decided to say yes.

"That's natural. You would be a fool not to. In the desert, everything conspires to kill us. Hunger, thirst, the sun, dune lions, scorpions. Dragons, of course. Even Eliran."

"Who?" Aric asked with a mouthful of cheese.

"Eliran, the desert witch," the old man replied as if everyone knew that.

"There's a witch in the desert?"

"Wherever there are dragons, there are wizards."

"But…why would she want to kill me?" Aric had never harmed any mage. He actually wished he was one.

"Ten years ago, the Empire killed everyone like her. Can you imagine surviving that? What would you do if you were in her place? Would you have any friends among the non-magical folk?"

Aric did not know how to answer that.

"The Guild will teach you to survive in the Mahar," the old man continued. "Where to find water, how to protect yourself from sandstorms, even how to kill a dragon. But they can't teach you how to protect yourself from

Eliran." He paused and there was a small silence. "Oh, many will tell you she doesn't exist. They'll tell you she's just a story to frighten young children. But she's real, and she's out there. So, if you see her...run, boy. *Run.* Or you won't live to tell the story."

Aric felt a chill drum down his spine but told himself it probably was just a story to frighten young children. Besides, he wasn't really going to Lamash. Corca would help him escape.

"You don't believe me, do you?" the Samehrian asked.

Aric replied with a shrug. "I have no reason to believe or doubt you. I just got to Nish. I know nothing about the desert, or witches, or about what a witch might want in the desert."

"Ah!" the old man said. His eyes shone. "That is the question, is it not?"

Was it? Aric wasn't sure he was still following the conversation.

"There is plenty that she might want in the desert. Come with me," he said, then stood up and left. He didn't even wait for Aric.

They went downstairs. The Samehrian didn't seem worried about the Paladins, but Aric could not avoid walking on tiptoes. They walked along two corridors until they arrived at a huge, barricaded door. Above the door, a small inscription had been scraped away and was unreadable, but the symbol of the Academy was still obvious – a flaming drop of water.

"We call the whole building Bloodhouse, but truly the *proper Bloodhouse* is down through this door," the man said. "There are many of these across the Empire, but none is as close to the desert as this one. When magic was forbidden, this Bloodhouse, like all others, was shut down. The city itself suffered a similar fate," he said longingly. "With the exception of a few spice traders, there is nothing left here to attract people, but once Nish was the heart of the magic trade in the Empire. Where there is runium, there is magic, and where there is dragon blood, there is runium. No other city in the Empire had access to as much dragon blood as Nish, and it was all transformed in there." He indicated the door.

"I saw no other Paladins beside the ones who brought me," Aric said. "Who guards this brewing chamber?"

"There is no need anymore. The brewing chamber was destroyed a couple of months ago. And before you ask, no, it was not an order from the emperor."

Aric was confused.

"So…who? How? Why?"

The old man chuckled.

"Exactly." He crossed his arms, hugging himself. "I woke up in the middle of the night. There was a scream; no…a shriek." His eyes were distant now. "Something no human mouth should be able to produce. It chilled my every bone. The other Paladins and I ran down here. The door was cracked open, and the two men who should have been guarding it were gone. We found them both inside, their naked bodies nailed to the wall above the blood pool, except that their bodies had been drained of all their blood and the pool had been smashed to pieces." The old man shivered. "I don't know for sure what happened, but I know it was magic and not the kind the Academy used to make."

That was the creepiest thing Aric had ever heard.

"Why are you telling me this?" he asked.

"You must know. All Hunters do," the old man said, shaking. "She is out there in the desert, and whatever she is doing is unnatural. She must be stopped." He looked downright terrified.

They heard someone clear his throat and both jumped, turning toward the noise. It was a Paladin – Corca.

After a small sigh of relief, the old man said, "Don't worry, sir. I was just showing the new recruit our facilities."

"The boy should rest," the Paladin said, pretending politeness. "Your fellow Guildsman could arrive tomorrow, and if so" – he nodded toward Aric – "it will be a long day for him."

Aric nodded back and agreed. The old man did not object, so shortly after, Aric was back in his room.

That night, Aric dreamt he was having lunch in the main hall of the Citadel with his mother, his father, and Fadan. The mood was joyful and there was no sign of Tarsus anywhere. Then, a dragon appeared in the sky above Augusta, and in the middle of the fire and destruction, Aric got lost from his family and ended up in a desert at the gates of the city. Suddenly alone, lost, and with the scorching sun searing his skin, he walked along the dunes until he found shelter beneath a formation of red rocks. He got scared after seeing a scorpion on the ground, and when he tried to leave, he saw another one, and then another, and another, and another. There were scorpions everywhere, sprouting from the rock itself. He searched for a piece of ground free of the deadly animals, but there was none. Then, he heard a sinister laugh, the laugh of a woman. She came from behind one of the boulders, her gray face like that of a cadaver floating above a white tunic that flowed shapelessly as if there was no body underneath it.

"You shouldn't be here, Hunter!"

He woke up covered in sweat, breathing heavily as if he had just run for hours. He shook his head, trying to remove that image from his mind, her scream still hammering in his ears.

Someone knocked, and Aric opened the door as he wiped the sticky sweat from his face. It was Corca.

The Paladin looked over his shoulder and said, "The Hunter has arrived. We are on our way, and you should leave soon as well." He looked over his shoulder again. "I'll follow you and as soon as the sun sets" – he nodded – "your prison time is over."

Aric smiled, feeling a mix of relief and excitement.

The Paladin turned to walk away, but Aric stopped him.

"Won't your friends notice you're missing?"

"My friends will be wasting what little they have on prostitutes and wine. By the time they realize I'm gone, we'll be at the gates of Victory."

"I thought they couldn't wait to get home."

Corca laughed.

"Their home is whatever brothel is cheap enough for our miserable salary. Don't forget, it will be tonight, so don't fall asleep. I might need help."

The Hunter was probably the strangest person Aric had ever seen. His clothes were a tapestry of metal and leather plates from which claws and fangs of all sorts of predators hung, along with feathers from exotic birds and other objects. His thighs were covered with overlaying steel plates. His hair had been shaven on the right side above his ear but grew down to his shoulder on the rest of his head, braided through with metal rings and colored ribbons. Beside these decorations, the man carried as many weapons as an entire Legion. Aric counted five daggers, one short-sword, four throwing knives, and a hatchet. He was even wearing brass knuckles on his right hand, and apparently he had cut himself with every single one of those blades. His face alone had three scars. One of them crossed his left eye, which, inexplicably, was intact.

The Hunter must have noticed Aric staring at that scar. "We still had mages back then," he said. "A damned physician would not have saved this eye."

Aric asked his name.

"Saruk," he replied. "Volunteer. Back in my day, most of us were. You could make a lot of money hunting dragons." His voice was rough and deep as if it came from a dark, endless well. "Now that runium is forbidden... let's just say the emperor should be more grateful that his skies haven't seen a dragon for centuries."

Aric wondered how many dragons this man had killed, but he was saved the question. Saruk wore the Hunter's mark on his right arm. Under the fire-branded *V* were ten triangles packed in a rectangle.

"Ten!" Aric blurted. "That's a lot of dragons...."

Saruk looked at his tattoo as if it were nothing.

"It's only hard the first couple of times. Most Hunters die from lack of experience. After your fifth, you learn to deal with the panic. That helps."

"How many survive until their fifth?" Aric asked. Maybe the stories about Dragon Hunters were a little exaggerated.

"Most never get to their third."

"Oh."

Once again, Aric felt grateful he was escaping later that night, but this time, it was different. In the middle of his relief, there was some guilt. After all, right beside him was a man who had volunteered to hunt dragons. Hundreds of cities across the Empire could sleep peacefully at night thanks to men and women like him. Aric himself had never even seen a dragon, and he could thank them for that.

He shook his head. There was no point in wasting time with those thoughts. Besides, Saruk himself had admitted that he had joined for the money, not some noble cause. But if that was the case, why hadn't he left the Guild after the Purge?

When the sun finally neared the horizon and the sky became smeared in red, that very question was still hammering his mind. Was it pure altruism, and if it was, what did that say of himself if he ran from that duty?

Saruk stopped his horse and told him they would be sleeping by the roadside tonight. They were already in the desert, but there was still some vegetation here and there. Cacti and other kinds of bushes were spread around them like spilled beans across a kitchen floor.

It shouldn't be long now. Aric caught himself scanning the landscape, hoping to find Corca hiding behind a rock. He scolded himself for that. Saruk could have noticed. It would have made him suspicious.

Aric decided to help the Hunter light the fire, and when the flames began to crackle, he couldn't handle his curiosity anymore.

"Why haven't you left? If hunting dragons isn't lucrative anymore, then why stay? You're a volunteer; you can leave."

Saruk smiled with half his mouth. "What for?" he asked.

That was certainly not the answer Aric was looking for.

"What do you mean, 'what for?' In the desert, everything conspires to kill you. Even Eliran."

"Eliran?" Saruk chuckled. "Eliran is a foolish story told by fools to frighten other fools. As for the desert…" He looked around, as if to an old friend. "It's not more dangerous than the Western Sea or the Shamissai Mountains." He tilted his head toward Aric. "Or the Citadel, wouldn't you say?"

Aric was still not happy. "But you have to risk your life hunting dragons. Ten or twenty dragons' worth of experience matters for nothing if one of them spits a fireball on you."

"That's true," the Hunter conceded as he finished skewering three sand sparrows. "But after you kill a dragon…what else is there?" He paused. "After you go through the anxiety of entering a cavern, not knowing if the monster sleeps or is waiting for you, after you feel the panic of facing a creature the size of a fortress…" He stopped, looking like he was at a loss for words. "Can you imagine its tail, capable of splitting a boulder, crashing down on you? Can you imagine its claws, bigger than a man, burying themselves in the rocky ground where you had stood moments before, its paws shaking the ground with every movement?" There was awe in his voice. "Nothing can prepare you for the moment you face your first dragon, but nothing compares to the frenzy of watching it fall at your feet." Saruk took a deep breath as if he was feeling it right then. "After that, what else is there in the world for you? It's weird, I know, but a man needs a horizon, something bigger than himself to look forward to, to follow or" – he shrugged – "to hunt." Saruk turned his sparrow skewer and the fire crackled. "Besides…" He smiled. "If I left, my wife would shove a lance through my chest. She's a Lancer," he explained.

He had a wife? Aric didn't even know Hunters married. On the other hand, why shouldn't they?

They ate in silence for a bit, lit only by the fire now that night had fallen. Aric gave up thinking about what Saruk had said. After all, he would soon be on his way north again. It didn't make any sense to worry about it now.

At that moment, he saw a shadow a few feet from Saruk. His eyes bulged, and he looked away immediately, fearing Saruk would notice something. To his satisfaction, the Hunter was still thoroughly focused on the bones of a sparrow he was chewing on.

This was it. He was finally going to escape. He had no idea how he would manage to contact his mother, but he would make sure Corca was well rewarded. It would be more than fair.

He casually glanced behind Saruk, who was still busy with his roasted bird. Corca's shadow advanced carefully, without making a sound. Aric realized he was holding a knife, obviously aimed at Saruk's throat.

What is he doing?!

Aric wanted to escape, sure, but not at the expense of the Hunter's life. He tried making a gesture, but it came out too timid for fear of alerting Saruk. Corca was already on top of him, and Aric decided that he had no choice. He jumped and, to his surprise, Saruk did the same. With his back to Corca, the Hunter grabbed the arm holding the knife as if he had always known where it was. He disarmed the Paladin with a swift, invisible movement that ended with Corca lying on his back.

Aric took a step back. He could run. Saruk did not look to be in danger anymore, but now Corca was.

Once again, he was wrong. The Paladin rolled to his right, just in time to miss Saruk's boot aimed for his face. It gave him enough time to stand back up. Without his knife, now in the hands of the Hunter, he unsheathed his sword and entered a guard stance.

Aric took another step back, feeling that this was his chance. He could easily escape now, but his feet refused to move. "Easy!" he said. "There's no need for this. Me and the Paladin can go and no one has to get hurt."

Saruk chuckled. "You're a conscript of the Guild, boy. You're not going anywhere."

"The kid is right," Corca said. "What do you care if he goes to your fortress or not? Are you going to die for a spoiled, useless recruit?"

"He's one of my brothers now. I'll do what is best for him, whether he wants it or not." He turned to Aric, but his knife stayed at the ready. "You don't want to spend the rest of your life as a fugitive. Sooner or later, you'll find yourself in the gallows and —"

Corca tried to catch him off guard with a thrust to his head, and the phrase was left unfinished. Using the knife he had taken from the Paladin, Saruk parried the blow at the same time as he unsheathed a second dagger from his belt, striking at his opponent's belly, all in one single, fluid movement. Corca managed to jump backward, evading the Hunter's blade by the thickness of a hair.

"I could use your help now, kid!" the Paladin said.

"Huh?" Aric wasn't going to attack the Hunter. It wasn't right.

"Listen, kid," Saruk said as he charged with his blades drawing long arcs. "I know who you are, and where you're from." His knives seemed to be everywhere. "In the Guild, we're all equal. All brothers. The Guild can be the home and the family you never had. Don't waste that."

As he finished the sentence, he struck a downward blow so powerful, it disarmed Corca and threw him to the ground, completely helpless.

Saruk raised one of his knives and Aric saw Corca lift a hand as if it could somehow stop the fatal blow.

"No!" Aric screamed. "I'll go with you," he promised.

Saruk froze. He looked at Aric and nodded, satisfied. Corca wasn't as merciful. He grabbed a fistful of sand and threw it at the Hunter's face. Blinded, Saruk staggered back, waving his blades randomly to his own protection.

The Paladin was quick. He recovered his sword, jumped back up, and attacked the left flank of the hunter. Blood burst from Saruk's arm, and the knife it was holding fell to the ground. Still unable to see anything, the Hunter spun, trying to parry the next blow with his other dagger. Corca did the opposite movement, placing himself on the other flank, but when he raised his sword, a burning log crashed into his face.

The Paladin let out a grotesque scream and instinctively stepped back.

With the flaming log still in his hand, Aric yelled, "Run! Get out of here! Quick, before I change my mind."

Corca did not need to be persuaded. He dashed away in a random direction, covering the burned flesh with his hands.

Aric dropped the log and turned to Saruk. The Hunter was still cleaning the sand from his face but could already see through a slit in his watery eyes.

"Dragon Hunter," Aric said in disbelief. "I'm going to regret this."

Saruk smiled. "You have no idea."

CHAPTER 6

The Dragon Hunters of Lamash

It took them three days to reach the mountain fortress. Three days under that merciless, scorching sun, the heat swirling up from the sand in waves. The *"never-ending desert"*, they called it. It was a great sea of dunes under an ever-clear sky, gold and blue for as far as far could be.

Night had fallen when they finally reached the home of the Dragon Hunters Guild, turning the desert into a silver ocean beneath the moonlight. Lamash could be seen from miles away in any direction; four mountain peaks as tall as demigods standing watch over the desert. Lights shone from the countless windows, balconies, and turrets draping the mountain. One of the peaks, wider and taller, stood proudly at the center, connected by long stone bridges to the other three.

A path wound up the mountain, leading to the main gate, and the sprawling dunes became smaller and smaller as they climbed.

The drawbridge opened, crashing against the rocky ground. There was no moat to cross, just a seven-hundred-foot drop into the cliffs at the base of Lamash. Aric had to force himself not to look down.

Their horses were taken by one of the sentinels, and Aric followed Saruk into the fortress. The entrance hallway was a series of archways. They marched between the slanted columns supporting the ceiling and their steps echoed a thousand fold. It felt like being inside a dragon's ribcage. The entire area had been carved from the cinnamon-colored mountain rock, but the walls had been polished to a gleam. Everything was so sharp and angular, Aric was sure he would cut himself if he leaned against a corner. Even the doorways stuck out like knives.

At the end of the hallway stood a glorious staircase that led them to the upper levels. They climbed it and went through a wide corridor until they arrived at a large black door. Saruk knocked, and shortly after, they heard someone granting permission to enter.

It was only a study but was as large as a dining hall. The walls were lined with shelves bursting with rolled parchments and books. Some of them were open on top of a large mahogany desk at one end of the room, but Aric's attention was drawn to something else: a massive, rectangular table bearing the largest piece of parchment he had ever seen.

It was a map, detailing every pass, hill, or rocky crag in the Mahar. Small wooden sculptures patrolled it, each one like a toy soldier holding a flag with a number.

"Grand Master," Saruk greeted. "The new recruit I picked up in Nish. Aric, this is the Guild's leader – Grand Master Sylene."

At first, Aric did not see who Saruk was talking about. The Grand Master was in a corner, reading from a book. She turned, and her black braids danced around her shoulders.

"Another conscript…" she said, setting the book down. "That's all we get these days. I'm supposed to protect the Empire with vagrants and thieves."

"I'm no thief, madam," Aric replied.

An eyebrow jumped on the Grand Master's face, and Aric felt Saruk's hand squeeze his arm.

"You will speak when authorized, recruit," the Grand Master told him. She looked at Saruk. "At least he has manners. I don't remember the last time someone called me 'madam'."

"Well," Saruk replied, "he is –"

"I know who he is." She paced along a line of book shelves. "Is he going to be any trouble, Saruk?"

Aric clenched his teeth. He hated when people talked about him as if he couldn't hear them. It reminded him of Sagun.

"I don't think so," Saruk replied. He looked at Aric. "He had his chance to run away, and didn't."

Grand-Master Sylene frowned. "He did?"

"Let's just say," Saruk replied, "the boy had a choice to make, and he made the right one."

The Grand-Master crossed her arms, pondering Saruk's words. She was very tall and lean, and wore black leather armor with a scorpion on her chest. The desert and her duties had clearly taken their toll, but she was remarkably beautiful nonetheless. She glanced at the table where the wooden Hunters stood watch.

"I don't care where you came from," she said, then looked him in the eyes. "It has no importance here. In fact, who you are, or even why you're here will have no impact on your life as a Dragon Hunter. You're one of us now. Any crimes you've committed or injustices you've suffered, they're forgotten."

She approached Aric and grabbed his shoulders tightly.

"Welcome to Lamash."

Crackling torches flickered in every corridor and tunnel of the mountain fortress. Each of their steps echoed a thousand times.

"The dining hall is on the main level, where we came in," Saruk explained. "These upper levels are the sleeping quarters."

Wind drafts whistled here and there, even though all doors were closed and there was no window in sight. It was almost surprising to look up and not see dripping stalactites hanging from the ceiling.

"Why are so many of these doors locked?" Aric asked.

"They're not locked, just closed," Saruk replied. "There was a time when dragons numbered in the thousands, and so did the Guild. But the world changed. Dragons no longer haunt the entire Empire. We've confined the scourge to the desert." He shrugged. "So, our numbers dwindle and our fortress becomes emptier every year." They turned a corner into an antechamber of sorts. "Even more so ever since magic was forbidden. Dragon blood used to be the most precious commodity in the Empire, and now a single drop can send you to the gallows. Turns out that's a terrible way to get new people volunteering to hunt dragons."

Saruk stopped in front of a large double door. Above it hung a tattered banner with the number twenty-three written in every language in the Empire. Aric could only read Arreline and Samehrian, but the Akhami and Cyrinian numerals were easy enough to understand.

"We're here."

Aric stared at the massive wooden door. "What's on the other side?" he asked.

"Your company's quarters. The people you will spend the rest of your life with."

That made Aric swallow dryly.

"They're trainees, just like you," Saruk continued. "The Twenty-third is a company we are re-forming. With you, it's now only two recruits away from being at full strength. At that point, you will begin your Dragon Hunting training."

Aric sighed.

"I don't belong here. I don't even know how to hold a sword."

"Trust me, nothing anyone could teach you outside this mountain could prepare you for a dragon." He paused. "Don't try anything stupid again, kid. You won't make it, and there will be a punishment this time."

"I know… I just wished…. I don't even know what happened to my father. Is he even alive?"

Saruk considered his words for a moment.

"How about this: The Grand-Master has contacts in the Citadel. She can find out, and she will if I ask her to. But you have to promise me that you won't try to escape again, no matter the news. Agreed?"

Aric pursed his lips as if he wanted to forbid himself from answering, but he gave up with a massive sigh.

"All right," he said. "Agreed."

Saruk pushed, and the door opened with a creak. On the other side, a dragon skull the size of a cow greeted them with sword-like fangs. It hung from the ceiling, and Aric felt his breath leave him.

"Wow!" he let out.

Saruk smirked. "Congratulations," he said. "Skully here scares the life out of most recruits the first time they see it. I've seen boys and girls older than you soiling their pants."

"May I?" Aric asked with a hand frozen a couple of inches from the massive jaw.

"Sure. Skully doesn't bite."

The surface of the bone was smooth and shiny. It had obviously been polished for better preservation.

"This must be worth a fortune," Aric muttered.

"Gold was never a problem in Lamash," Saruk said. "Until runium became illegal, of course. Come on, let me show you the place." He signaled Aric to follow him. "This is the common room; the dorm is through that corridor," Saruk explained as he pointed to his right. The Hunter pushed him through the dormitory's threshold. The room was a large rectangle filled with bunk beds. There were five windows, but they had been closed for the night, so the only available light came from a couple of lanterns casting long, twisting shadows all over the place. Two young boys were playing dice on the floor, and a tall, black bundle of muscles was dripping sweat from what looked like the one hundredth push-up in a row. Everyone else was lying on their beds, some sleeping, the rest about to.

"Anyone still awake?" Saruk asked.

The question worked like an alarm bell. Everyone jumped to their feet, forming a double line along the row of bunks.

"Guess so." The Hunter glanced around the trainees. "Goddess damn you, Tharius, how many times do I have to tell you this is not the freaking Legion? Stop saluting."

A boy with bushy black hair and blue eyes lowered his arm.

"I'm sorry, sir," he said.

"And stop calling me sir," Saruk replied. "From now on, I'll make you run up and down the mountain each time you do that again, understood?"

"Yes...Instructor."

"Good," Saruk paused and faced the room as a whole. "This is Aric, your new fellow trainee. Make him feel welcome." He grabbed Aric's shoulder. "Good luck, kid. And welcome home."

As the Hunter left, everyone quietly returned to their beds, except for the boy named Tharius. He offered Aric a hand.

"Hi," he said with a smile. "Are you a volunteer too?"

"No," Aric replied, shaking the boy's hand.

"I'm from Nosta. You?"

"Are there any free beds?" Aric asked instead. "I'm really tired."

"Yeah, sure," Tharius replied. "Those three are available. Just pick one."

Aric thanked him and found one of the free beds. It was right across from another bunk where a boy was reading quietly.

With a sigh, Aric dropped his satchel and removed the only thing inside – the leather parcel containing the glowstone and dragon-scale armor his father had gifted him. He untied the parcel and laid the cuirass on the straw mattress, running his fingers along the shiny scales. The incrusted shards of glowstone shone like frost on a sunny winter morning.

Someone whistled.

"That's beautiful," Aric heard someone say.

He turned around. It was the boy across from him who had spoken. He had closed his book and was now sitting straight. He had long, sharp features and his hair was cut in the Akhami fashion, with long braids in some places and completely shaven in others. The hairstyle was quite similar to Saruk's, except he didn't have any feathers, fangs, or jewelry hanging from it.

"Family heirloom?" the Akhami asked.

"Yeah," Aric replied.

It was more than just an heirloom, though. It was the only thing the emperor hadn't taken away from him, and that was probably only because the emperor didn't know about it.

"I'm Leth," the Akhami said. "I know you didn't ask, but Saruk already told us your name, so I thought we should take that out of the way."

"Uh, okay," Aric replied. "Thanks."

Leth gave Aric a "don't mention it" nod and leaned back on his bed, resuming his reading. Intrigued, Aric glanced around Leth's bunk. It had to be the neatest in the dormitory, probably in the whole fortress. It had a shelf attached to the bed, holding dozens of books as well as several statuettes, among them a dancing woman, a prowling panther, a bull's head, and a small dragon. He was also wearing a silk tunic, far too expensive for any plebian.

Somewhere, someone blew out one of the lanterns and the dorm suddenly became near dark. Exhaling loudly, Leth closed his book and slid under the bedcovers. Feeling his muscles ache from the trip, Aric decided to do the same, and soon the last lantern was extinguished, covering the dorm with darkness.

Despite being exhausted, he didn't feel sleepy at all. The room had apparently accumulated so much heat during the day that it was as hot as though they were inside a baking oven. Was it going to be like this every night?

Aric turned from one side to the other and tried every possible position, but sleep simply refused to come. The mattress felt weird and lumpy, the covers felt harsh and made him scratchy, not to the mention the countless snores coming from every direction.

It's like sleeping with a herd of bison...in heat.

He gave in and sat up. There were thin shreds of light seeping through the blinds in the windows, and he used them to guide himself out. Tiptoeing, he slid across the dorm and into the common room, making sure he didn't make any creaking noises opening and closing the door. Immediately, a cold gust of wind rustled his clothes, and the fresh air felt like home. He stepped toward the large window and sat on the thick parapet.

A huge silver moon hung in the sky, shedding its light upon the endless sea of dunes down below. Augusta was never this quiet at night. There was always some dog barking or the occasional yells and screams coming from the streets or one of the myriad towers of the city. This silence felt peaceful but also slightly creepier.

Another gust of wind swept in and Aric hugged himself.

"It's weird how it gets so cold all of a sudden, isn't it?"

Aric would have probably fallen off the window if the parapet weren't so large. He turned and saw Leth.

"Merciful Ava," Aric said. "You want to kill me?"

"Sorry. I thought you had heard my footsteps."

"No," Aric replied, then faced the desert once again. "You can't sleep either?"

"With the snore fest going on inside?" Leth snorted. "It's too damn early, anyway."

Aric smiled with half of his face. "It is," he said, facing the desert.

There was a small silence between them.

"It's a lot to take in, isn't it?" Leth asked.

Aric agreed. "How long have you been here?" he asked.

"Three weeks. Still not used to it." Leth leaned into the window beside where Aric was sitting. "I know who you are," he said after a while.

Aric's head spun so fast it almost snapped out of place. "You do?!"

"Every nobleman would recognize the empress's son, and my brother is Duke Carth of Nahlwar."

"Oh," Aric said, returning his gaze to the desert. "I see. Can't say I was expecting to find a nobleman in here, but your clothes are a bit of a giveaway."

Leth inspected his tunic. "Well, I might be stuck at the bottom end of the Empire for the rest of my life, but that doesn't mean I have to look like dung."

Aric chuckled.

"You're one to talk," Leth continued. "That armor of yours must be worth more than my brother's palace."

"You don't think someone will try to steal it, do you? I mean, someone from our company."

"No, everyone in here is too scared to break the rules. Do you know what the most common punishment here is?"

Aric replied with a shake of his head.

"They call it 'the pilgrimage'. Basically, you're dropped three hundred miles to the south, in the deep desert, without any supplies. If you make it back to Lamash, you are forgiven. If not, well, you die. Which is what happens to just about everyone, because even if you know what you are doing, and find some water before you dehydrate, the odds are a dragon will smell you, or hear you, and make a nice roast out of you."

"I see," Aric said. "That's good to know."

"This place is really messed up, let me tell you."

"Did you volunteer?" Aric asked.

"No," Leth sniggered. "I mean, officially, yes. But no, I didn't."

"What do you mean? What happened?"

Leth exhaled loudly. "What can I say?" he replied. "We can't all have perfect little families like yours."

Aric burst out laughing. Leth smiled as well.

"How much do you know?" Aric asked.

"Enough. The Legions may have unified the Empire, but gossip is what holds it together."

"It's funny," Aric said, "no matter how messed-up things were back in the Citadel, I still wish I was there."

"I know what you mean."

There was another moment of silence as the two of them contemplated the silvery dunes.

"Hey, want to see something really interesting?" Leth asked.

Aric shrugged. "Sure."

Leth grabbed a torch and signaled Aric to follow him. The windowless hallway was completely dark, filled only with the howling of wind drafts. On his way in, Aric had found the air current strange, but now it was downright scary.

"Where are we going?" he asked in a whisper.

"You'll see," Leth replied. "But why are you whispering?"

Good question.

"I… Old habit, I guess," he said. "I did this all the time in the Citadel with my brother. You know, sneaking out at night. It was the only way we could spend some time together. The emperor forbade us from seeing each other."

"You and your brother are close?" Leth asked as they turned a corner with moonlight flooding the corridor.

"He's my best friend," Aric said.

"Good. That's really good. Anyway, we don't have to hide if we walk around here at night. The Guild has rules for everything. Never spill water, the stables are off limits to trainees, don't spend more than one hour in the dining hall unless there is a feast, the kitchens and the lower levels are off limits to trainees, and so on. Surprisingly, though, no curfew."

"Why can't we go to the lower levels?" Aric asked.

They were now walking along a veranda of sorts, from which they could see one of Lamash's other towers. It was much thinner than the main one, albeit just as tall.

"I'm not sure," Leth replied. "I was told we will visit the lower levels as part of our training." He stopped at a large door at the end of the veranda. "This way." He pushed the door open and crossed it. "Grab on to the railing. It gets windy up here."

It was a bridge leading to the other tower. The wind sent Aric's blond curls into a wild dance and he had to turn his face so he wouldn't get sand in his eyes.

"I can't see any lights," Aric said. "Is the tower abandoned?"

"It is," Leth replied.

They reached the other end of the bridge, and the Akhami boy held the door for Aric. The interior had nothing to do with anything in the main tower. Instead of jagged walls and twisting columns, there were low relief sculptures everywhere. Women made of water and fire stood gracefully at the corners, prancing stags and prowling tigers chased after each other on the walls, and flowing ribbons framed every doorway. Even the doorknobs were small works of art.

"Welcome to the Mages' Tower," Leth told him.

Aric wandered around with his mouth open.

It was beautiful. There was some sand piling on the corners, and everything was covered with a thick layer of dust, but it looked magnificent nevertheless. He crossed into a large room with a long mahogany table at its center. Ten armchairs were lined up on one side of the table, facing a mirror as wide as the table was long. On each of its ends, a statue of a man made of smoke and stone held the mirror in place. It was framed in a silver ribbon, with dozens of incrusted glowstone shards shaped like jewels. Aric forgot how to breathe.

"It's a hypervisor," Leth explained. "Mages used it to communicate with each other over long distances. They could actually see and hear any other mage, no matter where he or she was, as long as they also had one of these." He approached the mirror and grabbed the silver frame. "It was powered by spells stored in these glowstone shards, but they must have run out years ago. It's just another piece of furniture now."

"You were right," Aric said, his eyes glowing. "This is incredible."

Leth smirked.

"We haven't got to the incredible part yet. Follow me."

Aric did not need any further encouragement. He followed Leth through a series of hallways and a wide staircase. Upstairs, the floor was like a giant puzzle, with each tile shaped differently, yet perfectly fitting each other. The painting on the tiles showed a twirling ribbon that transformed smoothly into a column of twisting smoke before ending abruptly at a tall double door. Leth pushed the door open and the smoke strand poured inside, becoming a trickle of water.

"What is this?" Aric asked, stepping into the room and looking around. It was larger than the main tower's dining hall and was packed full of row after row of empty bookcases.

"What do you think this is? It's a library, of course."

"Where are the books, then?"

Leth crossed his arms, looking disappointed.

"I told you this was the Mages' Tower. The books are gone, obviously."

"Right, sorry." Aric paced along the empty shelves. It would have been nice to have a library in Lamash. "What's so interesting about it, then?"

"That," Leth said, pointing at one wall.

Aric wondered if the Akhami had lost his mind. There was an archway protruding from the wall where Leth was pointing to, but nothing else. No object hanging there, no painting, carving, or sculpture of any kind. Just the same stone brick as everywhere else.

"Hum," Aric mumbled. "I don't think I follow…. It's a wall. What's so interesting about a wall?"

Leth threw his arms in the air.

"A wall?!" he yelped. "Are you blind? That's a passageway. And someone blocked it. Don't you see? It's a blocked passageway in the middle of a forbidden library! How much more interesting does it get?"

"I see," Aric said, tilting his head sideways. "So, you assume there's a cache of hidden books on the other side?"

"I don't know what is on the other side. That's the whole point. What I do know is the mages who lived here really didn't want whatever it was to fall into the hands of the Paladins."

"On the other hand," Aric said, "it might be just a wall."

Leth exhaled loudly.

"Look at the floor painting," he said, gesturing down. "The water trickle turns into a flame and then just…"

And then the flame was interrupted by the stone bricks.

"So, the painting wasn't finished properly," Aric said. "The painter must have miscalculated the distances. I've seen sloppier work."

"Come over here and place your hand there," Leth said, indicating the inner edge of the archway.

Aric obeyed. There was a clear interval between the arch and the stone bricks beneath it. Aric tried to slide his fingers through it, but they didn't fit.

"Wow!" he said. "I can feel air blowing through it."

"Exactly," Leth said. "Now look at it. Closer."

Aric removed his hand and inspected the tight gap. He got close enough to the bricks that he could feel the cold air blowing between them. What astonished him, however, was *what* he saw.

It was faint, but from within the crevice came a bluish hue.

"Fire take me!" he said. "There's glowstone in there."

"Yep," Leth agreed, smiling. "It's a glowstone lock."

"A what?"

"A glowstone lock. A door lock made of glowstone."

Aric looked at the archway, and the stone bricks under it.

"If there is a locking mechanism in there, where is the keyhole?" he asked.

"The only key that can open a glowstone lock is the exact counter spell," Leth explained.

"Well," Aric said. "I can lock-pick almost any door, but not something like this."

"You know how to pick a lock?" Leth asked.

"It's easier than it looks," Aric replied, "but this is hopeless. Even if we knew what the counter spell was, we're not mages. We wouldn't be able to cast it." He paused and frowned. "You're not a mage...are you?"

Leth chuckled. "Merciful Ava," he said. "No. I'm not *that* unlucky. But you're wrong; it's not hopeless. Glowstone locks might be unbreakable, but there has to be a way around it. I actually have a plan."

"You do?"

"Yeah." He aimed a finger at the ceiling. "We dig from the upper floor."

⌒

Sylene's quill ran dry midway through the sentence. She dipped the pen into the ink bottle and rewrote the half-written word. Again, the word remained incomplete. With a snort, the Grand Master looked at the ink bottle. It was empty.

"Edcar," she called, and immediately felt stupid.

It had been two weeks since she had released her former assistant. Edcar was an excellent right hand, and he was also leadership material. Sylene had been grooming him for years. Until the day Tyrek, the captain of the Twelfth Company, had gotten himself squashed by a dragon's tail. Edcar had been Sylene's only choice to replace him. She had always possessed the smallest staff of any Grand Master in the history of the Guild, but now she was running the mountain fortress all by herself.

She sighed.

I suppose getting the ink myself is no tragedy.

She was getting up when someone knocked on the door.

"Yes?" she said.

The door creaked and Saruk appeared.

"You summoned, Grand Master?" the instructor asked.

"Ah, Saruk, come in." She stepped from behind her desk and walked to the large map table at the center of the study. "I have good news for you." She crossed her arms. "You won't like it, however."

Saruk gave her a puzzled look.

"I imagine you saw the boy and the girl standing outside," Sylene said.

"New recruits?"

The Grand Master confirmed that with a nod. "Conscripts, of course. They're siblings. Orphans since the Purge, and have been living on the streets ever since." She strolled around the map. "The boy stole from a fruit merchant because he didn't want his sister to starve. So they ended up down here." She exhaled loudly. "You know, the usual."

"Are they for me?" Saruk asked. Sylene nodded. "It is good news, then."

"Yes." The Grand Master stopped and turned to face Saruk. "The Twenty-third is finally at full strength. I want them in the Frostbound within the week."

"What?!"

"You heard me, Saruk. Within the week."

"They're not prepared."

"Prepare them, then. I need the Twenty-third fully trained and ready to hunt, understood?"

"Prepare them? Half of them haven't been here for more than a week. Most of them are bakers and fishermen. One of them is a priest, for goddess's sake! I need more time."

"Look at this map," the Grand Master snapped. "Look at it!" She punched the table and the small wooden hunters jumped. One of them nearly tumbled. "It's practically empty. As we stand, we're barely able to maintain minimum patrols." She stretched her finger toward a portion of the map to her left. "Look at the eastern corridor. We haven't had a single patrol in Derrick's Pass for two months. If we keep this up for much longer, a dragon *will* get through. I need the Twenty-third in the field, Saruk."

"What would you prefer? Getting your new company a few more months down the road, or never at all? Because if they are not ready, they won't survive the training. It's too dangerous."

Sylene turned around and headed back to her desk.

"This is the Dragon Hunters Guild, Saruk," she said, sitting back down. "Danger is not optional."

After his little adventure in the Mages' Tower with Leth, Aric had no trouble finally falling asleep.

He dreamt of the desert witch again. She was opening the door Leth had shown him, except in the dream the library was much, much bigger and was completely frozen, with icy stalactites hanging from the ceiling. The witch waved her arms and green sparkles shot out from her hands. The glowstone lock clicked and hissed, and the door swung. As it did, Aric tried to hide, fearful that the witch realized he was watching her. But as soon as he took a step, her head snapped in his direction and everything went black.

He woke up with his heart pounding, sweaty and gasping. For a moment, it was very confusing not to wake up in his own bedroom. He saw Leth sitting on his bed, tying his boots, and suddenly remembered where he was.

A smiling Tharius greeted him. "Good morning," he said. "You should hurry. Instructor Saruk doesn't like it when we're late for muster."

The company broke fast at the dining hall. Each recruit grabbed a couple of flatbreads from a counter and sat at one of the long tables. Besides plates and mugs, each table was littered with jars, pots, and deep plates holding a myriad of dipping sauces. Red and yellow jams, a green, oily sauce that smelled of thyme, a black, sweet paste with pine nuts and sesame seeds, and even a white, creamy cheese. The lack of a good hot sausage and some eggs made it look like a strange breakfast, and the flavors weren't exactly familiar, but Aric was too famished to care. Apparently, so was everyone else. All thirteen members of the company were eating in silence with slow, sleepy movements.

Around the dining hall, the crowd of senior Hunters gathering for breakfast was as colorful as the dipping sauces on the tables. There were men with green braids and purple beards, and women with hair locks painted in every color of the rainbow. A thirtysomething black woman, probably from Cyrinia, walked by their table, and Aric counted twenty knives strapped to her leather armor.

"Half-Prince," a girl's voice said. Aric looked toward the sound and found a red-haired girl sitting to his left. "How does it feel to sleep and eat among the plebs?"

Is she talking to me?

"What did you call me?" Aric asked.

"Half-Prince," she replied as if it was the most obvious thing in the world.

"I'm sorry, what is your name?" Aric asked.

"Dothea," the red-haired girl replied.

"Dothea." Aric swallowed a piece of bread. "Why would you call me something like that?"

"Aric," one other girl called. "Leth already told us. All of us. We know who you are." She smiled. "I'm Clea, by the way."

She had olive skin and almond-shaped eyes. Her wavy black hair was cut just above her shoulders. Aric had the feeling he had never seen anyone so beautiful.

"He did?" Aric looked at Leth. "You did?"

"They were going to find out sooner or later," Leth replied. He was reading from his book and didn't even raise his head. "I figured it was better to get it over with."

Aric rehearsed a protest but it died out in his throat.

"So," Dothea said, "is it very different?"

"What?" Aric asked.

"To eat with the plebs," Dothea replied.

"Oh, uh…" Aric shrugged. "Back in the Citadel, I slept in the servants' wing and ate in the kitchens…"

"Better than sleeping in the mud and eating with the rats," a boy missing two teeth said.

"Or eating rats," Dothea agreed.

"Charming," Leth said beneath his breath.

"Shut up, Leth," Dothea told him.

The boy missing two teeth piled on. "Yeah, you rich kids are all the same. You should learn to respect people like us."

"Yeah, yeah," Leth sneered. "You're poor, we get it. Someone should make you a statue."

For a moment, Aric feared there would be a fight, but both Dothea and the other boy simply ignored Leth with a snort. Aric decided to defuse the awkward silence hanging over the table.

"So, um…have any of you ever seen a dragon?"

"I have!" Tharius said, raising a hand.

Dothea shook her head. "Sure you have," she said.

"It's true. It was my first week, before any of you got here. Saruk had me running across the dunes to test my endurance and then I saw it. It was flying north, several miles away. I ducked behind a dune and took a peek. It had turned west, putting me behind it, so I watched it glide off into the distance."

Dothea dropped a piece of bread onto her plate.

"Please," she said. "It was probably an eagle or something."

"I can tell an eagle from a dragon," Tharius replied. "It had a long tail, just like a lizard. It was no bird."

"It had to be," Dothea insisted. "Dragons don't come this far north."

"That's not true," Tharius replied. "If you paid any attention to Saruk, you would know there have been several sightings over the last few years."

"It's true," said a tall black boy. "Honor guards like me are sent on regular tours through the desert before joining the Guild. Last year, an honor guard younger than me spotted a dragon only a few miles south of Radir."

"What's an honor guard?" Aric asked.

"The Cyrinian version of volunteers," Leth replied. He had finally decided to close his book.

"In Cyrinia," the black boy told Aric, "all villages must provide the Dragon Hunters Guild with one volunteer per generation. They are called honor guards."

"Because it is considered a great honor," Tharius explained.

Dothea looked at him in utter disbelief. "I'm pretty sure the half-prince understood that part," she said.

Tharius was going to bark something back at her, but Aric interrupted. "Please, call me Aric."

"Okay," Dothea said, then shrugged. "But I'm still going to call you Half-Prince behind your back."

Aric sighed, deciding it wasn't worth arguing.

Then a thundering clap made them jump off their seat. Saruk had shown up from nowhere and was yammering like an alarm bell.

"Let's go, people! Time's up. This is no downtown tavern. We have work to do. Pick your asses up."

It felt like he was waking up from a bad dream for the second time that morning.

The instructor led them out of the dining hall and through the main gates. Silently, they marched down the mountain into the desert. As soon as the red rock of Lamash turned into the golden sand that surrounded it, Saruk chose a dune and spread the trainees along its slope as if it was an amphitheater. Only then did Aric realize he had a boy and a girl with him.

"This is Ergon and Lyra," he said before ordering the pair to join the rest of the company. "Your new fellow recruits."

The boy was blond and as skinny as a lizard, while the girl had short chestnut hair and big, watery eyes.

"I imagine you all know what this means," Saruk continued. "The Twenty-third Company is officially complete, and your dragon hunting training is about to begin. For those of you who have been here for a while, if you think you have any idea what training at Lamash is, let me educate you. You haven't got the first clue. From today forward, you will train day *and* night. You will run across the desert and learn to survive in it for weeks. You will practice with every weapon invented by man until you have mastered their every secret. You will scale mountains with your bare hands, and you will track dragons across the skies. But most of all, you will become a single cohesive and perfectly coordinated fighting unit. And by the goddess, you will learn to slay the world's most terrifying beasts and become one of the select few known as the Dragon Hunters of Lamash."

CHAPTER 7

The Empress's Ball

Tarsus walked quietly into the room. One of the Legionaries standing guard outside closed the door behind him. Cassia was standing by her window, watching the sun rise over the eastern hills beyond the city. There was another woman inside, thin and tall like a dagger. She jumped up from her seat and gave a deep curtsy.

"Imperial Majesty," the girl said, her voice shaking slightly.

"You're excused, Venia," Cassia said. "You may leave us."

"Yes, my Lady," Venia said, then turned to the emperor. "Your Majesty." She scuttled past Tarsus, her eyes low, and left the room after covering her platinum hair with an even paler hood.

"Who was that?" Tarsus asked as soon as the door closed behind him again.

"Someone beneath your notice," Cassia replied. She still had her back to Tarsus.

Tarsus cleared his throat. "I've been thinking," he said. "I...may have overreacted by placing guards at your door. I'll see that they are removed immediately."

"I don't see why," Cassia said. "We both know I'm your prisoner. Makes sense that they're out there."

The emperor frowned. "You are my *wife,*" he said. "The guards will leave."

Cassia followed a bird's flight across the sky. "Have it your way," she said. "It's not like it makes a difference."

Tarsus sighed, and there was a small pause before he said, "Sagun complained that you have not yet chosen the main courses for the ball. He says he must know by tonight if there is to be any food on the table tomorrow."

"He can serve his own liver, for all I care," Cassia replied. "I won't be attending the ball. You already gave me my birthday gift, Tarsus. I require no more."

The emperor stepped further into the room. "You *will* attend the ball," he said, his eyes burning. "Unless you want that traitor to die tomorrow, you *will* be there, and you *will* act accordingly. You are my *wife*!" Tarsus turned on his heel and stormed out, slamming the door behind him.

The room became absolutely still, and Cassia looked down to the letter in her hands. The Paladin's handwriting was clumsy, and there were, at least, three misspelled words per sentence, but the message was clear enough. Her boy had reached the desert and was beyond her help.

She crunched the parchment with her hands and closed her eyes, taking a deep breath. The air trapped in her chest came out in a sob and two tears rolled down her cheeks.

Keep calm, she thought. *Doric still needs you. Fadan still needs you.*

⁓

Beyond the great wooden doors, Cassia could hear the music. It went suddenly quiet and was replaced with the buzz of chatter until three loud knocks on the stone floor silenced everyone.

"Her Imperial Majesty, Cassia Ellara," the voice of the herald announced from behind the door. "Queen of Augusta and Samehria, Ultrarchess of Akham, and Empress of Arrel."

The wooden doors parted, and Cassia glided into the ballroom. A forest of nobles bowed and curtsied so deeply, some of them nearly kissed the floor. With gentle nods to one side, then the other, she walked toward the blue dais at the other end of the ballroom.

"Your Majesty looks beautiful," a fat duchess told her, curtsying.

"A most happiest of birthdays, Your Majesty," a Cyrinian count sang, making such a flamboyant bow, it was almost a pirouette.

The pleasantries followed her the entire way and didn't stop until she was in front of Tarsus by their thrones. The emperor kneeled, grabbing her right hand while looking into her eyes, then laid on it a profound kiss. Cassia wanted to pull her hand back and slap him across his face right there, in front of all his vassals, but she wasn't doing this for herself. Tarsus invited her to sit with a gesture, and the two of them sat on their thrones. Without a word, the music resumed.

The band sat atop a podium taller than any man, right in the middle of the hall. Above them, the Imperial banners that usually dangled from the ceiling had been replaced by the arms of Cassia's own House Ellara: A black eagle standing atop a black pine on a field of orange.

Most guests were at the center of the hall, dancing in concentric circles around the band's podium, while those not dancing mingled at the edges of the dance floor, eating and drinking from ten different counters where servants prepared their most peculiar requests.

"You look exquisitely beautiful today," Tarsus told her. "But when do you not?"

Cassia did not reply and simply kept staring at the crowd in front of her. There had to be at least a couple hundred people in there, celebrating her birthday as if they didn't know what had just happened to her son and former husband. As if *she* didn't know.

"How long will you keep this up?" Tarsus asked. "You can't just —"

"Back in my room," she said, cutting him off, "you said something. Before you left. You said that I was your wife." She finally looked him in the eyes. "You were mistaken. I *was* your wife. No more."

Tarsus opened an angry mouth and was going to shout something back at her, but never had the time.

"We had a deal, Tarsus," Cassia continued. "And you broke it. So I no longer have to keep up my end." She returned her gaze to the dancing crowd. "Our marriage is over."

The emperor moved in his throne and squeezed its armrest so hard, it was a miracle it didn't break beneath his grip.

"I did *not* break any deal," Tarsus said. "It was that traitor who broke it. For fifteen years, I kept my word. Why would I break it now?"

Cassia chuckled. "Why would Doric?" she asked.

"Because he got tired of waiting for you to run back to him, of course," Tarsus replied.

"Let me get this straight," Cassia said. "You're saying Doric got tired of waiting for me, so he…joined the rebellion?"

"There is no such thing as a *rebellion*," Tarsus replied, disgusted. "Just a handful of traitors with delusions of grandeur. And yes, I'm saying your former husband was conspiring to kill me. Which is why he has been sentenced to die."

"Which, in turn, is why I am no longer your wife," Cassia retorted. "In fact, I might announce that right now."

She was going to stand up, but Tarsus stopped her, grabbing her arm.

"You didn't let me finish," Tarsus told her. He took a deep breath. "I understand your grief. The punishment to your other son, although deserved, *was* severe." He removed his hand from Cassia's arm. "Under the circumstances, I cannot blame you for being resentful. Having said that, your former husband isn't dead *yet*, and I am nothing if not a reasonable man. So, if you are willing, I would be glad to meet you halfway."

"You're saying you won't kill Doric?" Cassia asked, frowning.

"I'm saying that our marriage is more important to me than anything else," Tarsus replied. "And for that reason, I'm willing to commute the sentence to life in prison."

Cassia weighed those words. "Why should I trust you now?" she asked. "The last time you made me a proposition like that, you used it to set Doric up and arrest him."

"I DID NOT!" Tarsus's eyes nearly jumped out of their orbits. He tried to calm himself, looking around to make sure no one had noticed. "I did *not*," he repeated quietly. "I admit the sequence of events might raise suspicions, but that is not what happened. Either way, the situation is what it is. I'm agreeing to spare the traitor's life. Is that what you want, or not?"

The empress considered that for a moment. "Are you willing to do the same for the others, including my cousin Hagon?" she asked.

The emperor sighed. "Very well."

"And you will bring back Aric?"

"Don't push it!" Tarsus snapped, twitching in his chair. "I'm bending the rules far enough already. This is the deal. I will revoke the death sentence on all of those traitors. For you, Cassia." He straightened himself in his throne. "Do you want it, or not?"

Cassia did not reply right away. "Yes," she ended up saying. "We have a deal."

"Good," Tarsus said, smiling. "Good. As always, my love, you make me very happy."

"Yes," Cassia replied, standing up. "I should mingle now." She stepped forward. "Talk to the guests."

Without giving Tarsus a chance to say anything else, she stepped down from the dais and allowed the crowd to swallow her. There was another wave of bows, curtsies, and pleasant remarks, but Cassia didn't even notice them. She felt dizzy. Dizzy and dirty. If there had been a lake in the hall, she probably would have jumped right in.

Three knocks on the floor woke her up.

"His Imperial Majesty, Fadan Patros," the herald announced. "Count of Capra, Prince-Duke of Fausta, and Crown Prince of Arrel."

The ballroom's doors opened and Cassia watched her son walk inside. As with her, the bows and curtsies piled on, but this time, there were some awkward glances and hushed whispers as well. Fadan looked like he had just jumped out of bed. His black hair was a mess, and instead of a gala uniform, he was wearing a simple brown tunic, as if this were just a regular day and he was on his way to a combat lesson.

Cassia rushed to his side, ignoring the courtesans who had approached her in the hopes of striking up a conversation with the empress.

"Are you all right?" she asked, placing a hand on Fadan's shoulder.

He nodded. "I'm fine," he said. "I tried to visit you, but there were –"

"I know," she said. "They won't be there any more after today."

Fadan nodded and the two of them went quiet.

"What is the meaning of this?!" the emperor demanded as he stormed up next to them. "Dressed like a servant… You're not even wearing a weapon. You're the host of this ball!"

"No," Fadan replied, facing his father. "You are."

For a moment, Cassia almost expected steam to come out of Tarsus's ears.

"This is not the time nor the moment," the emperor said. "We will have this discussion later!" He turned to Cassia. "Put some sense into your son's head." With that, he turned on his heel and left.

The two of them stood there, watching Tarsus march away.

"Aggravating your father won't bring Aric back," Cassia said.

"No, but neither will pleasing him."

A duchess with hair piled high above her head stepped next to them, pushing a young daughter toward Fadan. The girl was as thin as a reed and was shaking like one as well.

"Not now!" Fadan barked at them.

Mother and daughter grimaced, frightened, and scurried away without a word.

Cassia sighed. "None of this is any of that girl's fault," she said.

"I don't care," Fadan replied. "I don't care about that girl. I don't care about this ball. I don't care about my father —"

"Fadan!" Cassia pleaded. "Please, don't. You're angry, I know. No one understands you better than me. But I already lost your brother. I need you to keep yourself together."

"We didn't lose Aric," Fadan corrected. He reached into a pocket. "I have something for you."

Cassia grabbed the small pouch. Inside she found a necklace, where a glowstone shard as thin as a needle dangled. The empress immediately closed her fingers around the jewel and tucked it against her stomach, her head swiveling around and looking in every direction.

"Who gave this to you?" she asked urgently. "Where did you get this?"

"Doric gave it to Aric," Fadan replied. "When they met in the city. Aric was supposed to hand it to you that night, but…but then everything went to the abyss." He looked into his mother's eyes. "It was my idea, Mother. Please forgive me."

"What was your idea?" Cassia asked, confused. "Wait, you mean… You were there? With Aric and Doric? You were *there?*"

Fadan stared at the floor. "Aric was the only one who saw the soldiers, but he saw them too late. He only had time to save one person." His lips pressed against each other tightly and his eyes welled. "He saved me."

Cassia sent her arms around her son. "Oh, my sweet," she said, kissing his hair.

They stood like that for a little while until Fadan stopped sniffing. Cassia looked him in the eyes.

"Aric *will* survive the desert," she said. "You know him. There's no one stronger."

Fadan nodded. "I know," he said, weakly. "He's too stubborn, even for a dragon."

The two of them chuckled.

"He sacrificed himself for you," Cassia said. "You can't just start getting into all sorts of trouble now and let that sacrifice be a waste."

Fadan weighed those words for a moment. "I made him a promise," he said. "I intend to keep it."

"What promise?" Cassia asked. "You have to let *me* handle these things. Please."

"You don't have to worry about me," Fadan told her. "I can take care of myself."

No, you can't! Cassia wanted to scream at him. Instead, she stood there, helplessly watching her son flee back through the main door. "Merciful mother…" she muttered.

⌣⁓

The humming of music and chatter followed Fadan across several halls until it became just a distant whisper. He climbed to the top of the palace's north wing. It was such a remote location that servants never even bothered lighting up the torches and lamps hanging on the walls.

Fadan pushed against the attic's door and it opened with a *creak*. Silver moonlight streamed diagonally from the windows on the slanted ceiling, lighting the dusty piles of old books, paintings, and tapestries within. He sighed before stepping in. The last time he had been there, Aric had been with him, that night they had decided to rescue Aric's dad.

In hindsight, it hadn't been the most sophisticated of plans, but that did not explain why the Legionaries had been waiting for them outside of the sewers. The only explanation, in fact, was that someone had been listening to them that night.

Sagun... Fadan thought.

Did that mean the Akhami castellan knew Fadan had the Talent? No, certainly not. There was no way he would have kept this information from the emperor, and Tarsus clearly had no idea about it.

Still, there was no question the attic was no longer safe. He had to find a new place to hide the book and, more importantly, to practice. How else could he hope to spring Doric out of jail?

He was alone, and there was no one he could trust enough to ask for help. He also didn't have any of Aric's skills like lock-picking or knowing his way around the sewers. No, all he had was his Talent. He would have to learn how to use magic. The book should be sufficient. It was an introductory manual, after all.

Fadan walked over to the improvised secret stash he and Aric had created, a loose floorboard in a corner under a broken chair. Both the book and what remained of the runium they had stolen were still there. Fadan slipped the vial into a pocket, then shuffled the magic book into the middle of a pile of dusty books. Swiping some of the dust off the pile of books, the prince picked it up and left the attic, the old floor creaking beneath his boots.

Hauling such a load across the Citadel was a risky idea, but there would be no better time than now to do so. Everyone was distracted down in the ballroom, and the dark of night would help to conceal him.

Taking a peek around every corner, Fadan sped out of the main palace and into the service courtyard. Crates of vegetables, fruit, and wine were still waiting to be hauled into the kitchens and cellars. Making sure none of the books tumbled from the pile, he lurched from crate to crate, checking that the way was clear of any sentinels.

He followed into one of the streets that led out of the Core Palace, using the shadows of a file of cypresses as cover.

The Imperial Citadel was an entire district, walled off from the rest of the city. The Core Palace, where Fadan and the Imperial family lived, was just one of the many palaces inside, albeit by far the largest. The other palaces were spread randomly around the Core, marble-paved streets connecting their luscious gardens. Most of them were inhabited by the Augustan nobility, the descendants of those families who had been vassals of House Patros since Augusta was just another city-state. Other palaces belonged to the major landed Houses of the Empire, like those holding grand duchies or principalities, although these were mere expressions of wealth and power, and rarely housed anyone. Then there were the palaces of the high offices, like the Imperial Council, the Legion's Headquarters, and so on.

Lastly, there were the abandoned palaces, extravagant constructions harkening back to some of the most eccentric Emperors in history. There was the palace Torrus II had built, right next to the Imperial Council, for his twenty-two concubines. There was the one known as the Countess's Palace, built by Ambrosian Carva, a chancellor who had served a total of four different emperors, for his mistress, the Countess of Vastegat. There were also Fadan's favorites, a set of seven palaces built by Fastan III and his brother Marcius in a weird competition to determine who could achieve the most outrageous construction.

The list of empty palaces went on and on, some of which had been claimed by plant life after decades – in some cases, centuries – of vacancy. It was precisely one of these that Fadan was after. What better place to perform his experiments? Fadan didn't know the first thing about magic, but he had a feeling it was a loud, messy business.

The long line of cypresses came to halt at a square guarded by a tall statue of one of Fadan's ancestors; he couldn't recall which. He heard something like a squeal and froze for an instant before checking over his shoulder. He looked in every direction, scrutinizing every shadow around him, but there was no one in sight.

Steadying his breathing, Fadan tiptoed across the square, double-checking over his shoulder to make sure no one was following him. Then, as he turned to look forward again, he nearly dropped the pile of books from fright. How he managed to keep himself from screaming was a mystery to him.

Leaning against the other side of the statue's pedestal were a man and a woman. They were in each other's arms, kissing, but they must have heard his footsteps, because they turned to face him, startled. The man wore the elaborate garment of a noble, probably a marquis or a baron, considering the large, overcompensating hat. The woman, on the other hand, looked like one of the servants.

"What are you staring at?" the man asked.

The arrogant tone definitely belonged to that of a noble, but Fadan was certainly not used to being spoken to like that. He nearly told the man to watch his manners. Fortunately, he remembered his own choice of clothing earlier that day. He looked down at his chest and saw the simple brown tunic he was wearing, then bowed.

"Forgive me, Lord," he said, speaking through his nose. Then he spun on his heel and scurried away.

Behind him, the woman whispered something and the couple giggled, resuming their kisses.

Fadan turned a corner, leaving the noble and the servant out of sight, and followed through a narrower street, flanked by smaller palaces. Smaller by Citadel standards, that is.

These buildings were the rarest in the Imperial Citadel; mansions bought by extremely wealthy plebeians, like merchants and bankers, for the prestige alone. The area Fadan was looking for was just beyond this street, containing a block of nine palaces where no one had lived for at least a century. After all, who in the Citadel wished to be neighbors with the plebs?

The block of abandoned palaces seemed darker than the rest of the Citadel. Oak trees, willows, and pines grew thick and unruly all over the entire block. Hedges had turned to tall, wild bushes that spewed into the once-beautiful gardens. Vines and other climbing plants crawled along the walls and over the roofs as if the land itself wanted a palace of its own.

Fadan travelled along the abandoned buildings until one of them caught his attention. The trees in its garden had been trimmed, and leftover branches and twigs carpeted its main gate. It was perfect. No one would be back there for years.

He hurried inside, kicking the front door open, then pushing it shut again with his hip. The pile of books was starting to carve into his hands, so Fadan dropped them right in the middle of the lobby, keeping only the magic book in his hand. It wasn't like anyone would complain. Moonlight shone everywhere through the broken windows. There was an earthy, moist smell, and the floor creaked loudly with every step.

Good, an intruder alert, Fadan thought.

He climbed upstairs, moss-covered statues welcoming him. The first floor had several good candidates for a practice room. The areas were wide, and most of the furniture had been removed, although not all of it, which was handy. After all, he would need at least a place to sit, and he wouldn't mind a table, either.

With the magic book under his arm, Fadan paced through the different rooms. *Well, this all started in an attic,* he thought. *Why not keep it that way?*

Climbing two steps at a time, he went to the topmost floor of the manor.

It was *perfect.* The room was a wide rectangle that ran almost the entire width and length of the building, giving him more than enough room to work. The slanted ceiling was tall enough that he didn't have to hunch. There was also enough light to allow him to read without lighting a candle, but it all fell through a couple of skylights in the ceiling, which was impor-tant because, without any windows, he would be free to cast the brightest spells he could without turning the place into a lighthouse. Finally, there were several chairs lined against a wall, two tables stacked on top of each other, and even a porcelain dinner set.

Perfect for some target practice, he thought.

He could already picture himself conjuring bolts of energy, destroying plates and jars from across the room.

Fetching one of the tables and one of the chairs, he fashioned a desk for himself in one corner, placing his studying material on top of it – the manual on magic and the runium flask.

Sitting down, he grabbed the vial and inspected its contents. The runium looked like mercury, its streaks of red reminding him it had been made of dragon blood. Fadan grimaced, picturing having to drink that thing.

Well, I suppose I should start with the theory, anyway, he thought, placing the vial down and opening the book.

"By all accounts," Fadan read from the first page, "magic is as counterintuitive as breathing underwater. Learning to do it consists of teaching your body that everything it knows is wrong. Up can be down, fire can freeze, air can be solid, and so on and so on. It becomes all the more difficult considering wizards can't permanently be under the effects of runium – such experiments were made by numerous wizards throughout history, always with gruesome results. This effectively means that everything you retrain your mind and body to believe under a dose of the potion will immediately resume its state of falsehood as soon as the effects wear off."

Well…this should be easy, then.

"While the detrimental effects on your learning of magic, of not being under runium, will diminish with experience, one thing will never change. No spell, charm, *incantation,* or other form of magic can ever be learned without the influence of the dragon blood concoction. It would be like trying to climb a ladder without having a ladder to climb. Attempting to learn magic without first drinking runium is thus an exercise in futility."

All right, then… Fadan thought. *Straight to practice it is.*

Trying not to think too much about it, Fadan closed his eyes and tipped his head back, swallowing the runium in a single gulp.

It tasted like iron. Or was it blood?

At first, all he felt was a coolness coating his throat. Then, it began to warm further and further until his mouth, throat, and stomach were on fire. Fadan had drunk strong liquor before, but this was much, much more powerful. The burning kept increasing until it became almost too painful to endure. Fadan regretted not having some water to soothe it with.

The burning slowly turned into a choke, and Fadan had trouble breathing. He jumped up, grabbing his throat, and the chair fell backward. The world spun and blue clouds formed with his breaths, even though he felt like he was drowning.

What's happening to me?

He staggered sideways and his footsteps made the floor shake…no, the whole building. Then, suddenly, air flooded his entire body as he inhaled, and it was as if everything in front of him got closer, then backed away when he exhaled. The burning eased to a more tolerable level, and he felt himself swell and grow taller. Or was everything else shrinking?

He looked at his hands. They were pulsing with an indigo hue.

I'm powerful, he thought.

"I'm powerful!" he echoed out loud, staggering backward and forward.

There was something filling his chest, begging to come flooding out. Something so potent that he had to breathe heavily just to contain it.

"I can feel everything!" Fadan looked at the dinner set across the room and smiled wickedly. "I can tear it all apart!"

Eyes bulging, he flung his hands forward, commanding that force in his chest to pour through them.

A gush of blue light shot from his palms, but instead of following a straight line, the light surged in every possible direction, blinding him. A searing pain exploded in his chest as if he had eaten embers. He tried to scream, but his throat was ablaze. The world spun, accelerating and becoming a blur, then –

BAM!

He smacked his head on the floor, his whole body convulsing uncontrollably until darkness swallowed him and he blacked out.

CHAPTER 8

The Frostbound

Sand trailed after them as they ran atop the dunes. Relentless sun seared their skins. Aric felt his heartbeat hammering and his lungs and feet burning. He grabbed the canteen on his belt and raised it to his cracked lips. Nothing, not a single drop left.

Goddess damn it.

He tried swallowing to get some moisture in his throat. It felt like it had been covered with thick parchment.

"We need… to rest…" he said between heavy panting.

"Not until we find some shade," said Ashur, a blond boy from Samehria. "Toughen up, half-prince."

Aric looked for support among the others, but besides little Lyra, who had her brother to carry her, no one seemed as exhausted as him.

"Here," Clea said, holding her canteen toward Aric.

"No," he replied. "I can't drink your water. You're gonna need it."

"It's fine," she insisted, smiling.

Aric took a little sip. Just enough so she would let it go, even though he would have drunk a laundry tub if he had one.

Midday was approaching, and the sun felt hotter with every step. Aric's running became a stagger, and he began to fall behind.

"Rocks!" Nahir, the honor guard from Cyrinia, screamed from the front. "I see rocks up ahead."

There was a group of brown stones a mile to the northeast, jutting out from the sand like pillars. Aric would have thanked Ava out loud if he had found the breath to do so. The nearly vertical sun meant every shadow was as small as it would get, but those boulders were tall enough to create a decent resting area.

Aric was the last to reach the blissful shadow. His legs careened against his will, and he zigzagged on the last couple of steps until his foot caught in a small crevice and he crashed to the ground. Hands abraded, he remained on all fours, feeling his stomach turning. He tried to swallow but his throat clenched, and then suddenly, puke burst from his mouth.

"Ava Mother," Ashur said. "Get a grip of yourself, half-prince."

Aric felt a mess. Between the jets of vomit, the fact that he was already out of breath from the dune sprint, and the tears welling up in his eyes, it was like drowning.

"Leave him alone," Clea told Ashur. "He just drank too much water." She knelt besides Aric, placing a soft hand on his shoulders.

"I'm okay," Aric managed to tell her. This was all sufficiently humiliating without her feeling pity for him. Not only that, but she was right, too. Aric had already drunk his entire supply of water, and they were still hours away from the fortress. He had no idea how he was going to make it.

Ashur snorted. "Leave him alone," he muttered. "I wish he would leave *us* alone."

"What is that supposed to mean?" Aric asked, wiping his mouth.

"You're dead weight," Ashur replied. "You slow us down. Make everything harder for the company."

"I'm just not used to running," Aric said. "That's all."

"Bull crap!" Ashur said. "You suck at everything." He started counting with his fingers. "You suck at climbing, so we have to heave you up the walls; you suck at fighting, so your team is always one man down; you even suck at waking up! You're always late for muster and then we all have to do push-ups with you."

Aric stood up, clenching a fist. "I've never done these things! I'm learning."

That looked to be exactly what Ashur wanted. He took a step forward and stared Aric in the eyes, their faces a mere inch apart.

"Learn without screwing everyone else!" Ashur said, gritting his teeth.

Narrowing his eyes, Aric held Ashur's stare, praying that would be all he would have to do. After all, Ashur was a head taller than him. Not to mention twice as wide.

"Back off!" Leth's voice sounded like a snarl. He brushed past Aric and placed himself in front of Ashur.

The blond Samehrian chuckled. "The half-prince has a bodyguard. Figures."

"You're being a jerk," Clea told Ashur.

Ashur was going to retort with something but Aric cut him off.

"I'm fine!" he said, speaking to Leth and Clea at the same time. "I can take care of myself."

At the sound of that, Ashur's head jerked back and he burst into laughter. Aric began to tremble. He closed both fists so hard, the blood disappeared from his hands. It just made Ashur laugh louder. Prion and Jullion, who never left his side, joined Ashur's laughter. Aric's world became a blur. The whole desert was trembling with him.

He snapped, lunging toward Ashur. He pulled his fist back and smacked him right between the eyes.

⌣⟶

Aric, Leth, and Clea, standing against the corridor wall, cringed each time the muffled yells crossed the thick wooden door in front of them.

"You should have stayed out of it," Aric whispered. "They're gonna drop you in the deep desert for this."

"Well," Leth replied. "Three against one wasn't exactly fair."

"Yeah," Clea agreed. "Three against two didn't seem fair either."

"Are you kidding?" Leth asked, his whispers bordering on normal voice levels. "Me and Aric could have handled those idiots."

Clea chuckled. "Sure you could, blue eyes."

Leth glared. "Is it that bad?" He turned to Aric. "Does it look very bad?"

Mumbling something inaudible, Aric inspected the purple circles growing around Leth's hazelnut eyes. It was all the answer Leth needed, and he cursed under his breath.

"I hate Samehrians," Leth said.

"I think Jullion is Thepian," Clea told him.

"And Prion is Arreline, like me," Aric added.

Leth shrugged. "I don't care. Ashur is Samehrian enough for all three of them."

The door opened and Saruk held it with a blank expression. With their eyes on the floor, Ashur and his two minions left the room and kept walking without a word.

"Get in," Saruk's rough voice thundered.

Exchanging a quick glance, Aric, Leth, and Clea obeyed, and the door slammed behind them.

"You haven't been here a week and you're giving me this crap already?" Aric felt bits of saliva hitting his face.

"We just —"

"Be quiet!" Saruk aimed a finger at Leth and Clea. "And you two, what were you thinking?"

"We fell," Leth replied with a shrug.

"Oh, please." The Hunter waved an arm and turned his back to them. "The other three are as dumb as doornails, but you're even dumber if you think I don't already know what happened."

The three recruits exchanged another glance.

"I have no idea what you're talking about, Instructor," Aric said. "We were climbing these rocks and —"

"Stop that!" Saruk snapped, eyes glaring. "I'm not sending you on the pilgrimage if that's what you're worried about, so stop with the act. It's insulting."

"Forgive us, Instructor," Clea pleaded, joining her hands. "We were tired, hungry, and thirsty. We should have known better than to fight them."

Saruk scowled. "Yeah, right. I have to train a brand-new company in record time and these are the recruits I'm given." He crossed his arms, eyes swaying from Aric to Leth. "Even the noblemen act like tavern brawlers." He paced from one side to the other. "The three of you will have the privilege of telling your company the good news. The punishment will apply to all of them."

"What?!" Aric asked.

"The entire company must learn that you are in this *together.* Good and bad. Rewards and punishments." There was a small silence. "Tell your fellow recruits that the Twenty-third Company is to muster in the courtyard at sundown. No dinner."

In Lamash, unlike any other castle Aric knew about, the courtyard wasn't at ground level. Instead, it was perched up high on the mountain, like a balcony that ended on a massive cliff.

The moon hung low in the sky, and a soft wind grew colder and colder. Saruk paced in front of the line of recruits, staring each of them down. His orders had been simple – hold a spear out at arm's length. At first, it had seemed easy enough, especially considering this was a form of punishment, but it didn't take long before everyone's arms began to ache and tremble. After what felt like an hour, Aric was dripping with sweat, even though the desert heat was long gone for the day. He was gritting his teeth, trying to tuck the pain away into some forgotten corner of his mind.

"Recruit!" Saruk screamed. He stormed toward little Lyra. "Hold that spear up or goddess be my witness, I'll throw you off this mountain."

Tears dripped down Lyra's cheeks, but she obeyed with a quiet sob. Beside her, her brother Ergon faced Saruk with murderous eyes. Athan and Irenya didn't look much better than little Lyra, and Aric allowed himself some small pleasure in finally not being the worst performer of the company.

"What's the matter, priest?" Saruk asked Athan. "Are you tired?"

The boy tried to answer, but all that came out was a groan of pain.

"Have you forgotten how to draw your strength from the goddess?" Saruk insisted. "Has she abandoned you?"

Athan's back was buckling, his eyes were closed shut, his arms twitching. "Mother Ava," he managed to mutter, "never leaves my side."

"She must be bored out of her mind, then," Saruk replied, continuing along the line of recruits.

The instructor passed by Nahir. There wasn't a single drop of sweat rolling down his face. The tall Cyrinian looked so calm and still, he could have been mistaken for a statue. Beside him, Orisius, the green-eyed Arreline the girls in the company couldn't take their eyes off, inhaled and exhaled so loud and fast he sounded like a dog sniffing the dirt. Aric wondered how that could possibly help.

"You are all weak," Saruk announced, "and weak recruits don't survive their training." He paused and looked at Nahir. "Well, maybe not all of you."

The black boy smirked.

"The problem is, some of you are *never* going to be strong. So how do weak recruits survive in the Guild? Easy. They become a *company*, something you don't yet understand. But you're in luck. I will grant you the privilege of explaining it to you." At that moment, a torrent of Hunters flooded the courtyard and surrounded the recruits. "You will learn to appreciate each other's flaws and qualities as if they are your own, because that's what a team is. And this is the choice you have to make: either become one or die." Aric had no doubt Saruk was staring at him during the last couple of words, then he faced Nahir. "Including the strong. Is that understood?"

"Yes, Instructor!" the recruits replied in a powerful unison.

Saruk spat on the ground. "Pathetic. Here's another problem you have – I don't believe you."

Before any of the recruits had time to react, the circle of Hunters closed in on them, covering their mouths and noses with pieces of cloth.

Aric struggled uselessly with the large man tying his arms behind his back.

What are they doing?!

The piece of cloth had a funny smell, and it felt like it was clearing a path through his airways. The world began to blur, then spin, then everything exploded into white.

⌣⟶

With a groan, Aric sat up, hands gripping his head.

"Look, the half-prince is up," Tharius said.

"Finally," Ashur complained.

Massaging his throbbing head, Aric inspected his surroundings. It was a poorly lit room made of dark stone and…glittering walls?

"Where are we?" Aric asked.

"That's a very good question," Dothea replied. She was kneeling next to one of the walls. "Wherever we are, it can't be the desert. This place is covered in ice."

"Seriously?"

It sure *felt* cold in there.

"Also," Dothea continued, pointing at the glittering stone beneath the shiny layer of ice. "There's glowstone in there. My guess is that we're in the Shamissai Mountains."

"Not a chance," Leth said. "We must have blacked out for a few hours at best. It would have taken them days, if not weeks, to get us to the Shamissai."

That's when Aric noticed Leth was balancing a broadsword horizontally on his index finger.

"Where did you get that?" Aric asked.

"What, this?" Leth asked, indicating the sword. He threw it up, grabbed the handle, and swung it from side to side in a blur of twists and twirls until it disappeared into a sheath on his belt. "It's mine."

"Apparently," Clea said, holding a bow, "the instructors left us here with some of our personal belongings."

"Yeah," Ashur said. "Obviously, you got some jewelry." He tossed the glowstone and dragon scale armor onto Aric's lap. The cuirass landed with a clinking sound.

"Still better than what the priest got," Jullion said.

"I'm not a priest," Athan retorted. "I told you. I never took my vows."

"What did you get?" Aric asked.

Athan searched his pockets and produced a sphere made of red glass with a metal lid on top. He flipped the lid up and a pinky-sized flame flicked into existence.

"My prayer flask."

Jullion, Ashur, and Prion chuckled, but Athan ignored them.

"Are we just going to stand here doing nothing?" Dothea asked. "Everyone is up. Shouldn't we try to get out of here?"

"I still don't feel very well," Aric said, standing up. Then he froze and placed a hand on his belly. "I think I'm going to be sick."

"Don't you dare throw up in here," Ashur warned. "It'll stink up the place."

"Will you stop that?" Trissa said, placing her hands on her waist. "It was that attitude that got us in here the first place."

Ashur didn't like that. He stepped toward her, crossing his arms.

"Are you saying this is my fault?"

Trissa snorted. "You don't scare me, little boy."

"Maybe that's because you don't know why I was sentenced to the Guild," Ashur said, narrowing his eyes.

"No, I don't," Trissa replied, taking a step forward. "But I was sentenced for breaking a Paladin's leg and cracking another one's skull. So come and get it, little boy."

"Easy!" Aric slid in between them and pushed Trissa away. "Teamwork, remember? That's what Saruk was talking about before we blacked out. This is just another exercise. We need to work together to get out."

"This is not just another exercise." Nahir's powerful voice came from across the room. "Leth is correct; we are still in the desert. Which means…" He paused as if he was afraid of his own words. "We are in the Frostbound."

"What's the Frostbound?" Aric asked.

Leth made a dismissive hand-wave. "It's a Cyrinian legend."

"It is no legend, Leth of Nahlwar," Nahir said. "It is quite real, and we are inside of it. How else do you explain a frozen place in the middle of the Mahar?"

"Just because I can't explain the ice," Leth replied, "it doesn't mean it comes from the realm of the dead."

"The what?" Half of the group made that question in unison, and the other half didn't look any less curious.

Leth exhaled loudly. "The Cyrinians believe there is a gate to the underworld buried beneath the Mahar. It's supposed to be frozen because the cold seeps through the gate or something." He waved dismissively.

"Ava's mercy," Clea muttered, hugging herself.

Athan lit his prayer flask and began mumbling something inaudible. Irenya, Orisius, and Lyra joined him.

"Why would Instructor Saruk put us in a place like this?" Clea asked.

"Because, obviously, this is *not* the doorstep to the underworld," Leth said.

Ergon, Trissa, and Irenya decided to join the collective prayer.

"Oh, come on!" Leth protested. "This is clearly a sacred place, sure, there's glowstone and all, but let's be reasonable."

"Maybe you're the one being unreasonable," Clea said.

Leth snorted, shaking his head.

"It doesn't matter," Aric said. "Leth is right about one thing. There's no point in panicking. We need to calm down and figure a way out of here. Nahir, why do you think Saruk brought us here?"

"Isn't it obvious?" the black Cyrinian replied. "If we're ever going to kill a dragon, we'll need weapons made from glowstone. Look around you."

Aric obeyed, and so did everyone else. Nahir was right. The place was full of it.

⌒

"No, no, no," Irenya said, pointing at Ashur, Jullion, and Prion. "There's no way I'll be going with you three."

"Don't worry," Orisius said, smiling at her with his liquid green eyes. "I've got your back."

The girl nearly melted.

I wish I knew how to do that, Aric thought, taking a quick glance at Clea.

"Okay," Aric said, clapping his hands. "I, Clea, Leth, Nahir, and Athan will take the corridor on the right. Dothea, Tharius, Trissa, Ergon, and Lyra will take the one in the middle, and —"

"Me and Orisius are stuck with these three," Irenya said, frowning.

"Exactly," Aric smiled. "Good luck. We'll meet back here."

The three groups separated, and as Aric climbed the narrow stairs, the confusion of echoes from the other groups' chatter slowly faded until they became silent.

There were patches of ice covering the floor tiles like puddles, so Aric trod carefully. At the top of the stairs, a wide corridor stretched toward a massive wooden door. Hundreds of tiny glowstone shards dotted the walls like indigo stars in a clear night sky.

"It's beautiful," Clea said.

Leth pushed the door at the end of the corridor and the hinges wailed. On the other side was a round chamber with the statue of a warrior in the center.

"Look at that," Aric said, pointing at an inscription on the statue's pedestal.

"Runes," Nahir said.

"Yeah," Aric agreed. "Like the ones on a Bloodhouse."

"Why would someone build a statue of a warrior at the gates to the underworld?" Athan asked.

"I would answer that question," Leth said, "but I have a feeling I already did."

Aric moved to a door right across from the one they had come in through.

"We should keep going," he said, opening the door.

There was another wide corridor on the other side of the door. As before, it was lit by a myriad of glowstone shards set into the walls.

"Wait!" Clea said, stopping. "We're being stupid."

Leth crossed his arms. "I agree, but there's no need to be that hard on yourselves."

"I'm serious," Clea continued. "The walls are full of glowstone. Why don't we break the ice and pick the shards underneath it? There are enough crystals in this corridor alone to arm an entire battalion."

The five of them paused, weighing the idea.

"It's worth a try," Nahir said, unsheathing a blade. It was as long as Aric's arm, but in Nahir's hand, it looked like a kitchen knife.

The Cyrinian stabbed the wall, but the transparent surface remained intact, so he did it again and again. The stabs didn't create a single dent. With a grunt, Nahir swung the sword back, then hammered the wall so hard, it would have split a man two.

BOOOOM!

It was as if a ceiling had just caved in, except the wall remained intact while Nahir was sent flying backward across the hall. He cringed as he stood back up.

"Are you all right?" Clea asked.

The Cyrinian nodded while Leth and Aric inspected the unscathed layer of ice in utter disbelief.

"What just happened?" Aric asked.

No one answered. Instead, from somewhere within the bowels of that place, came a long, drawn-out screech that felt like cold hands wrapping around their spines.

"Ava Mother," Clea said, stepping backward.

Athan closed his eyes and began to pray.

⌐⌐⌐

Quicker than she could blink her eyes, Irenya jumped into Orisius's arms. By the time she realized she had done so, the sound had already faded away.

"I'm sorry," she said, letting Orisius go.

"That's okay," the green-eyed boy replied. "Nothing to be sorry for."

"Take it easy, little girl," Prion told her. "That's just the wind playing tricks with the tunnels."

"I know that!" she snapped.

"Well," Ashur said. "That is definitely the sun." He was perched atop a stone, peering through a small hole in what looked like a very large stone trapdoor. He jumped down with a satisfied smile. "Let's get this thing open and get out of here."

"What about the others?" Irenya asked.

"We'll fetch them when this is open," Ashur replied. "Come on, push." He placed both hands on the door and waited for the others to join him. "One, two...."

They pushed until their faces became bright red.

"Fire take this," Prion said, panting. "It won't move a hair."

They stopped to catch their breaths, then tried pushing again.

"It's useless," Orisius said, sweat breaking out on his forehead. "It won't budge." He sat on the ground, breathless. "I think we're entombed in here."

"Don't say that," Irenya pleaded.

"Sorry," Orisius replied, lying on his back. "I didn't mean it."

"Yes, you did," Ashur said. "Those sadists buried us here to die!"

"Why would they do something like that?" Irenya asked.

"She's right," Orisius agreed. "We just need to find some glowstone, like Nahir said."

Ashur kicked a pebble, cursing.

"I agree, Ash," Prion said. "It kinda makes sense."

"Nothing about this makes sense," Ashur replied, "but I agree that it's the best idea we got."

They started back through where they had come in, making a different turn before arriving at the chamber where they had woken.

Then another one of those chilling noises came from down the corridor, making Irenya jump.

"Did you hear that?" she asked.

"Hear what?" Orisius asked.

They had found a T-junction. Ashur signaled Jullion to inspect the corridor on the left while he turned to the right. Irenya stayed put, looking behind and hugging herself.

"Want my jacket?" Orisius asked her.

Irenya trembled a little. "No."

"Hey, guys," Jullion called from beyond the corner. "You should take a look at this."

Ashur emerged from the other corridor and they followed Jullion's voice. Their jaws dropped. Around the corner was the top of a stairwell from which you could see a massive cave opening. No, not a cave. It was a hall. The floor was tiled and there were dozens of warrior statues guarding a door as tall as a tower.

"I sure hope that door is not what I think it is," Jullion said.

"Maybe it's a vault," Orisius murmured, "where the glowstone is kept."

That sounded plausible enough. Or, at least, they all hoped it did.

Exhaling loudly, Orisius walked down the stairwell and the others followed. They meandered between the statues and the hall echoed with each of their steps. Blue lights, scattered above in the tall ceiling, sparkled like blue fireflies.

"Look at this," Jullion said, touching the metal surface of the colossal gate. It was covered with raised glyphs that reflected the blue lights in the ceiling. "I've never seen anything like it."

"Is it metal?" Ashur placed a hand on it and pushed. "It must weigh more than a dragon. What do you think these symbols mean?"

"These aren't symbols, you moron," Irenya told him. "These are blood runes."

"How would you know?"

"I was locked in a cell in the Bloodhouse of Capra before coming to Lamash."

"You were in prison?" Orisius asked.

Jullion swung around. "Did anyone see that?"

"It's...a long story," Irenya told Orisius.

"Seriously," Jullion insisted. "Did anyone see something over there?"

Everyone looked at where he was pointing but found nothing except shadows.

"It's just the statues," Ashur said, turning back toward the door. "I bet the crystals are in there. You know, like a treasure."

"Yeah," Orisius agreed. "We just need to find a way to open it."

"Merciful Ava!" Jullion screamed. He took several steps back. "There's something moving between the statues."

"Sure, Jules," Prion said. "They're coming to life."

Ashur laughed, but his chuckles were cut by a guttural screech that echoed tenfold.

Irenya felt her heart sinking through her stomach. "Run!" she yelled.

Dashing through the corner, Dothea stepped on a patch of ice. Her foot lost traction and she crashed to the floor. She heard something crack and howled.

Tharius was right behind her and he didn't as much as slow down. Grabbing the collar of her shirt, he heaved her up and spurred her forward. Trying to ignore the pain shooting through her arm, Dothea looked over her shoulder, making sure Trissa, Ergon, and Lyra were still following.

"Quick! They're getting closer," Ergon screamed, pushing Trissa and his sister forward.

Dothea kept running, scanning the floor ahead of her, careful not to step on the ice again. The arm she had fallen on felt funny, with a tingling sensation that seemed to be turning into pain. A savage growl disfigured her expression and she looked over her shoulder again. Whatever those things were, they looked hideous. She saw the three creatures chasing them turn the same corner she just had. One of them slipped on an ice patch and scraped its bluish, scaly skin against the wall. With swift, feline movements, it quickly regained its balance and resumed the chase, letting out a wolf-like growl.

The corridor turned another corner, and Dothea nearly crashed against a wall. What chamber was this? Where were they?

Oh, no, this is not where we came in.

Her head spun, checking the room for an exit. There was only one door. She tried it with the others in tow.

"It's locked!" Dothea told them.

They turned around. The creatures were closing in, snarling.

"Quick, the statues! Grab a spear!" Trissa said.

There was a statue on each side of the room. Two powerfully armored warriors were standing watch with spears at the ready. Trissa grabbed the one on the right; Ergon went for the one on the left.

"Oh, goddess," Lyra said, backing into the wall.

"We'll have to knock the door down," Tharius said, pushing Dothea out of the way.

"No," she said. "You'll just break a leg or something. Let me. I can open it." She removed a small leather pouch from her jacket's inner pocket. "I had this in my pocket when I woke up."

"What's that?" Tharius asked.

"My pickset," Dothea replied. She opened the pouch and removed a couple of thin metal tools. "This is what I did for a living."

"Here they come!" Ergon screamed.

"Help them," Dothea told Tharius. "I can do this."

Tharius nodded, still looking confused, then joined the others.

Closing her eyes, Dothea took a deep breath.

I'm on the beach, she told herself, kneeling in front of the door.

"Get ready," she heard Tharius saying from somewhere behind her.

I've done this hundreds of times.

She was so focused, she didn't even notice Trissa swinging a spear above her head and smashing it down on one of the creatures' necks. The thing fell to the ground, its head twisted in an impossible way, then hissed and quickly jumped back up.

Breathing steadily, Dothea inserted the torsion wrench into the lock, trying to ignore the pain in her arm. She turned the wrench, putting the lock into tension, then slid the pick along the locking opening, feeling each pin with careful strokes.

Behind her, the battle raged. Pushing Lyra behind his back, Ergon stabbed one of the monsters, sending it hurtling backward.

"Did you see that?!" Ergon screamed. "They don't bleed!"

I'm not here. I'm at the port. Seagulls are singing. Waves are crashing against the seawall. Click!

The first pin locked into position and Dothea exhaled loudly, her eyes still shut and a drop of sweat rolling down her forehead.

Roaring, Trissa smashed the butt of her spear against the jaw of a monster, sending it reeling. The swing made her lose balance and exposed her back to another creature standing right next to the one she had hit. It grabbed Trissa's neck and shirt, hissing.

"No!" Tharius screamed, kicking the thing in the gut. For a moment, he almost expected his foot to burst into flames or something.

Click!

Another pin locked into position. Dothea adjusted the pressure on the torsion wrench, being more careful than ever in her life. She couldn't risk having to start the process all over again. The pain in her arm, however, was getting a bit too hard to ignore.

Click!

Only two left to go.

Behind her, claws hacked and slashed wildly, barely kept at bay by Ergon's spear.

"Lyra, stand back," Ergon said.

His sister wanted to help. She was unarmed, just like Tharius, so she tried to mimic him and kick the monsters away. One of them grabbed her leg.

"Ergon!" she screamed.

Eyes widened, the boy wrapped an arm around his sister, pulling her. It left him with only one hand available to handle the lance, but the weapon was made of solid iron or something just as heavy. There was no way Ergon could wield it with just one hand. It left him completely exposed. One of the creatures attacked and four streaks of blood gushed from Ergon's torso. He screamed with pain but managed to head-butt the creature and free his sister from its hold.

At the sound of Ergon's cry, Tharius spun behind him, took the spear from him, and tripped the monster's with a swing. He wasn't even aware that he could move that fast.

"I did it!" Dothea jumped with her arms in the air. The door slid open. "Quick, through here."

She held the door open, rushing the others with hand waves.

"Go!" Tharius said, swinging his spear at the monster's legs, making sure all three of the beasts were either fallen or trying to get back up.

He was the last to get through, and just as he passed, Dothea slammed the door behind him. With a twirl, Tharius slipped the spear through the ring of the handle and placed it diagonally, barring the door from open-ing again. The door shook and trembled, horrible shrieks coming from the other side, but the spear kept it in place.

"Guys," Trissa called.

Dothea and Tharius turned around. Ergon was on the floor, bleeding badly.

"I need water," Lyra said, tearing the sleeve of her tunic. "I need water!"

"He won't able to walk," Tharius said, flatly. The sounds of punching and scratching and howling came from across the door. "We need to get out of here."

Lyra sniffed and wiped a tear from her eyes. "I have to stop the bleeding first."

The other three exchanged a glance.

"There's no time, Lyra," Trissa said.

Somehow, the screeching and thundering became louder.

Lyra sobbed, but her hands picked up speed, wrapping her brother's wound with her own rags. It made Ergon flinch and groan, but he didn't complain.

"I'll carry him," Tharius said.

"Are you mad?" Dothea asked. "He's too heavy."

"I need to stop the bleeding first," Lyra insisted.

Ergon grabbed her arm and forced her to stop.

"Sis, I need stitches. You can't stop the bleeding."

"I'll..." Lyra paused and her head spun around as if looking for some-thing. "I'll make a needle out of something."

Ergon shook her. "Sis! We need to get out of here."

"Lyra," Tharius said, kneeling beside her, "I'll carry your brother." He looked up at Dothea and Trissa. "Take Lyra and go on ahead. Find help. Me and Ergon will be right behind you."

⌒⌐

The screams echoing through the corridors were terrifying, but not nearly as much as the bestial growls that came with them.

"It's coming through here," Aric said aiming at one of three corridors in front of them.

The others agreed with anxious nods. They ran as fast as they could. Another set of screams and roars made Aric jolt with fright. He tripped on a patch of ice and would have fallen to the floor if Clea hadn't caught him.

"Are you all right?" Clea asked.

Aric froze in her arms. "Ye – yes, of course," he mumbled. "Thank you."

"Down there," Leth yelled. He was standing next to a stairwell. "The screams are coming from down there."

At the bottom of the stairs, they found another narrow corridor. The screams got louder and louder until the corridor gave way to a massive opening. Inside was a crowd of statues, but they could see people moving between them. And not just people.

"It's Irenya," Clea said. "And Orisius and...."

"What are those things?!" Leth asked.

The only answer he received was the sound of Athan's prayer flask lighting up, followed by the usual mumbling.

"We've got to help them," Clea urged.

The blade from Leth's sword rang out as he unsheathed it. Nahir mirrored him and drew out his knife, then looked at its tiny blade and snorted. "I don't think this is going to do," he said, sheathing the knife. He moved to one of the stone warriors and stole a massive battle-axe. It had to weigh as much as Nahir himself. The Cyrinian looked pleased. "Let's go."

Leth nodded and the two of them charged toward the creatures. Taking an arrow from her quiver, Clea looked at Athan and Aric.

"The two of you are unarmed," she said. "Best if you stay here."

Before Aric could reply, she was off.

She must think I'm a useless coward.

"We have to do something," Aric told Athan.

The former acolyte opened his eyes and faced him pitifully.

"I'm doing the only thing I know."

Shifting his weight frantically, Aric looked at the others and saw Ashur throwing a stone at one of the creatures. The beast was knocked down to the floor but jumped back up with catlike reflexes.

"You really think that will help?" Aric asked, indicating the prayer flask with his chin. There was no malice in the question. He truly wanted to know.

"No," Athan replied. "I don't."

Aric bit his lower lip as he saw Clea firing two arrows at one of the monsters. The creature merely stumbled back a little.

"Screw it," Aric said, then dashed away toward her.

Clea fired another arrow. This time, she hit the beast right between his eyes. It barely even flinched.

Aric saw her reaching for another arrow. The monster was an arm's length away from her. She fumbled around her quiver, gasping.

"Goddess!" she screamed.

Bam! Aric elbowed the monster, knocking it to the ground. He rolled to the side, trying to give himself enough room to stand back up. He knew the creature would slice him open if it got close enough. Except it didn't. Instead, the monster scrambled back, hissing before it ran away.

"I think," Clea said, astonished, "I think you scared it."

"I did?"

That didn't seem very likely. At the sound of a curse, Aric looked over his shoulder and saw Leth slashing a creature's torso open.

"Why won't they die?" Leth yelled.

"Because they are already dead!" Nahir replied, swinging his axe.

If it had worked once, why wouldn't it work twice? Aric gritted his teeth and charged. Leth heard him howling as he approached and barely had the time to dodge and let him by.

Bam!

Once again, he crashed elbow-first against the creature, hurling it to the floor. And once again, as soon as it caught a glimpse of Aric, it fled as quickly as it could.

Leth was rendered speechless. "What the —"

"AVA'S MERCY SAVE US ALL!" Athan screamed from the back. It was hard to tell if he was yelling or crying. The former acolyte must have been inspired by Aric's success, because he was charging with all his might, Ava's fire leading the way as he held his prayer flask firmly in his hands.

"What is that idiot doing?!" Leth asked.

Athan crashed against a monster that Ashur was barely keeping at bay with a lance and the two of them fell to the ground, wrapping around each other. Suddenly, flames erupted around Athan and the creature. The former acolyte jumped up, screaming and twirling as flames ate through his jacket. Hastily, he shucked the jacket off, throwing it away. Fire was enveloping the monster as well, except it didn't have a jacket to remove. It shrieked and howled hideously, hurtling from one side to the other as the flames consumed it.

"Fire!" Aric screamed. "They're vulnerable to fire!"

⌒⟶

Their scaled skins cracked and shredded beneath the flames until there was nothing left of those bone-chilling things.

"Goddess-damned beasts," Ashur spat as the last of the four monsters shrieked and squirmed.

"Put the torch out, Ashur," Aric said. "We should save the fuel until we're out of here."

"You put it out," Ashur replied, tossing the torch.

Aric caught it midair and swallowed a curse.

"Here," Clea said, taking her leather vest off. "Use this." The tunic she wore underneath the vest was bloodied.

"Are you all right?" Aric asked, wrapping the flames with the vest, carefully so as not to burn himself.

Clea looked down at the bloodstains. "These aren't mine; don't worry."

She smiled at Aric, and butterflies woke up inside his belly.

"Athan," he called, jerking his stare away from Clea. "How much fuel do we have?"

The former acolyte looked at his prayer flask. "A few more drops," he replied. "We'll have to make them count."

"Understood," Aric said with a nod.

Then, echoes of what sounded like a stampeding herd thundered from one of the many corridors feeding the hall.

"Oh, no," Irenya groaned with dread. "How many more of those things can there be?"

"It's not the creatures," Nahir told her. "It's Trissa and the others. Listen."

Everyone became quiet, trying to decipher the noise. Was that screaming?

"I think they're crying for help," Clea said.

"I think so too," Aric agreed. "They're trying to find us. Come on."

The group followed the sound and Athan placed his prayer flask at the ready. Tiny glowstone crystals lit the way across the tight tunnel as if they were inside a punctured box, and the echoing voices became clearer and clearer. A girl was crying for help. Actually, more than one girl. At least two of them.

With the torch at the ready, Aric guided them toward the screams. They took several turns and climbed a steep staircase.

Clea was the first to see them. "There!" she said.

"Quick! Help!" Dothea screamed.

The three girls were pushing a door, trying to close it, but several blue arms and legs were sticking out, keeping it from slamming shut. Trissa turned around, trying to gain more purchase on the ground, and blood dripping from her arm smeared the door.

Nahir, Orisius, and Clea rushed toward them, helping them hold the door.

"Athan," Aric called, "quick, give me light."

With trembling hands, Athan flicked his prayer flask open. He nearly dropped the red vial.

There was a pounding on the door so powerful, it made everyone pushing it jump.

"Quick!" Aric urged.

Steadying his own arm, Athan ignited the torch and fire quickly engulfed it.

"Okay, everyone," Aric called. "At my signal, get behind me."

The three girls hesitated, exchanging worried glances, but Nahir and Leth reassured them with a nod, and they decided to obey.

"Now!" Aric yelled.

The group jumped away from the door and the creatures burst through like a growling flood. Everyone ran behind Aric except for Nahir and Leth, who took positions at his side. The creatures charged and Aric torched the first one. All it took was a simple kiss from the flames and fire instantly spread across their blue bodies.

Strangely, none of the monsters tried to attack Aric, going for Leth and Nahir instead. It made the fight even easier, Nahir's axe and Leth's sword funneling all five remaining creatures toward Aric.

The last of the monsters was still hissing within the blaze when Lyra grabbed Aric's collar.

"You have to hurry," Lyra said, sobbing. "Ergon's hurt."

"Tharius stayed with him and we came for help," Dothea added.

Aric cursed. "Take us there!" he said. "Athan, the fuel. Stay close to me."

The former acolyte nodded, his milky-white hands wrapping around the prayer flask as if it were the most precious of jewels.

With Lyra in the lead, they ran across several passageways until she stopped, gasping. Aric felt a shiver. They had just entered another tunnel and there was blood smeared across the walls and floor tiles. At the other end of the corridor, pieces of wood dangled from the hinges of what had once been a door, but there was no one in sight.

No one dared to say anything for a while, until Clea pushed through the crowd and stepped into the middle of the mess of splinters and blood. She circled, trying to decipher the leftovers from the fight, and Aric joined her, the flame on his torch dancing nervously.

"The blood trails that way," Clea said, indicating the shattered door. "I think they have been taken."

Lyra bawled and her eyes welled once again.

"They're probably dead by now," Ashur said.

"Shut up, you idiot," Leth snapped.

If Ashur was going to retort, he changed his mind under the stares of the rest of the group.

It was Clea who broke the silence. "We can try to follow the blood trail," she ventured.

"We don't have to," Trissa said. "I think I know where they are." About a dozen puzzled looks turned to her. "When we were attacked, we had found a huge cache of glowstone. I think the creatures were protecting it."

Aric looked down at his own chest. "Maybe that's why they don't attack me," he said. "Because I'm wearing glowstone."

"So, they think you're one of them or something?" Leth said.

"Maybe," Aric said. "Trissa, do you remember where you found the crystals?"

"Yes. Follow me."

Trissa dashed away. She turned a corner and climbed a wide staircase, checking over her shoulder to see if the others were keeping up. She didn't seem to care that there were patches of ice everywhere. Aric almost asked her to slow down but quickly changed his mind when he checked the weakening flame on his torch. Then he heard a squeak from behind, followed by the sound of shattering glass.

Aric stopped, turned around, and saw a livid Athan, lying on the ground, staring at the remains of his prayer flask. What little liquid it contained was now spilled across the frozen steps of the staircase.

"I'm... I'm so sorry," Athan mumbled.

"Crap," Leth said.

Everyone quickly turned to Aric. The torch still burned in his hand, even if faintly.

"I think we'd better hurry," he said.

This time, Trissa didn't even reply, didn't even make sure the group was following her; she simply darted around a corner, curls of black hair bouncing on her head. Then she stopped right next to a threshold, doing a silent shush sign. The company lined behind her, backs against the wall, and she gestured for Aric to peek around the door.

It wasn't a room; it was a cave. Except, unlike any other cave, this one was blindingly bright. Massive glowstone crystals pierced its ground and ceiling like pillars. There were so many of them, it was impossible to count.

A cache of glowstone, Trissa had said. More like a mountain of it. There were enough of those crystals in there to build a palace. The most unsettling part was how the blue pillars felt like they were humming, even though Aric couldn't really hear anything. Between them, dozens of the scaled creatures walked around like restless ants, doing nothing except admiring the mighty structures. Twisting his head, Aric searched the cave for Tharius and Ergon.

"I see them!" he whisper-screamed.

The two boys were lying on the ground, appearing unconscious. A dark pool of blood spread beneath them.

"Aric," Trissa whispered. She pointed at his torch.

The flames were dying out. Only a few of patches of the torch's cloth still burned.

"I'm going in," Aric said.

Leth, Nahir, and Clea moved into position behind him. Aric stopped them with a gesture.

"No. There are too many of those things in there. I'll be fine. You saw how they always back away from me."

Leth glanced at the shiny dragon scale and glowstone armor on his chest, and gritted his teeth. "Just keep the torch in hand, all right?"

Aric nodded. "Stay here," he said, then swung and stepped into the cave.

The creatures noticed him immediately and a hundred fierce, unsettling eyes fell on him. Aric's entire body demanded that he flee. His stomach turned, his spine shivered, and the torch in his hand trembled like a branch in a storm. A gust of wind swept around him, the cold cutting his cheeks, and Aric took a slow step forward. Still, he almost slipped on the ice-covered rock.

Some of the creatures snarled, but none of them moved. Swallowing through a dry throat, Aric walked toward his friends.

"What are these things?" he whispered to himself.

A small semicircle was forming around him, but no creature got less than a couple paces away from him.

"Tharius," Aric called, kneeling beside him. "Tharius!"

With a twitch that shook his entire body, Tharius woke up, his blue eyes popping open. The boy grabbed Aric's arm and squeezed.

"Aric?"

"Yes. Are you hurt? Can you walk?"

Tharius's head spun around, panic writhing his mouth. "Wh – why aren't they attacking?"

Aric pushed him down. "Don't get up. Stay still." He looked at the torch in his other hand. It would go out at any moment. If those things attacked... "Can you walk?"

"I think so."

"What about Ergon?"

Tharius looked at the other boy lying next to him "I...couldn't help him," he said. His eyes welled.

"What?!" Aric dove and pushed an ear against Ergon's chest. A sigh of relief left his lungs. "He's still alive!"

That last sentence was a bit too loud. Around him, a small army of scaly monsters roared.

"I don't understand," Tharius said. "Why aren't they attacking you?"

"Because I'm wearing glowstone," Aric replied, tapping a finger on his cuirass. He stood back up, looked at the torch, and saw a last flicker of flame licking the charred ball of cloth. "Or at least, I hope that's why."

He threw the torch away and faced the circle of beasts, then took a step forward. Each one of them took a step back.

"Be still," Aric said over his shoulder. "Don't get up."

One foot after the other, Aric neared one of the gigantic glowstone pillars. Smaller crystals branched from the main one, some as wide and long as a log, others as short and thin as a kitchen knife. He tried grabbing one of them.

"Ouch!"

The crystal stung like an ice burn coursing through his veins, and Aric was forced to let it go. The monsters didn't like it and snarled again. One of them even took a step forward. Otherwise, the semicircle kept its distance.

"Yeah, yeah, be quiet," Aric told them. "You're even uglier when you open your mouths." He turned back to the crystals, ripped a patch off his sleeve, and then wrapped it around one of them. This time, he felt nothing except the jagged surface of the glowstone. He yanked hard and the crystal cracked away from the main structure. "Tharius," he called.

The other boy lifted his head slightly.

"Let's do an experiment," Aric said. "Catch." Hoping his aim had improved since the bow-and-arrow training a couple of days before, he sent the crystal circling through the air. Tharius caught it midflight. Aric felt rather pleased with himself.

The beasts rushed toward Tharius like a pack of famished dogs. Yelping, he rolled away from them and jumped up, holding the glowstone crystal like a dagger. The creatures froze, hissing. Were they afraid of it? They didn't look afraid.

"Fire take me," Tharius said.

"No," Aric replied, exhaling louder than ever in his life. "Fire take them. Literally. You should have seen it."

As soon as they stepped into the hallway where Ashur and the others had found the exit door, the glowstone shards lit up as if blue fires had suddenly ignited within them. And not just the pile of crystals they were carrying; every tiny shard on the walls of the tunnel burst to life, covering the group with a blue halo. As a response, the stone slabs in the ceiling cracked and a thin curtain of sand fell through the opening, immediately followed by a flood of sunlight.

There was a collective gasp of relief.

"How is this even possible?" Leth asked, staring at the slowly parting stone blocks.

"No one cares, rich kid," Ashur told him. "We're out."

Leth rolled his eyes.

"Has to be a spell stored inside the crystals," Aric said. He adjusted Ergon's weight over his shoulder with a tug.

"So, who stored the spell?" Leth insisted, taking a look at one of the crystals he was carrying. That one alone was the size of his sword.

"Maybe the Guild is harboring mages," Irenya said in an almost-whisper.

"I doubt it," Leth said. "The Guild hunts dragons. No one is as scrutinized by the Paladins as them."

"Maybe it's just...a simple spell," Aric said. "Simple spells can last for years, even decades if the crystal is big enough. And there's no shortage of those in here."

The stone slabs stopped and several silhouettes appeared on the other side.

"Who's there?" Aric asked.

Instead of answering, the figures lowered themselves, grabbed the recruits, and heaved them up.

"Is everyone okay?" It was Saruk.

"Ergon's wounded," Aric replied. "It's bad."

The open sky and the sun made Aric feel amazing. He turned around, taking a deep breath. It was a relief to be out, but everything was still wrong. A thin layer of frost crackled under his feet, and instead of the familiar, meat-cooking wind that had punished him for the past few days, he felt an icy breeze that made him quiver.

Where in the world are we?

A caravan waited for them and Ergon was lifted onto a large wheeled car being pulled by four camels.

"Congratulations," Saruk told them. "You've survived your first test and now own the tools of your trade. From this day forward, we'll teach you how to use them. But believe me, the tests *will* get harder." He turned around and climbed onto a horse.

"Harder?" Dothea complained beneath her breath. "It's a miracle we're all alive."

Tharius grabbed a handful of frozen sand and dropped it once again. "We're training to hunt dragons," he said. "What did you expect? Singing lessons?"

A few paces away from them, Saruk's horse stopped and turned back, whinnying.

"Oh, and one more thing," the instructor said. "It's about time you all start thinking about who will lead the company. You'll have to vote on it soon enough."

He smiled, then turned his horse back around.

"We get to decide that?" Aric asked.

Saruk was too far away to hear the question.

"Well," Clea said, placing a hand on Aric's shoulder. "I know who I'm voting for." She winked at him, smiling.

CHAPTER 9

The Docks District

Where am I? Fadan thought, blinking his eyes as the world refused to come into focus.

He rolled onto his back on the dusty hardwood floor. His muscles were sore and stiff. He could barely turn his head. The sun was shining powerfully above the skylights, its heat explaining why he felt so sticky with sweat.

The attic, Fadan remembered.

He looked at the floor where his face had been just moments before and saw a gooey, white puddle of some kind.

What is that, puke? he thought, grimacing and wiping his mouth with the back of his hand.

The attic was absolutely peaceful. Dust swirled inside the strips of light falling from the skylights, like curtains waving in the wind, except the air was completely stale. The tables, the chairs, and the porcelain dinner set all stood quietly in their places, intact, which meant his memory of some kind of explosion was obviously mistaken. He remembered drinking the runium, but the rest was a blurry, spinning mess of light. Something had gone terribly wrong, but what exactly? Had he cast a spell on himself by mistake? Had the runium poisoned him somehow?

Fadan stood up and nearly fell back down. His head was throbbing. He staggered to the desk where the magic book still stood open on its first page and sat down. At first, the letters began to dance before his eyes. He laid his hands on the pages as if he could force them to stand still.

The first chapter seemed to be an endless ramble about exotic concepts like cognitive entropy and other indecipherable terms.

Fadan sighed, leaning back in his chair. The room was still spinning slightly around him and he heard his stomach rumble. He was so hungry it ached.

I'm not going to accomplish anything like this, he thought.

He looked outside. Judging by the sun's height, it was around noon, which meant he had missed two meals at the Palace. His father would be furious.

Screw it! Let him wonder where I am, what I'm doing.

Trying to forget the demanding growls from his belly, Fadan walked downstairs to the kitchen, with the magic book under his arm. He picked up a pot from a pile, placed the book inside, covered it, and then slid the pot into the oven, burying it beneath a mound of old ash.

"There," he muttered to himself, wiping his hands together. "Just in case."

Now he had to find something to eat, and since he wasn't in the mood to face his father, going back to the Core Palace was out of the question, which narrowed his options considerably.

Making sure the way was clear, Fadan walked out of the kitchen and into the mansion's backyard. Grass had mostly claimed the cobbled walkway leading to the street, and he had to jump over a bush in order to reach the gate. Outside, Fadan nearly bumped into two Legionaries on patrol. The soldiers were too distracted to notice him scurry behind a bush, and he waited as they walked along the street, arguing over which tavern had the worst wine in Mount Capitol. Then, when they turned a corner, Fadan left his cover and ran the other way.

He crossed a wide street, flanked by the Lagons' estate on one side, and House Mantea's palace on the other, two of the richest, most powerful families in the Empire, and bitter rivals as well. At the end of the street stood the main gate to the Empress's Orchard, a garden that had been built by Empress Lessia, Fadan's great-great-great-grandmother. It was a beautiful place, decorated with flowers and fruit trees from all across the Empire.

Fadan picked a couple of red Thepian pears, a yellow Samehrian tangerine, and even a handful of thrystles, an Arreline flower whose pollen tasted like bitter cinnamon.

It wasn't much of a snack, and it vanished in a handful of bites, but it was enough to quiet his rebellious stomach. He had too many things swimming around in his brain to worry about eating.

What had gone wrong the previous night? Would he be able to decipher the book all by himself? And, most importantly, how was he going to find more runium by himself? He had already drunk the entire content of his only vial, and without it, he couldn't practice or learn.

Well, invading the Paladins' headquarters again is out of the question.

Fadan wandered aimlessly, running possible scenarios through his mind. Now that he was far from his hideout, it didn't matter if anyone saw him.

What are my options?

There was one obvious answer. He *could* buy some. Runium was illegal, but everyone knew it could be bought. It was dangerous, though, and runium traders couldn't exactly be found in street stalls, crying out their product's qualities. However, there was surely a way to find them. Fadan just had to find out how.

A series of nondescript palaces went by as he kept walking, his mind racing. Where in Augusta could he find a runium trader?

The docks, maybe? he wondered.

Everything was traded in the Docks District, why not runium?

Well, first of all, because that's where the customs officers check for contraband.

On the other hand, how else would runium get into the city? There was some land trade in Augusta, yes, but the sheer volume of ships coming and going up and down the Saffya would surely make it much easier to hide illegal goods.

Maybe I'm wrong, maybe I'm right, he thought. *The only way I'll know is if I check.*

Which raised another problem. How would he *get* there?

Being the prince obviously came with many privileges, but freedom of travel wasn't one of them. The Legionaries at the Citadel gate would never allow him to leave without express orders from the emperor himself.

I suppose I could ask if I came up with a good excuse.

But that would take time. Fadan's next encounter with his father was fated to result in some sort of punishment, not a gift. Besides, even if the emperor *did* authorize a stroll around the city, it would always be a supervised one. Attempting to purchase runium with a detachment of Legionaries breathing down his neck would probably be a bad idea.

Fadan halted as he realized he had walked himself to a dead end. He had reached the edge of the Citadel, and its massive stone wall rose in front of him like the face of a cliff. He decided to continue. The narrow steps climbing the wall didn't have a railing to hold on to, so he kept his back to the wall all the way up.

Wind rustled his black hair when he reached the top. The battlements overlooked Augusta, the Imperial city sprawling around in every direction. There were several other walls protecting Augusta. From the oldest ones at the bottom of Mount Capitol – on top of which the Citadel stood – to the more recent Flavillian wall, the outermost of all of them. Still, parts of the city spilled beyond them, reaching ever farther away as if trying to flee the emperor's grip.

Down to the south, on the section of the river that crossed into the Flavillian wall, stood the docks. It was the city's farthermost district from the Citadel, and not the kind of place where one should travel alone, by all accounts. Still, Fadan was determined.

What if I climbed over the wall? he mused.

It didn't look impossible, but it did look hard. Fadan leaned out, measuring the height. It was at least four stories high, and the only thing down there to cushion a fall was the wooden roof of some dwelling.

Well, if I had a rope, I could probably do it. The hardest part would probably be the return.

"Imperial Majesty!"

Fadan caught such a fright, he nearly tumbled over the battlement and fell. He turned and saw a tall nobleman give him a slight bow. The man smiled, a hand resting on the golden pommel of his sword. He wore a dark blue coat, as thick as armor, that barely moved as he sauntered closer to Fadan. The prince recognized him, of course, as one of the three younger brothers of the head of House Lagon. There were few families as fiercely loyal to the throne as them.

"Lord Fabian," Fadan said, faking a smile. "How have you been?"

"As well as an old man can be," Fabian replied. He looked over the battlement in front of Fadan. "Enjoying the view?"

"It is a wonderful view; wouldn't you agree?" Fadan said.

"Indeed. In fact, the best one in the Citadel." Fabian looked back and indicated the palaces with his chin. "Certainly much better than looking in."

Fadan frowned. There were a lot of things wrong with the Citadel, but being ugly was certainly not one of them.

"You do not enjoy the look of the palaces?" Fadan asked.

"The palaces?" Fabian asked. "Oh, the palaces are fine. It's the streets that bother me."

"What's wrong with the streets?"

Lord Lagon looked at Fadan. "They're empty," he said. "It's a ghost town. Look at it. Take out the Legionaries on patrol and there's not a soul in sight."

The man was certainly right. Fadan had just never thought about it like that. It was just the way the Citadel was.

Fabian sighed. "It wasn't always like this, you know?" he said. "Those marble streets used to be covered with young men and women chasing each other. Children playing and older people telling them to slow down before they hurt themselves. There was life here." He motioned toward the large gate leading to the city. "The gates were always open. Every day, we had a party, a ball, or an evening lunch to attend. It was…buzzing."

Fadan had no idea. He tried to picture the Citadel like that. It sounded nice.

"What happened?" the prince asked.

"Oh, many things," Fabian replied. "Things like the Purge, for example. When the nobility realized what Tarsus was capable of, they all decided it was best to keep their progeny someplace where the emperor did not hold the keys to every door."

"I see," Fadan said, looking away. He felt his cheeks warm. No one ever spoke of the emperor like this. He didn't even remember the last time anyone had so much as mentioned the Purge. Especially someone as loyal to the throne as Lord Fabian.

"No, you don't," Fabian told him. "Do you know who Faric Auron was?"

Fadan swallowed. This conversation was becoming beyond uncomfortable. "My brother's grandfather," Fadan replied after a pause.

Fabian nodded. "That's right. And the High Marshal of the Legions when your father was still the crown prince." He shook his head. "I was about your age when the Thepians revolted. They won battle after battle, and most of them without even drawing their swords. Our Legions simply surrendered, changed sides, or refused to march out of their forts. I remember my father saying the whole world was unraveling. Then Intila's father was captured in Nosta, and Faric was called to replace him at the head of the Legions. No one thought he could win. We all believed we were marching to our deaths when Faric led us out of Augusta that year. Our first battle was at Bregga; you know the one."

Fadan had no idea.

"There were ten of those bastards for each one of us," Fabian continued, his eyes somewhere far away. "By the goddess, did we chase them off that field! Don't ask me how. All I remember from that day is a furious blur. Dozens of people wrote books on Faric's military genius. His tactics, his resource management. There's even an idiot who wrote about Faric's *gentle* treatment of his men." He cackled amusedly. "*Gentle* treatment. One wrong look at the man and you'd get whipped."

He paused again, then shook his head, as if he were just waking up.

"Thanks to Faric, your grandfather kept his Empire, but it was hanging by a thread. That was what Tarsus inherited – a bankrupt, fractured, crumbling Empire." He looked into Fadan's eyes. "But your father didn't allow the Empire to disintegrate. A weaker emperor would have, but he kept it all together. It came at a cost, true. But he did it."

He once again glanced at the empty streets of the Citadel behind them.

"You and your brother were the last kids I ever saw playing in those streets." He paused for a while. "Just like me and my brothers used to before we went to war. That's life, you know?" He looked back at Fadan. "One day, you wake up, and instead of going out to play with your brothers, you have to go to war."

Fadan stared at him, his jaw dropped. No one had ever spoken to him of these matters so...candidly.

A Legionary on patrol walked by them. Fabian waited for the soldier to move away, then stepped closer to Fadan.

"You can't play with your brother anymore, and you want to go to war," the nobleman said. "It's written all over your face."

Fadan feigned a smile. "Lord Fabian, I —"

"Let me finish," the nobleman said, cutting him off. "Your father did what he had to do, and now you feel like you have to do the same. I understand. But you're alone, and you shouldn't have to be, so..." He took a look around, making sure no one was listening. "If you're ever in need of help, find me. I'll see what I can do."

"I... I don't know what you're talking about."

"Yes, you do," Fabian said. He looked down the battlements, at the rooftops several feet down below. "I don't know where you want to go, or why, but I know you'll break your neck if you try to go this way." Now he sounded like old Macael giving his sermons. "There are plenty of sewer tunnels beneath the Citadel. Your brother knew that. I thought you did too."

Fadan had no idea what to say. Fabian gave him a nod and, as if that had been an absolutely normal conversation, turned around and headed to the stairs.

"Wait!" the prince said.

Fabian halted.

"Did my father send you to spy on me?"

"No," Fabian replied. "But I wouldn't tell you if he had." He smirked. "Just like I won't tell him about this conversation."

The sound of dripping water echoed through the tunnel. The light from Fadan's torch played over the glossy black slime of the mold covering the stone wall. He walked alongside the black, stale river of sewage, its rotten smell nauseating. The place where Aric and Doric had been caught wasn't far. Fadan didn't know the sewers very well, but he knew that much.

He turned a corner and a rat ran over his feet, squeaking and startling him.

"Damn it!" Fadan muttered, steadying himself from the fright. "What in mother's name am I doing here?"

There was a manhole above him. He couldn't be sure he had walked far enough underground to have reached the other side of the Citadel's wall, but it was possible. He carefully set the torch on the ground, upright against the wall, and climbed the iron ladder.

The manhole cover slid out of the way with some effort, clanging against the cobblestone. Fadan peeked outside, hoping there weren't any Legionaries close by. His head swung around and he failed to recognize any of the houses.

I'm out, he thought.

The Citadel walls stood less than a hundred feet behind him, blocking the street and turning it into an alley.

Hurrying before anyone showed up, Fadan hopped out from the manhole and covered it once again, dusting his hands off. Up in the battlements, a couple of Legionaries walked by, chatting casually. Fadan raised his hood over his head and marched away.

Some of the main streets were still busy with pedestrians and even the occasional horseman, oil lamps flickering above them. Every merchant stall had been closed for the night, and windows were covered with wooden shutters. Nothing here felt familiar. The narrow streets and the closely packed buildings all looked the same and gave Fadan the impression that he was walking around in circles. Returning home would certainly be much easier. There wasn't anywhere in Augusta where you couldn't see the Citadel perched atop Mount Capitol like a crown. He decided to use the moon as a reference and make sure he kept going south. It should eventually lead him to the docks.

Fadan crossed avenues, squares, and plazas. Several people bumped into him without so much as an apology. He saw noblemen entering and leaving some of the shadiest buildings he had ever seen. Beggars, wrapped in ragged blankets, mumbled incoherently on most corners. Fadan crossed the gates of two of the inner walls, and on both of them, Legionaries were playing dice on wooden tables instead of standing guard. One of them actually looked drunk, and Fadan had to make an effort not to stare.

As he moved through the city, carefully cobbled streets were gradually replaced by mud paths, while stone houses, five or more stories high, were replaced by wooden shacks with three floors at the most. Then, the wide curve of the Saffya became visible. Ships of every shape and size were anchored to a tapestry of docking piers, wooden scaffolding rising here and there. Lamps and torches disappeared, and the streets became lit by the moon alone, helped by the massive, mirror-like surface of the Saffya. Barrels and crates seemed to be lumped together everywhere. Dogs rummaged through garbage piles, and cats fought each other in back alleys.

He had arrived at the Docks.

What was he supposed to do now, though?

There were plenty of shady characters lurking here and there, but Fadan couldn't bring himself to approach any of them.

A man walked past him, stepping into a puddle and splashing Fadan's boots with muddy water.

"Hey!" Fadan complained. "Watch where you're going."

If the man even heard him, he made no sign of it. He simply kept walking until he reached a door and opened it. Light and wild chatter poured outside until the door closed behind the man.

A tavern.

Fadan felt like going in there as well. Not to chase the man, of course. It should just be easier to strike up a conversation inside a tavern than in the streets. Someone in there would have to know something or someone that could help. He decided to go in.

Muffled sounds of laughter came through the wooden door. Hanging above it, shaped like a tiara, was a plaque that read The Boring Princess.

Fadan chuckled and walked inside. The air was thick with smoke and the tang of bad wine. Two long tables occupied most of the space, and a crowd of what Fadan guessed were sailors gathered around both of them, drinking, yelling, and laughing obscenely loud. There were other, smaller tables lining the walls, where a myriad of different patrons sat. Fadan chose one of the only two vacant tables and sat down, pulling his hood back. Behind him was a pair of old men playing cards, while at the table across from him, a Cyrinian tuned a sitar.

It was a strange, diverse crowd, certainly much different from what he was used to, but that was to be expected.

One of the girls waiting tables walked by but completely ignored Fadan. Not that he was in any hurry to try their wine. That was when he noticed one of the sailors at the long table staring at him with a wicked smile. The man scratched his chin, weathered skin under a couple days' worth of old beard. His hand had the thickest knuckles Fadan had ever seen.

The prince averted his eyes, pretending like it was nothing with him.

"Hey, you," a hoarse voice called.

It was the sailor. Fadan turned and the man widened his smile.

"You lost?" the sailor asked.

"I'm fine," Fadan replied. "Thank you for the concern." He averted his eyes once again.

"Nice boots you got there," the man insisted.

Fadan looked down and realized his mistake. Before heading for the sewers, he had sneaked into his bedroom to change his clothes. He had chosen something warm, dark, and simple. The idea was to blend into the crowd, of course. He had also grabbed a pouch of silver coins with which to buy the runium, and lastly, a dagger, just in case something went wrong. But he had forgotten to change his boots. They were dark, sure, but they were also made of the finest leather, with silver straps and rivets. Not even the muddied water that had spilled over them made them shine any less. No commoner would ever wear something like that.

"Thank you," Fadan replied. "I enjoy them very much myself."

"I think I would enjoy them too," the sailor sneered.

Fadan felt his heart speed up a little but stayed quiet, hoping the man would just give up and ignore him.

"You didn't hear me?" the sailor asked.

"Oh, leave him alone," one of the serving girls said, walking up next to Fadan. "What will it be, dear?"

"Uh…" Fadan mumbled, "a beer, please."

"Please?" the woman said, surprised. "You hear that?" She wasn't talking to Fadan anymore. "Boy has manners. *And* he's pretty like a button." She turned around and left, her wide hips bouncing. "I gotta find myself one o' these."

"Yeah," a white-bearded sailor said. "But you'd still need to find yourself a man!"

Half of the tavern burst out laughing and Fadan felt his cheeks warm. At least the sailor with the thick knuckles wasn't staring at him anymore.

The tavern woman returned a moment later with a wooden mug brimming with frothy beer. Fadan thanked her and took a sip. It was by far the worst thing he had ever tasted, and that included Aric's dares to try weird flowers from the Empress's Orchard. Fadan was forced to summon all his strength in order not to grimace.

"Will that be all?" the woman asked. "Maybe something to eat? We have the best pork stew in the Docks. Ask anyone."

Fadan was indeed hungry. He had skipped far too many meals that day. However, after tasting that beer, he wouldn't dare to eat anything prepared in that place.

"I'm not really hungry," Fadan said. "Thank you."

"All right then," the woman said. "That'll be a silver crown."

Fadan hesitated.

A silver crown? he thought.

There was no way he had any coin that small. He mumbled something incoherent as he rummaged through his pouch, trying not to draw too much attention to it. He finally found a smallish, twenty-silver-crown coin.

"Um…listen," he said, leaning closer to her. "I need some…information." He showed her the coin, making sure no one else saw it.

The woman frowned. "Information?" she asked, far too loud for Fadan's liking.

"Yeah," Fadan whispered. "I need to buy something."

The woman took a step back. "All we sell here is food and drink," she said flatly. "We have plenty of it, and you can obviously afford it. So, what'll it be?"

Fadan sighed. "Right," he said, leaning back away from her. "I'll...have some of that stew, I guess."

The woman swung around and left without another word.

Stupid! Fadan admonished himself.

Then, a body landed with a thump in the chair across from his. It was the thick-knuckled sailor who had talked to him before.

"Hello again," the man said, taking a sip from his beer. "Couldn't help but overhear."

For some reason, the man now had a rather pleasant smile about him.

"Oh, I bet you could if you wanted to," Fadan told him.

"What?" the sailor asked, confused. "Never mind. I know what you're look-ing for. You're looking for a drink. But not the kind they sell here, am I right?"

Fadan looked into the man's beady blue eyes. They made an eerie con-trast with his leathery skin. He was obviously offering to help, but Fadan wasn't sure he would like to be helped by someone like him. Problem was, what other kind of character would be involved in something as illegal and dangerous as the runium trade?

"Maybe," Fadan said. "Why? Are you in the...'drinks' business?"

The man smiled with all his yellow teeth. "I knew it," he said. "I always recognize your kind. Anyway, I am a...let's say 'middleman' in the drinks business. I don't actually *sell* drinks, but I know who does."

"Ah, I see," Fadan said. "And you'd be willing to introduce me?"

"Not possible," the sailor said. "You see, drink sellers, they're cautious people."

"What is it *you* do, then?"

"Well, you pay me the price of the goods," the man explained, "plus a small fee for my troubles. Then I go and fetch the merchandise and hand it to you."

Fadan chuckled. "You think I'm stupid?" he asked. "You'll just run off with my money."

The man put on a frown. "No, *you* must think I'm stupid. You people can never have enough of that thing. I know sailors that can go longer without rum than your kind without…" He never finished his sentence. "Why would I waste a profitable, steady business from a fine patron as yourself?" He leaned back and motioned toward Fadan's feet. "I mean, look at those boots."

That certainly made sense. The man did not look the least bit trustworthy, but he was clearly not an idiot, either. Finding himself a frequent runium buyer would be far more profitable than traveling the Saffyan route, and Fadan could certainly make it worth his while.

"All right," Fadan said after a while. "We'll make an experiment of it, see how it goes. If I'm happy with the transaction, I'll be back for more, and I'll even increase your fee."

The man opened his arms in celebration with a smile. "Excellent!"

"You'll find I can be a very generous patron," Fadan told him. "*If* you keep your end of the deal."

"Believe me, I'm very much looking forward to that generosity. Now, head outside, turn left, and then take the second turn on your right. You'll find this alley. It's discreet and quiet. We don't want anyone nosing around in our transaction. I'll meet you there in a moment."

Fadan nodded in understanding. "And then what? I give you the money and wait for you there?"

"Not for me, no," the sailor said. "A third person will come by and hand you the goods. It might seem convoluted to you, but trust me, this is the safest way to conduct this type of business."

"Let me guess," Fadan said. "That third person will charge me a fee as well?"

The sailor shrugged. "That third person will be risking his neck as much as me," he said. "He deserves pay."

"I won't argue with that," Fadan said. "As I mentioned before, I'm prepared to be generous." He stood up. "Very well, then. I guess I'll see you in a bit."

The sailor raised his beer mug as if in a toast, and Fadan left, tossing the twenty crowns onto the table.

Fadan felt a chill as he closed the tavern door behind him. A dog barked somewhere, but otherwise, the street was quiet. He followed the sailor's instructions, realizing he hadn't even asked the man's name. But, then again, the less they knew about each other, the better.

The alleyway was a muddied path squished between two abandoned houses. It smelled as bad as the sewers and was almost as dark.

Fadan waited, pacing around a dark puddle until he finally heard sloshing steps. The sailor walked into the alley and smiled, only he wasn't alone. Three men followed him, with clubs across their shoulders. Fadan took a step back.

"I thought you'd be coming alone," the prince said.

"Oh, me and these guys are inseparable," the sailor replied. "We always do our business together."

The four men surrounded Fadan with hawkish stares.

"I thought we had a deal," Fadan argued. "A long-term deal."

"Well," the sailor replied, "I understand your disappointment, but you should look at this as a learning experience. I'm actually helping you. In the *long term.*"

Fadan drew his knife. "Back off," he warned.

"Oh, cub's got fangs!" the sailor jeered.

All four men chuckled.

"Listen, kid," the sailor continued. "We don't want to hurt you. All we want is that fat pouch of yours. Just toss it my way, and we'll leave you be. As I said, it's a valuable lesson for you."

"Never to trust people like you?" Fadan asked, turning to keep all his attackers in sight.

"No," the sailor replied. "I mean, yes, if you're carrying enough money to buy a brand-new ship."

Again, the sailors laughed.

Fadan was going to reply, but one of the men swung his club at him.

Fadan parried the blow, but it left his back exposed and another of the attackers struck him on the back of the head. The world blurred and his ears started ringing. He staggered, swinging his knife blindly to keep the attackers at bay.

Never let yourself get surrounded, his instructor's words echoed in his mind. *When outnumbered, funnel your opponents.*

Roaring, Fadan charged the sailor between him and the back of the alley. The man swung his club but in a predictable angle, and Fadan ducked past him. He ran toward the wooden wall at the end of the alley, boxing himself between two piles of empty crates.

The four sailors closed in on him, eyes narrowed. Two of them hopped onto each of the piles beside Fadan as the others moved head on.

"All right," Fadan said. "I'll give you the money." He searched his pockets, hands shaking.

Then, out of nowhere, a club smashed against his chest, followed by another blow on his knees, and another right across his head. Fadan collapsed, the alleyway spinning over him. He heard muffled voices but couldn't understand a word. Hands tugged at his jacket, his trousers, and his boots.

Then, he heard yells as shadows moved around him until there was nothing but silence.

"Are you all right?" someone asked. It wasn't a voice Fadan recognized. "Hey, kid, can you hear me? Goddess damn it!"

The spinning alleyway became darker and darker, and the stranger's voice became farther and farther away until Fadan passed out.

CHAPTER 10

Tracker-Seeker

There had always been plenty of people who didn't like Aric. The emperor was obviously probably at the top of that list, closely followed by Sagun, the Citadel's castellan. Then there was that cook that always pushed Aric out of the kitchens before he could finish swallowing his dinner, not to mention just about every Legionary he had ever come across. He had become so accustomed to being surrounded by people who didn't like him, it was almost weird not having to hide from any.

In Lamash, he was just another recruit. Most senior Hunters loved to annoy recruits, cutting ahead of them at the food line in the dining hall, or making too much noise on the rare occasions Saruk allowed a nap. It was certainly irritating, but everyone could tell it was done in a spirit of camaraderie. It was the Guildsmen's way of welcoming them into the family.

Ashur, however, was a different matter altogether. He and Aric weren't exactly enemies – the exercises demanded that they rely on each other far too often – but that didn't mean they had to get along. In fact, Ashur had found the perfect attitude toward Aric – rivalry. For Aric, it was a baffling experience. Most of the time, it felt preferable to being constantly harassed by Sagun, but it was also much more intense. Especially considering that they spent every moment of every day together. From the sparring lessons where Aric had learned to disarm Ashur in a few quick parries, to the races across the desert where Ashur would push Aric down the tallest dunes. Even in the mornings, when the company woke up, Ashur always made sure to leave the dorm ahead of Aric, closing the door in Aric's face just to slow him down a little. It was almost as intense as Saruk's training itself.

"Come on, hurry up!"

There was only one thing that didn't change in Saruk's daily training—the morning sprint across the desert. The instructor was perched atop a small crag with Lamash standing starkly in the background.

As the last members of the company climbed the final feet of the small crag, Aric looked over his shoulder and counted the recruits lagging behind him. Every one of them felt like a small victory. Only Nahir, Leth, Clea, and Tharius were now faster than him, which was really impressive, considering he had always finished dead last up until only a couple of weeks before.

Shoving aside everyone in his path, Ashur pushed up to the front as if that could change the fact that he was now among the slowest half of the company. Aric was forced to hide a proud smile.

"Does anyone here know how to find a dragon?" Saruk asked as the gasping recruits lined themselves to face him. "Except Tharius."

Tharius lowered his arm with a disappointed look.

"I'm serious," Saruk continued. "One day you'll learn how to kill a dragon, but you have to *find* one first, and the Mahar is a huge place."

"I always thought dragons found us," Clea said. "Aren't they supposed to hear and smell us?"

"That's exactly right." Saruk jumped down from his rocky pedestal and landed beside a large leather case, a bow, and a quiver full of arrows. "But that is also a problem for you. Anyone knows why? Lower your arm, Tharius."

Tharius obeyed with a sigh.

"Because if we try to fight them out in the open, we don't stand a chance?" Aric ventured, his arm half-raised.

"Exactly!" Saruk clapped. "So, if we can't fight them out in the open, where do we fight them?" He picked up the bow and an arrow. "Go ahead, Tharius."

A smile swelled across Tharius's face. "We ambush them in their own lairs."

"That we do," Saruk said, nocking the arrow into the bow. "That we do." He stretched the bow, released the string, and the arrow flew away, disappearing as it dove into the dunes. "Now, Tharius, if you answer the next question right, I'll run down to the dunes and I won't return until I find that arrow."

Everyone in the company exchanged a hopeful glance. Saruk had spent the last month torturing them around the desert. A role reversal would sure be a welcome change.

"All right," Tharius said, raising his chest.

The others cheered him on.

"Come on, volunteer," Dothea told him.

"Yeah," Clea said. "Forget Aric. If you get this right, I'm voting for you to be our captain."

Tharius blushed.

"Let me make this more interesting," Saruk said, nocking another arrow. "If Tharius gets it wrong, the lot of you will have to find these arrows for me."

He released the bowstring and another arrow disappeared somewhere down into the sand.

"It's a trap," Leth said. "Don't do it, Tharius."

"Who said he had a choice?" Saruk asked, firing another arrow. "Here's the question. How in Ava's mercy do we *find* a dragon's lair?"

Tharius's mouth opened, and then closed again. Around him, hopeful smiles turned into sour frowns.

"Well, we…" Tharius mumbled, shifting his weight. "There's the…the rotation and…uh…" His eyes darted around and sweat broke out on his forehead. You could almost see his mind desperately at work. "Well, there are regular patrols, and the patrols, they…"

"Yes?" Saruk asked, letting loose a fourth arrow.

"Well…" Tharius followed the missile with a miserable stare. "I don't know."

Saruk chuckled.

Poor Tharius deflated like an empty wine bag as the rest of the company showered him with curses.

"All right, all right," Saruk said. "Get those murderous looks off your faces; I won't make you find the arrows."

There was a collective sigh of relief.

"No sir. I have a much better idea. I'll make you find some dragons."

The whistling wind brought grains of sand hurtling toward the recruits' mouths and eyes. Squinting, Aric pulled his scarf up to cover his mouth.

"What you are holding in your hands is a tracker-seeker," Saruk said over the wind. "They are the Guild's most precious pieces of property. The only glowstone devices we own whose charms still work." His desert robes flapped as he held out an opened leather case just like the ones each recruit was holding. "Let me rephrase this just to make sure you understand. The Grand-Master would rather lose any one of you than any one of those cases. Understood?"

"Yes, Instructor!" came the unison reply.

"Inside," Saruk continued, "you will find two objects — a glowstone pendant and a glowstone-tipped arrow. Your job is simple. Fire one arrow at a dragon, and return its corresponding pendant to Lamash. A company of senior Hunters will then follow the pendant back to said dragon. Any questions?"

"Yeah," Ashur said, raising an arm. "What does the arrow do? Poison the dragon?"

"Don't be ridiculous," Saruk replied. "Dragons can't be poisoned."

"How exactly will the senior Hunters follow the pendant to the dragon?" Jullion asked with a confused look on his face.

"It's a spell, you idiot," Trissa told him. "Didn't you hear the instructor?"

"Easy, Trissa," Saruk said. He pulled the Seeker pendant from his own case and moved it around. "As you can see, the glowstone shard on the seeker always points to its corresponding tracker arrow. So, if you fire the tracker into a dragon, the seeker will lead us back to it."

"That sounds a bit dangerous..." Irenya said, her hands shifting around as if she didn't know what to do with them. "I mean...how close do we have to get?"

"Dangerous?!" Saruk asked. "Of course it's dangerous. This is the Dragon Hunters Guild. What did you expect you would be doing, gardening?"

"Yes but," Orisius came to her defense, "we have no experience with dragons, Instructor."

"If, or rather *when* you find a dragon, you won't need any experience," Saruk told him. "You'll need to hide. In a cave, under a rock, wherever. Dig yourselves under the sand if you have to. Put your head out long enough to tag the dragon with your seeker arrow, then hide yourselves once again. Now, if there are no further questions I would like to address another issue."

He locked the gilded leather case and placed it on his belt.

"I told you recruits to think about who you wanted to be leading you. Your time to think is over." He paused, scanning his recruits as they exchanged nervous glances. "From here on out, you will train in teams, and teams will compete with each other. How will we choose the teams? Easy. Anyone who thinks he or she can make a good captain for this Company can step forward and will immediately become a team leader. Everyone else is free to choose the team they want to be a part of."

There was a small moment of silence until Ashur gave a step forward. "I can do it, Instructor."

Somewhere along the line of recruits, Trissa snorted. Everyone else remained quiet.

"Is that it?" Saruk asked. "No one else up for the job? If we have only one candidate, then the decision is made. Ashur will become company captain effective immediately."

Aric saw a smirk twisting Ashur's mouth. There was no way he would let Ashur be their captain.

"Go on," Leth whispered in Aric's ear. "We can't be stuck with Ashur."

"He's right," Clea agreed, tugging at Aric's tunic.

"Why don't you step forward?" Aric asked Leth.

"Are you kidding?" Leth replied. "I don't like anyone in this company. I'd make a horrible captain."

Aric turned to Clea. "You do it, then," he whispered.

She shook her head very quickly, glaring back at him. "No way!"

"Come on," Leth insisted. "You're an Auron."

"So what?" Aric asked.

"Isn't everyone in your family supposed to be a hero or something?" Leth said. "Think of your…your legacy or whatever. I don't care, just step forward."

Aric exhaled loudly. He pulled his scarf down and stepped forward. "I'll do it."

"Good," Saruk said. "We have ourselves a competition after all." He rubbed his hands together. "So, one of you two is going to be the captain of this –"

"No!" Tharius stepped forward. He looked angry. "They're not even volunteers."

"So what?" Saruk asked. "There's no rule against a conscript making captain. Are you stepping up to the plate as well, recruit?"

Tharius looked left and right, first at Aric, then at Ashur, as if he was measuring them. "I am," he said after a while. "I've been preparing for this my whole life."

"And so have I," the powerful voice of Nahir thundered as he stepped forward.

"Well, fire take me," Saruk said, "this is going to be more interesting than I thought."

"It will if you like boys-only taverns," Trissa said. A couple of the other girls giggled. "We need a girl to lead this company. There's a reason the Grand-Master is a woman, you know?"

Ashur snorted.

"You got a problem?" Trissa asked him.

"Nothing I can't handle," Ashur said without even looking at her.

"Trissa," Saruk said. "I could not agree with you more. Why don't you step forward?"

Irenya and Dothea agreed, spurring her forward.

"All right," Trissa said, hands on her hips. "I'm in." She stepped forward.

"Excellent! Anyone else?" Saruk asked. He waited a moment, and when no one else said anything, he continued. "All right, now the rest of you have to choose. Get behind the candidate you wish to follow."

Aric felt his stomach twist a little bit. He still wasn't sure if he wanted to be the captain, but he certainly didn't want to have no one choosing him.

That would be humiliating. Especially considering Ashur could count on Jullion and Prion. Those two would never choose anyone else.

Behind Aric, people shifted and moved. Some went straight to their candidates of choice, like Jullion and Prion, while others remained in their spot, scratching their heads.

A sigh of relief left Aric's chest when Clea walked behind him.

"What are you doing?" Clea asked Leth.

The Akhami boy hadn't moved yet and was looking from Tharius to Nahir. "What? I have a right to choose, don't I?"

"You're the one who told Aric to step forward!" Clea said through her gritted teeth.

"Because I didn't know there were other choices."

"Leth!" Clea warned, fists clenched.

"All right, all right."

"I don't want you to support me against your will," Aric said.

"Nah," Leth dismissed him with a wave of his hand. "You're fine, I suppose."

Aric looked at the others. To his great satisfaction, no one had chosen Ashur beside Jullion and Prion. Trissa hadn't done too badly either. Both Irenya and Dothea were standing behind her. Everyone else had chosen Nahir, which meant poor Tharius was left alone.

Ouch, Aric thought.

"Tharius," Ashur sneered, "the one-man company."

Jullion and Prion chuckled.

Calmly, Saruk neared Tharius and spoke in a low voice. "You may forfeit your candidacy if you like, recruit."

"I would rather not, Instructor."

"Are you sure? This is no easy mission. Certainly not for a single person."

"I'll be all right, Instructor."

Saruk nodded. "Good for you, recruit." With a twist of his heel, Saruk turned to rest of the company and raised his voice. "The rules are simple. First team back to the fortress wins. Last team loses."

Aric raised his hand. "What exactly do we lose, Instructor?"

"The chance to become captain," Saruk replied. "The leader of the losing team has to drop out of the race."

That wasn't so bad. Aric wasn't even sure he really wanted to be the captain.

"And what do we win, exactly?" Trissa asked.

Saruk smirked. "The support of the losing team, of course."

⌣⟶

No matter how many twisting dune tops they crossed, the mountains stretching across the horizon simply refused to get any bigger.

"That Saruk is a tyrant," Leth said. "And a sadist. He's a tyrant-sadist with an insatiable thirst for our misery."

Ahead of him, Aric looked through his binoculars. "There's no point in complaining. We just have to finish the mission as quickly as possible."

"What if Ashur wins?" Leth insisted. "We can't control how fast a dragon will smell his stinking armpits."

"Then all we can do is make sure we don't finish last," Clea told him as she scanned the horizon.

"We can't control that, either," Leth replied. "This is pointless." He fell to his knees and Aric sat beside him.

The torrid sun had turned their dirt-stiff clothes into cooking pans, draining their bodies with every step. With a leathery throat, Aric opened his canteen, only to close it right away. They would have to make their water supply last.

"We should keep going," Aric said. "I'm sure it was a dragon."

"How can you be sure?" Clea asked, dropping her backpack in the sand and sitting down beside the two boys."

Aric looked through his binoculars again and searched the horizon. "It was a dragon. Had to be. Besides, those mountains are probably dragon territory. They're tall and wide."

"We don't need to find a dragon's lair," Clea said. "Just the dragon, remember?"

"What we need is to get out of the sand," Leth said. "Sand is death. For all we know, there's a desert lion following our tracks." He stood back up and circled, searching their surroundings. "We should find a rock forma-tion. Rocks might mean a cave, a cave might mean water."

"Over there!" Aric said, his eyes glued to the binoculars. "Rocks."

Leth borrowed the goggles and looked through them. There was a set of outcroppings, brown boulders, each taller than a large house, huddled together amid the dunes.

"Great!" Leth celebrated. "We should head there."

"Yeah, you should," Aric said. He took off his backpack and handed it to Leth. "Here, hold this for me. I'll travel faster without it."

"What do you think you're doing?" Clea asked.

"I'm going to keep walking south for two more hours, try to get a glimpse of that dragon," Aric replied. "The two of you find shelter and rest. That way, we'll conserve water." Aric fastened his tracker-seeker onto his belt and the bow across his back.

"Wait," Clea said. "Here, switch with me; mine is fuller." She handed Aric her canteen, then stuck a hand into her backpack. She fiddled inside for a moment and picked up a small pouch. "Take the biscuits, too. You don't want to get too weak to get back."

"I'm not going to get weak," Aric said, accepting the biscuits. "Anyway, I should be back shortly after sundown. Try to get some rest."

"Best idea ever." Leth adjusted Aric's backpack over his shoulder, next to his own, with a huge smile. "See. I knew you'd make a great captain."

"Shut up," Clea told him. She turned to Aric. "We'll have some dinner waiting for you. *Be careful.*"

⌣⟶

The wind had picked up and flying sand was polishing Aric's cheeks, the only part of his face left exposed. He used his hand to cover his eyes and looked up at the mountain range to the south.

The peaks had finally started to look bigger. Or, at least, so it seemed. The dragon, however, was still nowhere to be found. Aric had first noticed its shape shortly after midday, and despite Leth's insistence that it was just a hawk, Aric had followed it south for most of the afternoon, until the waving silhouette had become a tiny speck in the immense, blue glass sky and finally disappeared.

Had it really been a dragon? What if Leth had been right all along?

A stronger gust of wind sent grains of sand into his eyes and he wiped them away with vigorous rubs. As he turned around, eyes watering, the mountains in the south seemed to shift.

"What the…"

Aric wiped his eyes again, making sure there were no grains of sand or tears left to impair his vision, then focused on the distant brown peaks.

That's no mountain! Those are clouds. Low-hanging clouds.

*H*e took two steps forward as if it could somehow help him see any better.

Yup, those were not mountains. They were dancing and shifting at the top, dissolving into the blue sky.

They're really dark, too. Could it be rain?

If it was, Aric was about to witness a moment of a lifetime. According to Saruk, it only rained every fifty to sixty years in the Mahar. There were records of entire centuries without a single drop of rain in the desert.

"Well, I guess my water problem is solved," he muttered to himself.

The problem was, so was every other desert creature's. According to the Guild's records, there would be a flash flood. Nothing dangerous, but it would bring out every living creature in the desert. Predators would have a field day, especially dragons.

I should get back.

Turning his back on the looming darkness, Aric felt the wind push him forward. At least, from this direction, there was no need to cover his eyes from the sand. His robes flapped wildly and he saw huge pockets of sand billowing ahead of him. Were desert rains supposed to be like storms?

Storms?!

"Oh, crap!"

The realization made his heart sink through his stomach. Those weren't rain clouds. That was a sandstorm.

He quickly remembered Saruk's survival instructions. "Soak your mouth cover," he repeated to himself.

Obeying his own instructions, he scrambled for his canteen. The rush made him spill far more water than he would have liked.

"Find cover," he continued. He needed a hole or a cave to protect himself, or at the very least a boulder he could hide behind; otherwise, he could end up buried beneath the relentless sand. And he had to find it quick, before he was caught by the storm and lost his sight.

Using the binoculars, Aric searched in every direction but found nothing except for dunes and more dunes.

I could try to run back to where I left Clea and Leth...

No, that was a terrible idea. No one could ever outrun a sandstorm. Instead, he ran along the sand crests and climbed the tallest dune around him. He scanned the distance with his binoculars again. The sand hurtling toward him was becoming almost painful. If it wasn't for the scarf around his mouth and nose, he would have swallowed a bucket of sand by now.

He looked, and looked, and looked until... There! He saw something! A small mesa, crowned by a curving rock that looked like an archway. There seemed to be an opening of some sort on its side.

"Thank the goddess!"

The only problem was, the mesa was in the same direction as that of the looming sand wall, so either Aric would get there first, or the storm would. There was no time to lose.

Aric dashed away, his feet burying in the sand as he raced up and down the dunes. He didn't even give himself enough time to figure a way atop the crests, but as if running through the sand wasn't tiring enough, some dunes were so steep that Aric was out of breath by the second one.

Can't stop. Can't stop.

Lungs burning, legs shaking, Aric pushed forward. The massive wall of sand kept rolling like a colossal brown wave, swallowing everything in its path. He leapt onto the solid surface of the rock as the deafening sound of rattling sand engulfed him. If he wasn't inside the storm yet, he sure would be very soon.

The small cave opening stood several feet above the ground. Aric grabbed onto the rock and heaved himself up to an outcropping. It would have been as easy as climbing a flight of stairs if it wasn't for the gusts of wind tossing him around, not to mention the rock outcroppings stopped about five feet away from the cave opening.

He didn't even think about it; he just jumped sideways and grabbed onto the ledge, heaving himself up into the cave, and just in time, too. The moment he found himself up there, a thundering roar flooded the cave, and a thick cloud of brown dust covered the world.

"Sweet Mother Ava." Aric said.

Panting heavily, he removed his scarf. The furious wind played tricks with the cave's entrance, howling and...barking?

Aric figured he had to be imagining things until he heard it again. It was a strange, high-pitched bark. Wind wouldn't sound like that, no matter how much it swirled inside a cavern.

He stepped closer to the opening, his hands not leaving the ragged stone wall. A turmoil of flying sand made Aric cover his eyes again as he peeked outside. At first, the sight made him jump backward. Then, when he peeked again, he saw a large cat trying to jump up to the cave. He was panicking, barking and whining as his paws scratched the wall uselessly. The cave was just too high for him.

Well, that's a first.

Aric had never seen a barking cat. And certainly not one that was this big.

He lay on the floor, belly down, and grabbed onto the cat's neck, timing his move to coincide with one of the animal's nervous jumps. The cat really was huge and heavy. Aric heaved with all his strength. It must have scared the poor thing even further because he scratched Aric's arms furiously until its paws finally found the ledge and the necessary purchase to jump inside.

Aric rolled away, getting out of the blinding swirl from the storm, and found himself staring at a set of really long, sharp teeth.

"Whoa, there!" Slowly, Aric stood back up.

The cat hissed. It wasn't really a cat. More like a lynx, with very large, pointy ears and wide hazelnut eyes.

"I didn't just save you so you could eat me, all right?"

The cat didn't like that Aric was getting taller. It hissed and pawed the air.

"Okay, I get it. You don't like me," Aric said. He looked outside where the sandstorm was raging on. "But I'm afraid you're out of luck, because we're both stuck in here for a while."

Making sure he kept his distance from the cat, Aric walked farther into the cave. The cracked walls grew darker and darker until everything disappeared into shadows after a few feet. Twigs and small animal prints covered the dirt floor around the charred remains of a campfire. They were obviously not the first visitors to this place.

Aric sat down, massaging his legs. An overwhelming feeling of exhaustion was taking over his body. A grumble echoed through the cave and Aric placed a hand on his stomach. The race against the storm had clearly spent everything he had.

Careful not to spill any more drops again, Aric drank a couple of sips of water, shaking the canteen to check how much he had left. It wasn't much. A third, maybe, though probably less.

Beside him, the cat had finally decided to relax and was licking his forelegs. Aric removed the biscuits from his belt pouch as he watched the feline lying down. The instant Aric took the first bite, the cat's head snapped toward him.

Aric chuckled. "You're hungry as well, huh?" He finished his biscuit and drew another one from the pouch. "Here." The cat didn't move right away but slowly extended its head, sniffing the air separating him from the biscuit. "What? Are you afraid of me?" Aric threw the cookie and it landed right between the animal's paws. The cat smelled the brown cookie, licked it, then tried a shy nibble. He must have liked it, because the following moment, the biscuit disappeared through his needle-sharp teeth.

Aric ate another biscuit and pushed it down with a sip of water. Goddess, he was hungry and thirsty, but he knew he should conserve what little food and drink he had, so he put the canteen and biscuit pouch away and leaned back. The cat mimicked him, resting his head on his paws, his tongue slapping the top of his already-wet nose.

"Are you as tired as me, boy?" Aric asked in a low voice. "Or are you a girl?" His eyelids were getting heavy as he hugged himself.

The cave was warm, almost damp. Outside, the sandstorm whistled and howled hypnotically. The sound became farther and farther away, and Aric's eyes became heavier and heavier until they shut and his head drooped to his chest.

⌒

A sharp pain on the back of his neck made Aric cringe as he woke. He straightened his head back and his stomach grumbled. Everything felt wrong, from the coarseness of his throat to the boiling sensation in his feet.

He looked up, and his heart almost jumped out of his chest when he saw the shape of the huge feline standing next to him. The animal had his head down and was chewing at something on Aric's hip.

"No!" Aric yelled pushing the cat away, but it was too late. "You thief! You miserable thief!" Aric held up the empty pouch, and a couple of cookie crumbles fell to the ground.

Fuming, Aric threw the pouch at the cat's face, but the feline merely licked the corners of his mouth.

"I saved your life, you —" Aric gave up on the sentence, cursing as he stormed toward the cave's exit.

The storm was long gone, and the endless sea of dunes was back to its torrid calm. He didn't have anything left to eat, but at least the way was clear for him to get back.

I wonder if Leth and Clea are still waiting for me, he thought.

But even if they were, how was he supposed to find them? Aric had some idea of the direction from which he had come, but without the compass on his backpack, there was no way to tell north from south, let alone navigate across the desert for a few miles.

Still, there was no point in staying in the cave. He jumped, landing on soft, warm sand. The next moment, the cat landed right beside him, but Aric turned away from him. The huge stone wall gave him an idea– maybe if he climbed up to the mesa, he would be able to see some distant point of reference.

For the first time since arriving at Lamash, Aric felt grateful for the merciless training Saruk had been putting them through. A month before, he would have never been able to climb such a wall. He looked down and saw his cave companion jumping over outcroppings and racing up impossibly steep portions of the wall. Apparently, without the storm to confuse him, the cat was an amazing climber.

"Are you following me?" Aric asked as he found a small ledge to place his right foot. "You already ate all my food, you know?" Using a couple of holes, Aric heaved himself up to the top of the mount, sweat dripping down his forehead. "Unless, of course, your plan is to eat me."

The top of the small crag was completely flat except for the stone arch. Aric walked under the arch and sat beneath its shadow. He wanted to conserve what little water he still had, but the climb had taken too much of a toll, so he took a small sip.

What now?

At that moment, he really wished for his backpack and the binoculars within. Instead, he covered his eyes with the palm of his hand and scanned the horizon. Sand and more sand surrounded the small island he sat on.

Sighing, he tied the canteen to his belt without taking his eyes from the horizon. There had to be something, somewhere, that could help him find his way back.

A tickling sensation on his hand made him look down, and the sight paralyzed him. A huge black scorpion had climbed onto his arm. Fearing that a sudden move might provoke a sting, Aric held his breath. Slowly, he turned his head, looking for a rock to hit it with. There was a decent-sized one to his left, but when Aric reached for it, the rock stayed a couple of inches away from his fingers. He tried to stretch his arm, but when he did, the scorpion tensed and its tail arched forward.

Oh, goddess.

He stretched his fingers again, making sure to keep the rest of his body still, but the rock was just too far away. Then, out of nowhere, the wheat-colored cat pawed the scorpion away. A gigantic weight disappeared from Aric's chest as he saw the cat pursuing the furious scorpion.

"No, leave it alone!" Aric screamed. "It's gonna sting you!"

The cat ignored his pleas and kept harassing the scorpion with lightning strikes, until suddenly, he struck with his fangs and ripped it apart.

Aric was speechless. He neared the cat, sure that he had been stung either on his paws or snout.

"Are you okay?" he asked, placing a soft hand on the cat's back.

The feline replied with a stare while chewing on the last pieces of the scorpion.

"Of course you are. You have your belly full." Aric smiled. "Unlike mine." He drew out his canteen. "I suppose I owe you, don't I? Here, wash it down with this."

The cat licked every last drop of water from Aric's hand, then froze. His back arched and his tail tensed.

"What?!" Aric asked. "What did I do?"

Was it another scorpion?

The cat hissed, stepping backward, and Aric realized that the hiss wasn't meant for him but for something *behind* him. Dreading what it could be, he looked over his shoulder and his stomach melted.

A black shadow slashed across the sky, roaring.

Aric lost no time at all. Grabbing the cat by the neck, he dashed toward the narrow slit between two rocks and only let the cat go when both were safe between them. The cat shrank against the wall and his ears flattened. Only then did Aric realize his arm was bleeding.

"Must you always make me regret helping you?" Aric asked.

He moved to the edge of the rock, but another roar made him freeze just before he peeked.

"Fire take this!"

Gritting his teeth, he took a deep breath and sneaked a peek.

Nothing.

Where was it? Had it flown away?

Another massive roar made both him and the cat jump almost a foot into the air. No, the dragon was still near. Backtracking, Aric made his way to the other edge of the rock, where the mesa ended in a sort of cliff facing the sand.

This time, a mix between a yelp, a scream, and a cry for help got stuck in his throat. There was a woman in the sand, her white robes flowing around her as she gracefully walked the dune crests. She had an arm stretched toward the lumbering shape of the outrageously large black dragon. The beast's wings flapped, sending several waves of sand flying into the air until the colossal beast landed.

Aric's eyes had never been so wide.

The dragon's head curved upward, and it let out a growl so rough and deep, Aric felt the ground shake. Even at that distance, and hidden as he was, Aric shuddered. The woman, however, just kept walking toward the giant beast, its head, neck, and back a forest of black thorns. The woman gracefully walked toward the dragon and the creature lowered its head toward her, each of its fangs nearly as tall as she.

What is she doing?

Slowly, carefully, the woman's arm reached forward, inching closer to the dragon's nose until they touched, and when they did, the beast roared so powerfully, it sent the sand beneath her feet flying away.

The woman did not even flinch.

Eliran...

It was almost as if she had heard Aric. The woman turned around, stepped away with her arms open, and – *whoosh!* She was no longer there.

The dragon, however, was still very much in the middle of the sand. Aric slid back behind cover, and from the desert came the flapping sound of the dragon taking off. Pressing his arms against the side of his body, Aric made himself small. If he had remained undetected so far, maybe there was a chance he could survive this. That was when he realized his hand was squeezing the leather case of the tracker-seeker on his belt.

The mission!

He had a mission to complete. Every nerve in his body told him to stand still and quiet, to not even breathe. But the mission...

He drew the bow from his back, opened the case, and picked up the seeker arrow. The tracker pendant immediately came alive, aiming at the arrow. Aric exhaled loudly and looked at the cat still squatting down beside him.

"Don't move," he whispered.

With a spin, Aric left the safety of his hideout, found the enormous shape of the dragon circling up toward the sky, and dropped to one knee. He nocked the seeker and aimed it high, taking a deep breath in order to stabilize his arm and take aim.

Twang!

The arrow flew away and Aric was behind cover long before it hit its target. If the dragon felt anything, there was no sound to prove it. The only evidence Aric had that he had hit his target was the dancing glowstone pendant on his neck.

There was nothing quite like the sunset on the Mahar when the amber sky nearly fused with the orange sea of dunes. It was the third one Aric had witnessed since his encounter with the dragon and the witch, but this time, it was accompanied by the black outline of Lamash. The sight nearly made him weep. He hadn't drunk a drop of water for two days now, and the only reason he hadn't starved for the same amount of time was his feline companion. The large cat had decided to follow him, and the previous night had even shared a tiny mouse, which Aric had promptly roasted on a crackling fire.

"We're home!" Aric let out, hugging the cat, who replied with a purr.

A sentinel sent for Saruk when Aric reached the main gate, and the instructor arrived with the whole company in tow.

"You're alive!" Clea said, wrapping her arms around Aric.

There were other displays of happiness, joy, and relief, but hers was the only one Aric heard. He had some trouble wiping the silly smile off his face after that.

Everyone else was there, which meant that he was the last one back.

"So, who's the big winner?" Aric asked beneath a weak smile.

Please don't be Ashur, please don't be Ashur.

"The one-man company himself," Saruk replied, placing a hand over Tharius's shoulders. "Our volunteer was back before the second night. Truly impressive."

Tharius turned red and Aric congratulated him. Boy, that was a relief.

"I guess you're my new team captain, then," Aric told him.

"I guess so," Tharius replied, smiling.

"Well, I'm happy that it's you." Aric took the Seeker pendant from his neck. "Here, Instructor. I might have been the last, but I did complete the mission."

"You tagged a dragon?" Leth asked him.

"So did we!" Clea said.

"That means we scored two dragons!" Leth said. "We can't lose if we scored two dragons."

"Aric has to be disqualified," Ashur interrupted. "He abandoned his team."

"I didn't abandon my team!" Aric replied. "I got lost in a sandstorm."

Ashur burst out laughing.

"What sandstorm?" Clea asked.

Aric was dumbfounded. "What do you mean, *what sandstorm?* I was only a couple of hours away from where I left you guys when it hit me. There's no way it didn't hit you as well."

"He must have confused it with the morning breeze," Ashur said, and this time, Jullion and Prion joined him in his laughter. "I'm sure that happens a lot."

"So the desert sun cooked his brain; who cares?" Leth said. "The truth is, he faced a dragon on his own."

"Leth is right," Saruk said. "That does count for something."

"What?!" Ashur demanded. "What about the rules? The last one back loses."

"The rules said that, yes," Saruk agreed, "but you also had to tag a dragon."

He turned around and looked at Nahir. The tall Cyrinian gave him a respectful nod.

"I'm sorry, Nahir. Even if your man was hurt, you could have sent him back with an escort while the others continued. Your team was certainly large enough."

"I understand, Instructor," Nahir replied. "It was a poor decision." The Cyrinian walked over to Tharius and bowed. "It'll be an honor to support your bid for captain."

"So," Aric said, "am I still in the race?"

"You are," Saruk replied. "And just like Tharius, you should be proud to have faced a dragon on your own."

"Actually," Aric said. "I didn't face the dragon on my own." He turned around and raised a finger toward a huge cat standing at the entrance to the fortress. By the look on everyone's face, no one had noticed him yet. "I made a new friend."

Too bad this was Aric's only witness. If he couldn't persuade the others about the storm, how were they going to believe the part about the creepy witch who could tame dragons?

CHAPTER 11

The Strangers

Flames crackled, waking Fadan up, but he was too sleepy to open his eyes. It was one of those mornings when he felt so tired, his body ached. He tried to roll to one side, but something stopped him, tugging at his wrists and feet. Opening his eyes just a tiny slit, Fadan looked at his hand and immediately woke fully.

There was a rope tied around both his wrists and ankles.

He looked around, dazed and confused. This wasn't his room. It wasn't even in the Palace. It was some sort of cramped single-room house with moldy, wooden walls. A man was sitting down by an open fire right next to the bed.

"Who are you?" Fadan demanded. "Untie me!"

The man stood up slowly, without a word.

"Who are you?" Fadan repeated, squirming as if he wanted to rip apart the bedposts he was tied to.

"Calm down," the man said softly.

Instead of obeying, Fadan tugged at the ropes even harder, but the man drew out a knife, freezing him. The blade shimmered with the reflection of the fire.

"I told you to calm down," the stranger said, speaking in no more than a whisper.

Fadan's eyes went wider as the knife came closer.

"No! Please, wait!"

The man placed the blade on Fadan's wrist and *snap!* The rope became loose. Exhaling loudly, Fadan looked at his unharmed and now-free hand as the stranger proceeded to cut the remaining ropes.

"You were having these spasms," the man explained, "while you were out. I just wanted to make sure you didn't hurt yourself further."

"Spasms?" Fadan asked.

"Head injuries can be messy," the man replied, sheathing his knife. "What can you remember?"

Fadan's eyes moved, looking for his latest recollections. "I was in the alley. Four sailors attacked me." He sat up and pain immediately shot through his ribs, legs, and skull, making him cringe. "Then you...saved me." He looked at the man. "Thank you."

Kind blue eyes beneath thick white eyebrows returned Fadan's stare. The stranger nodded and walked back to the fireplace. "Good," he said. "It's not as bad as I thought. You should be fine."

There was a pot boiling above the crackling flames. The man stirred it.

"You must be hungry," he continued. He picked up a wooden bowl and poured in a generous amount of whatever was in that pot.

A smell of meat and onions flooded the room, making Fadan's stomach come to life, growling.

"Um...yeah," Fadan said, accepting the bowl from the stranger's hand.

It was a thick, dark stew. Despite its smell, there wasn't any meat in it, at least not that Fadan could see. In fact, there was nothing swimming in that bowl. It looked more like porridge than it did stew, but Fadan was too famished to care. He started slow, with just a taste, but ended up devouring the whole bowl in a few rushed mouthfuls.

"It's delicious," Fadan said, gasping for air. He had been eating so fast, he had lost his breath.

"I doubt it," the man said. "But thank you."

The man quietly watched Fadan finish his food. He was sitting by the fire, his fingers poking through the tips of a tired pair of gloves, searching for the heat of the flames. His clothes reminded Fadan of Aric's patchwork quilts, except these seemed to have been used to wipe soot off a chimney.

"I'll pay for all this," Fadan said, scooping the last smudges of stew from the bowl. "I mean, not right now. My money was stolen."

"Not just your money," the man said. "They also took your jacket and your cloak. Oh, and your boots."

Fadan looked at his black woolen socks and cursed.

"Don't worry," the man said. "I have an old pair of boots you can borrow. You look to be about my size."

"Thank you," Fadan said. "I'll pay for all of this, I promise."

The man did not reply and instead just stared at Fadan intensely. It was a bit awkward.

"I…" Fadan mumbled, avoiding the man's stare. "I guess I should be going. I need to get home. My parents will worry."

"Oh, yes, of course," the stranger said as if waking up. He rushed to a worn-looking chest and removed a pair of old boots. "Here."

Fadan thanked him once again and put the boots on. They were riddled with holes and carved at his feet with the slightest movement, but it was still better than having to walk back home in his bare feet.

"I really am in your debt," Fadan said. "I *will* be back to repay you. I promise."

The man nodded quickly, mumbling something. He was either very shy or very distracted; Fadan couldn't decide. One moment he was staring awkwardly at Fadan, the next he was averting his eyes like a kid that had just been caught lying.

"All right, then…" Fadan said, not really sure how else to say goodbye to the strange man.

He headed for the door and was about to open it when the man called, "My name is Alman." It came out like a confession.

"Oh, it was a pleasure to meet you, Alman," Fadan said. "I am…" He hesitated. "My name is, uh…"

"I know who you are," Alman said.

Fadan smiled weakly. "I'm sure you have me confused with someone else," he said.

"My name is Alman Larsa." This time, it sounded like an explanation.

Larsa? That was vaguely familiar.

"My father," Alman continued, "was the Duke of Niveh."

Merciful Mother…

There was a good reason Fadan had trouble remembering House Larsa. They had been wiped out, branded as traitors during the Purge for refusing to kill Niveh's mages. They had even gone as far as closing the gates of their city to the Legions, but their rebellion had been a short-lived one.

"I… I don't…" Fadan mumbled.

"It was your mother's birthday the other day," Alman said, his eyes on the ground. He was smiling as if lost in some fond memory. "Ten years ago, I would actually have been invited." His smile vanished and he shot Fadan a serious look. "I know what you were doing at the docks."

Fadan swallowed. "I…simply got lost, that's all."

"No one finds himself with Durul's gang in an alley unless they're trying to do or buy something illegal." Alman stepped closer to Fadan. "You were looking for runium, weren't you?"

"Listen, I already told you I'll pay for your help and everything," Fadan said. "My business in the Docks is none of your concern."

"You don't understand," Alman said. "I can help you."

"You already did," Fadan replied. Then, as if putting an end to the conversation, he opened the door.

"Please, wait!" Alman begged. "Do you realize what this would mean for people like me?"

Fadan did, of course. If this man was telling the truth, he had once been rich and powerful. He should have gone on to inherit his father's duchy. Instead, he had become a fugitive, surviving in the slums.

"Were you looking for runium?" Alman asked, his eyes watery. "Please, I need to know."

Fadan sighed and closed the door. "Yes," he said after an overlong pause.

Alman covered his eyes and made a sound that was something between a giggle and a sob. Taking a deep breath, he returned his gaze to Fadan.

"I knew it," Alman said. There was wonder in his eyes. "The moment I recognized you, I knew it. I mean, if someone had told me, I would have never believed it but… Do you have any idea what this means? For people like me? For everyone who survived the Purge?"

"No one can know about this," Fadan said abruptly.

"Oh, I understand," Alman assured him. "I completely understand, Your Majesty. But that's exactly why you need my help. You can't just roam around the Docks asking for runium; it's too dangerous. But I can get you all the runium you need."

"So… You're a Mage?"

Alman shook his head. "No," he said. "I was never blessed with the Talent."

Or cursed, Fadan thought. *Although in your case, it didn't seem to make a difference.*

"But I work for a ship-owner," Alman continued. "I know exactly who to talk to about these things. I will need some silver, of course," He looked around. "runium is expensive and, as you can see, my…financial situation isn't ideal."

"Silver will not be a problem," Fadan said. "All I ask is discretion. If my father ever found out —"

"Of course," Alman said, nodding. "You have nothing to worry about." He paused, looking excited. "Oh, this is incredible! You have no idea." The man looked so happy, he seemed to be about to break into a dance. It was so contagious, it made Fadan chuckle. "Could I ask a question?"

"Sure," Fadan replied.

"How did you find out? About your Talent, I mean."

Fadan shrugged. "Not much to tell. To be honest, I never planned on finding out. The only reason I did was because my brother is as stubborn as an ox."

Alman laughed. "I see," he said. "So, who is training you? I wonder if it's someone I know."

"No one," Fadan replied. "I've just been experimenting with runium and this book I found, that's all."

"You don't have one?" Alman asked. "Your Majesty, runium is a *very* dangerous substance. You shouldn't be experimenting on your own."

"Trust me, I know," Fadan said. "But how am I going to find a mage?"

Alman smiled gleefully. "Well, you probably can't, but I can."

Fadan frowned. "You know mages?"

"Do I know mages? Your Majesty, my brother *is* one."

⌒⟶

Becoming High Marshal had always been Intila's dream, but it had quickly turned into a nightmare. A long, thoroughly documented and properly filed nightmare. Everything always felt to be on the verge of collapse unless he read, signed in triplicate, formally submitted a reply, and then wrote down a report on the matter. Producing parchment, he felt, had to be the most lucrative job in Arkhemia.

He missed the field. Leading a campaign as soon as the snows melted, chasing the enemy across the hills until the time was right to do battle, crafting a victory out of the worst possible odds. *That* was a worthy life.

Not that there was ever any shortage of conflict in the Citadel, but it was a very different kind of warfare. One of whispers and words not said. War had raged inside the gleaming hallways of the Core Palace for as long as it had stood.

This past week, however, had been far bloodier than usual. Far too bloody for Intila's taste, in fact. This level of violence, he felt, should be reserved to the battlefield.

"What is the point of an execution if the prisoners are killed beforehand?" Intila asked.

Chancellor Vigild stood beside him, flowing black robes over his tall, lean body. He shrugged. "The emperor ordered them tortured for twelve hours a day. What else did you expect?"

"I expected your people to pace themselves," Intila replied. "Look at them." He waved at the bloodied bodies in front of them. The pair dangled from the ceiling like old ragdolls. "The execution has been rescinded. They're to be kept alive."

The chancellor tilted his head, examining the hanging victims. "So, this is the famous Doric. All this mess over…*him?*"

"Will they survive the night?" Intila asked.

Vigild shrugged. "They might. My guess is the emperor won't care, so long as he can't be blamed."

"The emperor *will* care," Intila assured. "I have been told that —"

"High Marshal," Vigild interrupted. "Do not presume to know what goes on inside the emperor's head. You would also do well not to show such concern for the throne's enemies."

"What did you just say?" Intila asked.

If the chancellor was at all intimidated by Intila's tone, he did not show it. "The empress's concern for these traitors derives from emotional and personal attachment, and thus is easily understood. Yours is not."

For a moment, Intila actually considered drawing his sword and slashing Vigild's throat.

"Chancellor, I will concern myself with whatever pleases me," Intila said. "And since you are in a mood for exchanging advice, here is some for you. Do not *ever* question my loyalty again."

"Oh, please," Vigild sneered. "Spare me your displays of self-importance. They're tedious and predictable. I do not care for your honor; I care for the throne. The emperor might have made his promises to the empress, but he has not changed his mind about what is to happen to these traitors. You, just like the rest of us, are expected to understand this."

A rat's squeak echoed from some dark corner as Intila mulled over Vigild's words. That the emperor wanted Doric and the other prisoners dead was to be expected. That Vigild was so casual about it, not so much.

"This is foolish," Intila said after a while. "And it's not just about the empress. If these men die so soon, it will look like the emperor was lying. Something else for the Great Houses to resent him for. I'll have nothing to do with it." Intila turned on his heel. "I am removing my Legionaries from this dungeon. If the traitors die, it'll be *your* responsibility, not mine."

"As you prefer," Vigild replied with a vestige of a smile. "I will fetch additional Paladins immediately."

The night was still dark when they left Alman's shack, but the streets were much calmer. There wasn't a single person in sight. Even the cats and dogs seemed to have quieted down.

"My brother doesn't live far," Alman said, turning a corner.

"Isn't it a bit late?" Fadan asked. "I mean, he's probably resting. I can come back tomorrow."

Fadan wasn't truly sure he could. After two consecutive days of absence from the Palace, he was probably facing a severe punishment. However, if this man was going to be his magic tutor, Fadan would much rather meet him in a good mood.

"Don't worry," Alman replied. "Sabium is a nocturnal creature. Sometimes I think the moon is the brightest thing he can handle."

They turned into an alley that looked exactly like the one where the sailors had attacked Fadan, and Alman climbed the wooden staircase of a three-story building.

"This is it," Alman said as he reached the top of the stairs. "I found this attic for him a few years ago. It won't be much of a classroom, but the landlord doesn't ask any questions." He knocked twice on the door. "Oh, one more thing. Let me do the talking, all right? Sabium doesn't really... *approve* of some of my ideas."

"Who is it?" someone asked from inside the house. The voice did not sound thrilled by the intrusion.

"Sabium, it's me," Alman whispered.

The door swung open, revealing a tall man wearing black robes. He inspected Fadan with a quick, disapproving glance.

"What is this?" Sabium asked. "What do you want?"

"Not out here," Alman replied. "Let us in."

"I am *busy*," Sabium said without moving an inch.

"Well, you're taking a pause," Alman said, rushing past him and dragging Fadan by the sleeve.

Sabium grumbled something but closed the door behind him. The place was wide and spacious, but the slanted ceiling was so low, you could stand up only in the middle of the room. Window shutters were closed, and the only light came from a couple of candles melting over a mess of parchment on a desk. There was a bed in one corner – actually, not a bed, just a straw mattress – and several cabinets filled with so many books, its shelves arched downward.

"Who is that?" Sabium asked, waving toward Fadan. "Why would you bring someone here?"

"Shut up and let me talk," Alman said. "Do you recognize him?"

"Of course I don't recognize him," Sabium said. "I just asked you who he is."

"How can you not... Will you *look* at him?"

Sabium glanced at Fadan, who was inspecting the piles of books with his mouth open, seemingly not paying the least bit of attention to the squabbling brothers.

"Don't tell me it's another damned stowaway," Sabium said. "I will not babysit some illiterate orphan for you."

"Stowaway?" Alman asked. "It's the prince, you numbskull."

"The what?!" Sabium said.

Fadan turned to the old mage. "My name is Fadan Patros. I'm the Crown Prince of Arrel."

There was a moment of silence, then Sabium burst out laughing. "That's amazing!" he said, then faced his brother. "He's good. He's really good."

Alman gave his brother a serious look but didn't say anything. Fadan stepped forward.

"This is not an act," Fadan said. "I really am the prince."

Sabium's laughter quieted and turned into a weak smile before disappearing entirely. He looked from Fadan to his brother. "You're serious?" he asked.

Alman nodded.

"Ava Mother..." Sabium muttered. "What... why?"

"I'm here because I need your help, Lord Sabium," Fadan said, taking another step forward.

"*My* help?" Sabium asked his brother.

"That's right," Alman said, smiling. "His Majesty possesses the Talent. He wants you to teach him. Discreetly."

"You have the Talent?" Sabium asked Fadan. He was dumbfounded.

"You can test me if you want," the prince replied.

"You're mad!" Sabium said. "You're both mad. The emperor will find out. We'll be caught, all three of us. We'll hang."

"You have nothing to worry about," Fadan assured him. "I have my ways to enter and leave the Citadel unseen. No one will follow me."

"How could you possibly be sure?" Sabium asked. "The emperor's spies are everywhere."

"My father has many enemies, but I'm not one of them," Fadan said calmly. "He always worried that my brother would be a bad influence on me, but Aric is gone." He shrugged. "My father has nothing left to worry about."

"You're not one of your father's enemies?" Sabium laughed in disbelief. "You just walked into my house with a member of the rebellion!"

"A what?" Fadan asked.

Alman covered his eyes. "Goddess damn it, Sabium…"

"Oh, you didn't know?" Sabium asked. "My brother here colludes with rebels all the time, even though it will most likely end up leading the Paladins back to me. *A mage!*"

Fadan clenched his teeth. This was bad. Really bad. Releasing Doric from jail was one thing. Working with the people who wanted to murder his father was something else entirely.

"You should have told me this," Fadan said.

"Will you both please calm down?" Alman pleaded. "All I do is help the rebellion with supplies. I've never even met any of them in person. They're too cautious."

"And you're not cautious enough," Sabium said.

"I agree," Fadan said. "This was foolish. I need to leave."

The prince started toward the door nervously, but Alman blocked his way.

"Wait," the old man said. "Please, just listen to me."

Fadan exhaled loudly, but he waited.

"Fine, it's true," Alman said. "I'm with the rebels, but my brother isn't. If you want, I'll just disappear. You'll never see me again. There will be fresh supplies of runium in my brother's cabinets, but you won't even know how they got there. I promise."

"That's all very fine," Sabium said. "But I won't risk it. I refuse to train him."

Alman turned away from Fadan and walked to his brother. "The boy sneaked out from the Citadel and found his way to the Docks in the middle of the night for a vial of runium. You think he'll just give up magic because you said no?" He turned to Fadan. "Be honest, son. Are you going to forget about your Talent?"

The prince hesitated a little but ended up shaking his head. "No," he replied.

"Of course not," Alman continued. "The last time he tried to buy runium, I found him half-conscious in an alley. Next time, he'll probably get himself killed, but even if he does get lucky and manages to go back home with a bottle of runium, what do you think will happen?"

Sabium didn't reply right away. He shot his deep frown at Fadan as if the prince were guilty of all his misery.

"Come on," Alman insisted. "What do you think will happen?"

"Stupid kid will probably misfire a spell and blow himself up," Sabium finally replied. "If he doesn't poison himself first."

Alman opened his arms, closing his argument while Sabium walked to a chair and sank into it.

There was a moment of silence as the three of them exchanged glances. Fadan considered leaving. He wanted to learn magic, not join the rebellion against his father. But, then again, having a *real* mage to teach him was too good of an opportunity to pass on.

"All right," Sabium said. "I'll teach him. But if I get a single whiff of the Paladins, none of you will ever see me again."

"Fantastic!" Alman clapped triumphantly and turned to Fadan. "What do you say, Your Majesty? I will vanish into thin air. I guarantee it."

"If you think this will lead me to join your rebellion, you can forget about it," Fadan said. "I will not plot to murder my own father."

"Maybe not," Alman said. "Maybe the rebellion doesn't even have to murder your father. Replacing him with you would be more than enough for me." He smiled.

Fadan frowned. "I said I will not join the rebellion."

"And I said I would disappear," Alman said, moving toward the door. "The two of you are free to carry out your lessons."

CHAPTER 12

The Desert Flower

Aric led Leth and Clea up a tight, dark stairwell. Sometimes Lamash seemed like the crumbling castle of some bankrupt lordling, but then an opened door would lead to a gleaming hall with a ceiling as tall as a tower that would rise up before you. It was obvious that no architect had ever planned any of its design. The building had just gradually taken shape throughout the centuries as needed. You could even tell the older corridors from the younger by their walls' particular shade of amber.

"I'm not insane," Aric told them in a low voice. "I know what I saw."

"We believe you," Clea said hesitantly. "But…where are you taking us?"

"I'm not taking you anywhere," Aric replied, opening a door at the top of the stairwell. "You two are just following me."

They crossed the door into a barely lit storage room with flour bags in one corner and old wine barrels covering an entire wall.

"Well," Leth said, wiping a spider web from his head with a grimace, "you did tell us you saw a woman petting a dragon. Forgive us for wanting to make sure you didn't bump your head into something."

"My head is fine," Aric assured him.

"That's good to know," Clea said. "So why are we here?"

"Yeah," Leth agreed. "And why are we whispering?"

Aric didn't even acknowledge the questions. He opened a massive chest and dove inside, leaving Leth and Clea to exchange a confused glance.

"There!" Aric said, his legs the only visible part of his body. "I knew it was here." He reemerged with a victorious smile on his face and a large parcel in his hands.

"What's that?" Leth asked.

"Dried ostrich meat," Aric replied, leaving for the door. "Geric loves it."

"Who's Geric?" Clea asked.

"My cat," Aric replied as if it was the most obvious thing in the world.

"Wait." Clea raised her hands. "You *named it?*"

"Of course I named it," Aric said. "And don't just stand there; the cooks might come in any moment." He fled the room, trotting down the stairs.

Eyes widened, Leth and Clea looked over their shoulders to what they now realized was the front door to that storage room, then raced after Aric, closing the smaller backdoor behind them.

"You could have warned us we were aiding you in stealing from the kitchens," Clea said, catching up to Aric.

"I was going to," Aric replied, "but you seemed far more interested in my account of what happened in the desert."

"Yeah, about that," Leth said. "You're not going to tell that to Saruk or anyone else, are you?"

Aric shrugged. "I have to."

The stairwell came to an end and Aric turned left toward a door so small, they had to duck to get through it. On the other side, the desert swathed them in air like an oven.

"I really don't think you do," Leth said. "In fact, you probably shouldn't." He nearly didn't finish the sentence as a lean shadow darted past, sending him jumping backward. "What the —"

"There you are," Aric said, wrapping both arms around the huge cat. The two of them wrestled, Geric's paws slapping Aric around his neck. "Look what I got for you, look. What's this? Oh, you like this, don't you?" The parcel was barely open when Geric stuck his snout inside, devouring its contents. Aric giggled.

Clea neared Aric. "Will he bite me?" she asked, reaching out for the cat.

"Of course not," Aric assured her. "Go ahead."

Carefully, she moved her hand closer to Geric's fur. When her fingers brushed against the cat's neck, he snapped and one of his paws whipped Clea's hand away. The large cat finished his message with a hiss before diving back into his food.

"All right," Aric said, "maybe not while he eats."

"Can we please get back to the matter at hand?" Leth demanded.

Aric sighed as he stood back up, but he complied. "What do you want me to do? Keep this a secret?"

"Uh…yes."

"Are you serious?" Aric couldn't believe it. "There is a crazy witch out there that can tame dragons. The Guild has to do something about it."

Leth closed his eyes and pressed his temples as if a crushing headache had just struck him. "You do realize that if you start blabbering about women wandering around the desert with their dragon pets, you'll be the laughingstock of the whole fortress. If you're lucky."

Geric had just finished eating, and he was happily licking around his own mouth. Aric picked up the now-empty parcel and scratched behind Geric's ear.

"Don't worry," he told Leth. "I'll be fine."

⌣⟶

"So…" Saruk tried to weigh his words most carefully. "This woman was…*petting* the dragon. Is that it?"

Somewhere along the line of recruits came a muffled laugh.

"She wasn't petting him," Aric replied. He obviously didn't appreciate Saruk's condescending tone.

"And you say this woman was Eliran?" Saruk had a suspicious eyebrow raised. "The one from the scary bedtime stories."

Aric's mouth moved silently a couple of times. "I can't be sure it really was Eliran," he finally admitted. "But she was standing very close to the dragon and then…reached out."

"I see." He obviously didn't. "And the dragon simply stood there?"

Aric exhaled loudly, his cheeks glowing red. "You know I tagged a dragon; your Hunters traced my seeker arrow back to it."

"That's right," Saruk agreed. "A Mahari Black Dread, no less. Very impressive."

"Then why would I lie about the rest?"

"Because you've lost your marbles," Ashur said.

The crowd of recruits burst into laughter. Even Saruk had to hide a smile.

Feeling like there wasn't a hole deep enough for him to hide in, Aric looked to his left and found Clea trying to smile reassuringly at him. She was doing a terrible job of it.

"Listen," Saruk said, his hands asking for quiet. "Sometimes, when you're out there on your own, the desert plays tricks with our heads. Veteran Hunters with years of experience have come back from patrols swearing they had found the goddess herself. My own instructor, to the day he died, vowed that he had found the edge of the desert. That there was a city there with towers made of gold reaching up to the sun, and that some of the old gods still wandered there. As Grand-Master Sylene says, it comes with the job."

Aric didn't reply. He knew what he had seen, but it was clear that the conversation was over. Saruk turned his back on Aric, ordering the company to follow him out into the corridors. What else was he supposed to do?

Each team formed a line behind the instructor, marching down the great staircase leading to the main hall. Tharius seemed to have grown two inches overnight. He paraded himself along Lamash's hallways with his now-enormous team in tow as if he owned the entire Guild.

It was all right, Aric told himself. If someone deserved to gloat a bit, it was certainly Tharius. Ashur, however, wasn't as forgiving.

"Look at that idiot," Aric heard him whisper to Prion and Jullion. "Prancing around like a peacock."

It was funny how quickly Ashur's attention had shifted from Aric to Tharius, and it wasn't just him. Tharius seemed to be the only thing everyone in the company talked about since he had tagged a dragon all by himself. It felt kind of unfair, though. After all, hadn't Aric done exactly the same?

Saruk led the company to the lower levels of Lamash. The second challenge was to take place inside a damp cave somewhere within the mountain.

The bowels of the fortress were a frightfully large and dark place, and it was no wonder the recruits were forbidden to access them on their own.

One could easily get lost in the mess of manmade tunnels and natural caves. Saruk had even claimed that those who got lost in there were rarely found.

"This challenge is called the Silent Retrieval," Saruk said when they reached a large hollow where the sun could be seen shining through a crevice miles above them. "Your goal is to rescue a straw man laid inside. The trick will be to do it without waking up the bats sleeping within."

"Bats?" Lyra asked, grimacing.

"That's right," Saruk replied. "They're mostly harmless. *Mostly.* But they won't attack you if they remain asleep, which is exactly the point of the challenge. There are four candidates still in the race to become captain. Only three will remain by the end of today. Good luck."

Each team was placed in a different chamber, waiting for their turn to go in. Who would go first and who would go last, Aric did not know. He waited with Leth and Clea by the torchlight for well over an hour before Saruk came and told them their turn was up.

As they prepared to go in, Aric couldn't tell which was harder: dealing with the butterflies in his stomach, or pretending like he wasn't nervous at all in front of Clea.

"Are you all right?" she asked, firmly tying the leather straps around her boots.

"Sure," Aric replied, smiling weakly.

The challenge, however, went much smoother than Aric would have ever guessed. Clea seemed to feel quite comfortable in the darkness, and since lighting a torch was out of the question, Aric was more than okay with letting her lead the way. They were in and out in a breeze, and Aric was incredibly proud that none of them made a single sound. No one slipped or kicked a loose pebble. It was, as Saruk put it, a clean rescue. The only question was, had they been fast enough?

They were ordered to return to the company's quarters and wait for the results. By the time Saruk arrived with a rolled piece of parchment in his hand, Aric had nearly carved a trench in the stone floor of the common room from walking back and forth.

Please let us win, please…

Aric still wasn't sure if he really wanted to be captain, to have all that responsibility fall upon his shoulders, but the glory of winning the competition, however, was something he really wouldn't mind. For the last couple of days, he had found himself daydreaming of the moment that Saruk raised his hand in the air and announced him as the captain of the Twenty-third Company of Dragon Hunters. In Aric's mind, the announcement was always followed by loud cheers and applause. Sometimes, the whole company would rush to hug him; other times, they carried him upon their shoulders across Lamash. No matter how the news was received, though, the best part was always the way Clea's smile glowed when their eyes met.

Saruk opened his parchment roll and cleared his throat as every set of eyes locked on him. "The winner of this challenge," he said, "is Team Ashur."

Jullion and Prion jumped, screaming victoriously, grabbing and shaking a shock-frozen Ashur. Everyone else looked stunned.

"Oh, please," Leth begged uselessly. "Not him."

Aric agreed, but that wasn't the worst part. Losing would be bad in any case, but now it would mean becoming part of Ashur's team.

Oh, goddess…

"Congratulations, boys," Saruk said over the excited howls of Jullion and Prion. "Outstanding work."

Trying to look as if it didn't really matter, Ashur thanked Saruk, then leered at the other team leaders.

"Now the losers," Saruk continued.

Like a spell, those words made the whole room become silent in a flash. Aric saw Trissa close her eyes and move her lips in a silent prayer. Even Tharius had lost his recent smirk.

"I really wasn't expecting this, but…" Saruk said.

Oh, goddess…he means me.

"The losers are…" He made a face as if he was apologizing to the parchment roll. "Team Tharius."

"WHAT?!"

Every pair of eyes turned to Tharius. The poor boy was looking as if he had just been stabbed in the gut. Even his color was gone. Behind him, everyone on his team looked speechless. It was such a pitiful sight, Aric even refrained from giving a sigh of relief.

"Yeah," Saruk said. "I didn't see that one coming either." He rolled up the parchment containing the results and addressed the entire group. "Overall, everyone did well. I'm actually impressed. It came down to speed, and your team was the slowest, Tharius."

"But, but…" Tharius mumbled.

The poor guy never finished the sentence.

"Instructor," Trissa called.

"Yes?"

"I wouldn't mind knowing who came second," she replied. "Me or Aric."

"That would be you, Trissa."

If disappointment had a sound, Aric thought, that would've been it. It was still better than losing, though. Nahir and everyone in his original team couldn't even take their eyes off the ground. Losing two challenges in a row had to be rough.

"The three remaining team leaders are to report to the Grand-Master's study for the next mission's briefing. Dismissed."

⌣⟶

"We almost lost. Again," Aric said. It was the first thing out of his mouth since he, Leth, and Clea had left the company's quarters.

"We'll do better next time," Clea told him.

A piercing sound made them both jump.

"Goddess, Leth!" Clea cried. "What in mother's name are you doing?!"

"What does it look like I'm doing?" Leth said, indicating the pickaxe in his hand and the cracked stone slab he had just hit.

Clea fumed. "I've had enough of weird places in the fortress for today. Why did you have to bring us to this creepy old tower? And why in the world are you hacking at the floor?"

221

"I'm finding out the truth," Leth said as if making a solemn vow, then he stabbed the floor once again.

"What?!" Clea asked again, dumbfounded.

"There used to be a library on the floor below," Aric explained.

"What do you mean, *used* to be?" Clea asked.

"This being the Mages' Tower, obviously, the Paladins wiped it clean," Aric replied. "There aren't any books left."

"Then why is he trying to get in there? And what's wrong with using the front door?!"

"What Aric forgot to tell you," Leth said, wiping sweat from his forehead, "is that the library has a walled-off section. Who knows what the Paladins *didn't* wipe clean?"

Clea shook her head. "And you thought this was the best moment to begin your…excavation?"

"Well," Leth replied. "It's not like we've had lots of free time lately, have we?" He stabbed the floor once again, making Clea cringe.

Aric stood up. "Well, I have to go," he announced.

"Future captain's duties, huh?" Clea said.

Aric smiled faintly.

"I can't wait to learn what's next on Saruk's catalogue of tortures," Leth said, swinging the pickaxe above his head. He struck the stone slab again, his whole body lending strength to the blow. "Goddess damn this! What is this floor made of?"

"What are you expecting to find down there, anyway?" Aric asked as he walked toward the exit.

Leth lowered the pickaxe, resting his arms. "You never know," he said between heavy panting. "I might find the desert witch." He smiled devilishly and Aric smiled back.

"If the mages wanted that section to be a secret, it's going to stay a secret."

Aric ducked under a massive spider web and walked out the door, still in time to hear Leth screaming, "Dead mages are no match for the finest son of House Ranraik!"

It made Aric laugh out loud, even though he was already alone. He left the Mages' Tower and had to cover his eyes from the burning sun as he crossed the stone bridge leading back to the Main Tower. A company of senior Hunters was readying their gear in the Main Hall, and Aric recognized most of their faces.

That was the seventh company. Whitejackets was their nickname, although why, Aric did not know. He had never seen any of them wearing a white jacket. What Aric did know was that they had returned from patrol less than a week earlier and apparently were being shipped out already. None of them seemed very happy about it, either.

Trissa and Ashur were already by the door to the Grand-Master's study when Aric arrived.

"What are you looking at?" Trissa was asking Ashur.

The fair-haired Samehrian smirked. "Just wondering what your duties will be when I become captain."

Trissa looked away, shaking her head. "Idiot."

The three of them waited in silence for a little while until the black door opened with a creak and Saruk waved them in. They formed up in front of the huge table holding the map of the Mahari Desert, Grand-Master Sylene standing across from them like one of the marble statues of the Citadel. Slowly, she moved toward them, inspecting each one from head to toe, until she stopped in front of Aric.

"Is this the armor you were issued by the Guild?" the Grand Master asked.

"Yes, Grand-Master."

"What happened to your own dragon scale armor?"

"It's in my bunk, Grand-Master."

"Your bunk? Why?" Sylene asked. "Are you afraid it'll get damaged?"

"No. It's just…a bit flashy. Makes me stand out too much."

Sylene frowned and paused for a little bit. "Makes you stand out? What, are you trying to hide from someone?" she asked.

"Hide?!" What kind of question was that? "No. I –"

"That cuirass is the finest piece of equipment in this whole mountain. From this day forward, you will wear it at all times; is that understood, recruit?"

"Yes, Grand-Master."

"And what's this I hear about you adopting some kind of desert creature?"

"It's just a cat, Grand-Master."

"It's not a cat," Saruk intervened. He was standing behind Sylene like a bodyguard. "It's a desert lynx."

Sylene gave Aric a look of shock.

"He's harmless," Aric assured her. "Besides, Geric likes to hang out in the desert. He rarely even comes inside the fortress."

"Yeah," Ashur said, "but when he *is* inside, he likes to eat my sandals."

Aric had to fight back a smile. "It happened once. And I punished him for doing it."

"You punished him?" Sylene asked. "Let me get this straight. You named a desert lynx after a person and are trying to train it? Is that it?"

"I named him after my ancestor, Geric Auron, the conqueror of Saggad," Aric replied.

"I know who Geric Auron was; that's not the point, recruit! The point is a desert lynx is *not a pet.*" Aric was going to protest, but Sylene raised a hand, silencing him. "I don't care what you and your lynx do out in the desert, but he is not allowed inside my mountain, is that understood?"

"Yes, Grand-Master," Aric replied, his eyes on the ground.

"And I better not hear about any missing goats from the pens or you'll both find yourselves in serious trouble." Without even waiting for a reply, Sylene turned and moved toward the next recruit, Trissa. A smile grew on her face. "Oh, I like this one," she said. "There's some fire in her isn't there, Saruk?"

"I would say so, Grand-Master," Saruk replied.

"Reminds me a bit of myself when I was her age," Sylene added.

That managed to make Trissa grow a couple of inches taller.

"Let me guess," Sylene said. "Akhami?"

"Cyrinian, Grand-Master. But my parents moved to Akham after the Purge."

"Ah, runium traders, I imagine."

"My father was, yes."

"I used to do Blood Runs before the Purge. Before I became..." She moved an arm around, indicating her study. "Maybe we did business back in the day. What's his name?"

Trissa's eyes narrowed. "His name was Pashet, Grand-Master."

The smile on Sylene's face faded. "I see. Forgive me; I shouldn't have asked."

"There's nothing to forgive, Grand-Master."

Sylene nodded solemnly and stood in silence for a bit, then turned and moved to Ashur.

"You, I remember well. I don't get that many volunteers, after all."

Aric and Trissa's heads snapped, their eyes wide. Ashur was a *volunteer?*

"You know," Sylene continued. "There are only three kinds of volunteers. The ones that come for the money; the ones that come for the glory; and the ones that are insane. The curious thing is, Dragon Hunting isn't lucrative anymore, not since the Purge. So I wonder...exactly how crazy are you?"

"I...I just want to protect the Empire, Grand-Master," he replied.

Sylene chuckled. "Of course you do." She turned around and walked away. "But it doesn't matter. You're in the Guild now. Your past is gone. All that matters in your life now is the desert, this mountain, and your fellow Guildsmen. Nothing else. For now, however, the three of you must remain rivals. Saruk, if you'd be so kind."

"With pleasure, Grand-Master." Saruk took a step forward while Sylene leaned against her desk. "The next challenge will take place tomorrow. I like to call this one the Blood Raid, and it is quite simple. There are two crates filled with dragon blood hidden inside two different caves in the middle of the desert. Two crates for three teams. Which means the team that fails to return to Lamash with one of them, loses. Out of the two teams that do return with the crate, the first one back wins."

The Grand-Master picked up three pieces of parchment from her desk. "These maps contain the location of both crates," she said as she handed one of them to each recruit. "None of you or any member of your team is allowed to leave the fortress before dawn. At first sunlight tomorrow, the sentinels will sound the fortress's alarm and the challenge will start. Any questions?"

Ashur raised his arm. "If we'll be competing for the same crates, are we allowed to fight?" he asked.

The question made Aric shift his weight from one leg to the other.

"This is the Dragon Hunters Guild," the Grand-Master said. "I'm pretty sure that, by now, you have all realized the risks you face." She paused and looked each recruit in the eyes. "With that being said, however, you are all brothers and sisters now and are expected to act accordingly. So, if that is all, I —"

"Excuse me, Grand-Master," Ashur said, raising his arm once again. "But that does not answer my question."

"I was exceedingly clear, recruit," Sylene told him, her eyes narrowed. "If you failed to understand my words, then I believe that to be *your* problem."

"Grand-Master," Trissa said. "I disagree. I think that is *my* problem. Ashur here has nine people on his team. I have three. If he decides to beat my team into a pulp, there will be little I can do about it."

"As I've told you, recruit," Sylene said, "all of you should be familiar with the risks you face by now. However, if Team Ashur's conduct, or any other's for that matter, is deemed to be…outside the boundaries of reason, well…" Her head twitched in a most sinister way. "They will surely find themselves taking a rather long walk around the deep desert." She looked straight into Ashur's eyes. "The Guild might be in desperate need of manpower, but it has no need for thugs."

This time, it was Ashur who shifted his weight.

"Now, as I was saying before," Sylene continued, "you'll want to sleep so that you are well rested tomorrow, but if I were you, I'd spend some time tonight studying that map and planning a strategy. Oh, and one more thing. The crates we use to carry dragon blood are big and heavy. You won't be able to carry them on your backs. For that reason, on this challenge, you are allowed the use of horses, as well as carts and other tools like rope. Good luck, recruits."

When Aric returned to the empty room above the mages' library, there was no sign of either Leth or Clea. The fight between Leth and the stone slab seemed to be over, and the floor had clearly won, as the worn tip of Leth's pickaxe indicated.

With the next day's challenge swimming aimlessly in his head, Aric returned to the Main Tower and found his teammates on a balcony a few feet away from the company's quarters.

"They can't be serious!" Clea shouted after Aric explained the mission. "Ashur's team is bigger than ours and Trissa's combined. They might as well just send him straight to the last challenge."

"Blame Tharius," Leth said. "He's the idiot who lost the last challenge and gifted Ashur with six additional team members." He was lying on the balcony's parapet, one leg dangling outside the fortress.

"We just need to figure this out," Aric said, indicating the map Sylene had given him. "There's obviously a right way to go about this. I'm pretty sure that's what she was trying to tell us."

Like lightning, Leth stole the map from Aric's hands and looked at it as if there was a bad history between them.

"One cave is considerably closer than the other," Leth said. "So, either you risk going for the first in an attempt to be faster and win, or play it safe and go for the second, more distant one. The problem is, if everyone decides to play it safe, the second cave becomes the risky one and vice versa." He handed the parchment back to Aric and lay on the parapet once more, closing his eyes under the warm sunlight. "Basically, this is a dilemma. There's no right answer. They're just toying with us, as usual."

"So, you're saying the best strategy for this is *no* strategy?" Aric asked.

"No," Leth replied. "I'm saying that trying to come up with a strategy for this is as pointless as the pickaxe I left in the Mages' Tower."

That didn't convince Aric. There had to be something about this challenge other than randomness. The previous challenges had been tests on crucial skills like desert survival, dragon tracking, and stealth. So, the question was: what exactly was being tested in this particular challenge?

"I need to go for a walk," Aric said. "Think this through."

"I'll go with you," Clea said, standing up.

"No, I'd rather go alone." The words left his mouth before he even realized it. Had he just thrown away a chance to be alone with her?

What is wrong with me?!

"Are you sure?" Clea asked. "It's our job to help you. You don't need to figure this all by yourself."

"Yeah, I'm sure. It helps me think when I'm alone. I'm kinda used to it, really." At least that last part was true.

"If you say so," Clea said, sitting back down.

Awkwardly, Aric turned around and left, running up several flights of stairs until he found himself on a level he had never visited before. As soon as he started to walk around the empty hallways, the strange discomfort in his belly was gone.

He wandered around for hours. Lamash was so big and the number of Hunters left was so small that it was possible to roam around without bumping into anyone for ages. It was perfect, even better than the Citadel.

He tried to think about the challenge and the two-caves dilemma but had no success. At first, all that came to his mind were the thousands of ways he could have handled the conversation with Clea better. He eventually decided that Leth was right and he was an idiot.

The problem had no solution, which meant he could have taken the opportunity to spend some time alone with Clea. There were lots of amazing places with breathtaking views in the fortress where he could have taken her, like the small turret in the west wing near the abandoned quarters of the seventy-second company. The turret had a small vertical garden of purple desert roses. Someone took care of those flowers religiously, but Aric had no idea who it was. What he did know was that it would have been the perfect place to take Clea, maybe even gift her one of the roses.

Hours went by and the honey-colored sunlight pouring through the windows slowly turned red. Aric ventured into the inner corridors of the topmost levels, and the thoughts about Clea and that infuriatingly weird challenge vanished, replaced by images of the countless Hunters who had once lived in these halls. Aric found rooms filling with sand and dust around dozens of weapon racks. Some had had their blades removed – probably the glowstone ones – while others had become rusty and blunt. One room in particular caught Aric's attention. It was nearly as wide as the dining hall downstairs, and its walls were draped with the tattered banners of what he assumed were extinct companies. Each banner had its own set of colors, a number, and a name. Some names were hilarious, like the Ninety-eighth Company, Drunk Mules. Others were a bit scary, like the Nineteenth Company, Polished Skulls.

Eventually, Aric reached the highest level in Lamash and immediately headed for the outer corridor. The view up there had to be unbelievable. Only then did he realize that night had fallen and the moon had climbed to the sky.

What time was it? A sudden growl from his stomach told him it was much later than he thought. Still, there was no point in wasting the view.

He took a deep breath. It was a cold, silver night. It reminded him of home, except instead of shining down on the thousands of rooftops of Augusta, the moon shone above the wavy dune tops. *What has Fadan been up to lately?* Aric wondered. And what about Mother? She probably missed him like crazy.

Then, an image of his father locked behind bars came to his mind, and the whole desert beneath seemed to spin. He gasped and took a step back, fearing he could fall.

Shaking his head as if to throw the thought away, Aric turned around and returned to the stairs. It was best not to think of those things.

He ran down the stairwell, not stopping on any floor. When he finally recognized the floor of the Twenty-third's quarters, he was gasping and his head was swirling. He had to stop and rub his eyes just to make sure he didn't stumble.

"Can't sleep?"

Aric looked toward the voice, his sight blurry and covered with stars from the rubbing. It was Ashur. He was standing on a small balcony, the same where he had met Leth and Clea earlier that day. The bright moon behind him made him look like a shadow, but the contours of a bottle were clearly visible in his hand. Ashur took a sip, and black drops rolled down his chin.

"Just out for a walk," Aric told him. "Helps me think."

"Nah," Ashur said. "You have trouble sleeping. You always had. At least, ever since you got here."

"You're drunk," Aric said.

Ashur chuckled. "Not even close, half-prince," he said. "It's all right, though. We all have our demons. I get that. I bet you miss your palace or something." He chuckled and took another gulp from his bottle. "At least we have that in common." He looked around. "I *hate* this place. The heat. The sweat. That freaking instructor."

"Why did you volunteer, then?"

A smile twisted Ashur's face as if he was about to jump on an easy prey. "That must really mess with your head. The possibility that I might be a better person than you." He chuckled again. It was a rough sound, almost like a growl.

"That doesn't answer my question," Aric said.

Ashur's smile disappeared in a flash. "I don't answer to you, half-prince." He brought the bottle to his lips.

"Maybe not yet," Aric said. "But you will."

Ashur took three long, loud gulps and finished with a satisfied *Ah*. Then, slowly, he lay down on the parapet, just as Leth had done earlier, and closed his eyes. "Not even you believe that, half-prince," he said, cradling the bottle. "Not even you."

That night, Aric had a feverish mess of a dream. He was walking around Lamash, hand in hand with Clea. The best thing he had ever felt was glowing in his chest when all of a sudden, the floor cracked and the ceiling began to crumble. Aric tried to run, but Clea held him down, squashing his hand so hard, it turned white. He screamed that they needed to get out of there, but when he looked into her eyes, it wasn't Clea after all.

Eliran!

The witch's face was as gray as a corpse's, a silent scream frozen on her cracked lips, her hair bursting into flames.

"The skies will bleed!" she hissed.

Then the entire wall behind her collapsed, revealing the desert outside and a gigantic red dragon falling from the sky, spewing fire toward them.

Aric woke up covered in sweat, breathing heavily. Around him, the rest of the company was already up and getting dressed.

"Hey, you're up," Leth said. "I was going to wake you; the alarm should sound any moment now."

Rubbing his eyes, Aric stepped out of his bunk. "You could have woken me sooner," he said.

"It was really late when you came in last night," Leth replied. "I figured it was better to let you rest."

Leth was right. He still felt exhausted.

"Thanks," Aric said. "We should hurry, though. Get our equipment."

"No need." Leth leaned toward Aric and whispered, "I've taken care of it." Then he winked.

What was he up to?

"All right…" Aric said, his eyebrows raised. "I think." His stomach grumbled, reminding him he hadn't eaten anything since yesterday's lunch. "In that case, I'll rush to the dining hall and fetch some food for us. I'll meet you guys by the main gate."

With Leth's approving nod, Aric left, and a short while later, he was arriving at the fortress's gate with a satchel full of cinnamon biscuits, flatbread, and dried ostrich meat. He was just in time too, because the alarm had just been given, signaling the start of the challenge.

"What is that?" Aric asked, indicating a chest in Leth's hands. "And where's everyone else?"

"Oh, they just left," Leth replied. "They were in such a hurry —"

"Crap!" Aric smacked his own forehead. "We need to go!" He was climbing onto one of the horses but Clea held him back.

"Relax," she said. "By the way, did you manage to come up with a plan last night?"

"Uh…" That was embarrassing. "No, not really," he admitted.

"No plan?!" Leth shrieked. "What now?"

"I'm…" Aric's eyes darted left and right as if a plan might be lying around somewhere. "Don't worry, we'll…"

"Stop it." Clea was talking to Leth and laughing. "It's okay, Aric. Leth had an idea."

"You did?" Aric asked him.

"Indeed, I did." Leth held up the wooden chest. "And here it is."

"Uh…what is it, exactly?"

Instead of replying, Leth opened the chest, revealing two finely gilded leather cases. "Ta-da!"

"Tracker-seekers?" Aric asked, confused. Then, his eyebrows jumped. "You didn't."

"Oh, yes, he did," Clea said amusedly.

"This is the key to the whole thing, really," Leth said. "Think about it. The only way to make the right decision in this challenge is if you know what cave your opponents chose. So…now we do."

Looking exceedingly proud of himself, he set the chest down and opened the cases. The tracker arrows were gone. Only the seeker necklaces remained inside.

"Well, yes," Aric replied, scratching his head. "If they go for the same cave, that solves our problem, but what if they don't?"

"If they don't, we ambush them on their way back," Leth replied.

"We ambush Trissa, is what you mean," Aric told him. "There's no way we stand a chance against Ashur."

Standing back up with the two dancing necklaces in his hand, Leth exhaled loudly. "Listen," he said. "Trissa either has to deal with us or with Ashur. Except she doesn't get to choose, while we do. I'd say that's a pretty good advantage."

"Actually," Clea said, "we don't have to choose at all." She placed the map beneath Leth's seeker necklaces and aligned it with a compass.

"No way," Aric let out.

It really was hard to believe. Both necklaces were pointing toward the second, more distant cave.

"Wow! When did *we* get this lucky?" Leth asked.

⌒⟶

The closer they got to the first cave, the more Aric was sure one of the other teams would show up. Something could have happened to the tracker glowstone shard Leth had planted on Trissa's and Ashur's clothes. It could have fallen off or, worse, been discovered.

Despite all of Leth's protests, Aric insisted on sneaking up the small hill where the cave was located, and even though there was no one in sight for miles, Aric still told Clea to stand watch outside the cave while he and Leth got the crate. He even insisted Leth be as quiet and careful as the previous morning when they had infiltrated the bat-filled cave within the bowels of Lamash. But once again, there was no one inside. No ambush, nothing. The dragon blood–filled crate was just sitting there, waiting to be taken.

"I can't believe this," Aric whispered. "We might actually win this time."

"Come on, let's get this out," Leth said.

At the count of three, they lifted the crate using the metal handles protruding from the top and quickly went red.

"Dear goddess!" Leth complained. "This thing weighs more than a cow." Sweat broke out on his forehead immediately. "A pregnant one." They moved as quickly as they could toward the exit. "With twins."

They almost made it to the exit, but at the last couple of feet, the handle bars slipped through Aric's sweaty fingers and the crate crashed to the ground, knocking them both down.

"Ouch!" Leth yelped.

"Are you okay?" Aric asked. He had landed on his back and his bottom was hurting like crazy.

"I'm fine," Leth replied. "Just hit my knee on this damned thing. You?"

"Yeah, I'm all right. One inch to the left, though, and I would have lost a foot."

Then he froze. Right there, next to his foot, saved by some miracle from being squashed, was a tiny orange daisy. It was beautiful.

How had something like that grown out there in the desert?

Aric smiled. It reminded him of the roses he wanted to gift to Clea, except this one was far more special. A flower in the middle of the desert... He plucked the daisy and tucked it away in one of his pockets.

"Are you ready?" Leth asked.

"Yes, let's do this."

Looking as if they were about to blow steam out of their heads, they loaded the crate onto the cart and secured it with rope. And just like that, as quickly as they had arrived, they were on their way back.

Aric spent the whole journey to Lamash checking and rechecking the seeker necklaces. If the glowstone devices could be trusted, both Ashur and Trissa were still miles behind them. Aric, however, refused to believe they were safe until they crossed the mountain fortress's main gate. Their horse's hooves thundered against the stone floor and echoed across the Main Hall.

"Congratulations, Team Aric." Saruk greeted them with a smile. "You've won the challenge."

Aric couldn't believe it.

Leth shot both hands in the air and shouted as if he had just crushed all of his enemies, while Clea jumped to hug Aric.

"We did it!" she screamed.

Aric's face blushed like the desert sky at sunset. "We...we did it," he managed to say, a huge smile growing on his red face.

At that moment, he decided he really was going to give her the flower.

Just not now. Later.

Yes, that's what he would do. He would give her the flower later that night.

Aric was so famished, he could barely stand. He wanted to join Leth and Clea in the dining hall, but Saruk insisted on briefing him about the next challenge immediately. By the time they were finished, Leth and Clea were nowhere to be found, so Aric ate alone. Still, it felt like his first decent meal in weeks.

He wondered what sort of mood he would find in the dorm later that night. Unsurprisingly, Trissa had lost. Would she be all right with Aric being her new team leader? What about Dothea and Irenya?

Aric got his answer much sooner, when the three girls dragged their feet into the dining hall.

"Congratulations," Trissa told him. "I'm glad it's you."

"I guess we're at your command now," Dothea said. "Should we call you Captain or something?"

"No, of course not." Aric smiled. "I hope Ashur wasn't too hard on you guys."

Trissa shrugged. "We got to the crate before him. For a moment, I really thought we had it in the bag, but he was waiting for us down the hill behind a dune."

"We just surrendered," Irenya said, shaking her head.

"To that jerk," Dothea added.

Trissa stared at the floor. "I didn't know what Ashur was capable of, and… I decided it was better not to find out."

"It was the right decision," Aric told her. "But we'll get him on the next challenge; you'll see."

"I was so sure Ashur would go for the first cave, though," Trissa said, her eyes lost.

For a moment, Aric didn't know what to say. "Yeah," he ended up muttering. "I suppose this was an unfair challenge." He paused a bit. "The three of you should get some rest, though. It's been a long day."

At that moment, Ashur arrived in the dining hall, followed by his crew. He didn't even look at Aric; he just stormed along toward one of the long tables.

At the back of the file following Ashur, little Lyra hopped toward Aric with a big smile below her bushy brown hair. "Hi, Aric," she said. "Congratulations on your victory."

Ashur didn't enjoy hearing that. "Hey!" He turned around with murderous eyes. "Did your team win today?!" he asked Lyra.

The poor girl took a step back. "What? No, I —"

"Then why are you talking about victories?" Ashur was walking toward her, but Ergon, Lyra's big brother, stepped in front of him, stopping Ashur dead in his tracks.

The two of them exchanged an awkwardly prolonged stare until Ashur smiled and turned back.

"Tharius!" Ashur called, sitting down at a table. "Fetch me some dinner."

"Excuse me?" Tharius asked.

"He can't be serious," Aric heard Dothea say under her breath.

"Yes, dinner," Ashur told Tharius. "Fetch me some."

"What did you say, recruit?"

All their heads turned simultaneously. The voice belonged to a Hunter sitting a few feet away from Ashur, whom none of them seemed to have noticed until now. His leather vest displayed the Dragon Hunter's mark on his right shoulder, above dozens of tiny triangles indicating how many dragons he had killed. It was even more impressive then the dozens of claws and fangs that made up his necklace.

"You didn't hear me?" the Hunter asked after Ashur didn't reply.

"I...I said I wanted some food," Ashur mumbled.

"Oh, you're hungry?" The Hunter grabbed his own bowl of stew and sent it sliding down the table. It landed right beneath Ashur's nose. "There you go. Eat." He drew a gigantic knife from his leg and started slicing through dark corn bread.

Ashur looked at the thick, brown stew but otherwise did not move. "No, thanks, I —"

The Hunter struck the table with the knife's handle so hard that the bowl jumped, spilling droplets of stew around.

"I said *eat!*" the Hunter told him.

Hesitantly, Ashur picked up a spoon and swallowed a mouthful.

Behind Aric, Dothea and Trissa were doing a horrible job at hiding their chuckles, while Irenya begged them to be quiet. Across the table, Tharius, Ergon, Lyra, and Orisius had wicked smiles spread across their faces.

"Does it taste good, recruit?" the Hunter asked. "Do you like it?"

"Sure," Ashur replied without taking his eyes off the bowl. "It's fine."

The Hunter slammed the table once again. "No, it's not! It tastes like dragon droppings. In fact, why don't you ask the cook if he seasoned it with dragon droppings?"

Ashur didn't move, of course. He just stood there, gritting his teeth.

"Are you deaf, recruit?" the Hunter asked calmly. Too calmly. "I said" – he held his knife up – "ask the cook if he seasoned the stew with dragon droppings."

Ashur threw the spoon across the room. His face was so red, Aric feared he might explode. But he obeyed. With a jump, Ashur stormed toward the food counter.

A moment later, a cook's fist fell between his eyes and Ashur collapsed.

⌒‿

"Oh! You should have seen it," Aric said. He was laughing so hard, tears rolled down his cheeks. "The cook didn't even say anything."

"Stop it!" Leth begged, holding on to his belly. "Please, stop it." He was rolling on the ground from one side to the other.

It took a while for the laughter to subside. They were back at the small balcony near the company's quarters. A cold wind blew in from the moonlit desert. Aric had gone there looking for his teammates but had found only Leth.

"Where did you guys go?" Aric asked when he finally found his breath. "I went back to the dining hall but you guys were gone."

Leth shrugged. "We finished eating and left. I didn't know how long you'd be."

"So... Where's Clea?"

"I don't know," Leth replied. "Sleeping, maybe."

"Already?" Aric asked.

That was too bad, Aric thought. *I guess I'll give her the flower tomorrow.*

"Hey, Leth…" Aric began hesitantly. "Do you mind if I ask you something?"

"What?"

Aric took a deep breath. "What do you think of Clea?"

Leth's expression froze for a moment, then he said, "Oh, I was not expecting that…" He cleared his throat. "I think… I think she's great."

"Yeah," Aric said, smiling. "I think so too." He paused. "Do you, hmm… Do you think I would have a chance with a girl like her?"

"With a girl like her?" Leth echoed. "I… I don't see why not."

That made Aric smile. "Thanks," he said. "I needed to hear that."

"Yeah, sure. No problem." There was a moment of silence. "So, what about the challenge? What are we up against this time?"

Aric rolled his eyes. "Oh, you're gonna love it," he said. "Saruk calls it 'Capture the Banner'. But it's really just an outright battle."

Leth leaned into Aric. "A battle?"

"Kind of. Apparently, on the topmost of the lower levels, there's this place they call the Gauntlet, which is some kind of…maze or something. And here is where it gets better. This Gauntlet is where recruits used to train before heading to the Frostbound."

"You're joking!"

Aric shook his head. "That's what I said. Do you know how Saruk replied?" He put on his best impression of Saruk with a deep frown and a hoarse voice. "*The Frostbound used to be a lot more dangerous, kid. There's no need for that these days.*"

"Unbelievable."

"So, apparently, they now use the Gauntlet to stage battles between recruits. Like the ancient fighting pits."

"What do you mean, *battle*?"

"What do you think I mean? We're gonna get the crap beaten out of us tomorrow; that's what I mean."

The next morning brought the cloudiest day Aric had ever seen in the desert. Clouds didn't necessarily mean rain; in fact, the odds of it were pretty low, but it did make the day feel oddly less warm.

Hardly anyone said anything as they dressed up. The two teams formed two separate blobs around each other as if they were afraid to look the others in the eyes. Aric explained the brief in a low voice, but he didn't really have enough information to come up with a strategy yet, so he simply told everyone to dress for a fight. And to prove that he meant it, instead of the usual standard-issue leather cuirass everyone else had, Aric put on his own dragon scale armor. He didn't like how the glowstone shards made the cuirass shine like a lighthouse in a foggy night, but even he had to admit it made him look threatening, and right now, that was useful.

A senior Hunter they hadn't met yet showed up in the company's quarters and quietly escorted them through the thick gate that led to the lower levels. Dozens of hunters were waiting for them downstairs, with Saruk at the head.

"Twenty-third Company," Saruk greeted them when both teams finished forming a double line. "Welcome to the Gauntlet."

Aric looked around, but there wasn't much to see. They were standing in some sort of antechamber with a very wide, grated door, like that of a disproportionally large prison cell. On the other side of the gate was a wide corridor from which dozens of other corridors fed.

"Five teams began this contest," Saruk continued. "Only two remain. Which means that by the end of this challenge, your company will have its captain. One that has earned his position, as is the Guild's custom. You will enter this gate divided, but you will emerge united under a single leader. Aric, Ashur, are you ready?"

"Yes, Instructor," came the unison reply.

"To win this challenge, you must capture the other team's banner and place it at this gate. You are not allowed to move your own team's banner, only your adversary's. The only weapons available to you are blind bombs." He removed a sphere the size of an orange from his pocket. "One of the most useful tools of a Dragon Hunter." Saruk threw the bomb a few inches into the air and caught it again. "Throw them against a wall or the floor and they shatter, releasing a cloud of white dust that will blind your opponents for a while. These things are capable of blinding a dragon, so yes, they sting like Ava's wrath, but they won't cause you any permanent harm. To ensure the rules are kept, Senior Hunters will be placed on watch points above the Gauntlet. They will monitor the entire challenge. Good luck."

With a nod from Saruk, the crowd of senior Hunters turned around and climbed the metallic ladders sticking out from the walls.

Aric looked to his left. Ashur was staring at the gate as if he wanted to tear it apart. That sort of grit was surely intimidating; it was exactly how Aric pictured the dozens of heroes in his family line. There was also the problem of numbers. Even with Trissa, Dothea, and Irenya, Aric's team was still three people short of Ashur's. But it was too late to do anything about that now.

The gate opened and Saruk waved them in. Silently, each team was guided toward one of the opposing corridors: Ashur's to the left, Aric's to the right. Inside, the Gauntlet felt like a mix between a maze and a cage. The stone walls were lit by occasional torches, just like everywhere else in the fortress, but instead of a ceiling, there was an iron grate, on top of which the senior Hunters walked around, standing watch. One of them directed Aric toward a room located on what seemed to be the edge of the Gauntlet.

"This is your base," the Hunter told them. He had hair locks growing as far down as his waist. "And that is your banner." He was talking about a blue banner hanging from a pole in the middle of the room. The banner had the number twenty-three written in every language of the Empire. "You cannot move it, but you can protect it. The blind bombs available to you are inside that wooden chest." It was the only other thing inside the room besides the banner. "Now get ready. At the sound of the horn, the challenge begins."

That had to be the scariest thing Aric had ever heard, and Aric had heard a dragon roar a few feet away from him. What was he supposed to do now? The whole team was staring at him, waiting for instructions. What should he say?

What would Maric Auron say?

He decided to inspect the wooden chest. It was packed full of spheres just like the one Saruk had shown them outside.

"Has anyone ever used one of these?" Aric asked.

Everyone told him that they hadn't, but Aric already knew that.

Stop stalling, you idiot!

"Okay," he said, clapping his hands together. "We are outnumbered, so we'll have to be bold." The reaction he got was far more enthusiastic than he would have expected. It felt good. "We need be on the offensive, grab the initiative." He paused, his eyes dancing and his fingers twitching. "We can't leave more than one person behind," he concluded. "Yes, we'll need everyone else on the attack." He paused and studied the faces available to him. "Trissa, I need that to be you."

"What do you mean?" Trissa asked.

"You'll stay behind," Aric explained. "I'm sorry. You'll be our only defense, but for this to work, I can't spare anyone else."

The black girl glared and exhaled loudly but ended up nodding in agreement. "Sure," she said. "Whatever you need."

"We'll leave you with most of the bombs," Aric continued. "If they come – or, rather, when they do – give them the wrath of Ava. I don't expect you to hold them forever, but every moment you delay them will be precious."

"Understood."

"What about the rest of us?" Leth asked. "Are we just going to attack them head on?"

"No," Aric replied, moving to the crate and starting to hand out the bombs. "I have an idea, but we'll need to scout them first."

"What is that?" Clea asked, lunging toward the weapons crate.

From under the pile of bombs, Clea dug out a bow and a quiver. There were also five arrows inside the quiver, but they were very odd, with a bulbous head instead of the usual metal tip.

"I've never seen anything like it," Aric said. "But if it involves a bow, you're definitely keeping it."

Everyone agreed. The only person that even came close to her in marksmanship was Orisius, but he was on Ashur's team, and even he had never come close to scoring as well as Clea in archery training.

"Those are blind bombs too," the Hunter above them said. "They're mounted on an arrow, but they're the same. Blind bombs are all you get in this challenge."

Aric nodded in understanding. Then the wail of a horn echoed though the walls.

"That's the signal," the Hunter told them. "You can leave your base now. Have fun."

Something about the way he said the last words made Aric shiver.

Moving his arms like lightning, Aric handed out the bombs. Trissa received ten while everyone else had to settle for two.

"Let's go," Aric called, dashing out. "Trissa, give them Ava's wrath."

"Don't worry," Trissa said, lobbing a bomb in the air. "This banner will cost them."

They ran through corridors lined with flickering torches. At every turn, Aric expected to run into Ashur and his team. He decided to swerve and circle right, trying to avoid the most direct route. The strategy didn't work.

"There!" they heard someone scream. It was Jullion. He had several people behind him, but the distance made it hard to tell exactly who and how many they were.

"Quick, this way!" Aric said, escaping through a narrow corridor.

"They're chasing us," Dothea grumbled. "Those idiots are chasing us instead of going for our banner."

She was right. Aric could hear their footsteps and shouts. Boy, were they loud.

"Crap!" Aric let out. "We're wasting time." He stopped, raising his hand, ordering the others to do the same. He gritted his teeth, struggling with what he had to do. "Damn this!" he exploded. "Leth, I need you to lead them away."

The Akhami boy stared back at Aric in silence, as if he needed to be sure Aric wasn't joking.

"You're serious," Leth said eventually.

"I am."

Leth's head fell lifelessly on his chest. "I hate my life," he muttered, then he quickly straightened up. "All right, boss. Here I go."

"Leth, wait," Aric called. "Here, take these." He handed Leth both of his blind bombs.

"Are you sure?" Leth asked.

"Of course I'm not sure. But take them anyway."

Leth stowed both blind bombs in the leather satchel on his back, nodded, then darted away. Moments later, they heard Jullion shriek, and the footsteps moved away, followed by the shouting.

Silently, Aric signaled his remaining team to follow him and pressed on. They sprinted down a series of hallways, checking every door to make sure they didn't miss the enemy base. Clearly, finding Ashur's banner was going to be harder than he had anticipated. Occasional screams echoed every once in a while, and Aric pictured Leth torturing Jullion across the Gauntlet's corridors. It made him smile.

He could do this, he thought. He *had* to.

A couple of turns later, they ran into a dead end, so Aric backed away. His sense of direction must have gotten confused, because when he got to what he thought was the corridor he had come through, he saw an open door from which someone's shadow stretched along the floor. Aric froze and shot both hands up, forcing his teammates to stop as well. Tiptoeing, they backtracked to hide behind a wall.

"That's their base," Aric whispered.

"How can you be sure?" Dothea asked, her voice just as low.

"Has to be," Aric replied.

"All right," Clea said. "What's your plan?"

Aric thought about it for a while, then: "I didn't get to count how many people were with Jullion when we ran into him, but I'm pretty sure Ashur will have at least four people defending his banner."

"Well, there's four of us right here," Irenya said. "Should we attack?"

"No," Aric told her. "It's too risky. What we need is a diversion."

"What do you mean?" Irenya asked.

"Dothea, Irenya," Aric said. "Could you two draw the defenders away?"

"Hmm." Dothea didn't look very pleased with that thought. "What happens if I say no?"

"I'll ask you to do it anyway," Aric replied.

"Then sure. We can do it."

Aric looked at Irenya for confirmation. The girl sighed but nodded as well.

"Okay," Aric said. "Go. Now."

After taking a couple of deep breaths, the two girls rushed out and Aric waited. His heart was pounding so hard he feared the others would hear it.

There was a crash, like the sound of a plate falling to the ground, followed by shouts, curses, and heavy coughing. Dothea shouted something and Irenya replied, adding to the mess of sounds.

"Where are they?" a rough voice asked from somewhere around the corner.

"I can't see squat!" another one complained.

"I see them!" That was clearly Prion. "Quick, after them!"

Aric peeked out from his hiding place and saw Nahir and Ergon chasing after a couple of fleeting shadows.

"Prion stayed behind," Aric whispered to Clea. "But I think he's alone."

"What now?" she asked.

"Ready your bow." Aric steeled himself. "I am going to run, and I am not going to stop, all right? Whatever happens, I will keep going until I am through that gate. Do you understand me?"

Clea gave him a comforting nod. "You can do this," she said.

Aric wanted to believe that as well. "I need you to stay close and keep them at bay as best as you can."

"They won't even see you," she told him, then smiled. "Get it?" She motioned toward the blind-bomb tip of one of her arrows. "They won't even *see* you."

Aric had to muffle his own laughter with a hand. Then he closed his eyes, took a deep breath, and reopened them.

I am not gonna let her down.

And off he went. He galloped down the hallway so fast that when Prion finally saw him come, Aric was already halfway there. The sight stunned Prion, but only for a brief moment. Aric saw him reach for his belt and grab a bomb.

This is going to hurt, he thought.

But it didn't. Prion never even had the time to throw it. One of Clea's arrows flew past Aric and exploded on the wall next to Prion, swallowing him in a white cloud of dust. All that was left of the guardian were his desperate screams.

Closing his eyes and holding his breath, Aric sprinted through the white cloud. When he reopened his eyes, he was standing in front of a red banner. It felt like conquering an enemy castle. Aric grabbed the banner and ripped it from the pole in one swift tug.

"I was waiting for you, half-prince."

That voice made every bone in Aric's body turn to frost. He swung around and saw Ashur standing in a corner, smiling like a bird of prey. He dove toward Aric, his hands reaching for the banner, but he never got to either of his targets.

Another one of Clea's arrows exploded right between Ashur's feet. This time, Aric was caught in the blinding haze as well. The burning made it impossible to so much as open his eyes, but he didn't care. He could still remember where the door was, so he ran toward it. His shoulders brushed against what was almost certainly Prion, then he turned right and kept going. With tears running down his face, Aric ran for a dozen paces until he inevitably slammed, headfirst, against a wall.

"Aric!" Clea shouted.

"Where to?" he asked.

"Left."

That was all he needed to know. Without slowing down even a bit, Aric obeyed and ran left.

"Now right," Clea shouted. She was following him closely.

Using the banner as a towel, Aric cleaned his eyes as best as he could, stumbling from one wall to another, using Clea's instructions to keep going. The question was: were they headed in the right direction?

Some shapes started to form as Aric's eyes cleared. Not enough to actually see what was in front of him, but enough to keep him from banging his head against the walls.

He reached a gigantic, square hall, much wider than any room he had been in yet. At least ten different corridors fed from it, and Aric looked from one to the other.

Panting, Clea finally caught up with him. "What happened to not stopping no matter what?" she asked.

"I…" Aric was having trouble coordinating his breathing with his speech. "I don't know where the gate is."

"There!" Aric heard someone yell.

It was Ashur again. He had somehow trailed him.

Cursing, Aric fled through a random corridor. Behind him, the sound of an arrow being fired was followed by the crackling sound of shattering stoneware.

"I think I missed!" Clea shouted.

"Hit them with another one!" Aric replied.

This time, there were painful screams when Clea fired her arrow, and Aric allowed himself to stop again when he reached a bifurcation.

"I'm down to my last one," Clea said as she caught up with Aric once again.

"What do you say, left or right?" Aric asked.

They had to be close to the exit now. They *had* to.

"How should I know?!"

"Just say one at random."

"Oh, goddess damn this," Clea complained. "All right, left."

Aric grabbed her hand and darted left.

This corridor was much narrower than the previous ones. It snaked left and right a couple of times until it turned into a straight line, at the end of which stood the grated gate that led outside the Gauntlet.

That was it. One final sprint and he would win.

Aric let go of Clea's hand and raced forward, his fuzzy eyes completely focused on that gate alone. Until he caught movement from the corner of his eyes.

His heart sunk for a moment, but then he recognized Leth. The Akhami had come through one of the several doors leading to the hallway and stopped midway between Aric and the gate. He looked at Aric, then over his shoulder.

"Oh, crap!" he said.

The meaning became instantly apparent. Jullion and the others were still chasing him, and he had just led them straight to Aric.

I'm not stopping for anything.

Roaring, Leth turned around and rammed Jullion to the ground, dragging Orisius and Athan with them. An instant later, an arrow landed next to them, wrapping the group in a thick white blob.

"I'm out," Clea shouted. "Run!"

But she didn't have to say it because nothing on this side of the sun or beyond it would stop Aric. He zoomed past the pile of blind recruits and saw the gate slide open.

Three more steps.

He tripped, lost his balance, and crashed spectacularly.

It didn't matter, however. He was already outside.

⌐

"You were incredible!" Clea said, her eyes glowing.

Aric was surrounded by the entire company, getting everyone's congratulations. Well, maybe not *everyone's*, but at least this time, Ashur wasn't barking at his own teammates for congratulating Aric. Even Prion and Jullion shook his hand.

"Good job," Leth told him, winking.

"Good job yourself!" Aric replied. "That was brilliant!"

Leth shrugged. "Well, you know me."

The two of them laughed, slapping each other's backs.

"Settle down," Saruk demanded, his hands in the air. "You'll have plenty of time to celebrate. In fact, you all get the day off."

The whole company howled as if a pile of gold had just been handed to them. Saruk asked for silence again.

"As I said, the celebration can be done later. Right now, your new captain needs to be sworn in."

"What does that mean?" Irenya asked.

"It means Aric needs to fill in an entry on the Guild's record about himself and the company," Tharius said before Saruk could answer.

"Wait," Jullion said. "You mean he has to write? What if Ashur had won? He can't write."

All recruits burst out laughing, except Ashur, who punched Jullion on the shoulder.

They all left, the mood far brighter than it had been on the way down.

Tharius had been right. Aric was escorted to the Grand-Master's office, where he was handed a massive tome. When he opened it, every page was blank. The only thing written on it had been engraved on the leather cover:

LOG
TWENTY-THIRD COMPANY OF DRAGON HUNTERS
FOURTH BANNER
UNDER CAPTAIN ARIC AURON

"Start by filling out the date," Sylene told him, handing him a quill and some ink. "Then state your name, date, place of birth, and, since you are a noble, ascendancy, rank, and place in line for the throne."

Aric started scribbling quietly but fast. Everyone was celebrating his victory and he was stuck in there.

"State that on this day you won the right to captain the company, then briefly describe each of your Hunters."

Aric's quill stopped. "Briefly describe?" he echoed. "What exactly should I say?"

"Ideally? Everything you know about them."

What?!

This was going to be a long day…

"This log is now your most important possession," Sylene said. "Upon your death, it will be taken to the Guild's records in the lower levels and added to our accumulated wealth of wisdom. You must register all of your experiences as a company. Omit as little detail as possible. You never know how many lives your words may one day save."

"Yes, madam," Aric replied, writing furiously fast.

The Grand-Master slammed the palm of her hand on the table in front of Aric. "I'm serious," she said. "This is one of your most sacred duties as a captain."

Aric held her stare. Her eyes were burning.

"I understand, Grand-Master," Aric said. "I do."

"Good," she said, slowly retracting her hand.

"Is this enough detail?" Aric asked. He had just finished describing Leth.

Sylene inspected the paragraph and snorted. "How did he react to your orders as your teammate?" she prompted. "How was his overall performance in each challenge? Does he eat a lot, wake up on time? Come on, Captain. Be specific."

Oh, dear goddess…

This was going to be worse than any class he had ever had in the Citadel, and it was, if not worse, certainly longer. By the time he was finally done describing the company to Sylene's liking, the sun was already setting. The day – his day – was gone.

He closed the log with a sigh and Sylene sent him on his way, finally congratulating him for the victory as she closed the door to her study.

Aric rushed to the company quarters, but instead of a large, ecstatic welcome, all he got was a white banner hanging from Skully's teeth. It said: Welcome to the Twenty-third Company – The Half-Princes.

"You like it?"

It was Trissa. She was in the common room, but she could see Aric standing in the vestibule from where she was sitting.

"Have we been officially named?" Aric asked, joining her in the common room. To his disappointment, there was no else in there.

"No," Trissa replied. "But that's what most of us think we should be named. We took a vote. 'The Desert Farts' nearly won."

Aric chuckled. "Sorry I left you alone out there."

"Are you kidding me? You guys did all the work; I just stood there."

"What do you mean?"

"No one came, Aric," Trissa said, smiling. "I just stood there waiting. The whole time."

"You're kidding me!"

The two of them burst out laughing.

"I'm serious," Trissa said, wiping away a tear. "I just sat there holding ten blind bombs and nothing happened."

"Oh, goddess…" Aric exhaled, gasping from the laughter. "Where is everyone?"

"Most of them have gone to sleep," Trissa said. "Dothea made Tharius drink an entire bottle of wine by himself. The poor guy passed out hours ago."

Aric grimaced. "What about Clea and Leth?"

"Hmm… I think I saw Clea on that balcony outside."

"Oh, yeah, I know the one." That was perfect. He could still give her the daisy. Tonight would be the perfect night to do it – *his* night. "There's this thing I need to discuss with her." Aric was already on his way out.

"Sure," Trissa said. "Hey, Aric?"

He turned. "Yes?"

"Congratulations."

Trissa smiled, and Aric found himself smiling back. He had never been this proud of himself.

With his chest swelling, Aric sauntered out of the company's quarters and headed for the balcony down the corridor. He tried to picture the moment and rehearsed his speech a couple of times. Carefully, he removed the daisy from the small pocket he had kept it in. The tiny flower had flattened a bit, but with some careful prodding, Aric restored the daisy to its former beauty. Clea would love it.

As he neared the balcony's threshold, he stopped, straightened his clothes, and ran his fingers through the curls of his hair. Finally, he cleared his throat and crossed out to the balcony.

The sight stopped him dead in his tracks, and for a moment, it was as if all the air had been sucked out of the world.

Leth and Clea were in each other's arms, lips touching.

A hand reached inside Aric and ripped out everything inside his chest. His whole body felt like a hollow casket.

At first, Leth and Clea didn't notice him, and Aric was too shocked to do or say anything. When the two of them finally noticed him, they caught the fright of their lives. Leth nearly fell off the balcony.

"Aric!" Clea squeaked.

"Ava's mercy," Leth said, gasping. "You want to kill us?"

"I…" Aric's mouth moved but nothing really came out. He put his hand behind his back and crushed the desert daisy between his fingers. "I'm sorry."

If Leth and Clea said anything else, Aric did not hear it. He just spun around and disappeared.

CHAPTER 13

The Lessons

The Legionary waved Fadan into the room. The man looked extremely uncomfortable with what he was doing, but not enough to disobey his orders.

Fadan walked inside and heard the lock clicking shut behind him. The room was quiet and peaceful, a gentle draft swaying the window's curtains. He walked to his bed and let himself fall onto the soft feather mattress, his eyelids suddenly impossibly heavy. He hadn't even realized how exhausted he was until this moment.

His mind drifted, surrendering to sleep, and soon he was dreaming about the tavern. He was inside, surrounded by a loud group of sailors, but the tavern looked exactly like the Imperial Palace's Great Hall. The sailors cheered, toasting with wooden mugs brimming with beer. They screamed at Fadan, laughing obscenely.

"Look at his boots."

"Look at his legs!"

"Ha! Skinny as a little girl."

"Pretty as one too."

Fadan wanted to leave, but the circle of sailors tightened around him as if the crowd was about to swallow him.

Three knocks on the door woke him up. Fadan looked around, his fuzzy eyes finding his room instead of the mocking sailors. He got up slowly, his leg muscles complaining from the effort. It felt like one of those mornings after a particularly painful session with the weapons master, but when he looked out his window and found the moon perched high above the Palace's towers, he realized that he had only been asleep for a couple of hours at most.

There were three more knocks on the door.

"Fadan, it's me."

The prince recognized his mother's voice coming from the other side of the wood. "Come in," he said.

The door creaked open and the empress glided inside. One of the Legionaries standing guard outside quickly closed the door behind her, and the two of them stared at each other in silence.

"You were sleeping?" Cassia asked awkwardly.

Fadan shrugged. "Not much else to do in here," he replied.

"Of course." The empress glanced around as if she hadn't been in this room thousands of times before. "I tried to soften your punishment as much as I could, but to be honest, for once I have to agree with your father." She stepped toward her son. "Why would you disappear like that, Fadan?"

Fadan sighed, looking down. "I already said I was sorry."

Cassia shook her head. "Aric used to be the rash one, not you."

Fadan walked to his window. "Even you are siding with him now?"

"What are you talking about? Fadan, you disappeared for *three* days!" She received no reply from her son. "Why are you doing this?" she asked. "Because you're angry? You think you're angrier than me?"

"I'm not *doing* anything," Fadan replied. "I came back, I apologized, and I've accepted my punishment. What else do you want?"

"I want you to be safe," Cassia said gently. "I want to make sure I don't lose another son."

"I've told you, you don't have to worry about me."

"Yes, you did tell me that," Cassia said. "And then you disappeared for *three days!*"

Fadan sighed. "I disappeared for two days and a few hours," he said. "And as you can see, I'm fine."

"Fine?! You have blood on the back of your head, Fadan."

"What?" The prince sent a hand behind his head and felt a crust of dry blood sticking to his hair.

Damn it!

"This is… This looks worse than it is…"

"Stop it!" Cassia demanded. "If you're going to lie to me, then I'd rather you stayed silent."

Fadan opened his mouth to say something but ended up obeying his mother.

"I've lost Aric," the empress said, her voice shaky. "I might lose Doric at any moment. Please, Fadan, I can't handle being afraid for you as well."

"You haven't lost Aric," Fadan said. "He's still alive."

And I've made him a promise, he thought. *Two, in fact.*

"Please, just promise me you won't do anything foolish," Cassia said, bringing her hands together in a plea.

Fadan swallowed. What was he supposed to do? He surely couldn't confess his plan.

"I… I promise," he ended up saying.

And there it was, another promise, though this time he didn't even intend to keep it.

⌒

For the first time in his life, the prince arrived at Macael's classroom before his tutor. The old man frowned at Fadan, already sitting in wait as he walked inside, but made no comment. The morning went by, and Fadan did a wonderful job pretending he was paying attention to the mathematics lesson, or, at least, he assumed he did. The truth was, the only lesson on his mind was of a very different kind.

After lunch, Fadan attended his history and philosophy classes, and this time, he was pretty sure both tutors realized he wasn't listening to a single word they said. Not that Fadan cared. He had far more important things to worry about, like how exactly he was going to flee his room with two guards stationed outside his door.

As the sun began to set, Fadan went for a walk, skirting the perimeter of the Core Palace. He used every trick he could think of to make sure that he would detect anyone who might be following him. He doubled back without warning three times, sneaked behind bushes after turning a corner, then waited for someone to come following him. He even used the blade of his knife as a mirror to check behind him.

Unable to shake the feeling that he was being watched, Fadan studied the wall outside his bedroom. The Imperial family's hallway was on the third floor of the Palace, which meant getting out through the window would require some climbing. Unlike other wings of the Palace, this wall had no odd bricks sticking in or out that could be used to climb. Everything was beautifully even. On the other hand, there were ribbon-like low relief sculptures framing the windows, as well as wooden window shutters, all of which could very likely handle Fadan's weight. These ledges of sorts were farther apart from each other than what would be ideal, but they could be used as a ladder.

The problem was, Fadan could bet there would be someone stationed outside his window that night. It had been the reason he had postponed his return to the Palace. For as long as his father remained angry at him, there would be people watching his every move.

Throwing one last glance around him, trying to notice if anyone was watching, Fadan left toward the Palace's main gate and, just as he turned a corner, bumped head first into someone.

It was Sagun. "Your Majesty, what are you doing here?"

Of course, Fadan thought. The Akhami Castellan had probably been looking for him.

"That's none of your business, Sagun," Fadan said.

"Ah, I see," Sagun said. "The prince has forgotten about his punishment. No wonder he's disobeying his father's orders."

"I'm not disobeying anything. I'm free during the day."

"I'm afraid Your Majesty is only free to attend your classes, nothing else."

Fadan did not reply this time. He stood there, holding Sagun's stare.

"Will Your Majesty allow me to escort him back to his room?" the Castellan asked after a moment.

"I know the way back to my room, Sagun. I'm sure you can make yourself useful somewhere else." And with that, Fadan brushed past the castellan.

Grumbling something inaudible, Sagun followed the prince back to the Palace but made sure to keep a few respectable paces of distance. Fadan considered running and disappearing through one of the myriad corridors of the Imperial residence, but he was trying to keep a low profile. And with good reason. Besides, it wouldn't be long before nightfall. His waiting was nearly at an end.

Back in his room, Fadan did not have to wait long before the Legionaries escorted him back down to the Great Hall for dinner.

Lord Fabian was one of the guests that evening, along with the rest of House Lagon, a pompous group of men and women who droned on and on about commercial rights contracts, financial investments, and tax exemptions. No one would have guessed how fabulously rich they were, considering their ceaseless complaints. Apparently, the market was dreadful nowadays.

Other guests included the Count of Belleragar and his wife, seven high-ranking officers from the Paladins, and most of House Portar-Ravella, which included a niece of Lord Calva named Livia, a pretty, blond girl from Aparanta who was visiting the Citadel for the first time in years. The girl spent the whole meal sending Fadan odd stares. By the time the prince was done with dessert, he looked redder than the raspberry pudding.

As dinner approached its end, the courtesans rose. Not to leave, though. Imperial dinners were usually divided into two phases. Fadan thought of them as the public and the private dinners. During the first, everyone sat together at the table, while in the latter, guests mingled in smaller groups. Tiny tables, covered with all sorts of liqueurs, brandies, and vermouths, were set inside the open-sided hallway built around the hall. Guests casually walked around, gathering for more discreet conversations over a glass of some exotic beverage. This part of dinner was exactly what courtesans looked most forward to. In fact, for some of them, it was the only reason to ever come. The curious thing, Fadan found, was that for the first time in his life, he had actually been looking forward to it as well.

"Lord Fabian," Fadan greeted the old soldier after dodging one of Livia's approaches. "So nice to see you."

Fabian and a small group of his cousins bowed. "Your Majesty," he said.

"Remember the conversation we had the other day?" Fadan asked. "About military logistics in the northwestern campaigns?"

"Of course," Fabian replied.

"I have to say, I found the subject fascinating," Fadan mused. "I wonder if you could elaborate further on the matter."

"It would be my pleasure, Your Majesty," Fabian said.

Sensing a boring conversation, Fabian's small entourage immediately excused themselves. They hadn't come to the Citadel to entertain the prince.

Fadan waited until they were alone. "I'm going to need your help," he said.

"Already?" Fabian asked.

Fadan shrugged. "I need to be somewhere tonight, and as you may have heard, my freedom of movement is…" He looked at Sagun, hunching next to the emperor across the hall, whispering something in his ear. "Let's say *limited.*"

"May I ask where you must go with such urgency?"

Fadan shook his head. "I'm sorry," he said. "Also…it's not just for tonight."

Fabian frowned.

"It'll be every night from now on," Fadan continued.

"You're going to make me regret helping you," Fabian said.

"Can I count on you or not?" Fadan asked.

Fabian exhaled loudly. "You'll need to come out through your window," he said.

"I had figured as much. What I don't know is if my window is being watched."

"It is," Fabian replied, "but I can handle it. Wait by your window. No candles or lamps. I'll signal when the coast is clear, so pay attention to the courtyard."

"I will," Fadan agreed, nodding.

The Count of Belleragar walked by and the two of them fell silent, politely greeting him.

"I assume you can find your way once you're out of your room," Fabian said when the Count was gone, "and that you'll be back before morning. Otherwise, there is nothing I'll be able to do to help."

"Don't worry, I will. But how will I know if the coast is clear when I do?" Fadan asked.

"Just make sure you're back before dawn," Fabian replied. "I'll take care of the rest. If the worst happens, we'll just say you were out seeing some girl." He motioned toward the statue of a general beside which Livia stood, staring penetratingly at Fadan. "Which is what you should be doing anyway."

Fadan blushed. He saw the girl smile, then start toward him. Like a cornered animal, the prince looked around. Where had Fabian gone? He swallowed.

Oh, goddess.

⌒⸲

"You're late," Sabium said as Fadan walked into the house.

The old mage was sitting in an old rocking chair, its wood creaking each time he swayed himself back and forth. Candles burned here and there, casting flickering shadows across the entirety of the apartment.

"I got delayed," Fadan replied, closing the door. "This girl just wouldn't let go of me."

"Poor you."

"It's not like that," the prince said. "I wasn't interested in her at all. I would've gotten here sooner if I had managed to ditch her, believe me."

"Well, you should've ditched *me* instead. I can promise you'll regret you didn't." Sabium pushed himself up, flinching from the effort, then ambled to one of his wooden chests. "Alas, that's what youth is. An opportunity for stupidity." He began rummaging inside the chest.

"What is old age, then?" Fadan asked, annoyed. "Confusing hindsight with wisdom?"

Sabium looked at Fadan, narrowing his eyes. "Yes," he replied after a while. "And complaining a lot. Here, put this around your neck." He handed Fadan a strange wooden necklace.

Fadan obeyed. "What is it?" he asked.

"A young mage's lifeboat," Sabium explained.

It was an ugly old thing. Unevenly shaped wooden plates with glowstone shards encrusted on them, all tied together by rusty metal rings that looked about snap.

"It's called a transmogaphon," Sabium continued. "The spells on those shards will help me monitor your progress and, most importantly, keep you from killing yourself. You are to wear this anytime you practice magic, especially if I'm not around, but be careful. Paladins are trained to recognize transmogaphons. Conceal it as best you can." Sabium grabbed a runium flask from a drawer, drank half of it, and handed the rest to Fadan. "Bottoms up."

Red strands swirled inside the metallic liquid as Fadan looked through the vial's glass, frowning. The last time he had drunk runium, the experience had been less than enjoyable. The prince took a deep breath, then swallowed the reddish liquid in a single gulp. A burning sensation spread though his body, and he began breathing out blue puffs. He braced himself for the overwhelming experience he had been through the last time, but nothing else happened. His vision remained the same, his mind stayed clear, and there was no loss of balance.

"Surprised?" Sabium asked.

"Yes," Fadan replied. "The last time I felt...powerful. A little overwhelmed but powerful."

"Powerful?" Sabium chuckled. "Well, wine will do that to you as well. It's the transmogaphon." Sabium pointed at Fadan's chest. The glowstone shards were glowing powerfully. "It's keeping you balanced, keeping the runium's effects in check. Which reminds me. Do you have a place to practice in the Citadel?"

Fadan confirmed it with a nod.

"Good," Sabium continued. "Practice as much as you can, but always remember to bring the transmogaphon back to me so I can recharge it. Each time I do, I will make the spells weaker, until there is no magic in the transmogaphon at all. This way, you will learn to control runium and magic intuitively."

Fadan nodded.

"Now, some ground rules," Sabium continued. "Rule number one. I talk, you listen. If you have a question, raise your hand, but *never* interrupt me. Never.

"Rule number two. Don't pretend you understand something if you don't. You'll be wasting both our time if you're just waving your arms around like an idiot, not really sure what you're supposed to be doing.

"And finally, rule number three. Never be late again. I don't care if half the damsels in the Empire are after you. I'm not one of your servants, and magic isn't your fresh new hobby. It is the grandest of human endeavors, and you will show adequate respect." Sabium paused, but his frown did not soften. "Understood?"

"Yes," Fadan replied.

"Yes, *Master*," Sabium corrected.

"Yes, Master."

"Good. Let's move on. I remember you saying you had a book on magic; is that correct?" Sabium asked.

Fadan nodded.

"Then you must know a thing or two about magic already," Sabium said. "In theory, at least."

Fadan smiled uncomfortably. "I'm afraid I don't. To be honest, the book read like gibberish."

Sabium rolled his eyes. "Of course it did." He began pacing along the room. "From the start, then. What is Magic?" Obviously, no answer came from Fadan, but Sabium didn't look like he was expecting one anyway. "Magic is the ability to manipulate, control, or change things, material or otherwise, through will alone. Conversely, magic is *not* the ability to do it permanently. This is why spells stored inside glowstone shards wear off with time. Yes?"

Fadan's hand had just shot into the air.

"You said through will alone, but that's not true," Fadan said. "Runium is required."

Sabium stopped pacing. "Correct. Runium is the fuel which your will must burn for it to produce magic. In fact, the amount of runium in your system determines how much magic you are allowed to cast. Simple spells, like moving a pebble, will consume very little runium. Moving a mountain, on the other hand, would take more runium than any man or woman could possibly consume."

"What about experience?" Fadan asked. "Are we able to learn how to use our runium more efficiently with experience?"

"Yes and no. All beginners tend to be clumsy in the way they burn runium, but it doesn't require full mastery of the magical arts to burn runium at optimal efficiency. What experience, and most importantly, knowledge grant you is the ability to cast more sophisticated spells. You see, any idiot can set a house on fire, but it requires a degree of finesse to gently warm up every cup of tea in a party."

"So…how exactly do I do it?" Fadan asked.

"We will begin with a simple exercise." Sabium grabbed his rocking chair and dragged it in front of Fadan, then placed the empty vial of runium on top of its seat. "I want you to move that flask."

Fadan's eyebrows jumped in the air. "Using my will?" he asked skeptically.

"Using your will," the old mage echoed.

"All right," Fadan said, relaxing his arms. "Here goes,"

A slew of wrinkles appeared on the prince's forehead as he frowned and gritted his teeth. His eyes narrowed, focusing on the tiny piece of glassware.

Move, he thought.

"No, no, no," Sabium said. "I don't even need to read your mind to know you're doing it wrong."

"You can read my mind?" Fadan asked, suddenly worried.

"I'll teach you how to protect yourself from that later, but don't worry, I'm not doing it. I can *tell* you're giving orders. Don't you see how ridiculous that is? Even if you could already perform a spell as complex as telepathy, that is a flask. An inanimate object. It can't understand human language. You have to *will* it."

"What does that even mean?" Fadan asked heatedly.

Sabium raised his hands. "All right, calm down," he said. "There's no need for this to be frustrating."

Oh, really? Fadan thought. *Who would've known.*

Calmly, Sabium walked behind Fadan and placed a hand on his shoulder. "Close your eyes. Try to visualize the chair in front of you. Do you see it?"

"Sure."

"Imagine it exactly as it is. How far away is the chair from you?" Sabium asked.

"A couple of feet," Fadan replied.

"Very good. Now I want you to visualize the rest of the room. The hardwood floor beneath our feet, stretching toward the chair. The cabinets lining the walls. The bed at the other end of the room. Do you see it?"

"I do," Fadan replied.

"Excellent," Sabium said. "Now visualize the vial sliding across the seat of the chair. It doesn't matter which direction it slides; just chose one at random and watch it move. That's right, very good." He slapped Fadan on his back. "Now open your eyes."

Fadan obeyed, and his jaw dropped. The flask had moved a couple of inches to the left and was now teetering on the brink of falling to the ground, just as he had pictured in his mind.

"That wasn't so hard, was it?" Sabium asked.

"I... I moved it," Fadan mumbled.

"You certainly did," Sabium said, stepping toward the chair. "I actually expected you to shatter the flask. It's what most people do on their first attempt. Don't let that go to your head, though. Some of my best students showed no potential whatsoever when they were beginning, and I can also remember a couple of worthless mages who could have rearranged this whole room's furniture on their first lesson."

"So, you mean each mage has a different amount of…what, aptitude?" Fadan questioned.

"Oh, yes," Sabium replied. "We are all made differently. Some of us are smart; some of us are dumb as a doorknob. Some of us have a knack for music, others for physical tasks. Why would it be any different with magic? Having the Talent means you can use runium for more than just hallucinating, but not all mages are equally powerful. Some people are born to be Arch-Mages. Others will never be more powerful than the average Novitiate."

Fadan nodded. That certainly made sense. "What was your rank?" he asked.

Sabium grabbed the chair and dragged it back into its place, staring at nothingness. "I was ordained Grand Sorcerer, first class, three weeks before the Purge edict was issued." He cleared his throat. "Let's carry on. I want to teach you to cast fire. The technique is —"

Sabium was interrupted by a cacophony of tumbling crates and cracking wood from outside the apartment. Both Sabium and Fadan froze.

"You were followed," Sabium hissed.

Fadan shook his head. "No," he said. "That's not possible."

"This was stupid," Sabium growled, marching toward the door with a closed fist and a blue aura glowing around him. "We've doomed us both."

"I…" Fadan staggered back. "It can't be."

Sabium grabbed the doorknob, sparks flying from his free hand. He swung the door open, far too fast for his age, then jumped outward.

"You?" Sabium asked.

Fadan stood on tiptoes, trying to look outside, but saw nothing besides the dark shape of his master. Someone replied something inaudible, and Sabium turned around to face Fadan.

"Look who came for a visit," the old mage said, pushing someone's bulky shape into the house.

Alman came stumbling in, looking like a brat who had just been caught doing something he shouldn't.

"You were supposed to stay away," Sabium added, this time speaking to his brother.

Fadan shook his head, crossing his arms. "I knew it… I shouldn't have trusted you."

"I was just curious," Alman said. "I wanted to see how you were doing, that's all. I wasn't going to interrupt or anything."

"Except you *did*," Sabium grumbled, sinking into his chair.

"Well, I tripped," Alman said. "Have you seen the mess you have outside? You should really tidy up a bit."

"This is ridiculous," Fadan said, walking to a corner and picking up his cloak. "I'm leaving."

"No!" Alman begged. "I'll leave. You stay."

"There's no point, you know?" Fadan said. "You think you can persuade me to join your rebellion? I know that's why you want me to learn magic, but you're wasting your time."

The prince stormed to the door, but Alman stepped in front of him. "Please wait," the old man said. "You're right, I shouldn't have come, but there is nothing for you to be mad at. I do want you to join us, but only to do what you already plan to."

Had the old man lost his mind?

"What are you talking about?" Fadan asked. "I have no intention of conspiring against my father."

"I'm talking about releasing Doric and the other prisoners," Alman replied. "The rebellion is planning a rescue operation."

"A rescue operation?" Fadan asked. "In the Citadel dungeons? Are they *mad*?"

"Are you?"

"That's completely different," Fadan said. "I'm the prince. I'm supposed to be in the Citadel."

"But not in the dungeons," Alman said. He stepped toward Fadan. "You and your brother already tried to release Doric once and failed. You *need* our help."

Fadan stepped away from Alman. "How do you know that?"

"We have an agent in the Paladins," Alman replied. "We know the guard rotation, what cells the prisoners are being kept in, I could even tell you what they had for breakfast yesterday. We already have a plan, but we're missing someone else on the inside. Someone who knows the Citadel and can move freely about. Someone who could hide us in one of the empty palaces both before and after the rescue."

"After?" Fadan asked, confused.

Alman smiled. "Exactly," he replied. "Hiding. That's what you and your brother did wrong. You went for the exits, and that's exactly what they were counting on. The moment the alarm was sounded, you had only one shot at not being found."

"That's ridiculous," Fadan said, but he didn't sound too sure of himself. "They will look everywhere, even the empty palaces, I'm sure."

"Are you? If you could keep us supplied with food and water, we could remain hidden under the emperor's nose until the dust settled. It might take a week, maybe a month, who knows, but it *could* be done. And in the meantime, the Paladins will be running around like headless chickens, trying to find us in all the wrong places."

The prince did not reply. He shuffled his feet, his hands fidgeting restlessly, then glanced at Sabium, who refused to return his gaze.

"I'm..." Fadan sighed, turning back to Alman. "I'm sorry. It just feels wrong. I can't help you. You'll need to find someone else." He looked at Sabium once again. "Am I excused, Master?"

The old mage gave Fadan a wave and the prince fled out the door without so much as looking at Alman, leaving the two siblings alone in the twilight of Sabium's candles.

"You just couldn't give it up, could you?" Sabium asked after an overlong pause.

"No," Alman replied, heading for the apartment's door. "That would be your department." He slammed the door behind him.

CHAPTER 14

The Blood Carriers

Aric's first day as captain of the Twenty-third Company had begun mostly without incident. Saruk had decided that they should start out slow, giving Aric a simple half-day desert patrol. Nothing the recruits couldn't handle. Aric's troubles, however, had more to do with his unexpected encounter the previous night.

All recruits had gathered at the fortress's main gate, getting ready to move out, when Leth tried to give Aric a morning greeting. Without stopping his inspection of the company's gear, Aric simply looked the other way and pretended not to hear him.

Soon, the company was on the move and Aric got to empty his mind with the race across the sand and the vastness of the desert. It was funny how a place this dangerous could feel so calm and peaceful. Later, during a short resting pause under the shadow of a tall ridge, Leth approached Aric.

"Can we talk?" he asked.

"Pull your scarf up," Aric replied. "You'll dehydrate faster if you don't cover your mouth." Then he turned his back and signaled the company to move out.

Leth, however, wasn't about to give up that easily. The patrol ended shortly before nightfall. As soon as they arrived, some of the recruits dove straight for the water fountain in the fortress's lobby while others shook sand off their clothes. Leth neared Aric as he took off his weapons and laid them in a small pile.

"Aric?" Leth said. "Aric, can we please talk?"

Leth received only a quick glance.

"Tharius," Aric called. "You're on weapons duty today. Get everyone's blades to the storage room." He received a 'Yes, Captain', then turned around and walked away.

Groaning, Leth chased him. "I was talking to you," he said. "I know you heard me."

"Yeah," Aric replied at last without slowing down. "I've noticed your sudden interest in talking," he said. "Too bad you didn't feel like that sooner."

"What is that supposed to mean?" Leth asked.

"Well…" Aric said as he began to climb the great staircase leading to the dining hall. "You had plenty of opportunities to let me know about you and Clea. But I suppose it was a lot more fun to watch me make a fool of myself."

"There was nothing to let you know about when we last talked."

"Oh, no, of course not," Aric said. "The two of you just developed a relationship overnight."

"Actually, yes. That's kind of what happened."

Aric rolled his eyes so far up, they nearly disappeared into the back of his head. "Right," he said, turning his back on Leth and pushing the door to the dining hall open.

"Will you grow up for a moment?" Leth asked.

"Oh, so now I'm a child?" Aric chuckled. "Is that because I thought I could trust you, or because I asked for your advice?"

"Listen to me," Leth said, stabbing Aric's chest with a finger. "I did nothing wrong." At that moment, the rest of the company walked into the dining room as well and Leth was forced to lower his voice. "You're mad at me because you like a girl and she chose me instead. Well, I'm entitled to like her as much as you, so deal with it."

"Is something wrong?"

It was Clea. She had walked up behind Leth. Aric froze, unable to answer.

"Everything's fine," Leth assured her. "We were just…discussing an issue with today's patrol." He turned to Aric. "Will you take what I've said into consideration, Captain?"

Aric didn't reply right away. "I don't think we were talking about the same issue. Now, if you'll excuse me, I'm getting something to eat."

Aric mindlessly filled a tray with flatbread, dried dates, and some cheese he didn't even like. Calculating how far he could sit away from Leth, he walked to the company's usual table to find them huddled around something instead of sitting down as always.

"Is anything wrong?" Aric asked.

"Look, Aric," Clea said. "Tharius found it in the weapons storage room."

"It was on one of the top shelves," Tharius confirmed. "Behind a sharpening wheel."

Pushing Prion out of the way, Aric found what that fuss was all about – a lagaht board.

"I bet you and Leth are really good at it," Tharius told Aric, his eyes gleaming.

"Yeah," Clea agreed. "It would be really exciting to see a match between two serious players."

"What do you expect will happen?" Leth asked Clea and Tharius. "Just because we're nobles doesn't mean fireworks will go off every time we make a move. Besides, I don't think Aric will want to play."

"Aww, I'm sure he would," Clea said. "Wouldn't you, Aric? I bet you would love to beat Leth's ass." She smiled.

It made Aric smirk. "Oh, I wouldn't mind that."

"As if," Leth said, shaking his head.

"You think you can beat *me?*" Aric asked.

Leth didn't answer right away. Slowly, he looked at Aric and said, "Wouldn't be the first time I beat you at something."

Aric's eyes narrowed. "Tharius, take the board out."

There was a collective cheer. Clea even clapped. The two players sat across from each other as Tharius placed the lagaht board between them. The company gathered around, and even some senior Hunters eating nearby joined them, looking curious.

"Looks fancy, doesn't it?" Tharius said, placing the game materials on the table.

"Looks like Samehrian dung," Leth replied.

Aric was forced to agree. This was certainly not the kind of board made for a duke or an emperor. It was an ugly old thing, with washed-out paint and ridiculous woodcraft. The horses had bulgy, disproportionate eyes; the spears looked mostly like swords, and the swords looked mostly like spears. Not to mention that every single piece was chipped in places or outright missing something. Its problems, however, weren't merely esthetic.

The deck of spell cards, for example, was extremely small, with only forty cards, the bare minimum allowed in a lagaht board. The cards themselves were also as bland as lagaht spell cards could get. Aric flipped through the deck three times and didn't find a single one that could really make a difference. Then, there was the layout of the board itself, an extremely basic design with only a couple of choke points. The sort of board that would make for predictable matches after a while. Still, since none of them had ever played on it, that shouldn't be much of a problem. And, at the very least, it did look fairly balanced.

Well, at least this way, he can't complain about luck.

That had always been Fadan's excuse. What Fadan had never known, however, was that Aric had read just about every single book on lagaht in the Citadel's library. Some of them twice.

"I shuffle, you cut?" Leth asked.

"Sure."

The cards moved swiftly between Leth's fingers. He had obviously had a lot of practice. Then, with a thump, Leth placed the deck down and Aric cut it. It was a rushed movement, and Aric regretted it immediately. He had just split the deck into two highly uneven piles, one being at least twice as big as the other.

Leth chuckled. "Well, well… Someone's feeling confident," he said. "Suit yourself; I'm not stupid." He promptly grabbed the taller pile of cards.

Making a huge effort to hide his gritting teeth, Aric grabbed the remaining pile of cards and flipped through them. Thirteen cards. Thirteen lousy cards. It didn't give him much choice, considering he could only keep ten. Still, there wasn't any point in complaining now. The overall quality of the deck was so bad that the lack of choice would hardly make much of a difference.

After discarding the three spell cards he felt were least useful, Aric began laying out his pieces on the board. He picked the blue pieces, took them out of their wooden case, and then used the case as a screen to keep Leth from peeking at his formation.

Aric had decided on a strategy the moment he had seen the board, so it didn't take him long to knock on the table, signaling he was ready. It also meant he would get to move first. Leth, on the other hand, had decided to take his time. He carefully placed his pieces one by one, arranging and rearranging them over and over again.

"Think you'll be ready before dawn?" Aric asked.

"I'm almost done."

Aric made a sleepy face and pretended to yawn.

"Only fools trade moving first for a better starting position," Leth retorted.

It made Aric roll his eyes. This was typical of players who thought they were better than they really were. Fadan was the same, confusing indecision with thoughtfulness.

At last, Leth signaled he was ready and the two of them revealed their formations. Leth had clearly gone for an aggressive approach, with most of his horses at the front.

He's going to rush for the center choke point, Aric thought.

The logic was sound. Controlling that choke point was key to victory on a board like this, and horses did have the most movement of all three kinds of pieces. But without cover from other units, horses were useless. Aric's spears would make short work of those horses if they found them isolated.

Which means he built a hand to protect horses.

And there it was. Leth hadn't even made a move and Aric already knew exactly how the game would play out. This was the problem with players like Fadan and, apparently, Leth. They always overplayed their smartness.

The initial rounds played out without incident as both armies marched forward. As predicted, Leth moved his cavalry forward, rushing to the choke point.

Not wishing to disappoint him, Aric sent some spears to meet Leth's horsemen.

Always good to allow an enemy to commit to the wrong strategy.

The first pieces began to fall as Leth's cavalry clashed with Aric's spearmen. This was also the moment the first spell card came into play. As always, the card's instructions were simple but effective – *Enemy spears cannot move for two consecutive turns.* It saved some of Leth's cavalry, but not for very long.

Dead pieces piled around the board as they were removed from play. The initial orderly formations had been replaced by an apparent mess of blue and red pieces. Aric played a card that allowed him to teleport three pieces and used those to punish Leth's rear. It wasn't the final blow yet, but it wreaked havoc on Leth's lines.

Then, suddenly, the balance seemed to shift. Although outnumbered, Leth's forces remained fairly balanced, with the same number of each kind of piece. On the other hand, while Aric's cavalry remained intact, he had lost most of his swords and spears. To compensate, Aric was forced to spend several spell cards protecting his vulnerable pieces.

Aric looked across the board and found Leth smirking at him. Had he purposefully sacrificed numbers in order to get Aric off-balance? That smirk certainly said yes.

We'll see who laughs last.

This wasn't the ideal situation Aric had planned for, but then again, no plan ever played out exactly as predicted. The game was still well within his reach.

"Been a good game so far, hasn't it?" Aric asked, smiling.

Leth shrugged, smiling as well. "Can't complain."

"If you don't mind, I'm going to finish it now."

"By all means," Leth said.

Aric was going to have fun wiping that smirk off his face.

He played his final card, allowing six of his pieces to traverse mountains – impassable terrain. The plan was deliciously simple: use that card to send his abundant cavalry around the choke point Leth controlled, and smash the swords Leth had been carefully protecting beyond it. From there, the game would be all but finished.

A frown grew above Leth's eyes as the stratagem unfolded. He could obviously see what was about to happen. He made some adjustments, retreating a couple of spears and horses, but it was useless. Those units would never get there in time. Leth's army was doomed. Aric could only smile.

Then, at the last moment, as Aric prepared to charge, Leth played his last spell card as well.

"I turn my swords into spears," he said, holding the card at Aric's eye level.

"What?" Aric mumbled.

"That's right. Your entire cavalry force is as good as dead, and my army is free to hunt down what little is left of yours." Chuckling, Leth placed the card on the table and leaned back. "But you don't have to be dragged on hopelessly for the next few turns. You can just yield."

"That's not possible," Aric said, livid.

Leth didn't reply, though. He simply shrugged smugly.

"You cheated!" Aric yelled, jumping to his feet.

"What?"

"You sneaky rat! You reached into the deck while I wasn't watching."

"I did no such thing!" Leth replied, getting onto his feet as well. "You take that back right now."

"How else would you possibly have that precise card at this precise moment?!" Aric asked. He swung around, looking for support. "Did anyone see it? Did anyone see him reach for the deck?"

"You're pathetic!" Leth said. "Did you consider just for a moment that I might have planned this from the start?"

"Impossible. You'd have used that card by now if you had had it from the start."

"What a spoiled little brat you are," Leth said.

"And you're just a selfish, greedy narcissist who'll do anything for his own gain."

It was as if an arrow had been fired at Leth's heart. His arms fell, and all color abandoned his face. "Take that back," he said lowly. "You take that back right now."

But Aric wasn't going to. Instead, he stepped forward defiantly. "Admit you are a cheat."

"You know what?" Leth asked, disgust twisting the corners of his mouth. "You're just a pitiful little guy that knows nothing except feeling sorry for himself. But I suppose that's all your mommy had to teach you."

Aric's eyes went blank with rage, his face turned red, and a ringing began in his ears. With a jump, he lunged over the table, stomping over the lagaht pieces and diving toward Leth's neck.

The two of them crashed to the ground, rolling over each other, punching and kicking until a group of senior Hunters jumped in and separated them.

Aric could barely see. He tried to free himself, but the choke hold the Hunter was using on him didn't give him a chance. Leth was beyond his reach.

⟵⟶

The wounds on Aric's face had gone sore a little while before. He could feel a lump growing on his lower lip that made it hard to close his mouth, but at least the sickening taste of iron from the blood was gone.

The door opened and Saruk peeked inside.

"Are you hungry?" he asked.

Both Aric and Leth replied with a suspicious yes.

"Good," the instructor said, then slammed the door shut again.

Leth cursed. "How long have we been in here?"

Aric didn't say anything; he just looked the other way.

"Oh, right, you're not talking to me now." Leth sighed. "You're the one who hit me first, you know? If anything, *I* shouldn't be talking to *you.*" Once again, Aric didn't reply. "All right, fine. I shouldn't have said those things. I'm sorry. But for the record, I did not cheat. I just goaded you from the beginning. It's your own damn fault for underestimating me." He felt his left cheekbone and flinched from the pain. He would have flinched even further if he could have seen how purple it had turned.

"I'm sorry too," Aric muttered at last, his eyes on the ground.

Leth tried to hide his shock. "Good," he said.

"No, it's not," Aric continued. "I was an idiot. I mean, I was just… I don't know what came over me." He was having a hard time deciding what to say. "I know you didn't cheat. And…yeah, I think we both know what my problem was."

Leth nodded. "Well…I did play a really good match," he ended up saying after a bit. It managed to make Aric laugh, and Leth looked obviously pleased with that. "Listen, I know this doesn't change much, and you'll still feel like crap but… That kiss you saw, between me and Clea… It really did come out of the blue. I don't think she was expecting it any more than I was. We haven't even talked about it yet."

"What do you mean?" Aric asked, finally getting the courage to turn and face Leth.

Leth shrugged as if he was baffled. "After you saw us, we just stood there like a couple of idiots, staring at our hands and feet until one of us had the brilliant idea to say 'I guess I'm going to sleep now' and we left."

Aric chuckled.

"I'm serious," Leth said. "I can't even remember who said it."

Aric's chuckle turned into laughter and Leth joined him. Then, suddenly, the door swung open and Saruk appeared on the other side.

"Am I interrupting something?" the instructor asked. He didn't really give them a chance to reply. "Out. Get out."

They had been locked in that little cupboard in Saruk's office for what felt like hours now. Without another word, the instructor escorted them out and across the halls, taking them through the narrowest, darkest tunnels they had ever been through inside Lamash. Then, after climbing down a couple flights of stairs, a shrill scream echoed around them, freezing them. Even the flickering flames of the torches seemed to cower at the sound.

"Who told you to stop?" Saruk asked, a murderous look in his eyes.

Leth and Aric exchanged a glance. Aric didn't know what Leth was thinking about, but he had a pretty good guess it was running away. Then, a second, even more terrifying scream almost persuaded him to really do it, but Saruk reached out, grabbed them both by their collars, and tossed them through a door.

The two recruits landed on the stone floor, screams filling the room around them. Aric looked up and saw a man being held down on a black table, blood dripping from him and over the table's edge like a waterfall.

"What the —"

"Don't you even dare," Saruk said, forcing him and Leth to not look away.

The sight was disturbing. The man being held down had a horrible gash across his abdomen and another man had both his hands deep inside of it, blood reaching up to his elbows. All five people holding the man down had wounds of their own, with so much blood everywhere, it was impossible to tell whose it was.

Aric felt like puking, but he kept it in as best as he could. That man was clearly about to die; the least Aric could do was not to throw up on the people who were trying to save him.

The wounded man's screams became even higher-pitched and his howling turned hoarser and hoarser until he passed out. At least it made him become still, which helped the surgeon finish his job. The rip in the man's flesh was sewn closed and then washed with something that, from the smell of it, had to be the strongest liquor in all Arkhemia.

Saruk kneeled in front of his recruits, their eyeballs ready to jump out.

"This isn't over for him yet," the instructor said. "If this man is lucky, the wound won't infect and he will survive. And that's hoping he didn't lose too much blood. In any case, the next few weeks will be nothing but pain for him. But there is more. Next door, there is another Hunter getting his leg sawed off. And somewhere down in the Main Hall is a dead woman everyone's been too busy to carry away."

Aric could only swallow.

"This" – Saruk aimed a finger at the gasping, bleeding, cringing Hunters behind him – "is the life of a Dragon Hunter. This is *your* life. You might not have chosen it, but it's what you have. One day, you'll have to step inside a dragon's lair too, and when that day comes, all you'll have is each other. That's it. So you better learn −"

"I'm the sole responsible," Aric said, cutting Saruk off. "I hit Leth; he was simply trying to defend himself."

Saruk nodded. "Good," he said, getting on his feet.

Both recruits followed him up.

"Instructor," Leth said, "That's not really what −"

"Shut up!" Saruk barked. "Your captain has assumed responsibility, as is his duty. So shut up and get out of my sight."

"I −"

"NOW!"

Not looking very pleased with it, Leth turned around and left.

"You will stay here," Saruk told Aric, "and help these people."

Aric nodded obediently.

"When that is done, you will return to your company and let them know that tomorrow you will all be doing a Blood Run. You will load all blood crates in the stockpile onto horse carts, take them to Nish, and unload them at the Bloodhouse. All by yourselves. No one will give you any help whatso-ever. You will let your company know this is *your* punishment and that they are all paying for something *you* did."

"Understood, Instructor."

"Good," Saruk said. "Now find yourself a bucket and start cleaning this mess."

⌒

The Guildsmen in charge of the blood stockpiles laughed every time one of them fell or let a crate slip through their fingers, nearly squashing their feet. These Guildsmen were reservists, just like the cooks and the rest of the fortress's staff. They had all been Hunters once but for some reason or another had been considered unfit for desert patrols. Some limped heavily, others were missing a limb or maybe even two.

For safety reasons, the blood stockpile was located deep inside the mountain, which meant each crate had to travel about a mile inside the halls of the fortress before they reached the loading bay next to the Guild's stables. However, the wheeled pushcarts had mysteriously disappeared and the elevator's ropes had been cut just above the counterweights. All very unfortunate, as the man responsible for the stockpile had put it. Add to that the fact that everyone they passed through the halls kept asking how they liked that their captain had turned them into mules, and Aric was having a tremendous day. By the time all the crates had been loaded into the carts, there wasn't a single recruit who hadn't come up with his very own name for Aric, and none of them were either charming or flattering.

"The least you could do is have your pet stay away," Ashur complained.

Geric was having a lot of fun chasing pebbles between everyone's legs. Nahir nearly tripped over him twice, and Athan almost got bitten when he stepped on Geric's paw. Eventually, Aric managed to get the cat to stay away by sending him chasing an empty blind-bomb shell down the mountain.

The convoy left at midday, the peaking sun frying them under their cloaks. Only Leth and Geric seemed willing to sit with Aric on the front cart. Even Clea decided to go for one of the others.

"Don't worry," Leth said as they started down the mountain. "They'll forget about it soon enough."

However, Aric wasn't so sure.

As they were riding on horse-pulled carts, the journey across the dunes was certainly far more comfortable than their usual desert runs. Or, at least, it would have been if their muscles didn't hurt so much. And they still had to unload their cargo once they arrived in Nish, as well.

Night fell and they made camp on a plateau. Gathering the carts in the center, Aric spread the company around them in a protective formation. A fortune could be made in the black market with all that blood, and raids on blood convoys weren't rare.

"Think there'll be Paladins at the Bloodhouse?" Aric asked Leth by the crackling fire.

Around them, the rest of the recruits had fallen asleep.

"Don't Paladins oversee the destruction of dragon blood?" Leth asked.

"Yeah, I think so."

"I freaking hate Paladins," Aric said, scratching behind one of Geric's ears.

"You know what?" Leth said. "I don't think I've ever met a Paladin that wasn't Samehrian."

Aric tried to muffle his own laughter before he woke anyone up. "That's not true," he said.

"I swear by the first of my ancestors," Leth said, but his smiled betrayed him. "In fact, I'm sure Ashur would have been a Paladin if he hadn't joined the Guild."

"Hey, that reminds me," Aric said, his eyes suddenly focused on something far, far away. "Do they need the brewing chamber to destroy the blood?"

Leth shrugged. "No idea."

"'Cause the brewing chamber in Nish was destroyed."

"What?!" Leth clearly didn't think that was plausible.

"Seriously," Aric assured him. "On my way to Lamash, I stopped at the Bloodhouse, and there was this really old guy, a Guildsman. I think he is the keeper of the Bloodhouse."

"What about him?"

"Well, out of nowhere, he takes me to this huge, barred door and tells me the brewing chamber was on the other side, but it had been destroyed a few days back."

"Wait, is this the same guy that told you about the desert witch?"

Aric sighed. "I *saw* Eliran with my very own eyes."

"Yeah," Leth smiled. "On the same day you hallucinated about a sandstorm."

Aric dismissed Leth with a hand wave and leaned back, closing his eyes.

They arrived in Nish two days later. Their horse carts rolled across the city's brown walls and into its cobblestone streets. Just as Aric remembered, the city looked mostly deserted, but a couple of citizens here and there were forced to make way for the convoy. They crisscrossed around a couple of blocks until Aric had to stop at a junction to ask for directions. Those empty streets made it feel even more like a maze.

A fat man with a greasy smile approached Aric's cart. With a thick Cyrinian accent that made Nahir sound like a native Arreline, he gave them some vague instructions. Aric decided it might be a better idea to ask someone else. Across the street, at the end of a block, Aric saw a woman walking briskly, a white veil covering her head.

"My lady, excuse me!" Aric called.

"My lady?" Leth asked, chuckling.

"Right," Aric agreed. "Madam? Madam, wait!"

The woman turned around and Aric felt like a bolt of lightning had struck him down. Locks of copper hair danced around a face so pale, it seemed to meld into her veil, making her blue eyes seem like lagoons glistening under the midday sun.

"Eliran…" Aric mumbled.

"What did you just say?" Leth asked.

But Aric didn't even hear him. He just stared at the woman as she turned away and disappeared into some tavern or inn on the side of the street.

"We're lost, aren't we?" Ashur said. He had walked over from his cart and was standing next to theirs, looking his usual charming self.

"It was Eliran." Aric didn't seem to have heard Ashur. "The woman I saw in the desert."

"He's joking," Leth assured Ashur.

The Samehrian shook his head and turned to the other carts. "Our brave captain is hallucinating about the desert witch again."

There was a wave of disbelief from the rest of the convoy, but once again, Aric didn't seem to hear it. "That was Eliran," he told Leth. "That was *her.*"

"I think maybe you should focus on finding the Bloodhouse instead," Leth advised carefully.

The yells from the other carts grew louder and more impatient. It seemed to do the trick – Aric snapped out of it.

"Right," Aric said. "We'll just do what the fat guy said." He grabbed the reins and spurred the horse forward, but he made sure to drive past the door the strange woman had gone through. A plaque hanging above it was shaped like a flagon and read: The Thirsty Dragon.

It turned out they weren't that far from the Bloodhouse after all. Aric recognized it after only a couple of turns. With a whistle, he ordered everyone to dismount and begin unloading the cargo.

The wrinkled face of the old keeper came out to meet them before the first crate was out of the cart.

"Who are you?" the old man demanded to know. "Where is Muric?"

"My name is Aric. Hey, get out of here, Geric." The cat had frozen behind his legs, blocking him just as he was heaving a crate from his cart."

"I don't know you," the old man said. "You're not Guildsmen; none of you are."

"We're recruits," Aric told him. "Saruk sent us to do the Blood Run this time. Come on, Geric, get out." The cat was still refusing to move.

"This is most unusual," the old keeper said. "I wasn't informed of any changes."

"Geric!" The blood crate was starting to hurt in Aric's hands, so he kicked the desert lynx away.

Like a spring, the cat dropped down to a crouch, hissing and baring his fangs. But not at Aric. No, Geric was facing up, toward the sky.

He looked up in the same direction as the cat and every drop of blood in his body froze.

"Run!" he screamed, dropping the blood crate to the ground with a *slam*.

"Hey!" Leth protested, holding the other end of the blood crate. "You want to smash my legs or something?"

"Everybody run into the House!" Aric ordered. "NOW!"

A thundering growl burst from the sky, sending everyone reeling back into the nearest object. Right there, a mere few feet above the ceilings of Nish, a gargantuan dragon swooped down, opening its mouth and gushing out a river of flames. The skies were bleeding.

CHAPTER 15

The Spies

"No, no, no!" Sabium said, his hands on his forehead. "For the tenth time, *focus.*"

Fadan grabbed a bandage and wrapped it around his bleeding fingers, gritting his teeth.

For the past couple of weeks, lessons with the old mage had grown increasingly frustrating. Fadan seemed to be making less progress every day. In fact, it actually felt like his abilities had decreased. A month earlier, he had been able to easily light every candle in the apartment with a snap of his fingers, but just the other night, he had nearly set his bedroom on fire trying to ignite an oil lamp.

"I told you this was a bad idea," Sabium continued, helping Fadan clean his wound. "When I agreed to teach you, it was on the assumption that we would do it *my* way. This is far too advanced for you."

"I thought you said becoming invisible was too advanced, but this was not," Fadan retorted.

"No, I said that I refused to teach you invisibility because you were not ready."

"Yes, and then you suggested traversing walls instead," Fadan said.

"Because you wouldn't shut up about it!" Sabium grabbed Fadan's wounded hand. "Let me see that." The old mage carefully unfurled the bloodstained bandage and inspected Fadan's bleeding fingers. "You were lucky," Sabium grumbled. "It missed the bone and the tendons. I think I can fix it."

Muttering something beneath his breath, Sabium closed his eyes and placed the palm of his hand a couple of inches from Fadan's gash. Then, something sparkled and the bleeding stopped.

Fadan felt a rush of relief as the pain subsided, replaced by itching.

"Grab me that jar of water," Sabium said without taking his eyes off the wound.

Twisting so as not to take his wounded hand from Sabium's healing touch, Fadan grabbed the jar with his other hand.

"Pour it over the wound," Sabium instructed.

The prince obeyed and watched as the blood was swept away. Somehow, the water's freshness made the itching even worse, and then his jaw dropped. The V-shaped gash where his fingers had nearly been severed began to close, filling in like a hole in the sand whose walls had collapsed.

"You need to drop this madness," Sabium muttered as Fadan's pink skin finished healing. "You're going to get yourself killed."

"You said I could learn this," Fadan insisted.

"Obviously, I was wrong." The old mage took a deep breath, releasing Fadan's now-healed hand. "Listen, you're still no more capable than a Novice. Traversing walls is something even an Initiate would struggle with. This is *dangerous* stuff. If the spell breaks, or you lose your concentration like you just did, you can find yourself materializing halfway through a door or something. Believe me, it wouldn't be a pretty death."

"At least it would be a quick one," Fadan said, smiling.

"This isn't funny," Sabium told him, looking not the least bit amused. "Just drop it and let's resume your lessons. The regular ones."

Fadan's smile disappeared. "Master, I can't just drop it. Not while Doric is still in the dungeons."

Sabium exhaled loudly. "It's because of my brother, isn't it? He got into your head."

"No, it's because of mine," Fadan said. "I made Aric a promise, and I intend to keep it."

"Promise," Sabium snorted. "You also promised your brother you would rescue him from Lamash, but I don't see you rushing off to the desert."

The prince sank into a chair. "One promise at a time," he said, looking down. "In fact, that's precisely the point, Master. I'm already taking too long as it is. If I stick to your program, it'll take me years of training before I'm ready to do anything. Doric will rot in jail and my brother will get eaten by a dragon in some forgotten cave."

"So you'll just kill yourself instead?" Sabium asked. "Let me teach you the *proper* way. It'll take a long time, but it'll be worth it. You have potential, I've seen it, but you'll waste it if you insist on learning without structure."

Drafts seeping through the poorly built window shutters made the candle flames quiver. Winter had settled in Augusta for a couple of weeks now, and Fadan hugged himself against the chill.

"Maybe you're right," the prince said. "I guess there is another way to save Doric." He looked up to face his master. "I could ask the rebels for help."

"Oh, dear," Sabium said, turning around and heading for his bed before snapping back toward Fadan. "You *do* realize the rebellion isn't exactly a wine merchant, don't you? You can't just purchase their services when you need them and then forget about it. If you join the rebellion, you don't leave. And you do it on *their* terms."

"You know, there's something I never quite understood," Fadan said. "I mean, you're the mage, not your brother. Why is he with the rebels instead of you?"

Slowly, Sabium walked back away from his bed. "Alman is a fool," he muttered. "Always was. Maybe the rebellion gives him a sense of purpose; I don't know." He stopped in front of his pupil, staring into the boy's eyes. "What I do know is that the Purge cost me everything except my own life, and I'm not willing to sacrifice anything more for someone else's political gain. Even if the rebels *are* the emperor's enemies, that hardly makes them my friends."

"I thought the saying said otherwise," Fadan said.

"Well, the saying is wrong. Now, shall we learn something today or not?"

Fadan sighed. "I suppose you're right. They might not be your friends, but they definitely are my father's enemies. I'll never have any business with them. I just want Aric and Doric to be safe; that's all. Besides, the Academy believed in some really creepy stuff. If the rebels share those beliefs, I *really* don't want to join them."

Sabium frowned. "What are you talking about?" he asked.

"Oh, right," Fadan said. "I'm sorry. I know you were a member of the Academy, but I have to be honest. Some of the stuff in that book creeps me out. I fully intend to restore the Academy once I'm on the throne, but I will not accept those kinds of ideas."

"What ideas?" Sabium's frown had grown deeper. "Are you talking about your magic book? I thought it was all gibberish to you."

"The sections that try to teach magic, yes. They're gibberish," Fadan replied. "But the philosophical passages are easy enough to understand, albeit very hard to agree with."

"What are you talking about? There is no philosophy in any of the Academy's manuals. I should know; I taught them. All of them."

Fadan shrugged. "All right, call it whatever you want. It's still creepy to me. What's that phrase that keeps repeating? It sounds like a mantra: 'If we keep the world from burning, all that will be left is darkness'. Do you agree with this? 'Cause to me, it just sounds like…"

Fadan cut himself off. Sabium had turned pale.

"Master, are you all right?"

"What did you just say?" the old man asked, his voice weak.

"What? About the book? The mantra?" Fadan took a step forward, readying his hands. Sabium looked about to faint or something.

"Where did you get that book?" Sabium asked.

"I told you," Fadan replied. "It was in an attic in the Core Palace."

Sabium exploded forward, grabbing Fadan's collar. "*How* did you find it? Was it hidden?"

Fadan staggered backward. "It…it just fell from the ceiling."

"*Fell?*" Sabium echoed. "How did it fall?"

"I… I don't know. My brother and I had our backs to it when we heard it fall to the floor. It must have tumbled from the beams on the ceiling."

Sabium released Fadan and began to pace the room as if he was looking for some way out of there. "Merciful Ava!" He stopped and turned to Fadan. "Listen to me *very* carefully. You are going to return to the Citadel, right now, and you are going to set that book on fire. Do you understand me?"

"I… Yes, but why? What's happening?"

"What's happening is that you have found something you shouldn't have," Sabium said, his eyes wide. "Now go!"

Instead of obeying, Fadan stood still, looking defiantly at Sabium. "You sound like a madman," he said. "I'm not going anywhere or burning anything unless you explain what is wrong with that book."

The old mage swallowed visibly. "I'm sorry," he said, looking tense. "I'm just not used to dealing with this sort of…thing."

"What *thing*?" Fadan was losing his patience.

"Most people don't know about this, but the Academy wasn't the only place where magic was taught. It was just the only place that did it legally. That phrase you mentioned, it's not a mantra. It's a prayer."

"What?" Fadan asked. "There was no mention of Ava anywhere in the book, Master."

"That's because the people who wrote that book do not worship her," Sabium replied.

"What do you mean? Who do they worship, then?"

"Fyr. The dragon goddess."

⌒⌐

Tarsus was a heavy sleeper, but nonetheless, Cassia made sure she closed the door without a sound as she left his room. It was impossible to avoid his bed when the emperor summoned her. It was what kept Doric alive, she kept telling herself. That didn't make her feel any less dirty, any less nauseated.

Tiptoeing, the empress returned to her room, opening and closing its door as silently as she had done in Tarsus's room. A shadow awaited her by the bed, the glint of a blade sparkling in its hand.

"Easy, Venia," Cassia whispered. "It's me."

The shadow sheathed its blade and sat on a chair besides the bed. "Will you be needing a bath, Your Majesty?"

"I will." The empress used a flint to light up an oil lamp. "But tell me of Fadan first."

"He is out again, like every night," Venia replied. "I am now sure someone is covering his comings and goings from Sagun's men, but I'm not sure who it is."

Cassia sighed and poured a jar of water into a basin. "I know I shouldn't keep thinking about him as a child, but…" She leant forward and splashed some of the basin's water on her face, scrubbing her cheeks, her mouth, and her neck. "I don't know… It's just strange that my son has his own spies, isn't it?"

Venia shrugged. "If you say so."

"Do you think I should confront him?" Cassia asked, a white towel softly muffling her words as she used it to dry herself. "Beg him not to do it?"

"Why would you do that?" Venia asked.

"Why?" The empress tossed the towel besides the basin. "Because whatever he is doing is obviously very dangerous."

"Whatever he is doing is requiring a tremendous amount of effort, Your Majesty," Venia said. "He barely even sleeps. It obviously means a lot to him."

"You're right," Cassia said, walking toward her bed. "I need to know what he is doing before making any decision. Can you follow him?"

"I have tried to," Venia replied. "Three times. I always lose him in the sewers."

"Interesting."

"Not interesting, Your Majesty. Annoying." Venia paused. "There is, however, a rumor."

"Rumor?" Cassia asked.

Venia confirmed with a nod. "Some of the servants whisper about the prince having an affair. With some girl. Either a Mantea or a Strada."

"Oh…" Cassia was expecting a lot of things, but not that. "Well, that's great." She frowned. "I think –"

"I wouldn't get too excited," Venia told her. "It's too convenient. My guess is it's a planted rumor. Something to fall back on in case the prince is caught during one of his escapades."

Cassia wilted slightly. "I see," she said. "Will you keep trying to follow him?"

Venia nodded. "Of course, Your Majesty."

With a huge sigh, Cassia let herself fall into her bed. "Oh, Venia… What would I do without you?"

"Not much," Venia replied matter-of-factly.

The spy rarely had any problems speaking her mind. It amused Cassia to no end. The empress chuckled, sitting back up.

"Don't worry, Your Majesty," Venia assured her. "Relying on spies seems to be a common trend among people of your station."

Cassia snorted. "I had no need for spies when I lived in Fausta. When I was married to Doric."

"Yes," Venia said. "And that sure turned out great."

Cassia chuckled once again. "I'll be wanting that bath now, Venia."

"Yes, Your Majesty," Venia said, standing up. "A steaming bath coming up. Lots of soap."

⌒⟩

Sabium's words still rang in his head. Fadan had left his master's house immediately after the old mage's breakdown, but he had not arrived at the Citadel in time to do as bidden. With the sun nearly up, all Fadan had been able to do was climb back into his room. Burning the book would have to wait until the next day.

That night, the prince dreamt of a dragon's statue, its feet drowning in melted wax from a forest of candles burning around it. About twenty hooded figures encircled the statue, humming and chanting eerily, their shadows flickering behind them over a blood red floor.

In the dream, Fadan had stood in a corner, making his best effort to keep quiet and invisible. Then he had looked at his hand, realizing he still hadn't mastered the invisibility spell. It had been as if his thoughts were heard by the hooded figures, because their chants immediately died as they turned to face him.

He tried to look for some way out but found himself paralyzed. He tried using the spell to cross walls, but that didn't work either. One of the hooded figures walked slowly toward Fadan, reaching out with his index finger until he touched the prince's forehead. It had felt like being touched by ice. When he woke up, Fadan could still feel the ice-cold touch right between his eyes, a coldness that somehow spread to the rest of his body.

Fadan shook his head, pushing the dream's memory away, and got out of bed. He dressed up in a blue uniform with his ducal insignia on the chest – Fadan had already inherited his mother's duchy – and the golden chevrons of a general on the shoulder. He had always felt ridiculous about having such a high military rank, considering he was still learning how to swing a sword, but the emperor always insisted on obeying the formalities. All children of House Patros were the supreme commanders of the Legions. Their age was irrelevant.

Fadan rarely wore his uniforms, but it was something that pleased his father, and ever since he had begun his magic lessons, Fadan wanted to make sure he stayed on the emperor's good side.

Today was a relatively light day for him, with very little on his schedule besides the usual official meals. Sagun would surely barge into the room momentarily to let him know just that, but these days, Fadan always made sure he was aware of his daily program. It was a necessity now that he had less than two hours of sleep per night. Days like today were the only reason he had been able to maintain sanity during the last month. They were rare, but not too rare, and allowed him to catch up on his sleep at least once every other week.

Today, however, he had one little thing to care of before taking his nap – burning the magic book. Fadan had a hard time seeing how a simple book could be so dangerous, even if it did belong to a creepy group of people, but his master had looked scared enough that he wasn't about to take any chances.

There was a knock on the door.

"You may come in," Fadan said.

Sagun walked in, his colorful Akhami robes fluttering behind him. "Ah, an extremely appropriate choice of attire, Your Majesty," he said.

"Good morning to you as well, Sagun," Fadan said as he finished buttoning his uniform's jacket.

The castellan reddened. "A thousand apologies, Your Majesty," he said. "I was simply surprised that you were already wearing what I had come to suggest you would."

"I know, I know," Fadan said, heading for the glass cabinet containing his swords. "My father likes it when I dress like him."

Sagun rose to the tip of his toes and peeked at the sword collection. "Might I suggest the Aparantan saber, Your Majesty? The silver-bladed one."

Fadan nodded and grabbed the suggested sword. It was a magnificent weapon, with a gilded sheath, a golden head of an Imperial lion on the pommel, and a filigree guard so exquisitely sculpted, it made the High Priest's cloths look mundane. It had been a gift from his Aparantan cousin on his father's side and was a little too flamboyant for Fadan's taste.

"However," the castellan added, "it is not your father's preferences that directed my wardrobe advice for today."

Fadan sent him a suspicious look.

"I'm afraid next week's petitioning has been moved forward," Sagun said. "And your father insists on having you by his side, of course."

Oh, dragon crap.

How in the name of Ava had he missed that on the daily schedule?

"I don't remember anything about the petitioning being moved forward," Fadan said, a little too much frustration seeping into his tone.

"I may have forgotten to update the prince's agenda," Sagun said in an obviously fake apologetic tone. "I hope it is not an inconvenience."

How was he going to get any sleep today? Or worse, how was he going to keep himself from falling asleep halfway through the damned thing? Petitioning could last an entire day. It was one of the reasons his father held so few. Of course, the fewer petitionings the emperor held, the longer the ones that he *did* hold became, as petitioners simply accumulated further and further.

"You could have at least told me last night," Fadan said.

"Why, Your Majesty, was there, perhaps, something special you were planning for today?"

What is that supposed to mean? Fadan thought.

"I'll be right down," he said. "You may leave."

"Yes, Your Majesty." The castellan gave a deep bow, then turned on his heel to leave, his long, dark braid dancing behind him.

I'll need to have a chat with Fabian about this. And the book will have to wait until tonight. Fadan massaged his temples. And my sleep will have to wait until tomorrow.

Sighing, the prince left his room, heading to the main hall and making sure to keep to the narrower back corridors, as the main hallway would be packed full of petitioners and everyone accompanying them. The problem was, he hadn't slept more than two hours a night for almost two weeks. He was so sleep-deprived that he actually had a hard time walking in a straight line.

I have to sit as soon as I enter the Great Hall.

To his great relief, Fadan's smaller prince's throne had been added to the main hall's blue dais. Next to his father's and his mother's thrones, whose blue satin–covered backs stretched up to the ceiling, Fadan's throne looked like a wooden kitchen stool, not that he would complain. All he needed was something that kept his legs from betraying him. Once, he had been forced to stand through all nine hours of a petitioning for being caught playing catch with Aric in the courtyard.

"Father, Mother," he greeted them, bowing slightly as he climbed onto the dais. "How are you this morning?"

"Ah, son," Tarsus said, lifting his head from a roll of parchment. "Sit, sit. Food should be along shortly."

"Good morning, Fadan," Cassia said. "I hope you slept well."

"Well enough," the prince replied.

Oh, goddess.

"We are ready to begin, Your Majesty," Fadan heard someone say. It was Chancellor Vigild, who received an approving nod from the emperor and placed himself behind him.

Beneath the dais, Secretary Fressia and Seneschal Daria took their seats at a very large mahogany table overflowing with parchment rolls. Legionaries moved to their positions, creating a rectangle that stretched from the gate to about a third of the way to the Imperial throne.

"Open up," Tarsus ordered.

Two Legionaries pulled the large wooden gate of the hall open. The noisy crowd poured inside. Only nobles were allowed to petition the emperor, as it would have been impossible to attend the petitions of every citizen of the Empire. Plebs had to settle with regular courts, no matter how long those took to settle most matters. Some minor nobles, however, accepted small fortunes by rich plebeians, like merchants, to present their cases to the emperor. This practice was known as advocating and was actually the only way some nobles could avoid abject poverty.

The ceremony was a very straightforward affair. Secretary Fressia called each petitioner by name and the person presented their issue. Sometimes, the emperor exchanged some words with the petitioner before making his decision. Other times, he simply uttered his sentence after hearing the matter and the petitioner was quickly sent away. There was rarely the chance for an appeal.

Fadan knew that his father loathed the petitioning. Tarsus found it beneath an emperor to be forced to deal with such lowly concerns. Fadan, however, liked the idea of Imperial subjects having the right to discuss their problems in person with their ruler, even if it was so seldom an occurrence. It seemed just to him.

The first petitions of the morning turned out to be a succession of the usual squabbles between barons, viscounts, and other petty nobles. One marquis had come to petition for a temporary exemption from taxes because of a weak crop. The emperor fined him twenty thousand gold crowns for being a poor farmer and hurting the Empire's food supplies. An unlanded Thepian noble, claiming that each and every one of his ancestors were great military heroes of the Empire, begged the emperor for a job in the Legions. Tarsus sent him to do latrine inspection in the expeditionary Legions stationed in Northern Aletia.

It was all either boring or depressing, and Fadan's eyelids grew heavier and heavier.

"Lady Margeth Abyssaria, Archduchess of Pharyzah," Fressia called.

That managed to wake Fadan up. What was such a high-ranking noble doing in a petitioning? Their affairs with the emperor were usually dealt with much more privately. Tarsus's dinners served that very purpose.

This should be good, Fadan thought, looking forward to anything that would keep him from falling asleep.

"Your Imperial Majesty," the Archduchess greeted Tarsus, curtsying deeply.

Instead of the flamboyant dresses ladies usually wore to important occasions, Margeth wore the feminine version of an archducal uniform, much like the one Fadan himself was wearing. She was in her late thirties, and even though she was far from beautiful, something in the way she stood was deeply attractive. Dark hair fell over the golden chevrons on her shoulders, and the ivory white of her uniform was a stark contrast against the olive hue of her skin.

"Lady Margeth, it has been too long," Tarsus said flatly.

"I was unable to attend the empress's birthday ball," Margeth explained. "My presence was required in Pharyzah, Your Majesty."

"I'm sure you had a very good reason not to come," Tarsus retorted. "Please, proceed with your petition. As you can see, the line behind you stretches endlessly."

"Of course," the archduchess said, removing a document from inside her coat. "It has come to the attention of several Great Houses of the Empire that Your Majesty has been working on the draft of an edict that seeks to limit the right of nobles to muster their own military forces."

The hall became suddenly very quiet.

What?! Fadan thought.

The prince was no fan of his lessons on law, but he was competent enough with the subject to understand what the archduchess had just implied. If such a thing were true, his father would be violating at least five main tenets of the Unification Charter, the very document that bound the Empire together.

"You are exceedingly well informed, my Lady Archduchess," Tarsus said. His face was the perfect likeness of calm. "I wonder how you came by such information."

"I have come to present you with this," Margeth said, ignoring the emperor's question and presenting him the document in her hand. "Your Majesty's proposed law is highly illegal, to say the least."

Fadan had not met many people brave enough to speak to his father that way. In fact, this woman was probably the first. What was truly troubling, though, was that Tarsus looked thoroughly unfazed by it.

"As is our right," Margeth proceeded, "I and nineteen other landed nobles of the Empire hereby request that a Landeen be called to discuss and decide upon this matter."

There was absolutely no sound in the room for what felt like an eternity.

Fadan turned to his father, still in shock. It was no secret to Fadan that many regarded his father as a tyrant. His own mother had been coerced to divorce her husband in order to marry Tarsus. And, of course, there was the Purge, the dreadful time when Tarsus had slain just about every mage in the Empire. But it was one thing to hear about these stories; it was a completely different thing to witness his father's tyranny firsthand.

Fadan saw Vigild lean into the emperor.

"You think she has the votes?" Tarsus asked in a nearly inaudible whisper.

"We'll see," Vigild replied in an equally low voice. "If any of those signatures belongs to one of the lower Houses, she might. If not..."

"We cannot take any chances, Vigild," Tarsus said, his whisper almost turning into a growl. "If the Landeen blocks this law —"

"Relax, Your Majesty," Vigild told him. "With the right...'persuasion' techniques, we can be sure that a sufficient number of the lower Houses become tired of being bullied by their cousins' armies."

The emperor nodded, calm returning to his features. "Lady Margeth, as you know, I am an incorrigible formalist. You will forgive me if I fully observe the bureaucracy." He waved one of the aides forward.

"By all means, Your Majesty," Margeth said, handing the parchment to the aide.

Fadan watched as Chancellor Vigild quietly stepped down from the dais and collected Margeth's document. He squinted as he analyzed the parchment before rolling it closed and turning to the emperor, his back to the assembly of nobles. The chancellor smiled triumphantly.

"It seems everything is in order," Tarsus told Margeth, his calm expression masking the victory Vigild had just communicated. "However, I'm afraid I must disappoint you."

The archduchess frowned.

"I dread to inform you that you have made this long trip to Augusta for nothing. I already had every intention of calling the Landeen." The emperor smiled. "My dear lady, do you really believe I would even consider passing such a fundamental law without the consent of the nobility?"

The archduchess scoffed in disbelief. "You can't seriously expect the nobility to approve such a notion. It will mean the end of the distribution of power."

"My lady, I look forward to the opportunity to explain to you, and rest of the Landeen, why this law upholds the greater interest of the Empire. Chancellor," Tarsus called, "it would be impolite to allow the archduchess to leave Augusta empty-handed. How soon can we hold the Landeen?"

"Oh, dear," Vigild acted the part of a flustered man. "It's such a complex thing to organize, Your Majesty. The security alone is a nightmare."

"Chancellor, I'm sure the archduchess expects the Landeen to be convened as quickly as possible, and I will not disappoint her," Tarsus said. "Isn't that right, Lady Margeth?"

The archduchess seemed lost. She actually shuddered when she heard her name. "Uh... yes, of course. As soon as possible."

"You see?" Tarsus asked Vigild. "How about three months? Can we do it in three months?"

"If that is your wish, then it shall be done, Your Majesty," Vigild said, bowing.

"Excellent," Tarsus replied. "Let it be known that the Landeen will gather in Augusta in three months' time, counting from today. Archduchess, I bid you a safe and pleasant journey back to Pharyzah."

"I... Thank you, Your Majesty," Margeth said, curtsying. She turned around, still looking stunned, and started toward the door.

"And, Lady Margeth," Tarsus called.

The woman stopped and looked back.

"Send my regards to your...co-signatories," Tarsus continued.

Margeth's head straightened up a bit. "I will, Your Majesty."

A chilling wind rustled the trees around Fadan, slivers of moonlight flickering everywhere from the shaking branches above his head. He mindlessly adjusted his uniform's jacket, as if the small tug could somehow make the jacket more adequate against the cold.

"What are you doing out here?"

The question startled Fadan. It was Fabian. The old general walked into the small garden clearing with his head swinging from side to side, searching the shadows.

"What, you're replacing Sagun now?" Fadan replied. "I can stay out here whenever I want. That stupid punishment has been over for weeks."

"That's not what I meant," Fabian said. "I was just wondering why you are standing here staring at nothing. Aren't you going out to wherever you go every night?"

"So you were following me?"

"Of course I was following you," Fabian told him. "How do you think I keep your father's spies away from you?"

The prince sighed. "Forgive me," he said. "I'm a bit edgy."

Fabian nodded. "That's all right. What's bothering you? Anything I can help with?"

"I doubt it," Fadan replied. He sighed again. "Well, maybe you can tell me why my father is trying kill off the nobility."

"He's not trying to kill the nobility," Fabian said.

"Oh, no? Then why is he so interested in making sure they're not armed?"

"He thinks he can put an end to civil wars," the old general replied. "I fought in one. Believe me, they're not pretty."

"Oh, please!" Fadan snapped. "Spare me the propaganda. I know my father."

Fabian was left with nothing to say, so the two of them just exchanged a stare for a little while until Fadan looked away, snorting his disapproval.

"Why do you even pretend to agree with him?" Fadan asked.

"He's my emperor," Fabian explained.

"But you help me! And you know you're helping me do things he would not approve of, even if you don't know what these things are."

Fabian shrugged. "You're my prince," he said.

The prince rolled his eyes. "So, it's that easy for you, huh?" he asked. "You're with both sides and you're betraying no one, is that it?"

"What sides are we talking about, exactly?"

"Oh, come on!" Fadan cried, turning his back on Fabian. "I'm in no mood for games. Please leave me. I have things to attend to."

"Then attend to them," Fabian said. "There's no point in standing around sulking. If you have a decision to make, make it and stick with it, no matter how distasteful it is. Your father may have many flaws, but at least he does not hesitate. Even a bad decision is better than no decision at all." He turned to leave but paused. "Just do what you have to. Whatever it is, it won't get any easier by waiting."

I can't, Fadan thought as he watched Fabian disappear between the shadows. *I can't give up on Doric. I can't join the rebels. I can't master the right spells in time to do anything useful.*

He kicked a pebble away then looked back in the general direction of the empty palace he had chosen as his hiding place within the Citadel. At the very least, he could take care of the damned book. Maybe that would calm Sabium down a bit, convince the old mage to help him learn the spell to traverse walls. If Fadan could master at least that one spell, he would be able to get Doric out. He just knew he would.

"All right, creepy book," he told himself beneath his breath. "Time to burn."

⌣⟶

The cold made Venia shiver. She licked her lips, and the cracks she found with her tongue stung a little. It bothered her that she found this tiny pain so uncomfortable. All these years serving in the Citadel were making her soft. If this had been just a regular assignment, she would have requested a transfer long before, but it wasn't.

The sounds of conversation had died out, so she decided to move out. She stepped on a branch, but Venia had long learned how to step lightly enough that even twigs did not crack beneath her feet. Besides, a strong, cold wind was rattling the bushes and trees in the garden so hard that no one would ever have been able to hear her.

Unfortunately, it had also prevented her from overhearing the prince's discussion. She had, however, seen who he had been talking to. Lord Fabian Lagon, a retired general and a veteran of the Thepian revolt. He was the second in House Lagon's hierarchy and a stalwart of loyalism. Few nobles so accurately represented the ideals of an Arreline aristocrat as he. He was also the Viceroy of the Information Scriptorium, which meant he was Venia's boss and High Marshal Intila's right-hand man. The young prince hadn't just enlisted a spy; he had enlisted the *king* of spies. The man was so good at it, most people in the Scriptorium didn't even know he was the one running the show.

Not bad, kid, Venia thought. *Not bad at all.*

A thin layer of pine needles and other leaves covered the damp soil, but it wasn't hard for Venia to find the prince's trail. There was, of course, the chance that either Fabian or one of his people were also following her, but she didn't have a choice. She was either going to follow Fadan or not, so besides giving up, all she could do was to be careful, which she always was. After all, she hadn't been assigned to the empress because of her pretty blond hair. At least, she had always hoped not. There had always been the possibility that they had wanted someone inept for the job. Luckily, Venia had never been prone to that sort of insecurity.

The prince's trail ended at the garden's exit gate, where a dirt path turned into a marble-paved street wide enough to fit two Imperial carriages side by side.

Where had the kid wiped the mud off his boots?

Venia looked around, trying to find a fleeting shadow, either from Fadan, or a hypothetical pursuer. She saw no one, but she did notice a small patch of dirt on a mound of grass.

Ah, he covers his tracks, she thought. *Good boy.*

Walking out of the Empress's Orchard and into the marble street, Venia took off her dark robe, turned it inside out, and put it on again, turning a suspicious-looking hooded figure into just another maid in her light blue dress, surely running an errand for her mistress.

Now, where did you go, Your Majesty? Venia canvassed the shadows around her. *Probably the sewers. Which means I've lost you again. Unless…*

The beautifully paved marble street stretched for several yards in front of her, but to her left was another, not so pretty street, a cobbled boulevard feeding a neighborhood of abandoned palaces.

I wonder…

Looking over her shoulder, Venia turned left, into the shadows of the unkempt trees flanking the boulevard. Six once-radiant and now vegetation-covered palaces grew beneath the silvery moonlight. Each and every one of them was a perfect place to stay away from unwanted eyes. But which one?

There was only one way to find out.

Venia slid into the courtyard of the first one, making sure her clothes didn't get stuck in one of the wild bushes that had claimed the place. It was a particularly large palace, even by Citadel standards. At its prime, it would have rivaled even the Mantea or the Lagon estates, and that was saying something. Whichever Great House had called this place home, they had fallen from a very high place.

With deft hands, she removed her garment and turned its black side back out again before putting it on once again. The palace's front door wasn't locked, and Venia pushed it open slowly so it didn't make a sound. Unfortunately, the first foot she laid inside made the hardwood creak.

She closed her eyes, cringing. *I* hate *old floors*, she thought.

Venia was forced to walk nerve-wrenchingly slow to make sure the floorboards didn't betray her again as she explored the enormous four-storied mansion. There was no sign of the prince inside, so she moved to the second palace, still keeping to the shadows, still stepping like a feline on the prowl.

At this rate, it'll be dawn before I'm finished.

Once again, there was no sign of Fadan anywhere in the Palace. The third one was slightly smaller than the other six, but it was still just as tall and infuriatingly large, considering how slowly she had to move.

There was no one on the first or the second floors. Wind swept in from the broken windows, sending shredded curtains into a wild dance. Venia climbed to the third floor and, once again, there was nothing indicating someone had been there recently. It was then that she caught the scent of something burning. Pine and...parchment?

She found a stairwell leading up to what she assumed was an attic. She walked carefully, her hands to the wall to make sure she didn't trip. There was absolutely no light after the stairwell made the first turn.

The burning smell grew stronger and Venia shrank against the wall as she reached the top of the stairs. There was definitely something burning on the other side of the threshold. She could hear the flames crackling softly.

Venia tilted her head only enough so that she could peer into the attic. It was a long, wide room, empty save for some furniture pushed into a corner and a dinner set lined against a wall.

The prince was not inside. Instead, there was a bucket right in the middle of the room, smoke and an orange hue rising from it.

Carefully, Venia walked into the attic, then spun around like lightning, as if she expected to be jumped from behind, but there truly wasn't anybody inside.

The prince had been there, set something on fire, and then left. Venia stepped up to the bucket. There was a book inside, flames eating away at its pages and hardcover.

Very careless, kid, she thought. *Not such a good boy after all.*

She ripped a large patch of her skirt off, then kicked the bucket, its burning content spilling over the floor. In a quick motion, Venia covered the book with the piece of her skirt, then stepped on it repeatedly until she was convinced the flames were out.

A small cloud of smoke puffed into the air when Venia lifted the cloth. The book had nearly disintegrated, but not completely. Its bindings remained stubbornly intact, and so did its cover, despite the cindered look.

It was strange. Venia had never seen a book cover made out of wood. As for the pages, none remained intact, and most of them had burned away completely. A few of them, however, the ones at the center, still had portions where the text was still readable, even if most of the sentences were now cut by at least two thirds.

Venia's fingers ran through the pages with the softness of a caress. She wanted to be sure she didn't damage the book further.

"Fire take me!" she heard herself say as she read. "What *is* this?"

CHAPTER 16

The Battle of Nish

Aric slammed the door shut. Outside, clamoring bells joined a rising chorus of terrified screams.

Geric ran under a table, and the whole group shrank as the dragon's deep, rolling roar appeared to fly over the Bloodhouse. Even the beams on the ceiling seemed to tremble.

"Shouldn't we go underground?" Jullion asked, looking as pale as a ghost. Like a reply, the shattering sound of a crumbling building exploded nearby.

"Jullion is right!" Ashur said. "We need to hide."

"I could open the door to the brewing chamber," the old keeper said.

"Do it!" Ashur ordered.

The old man turned to comply, and was already on his way with several of them in tow when Aric said, "Wait!" He paused, looking at the group with steely eyes. "We can't just hide. We have to *do* something."

Feet shifted and nervous glances swung from one side to the other.

Ashur was going to yell something in return, but Irenya cut him off. "Aric, we're just recruits," she said softly. "We're not even halfway through our training."

"I know," Aric said. "But there's a dragon out there and we are the closest thing to a Dragon Hunter for miles."

For a moment, no one knew what to say.

"It's…a dragon, Aric," Orisius eventually uttered. Everyone else seemed to be thinking the exact same thing.

"Yes, it is a dragon," Aric said. "It will set the whole city on fire and kill anyone in sight. By the time that thing is done, there will be nothing left but ashes and rubble. We have to do something."

Irenya and Orisius opened their mouths to reply but said nothing.

"Aric is right," Clea said. "We have to do something."

Her plea received no echo. Aric saw Athan reach for his prayer box, while Nahir and Trissa closed their eyes, mumbling something inaudibly.

"It's suicide!" Ashur declared. He took a step forward. "What exactly are we supposed to do?"

Somewhere in the city, high-pitched screams followed the thundering sound of what was probably the collapse of some other large building or tower.

"We have glowstone weapons," Clea replied, her hand reaching for a sword handle at her hilt.

"So what?!" Ashur asked. "Even if we *were* fully trained, you can't fight a dragon if it's flying."

"I'm afraid the young man is right," the old keeper told Clea. "Airborne dragons are almost impossible to defeat. That's why we only ever attack them inside their lairs."

"Exactly," Ashur said, turning to Aric. "Listen to the old man if you don't want to listen to me."

"I'm not saying we attack the dragon," Aric said.

Ashur looked stunned. "Are you making fun of me, or have you just gone mad?!" he asked.

"Settle down," Leth told him. "What are you saying, Aric?"

"I'm saying we go after the witch," Aric replied. He raised a hand, stopping the chorus of protests before it erupted. "Yes, I know. You all think I'm crazy, but I'm not."

He looked at Leth and Clea. At least those two had to believe him.

"I know what I saw out in the desert. A woman walking toward a dragon as if it was no more intimidating than an untrained stallion. I understand how insane that sounds, and I probably wouldn't believe it either if I hadn't seen it myself. But today I saw her again. I saw her just as clearly as I can see all of you right now. It was the same woman I saw in the desert. She walked into a tavern a few blocks from here, then, moments later, a dragon swooped down from the sky and attacked the city." He shook his head. "I don't care how crazy I sound, because either I'm right or my hallucinations have the power to summon dragons, and *that* sounds much crazier."

That was a good point. Aric could see it in their eyes, even if no one wanted to admit it.

"So what?" Ashur asked. "We go after this…witch? What happens when we find just some random woman?"

Aric ignored him and instead addressed the whole group. "We might be just recruits, but *I* am your captain. That means I don't need you to agree with me before I give you an order. However, I can't be your captain in name only. I can only lead you if I have your trust, and I know I haven't earned it yet. So…" He paused, taking a deep breath. "Let me prove myself to you. Follow me and I'll show you this witch. I'll show you she's real, and together we'll stop her. I'm not asking you to commit suicide. I'm telling you that even though we are only recruits, *we* can save this city from that dragon." Aric swallowed through a dry throat. "What do you say? Are you with me?"

A frightful silence took over the room, interrupted by muffled, distant screams.

"I am," Clea said.

Aric felt like jumping to her and hugging her but instead gave her a calm nod.

"Well," Leth smiled, "between insanity and fear, I will much rather have the first, thank you. Count me in."

"I'm in as well, Aric Auron," Nahir said. "A Cyrinian Honor Guard will always follow his captain."

Three yeses in a row; Aric would have felt proud if it hadn't been for the spine-chilling growls and screams outside. They had to hurry.

"I don't need to be a Cyrinian Honor Guard to be loyal," Tharius said. "I'll follow my captain."

"Screw that," Trissa said, her hands on her hips. "The only thing Aric said so far that I agree with is that he hasn't earned my trust yet. But…"

She sighed and looked at Aric. "Clea's right. We have to do something, and I'd rather go on a witch hunt with you than stand here looking like a jerk."

"I would rather look like a jerk and live than go on a witch hunt and get roasted by a dragon," Dothea said. "But, you know…if you are all going, then I suppose I'm in too."

A smile grew on Aric's face. "What about you, Athan?" he asked. "We need the goddess's favor if we are to pull this off."

"For the thousandth time," Athan pleaded. "I'm not a priest!"

"Who cares?" Leth said. "We're not Dragon Hunters, either."

There were some smiles. Athan even laughed. "Well, anyone fighting a dragon has the goddess's favor. That's why I joined the Guild in the first place. To fight Ava's enemies, not to hide. So, yes. I'm with you, Captain."

"Thank you," Aric said. He looked at Orisius and Irenya and wondered if the two of them realized their hands were together. Not that it mattered. Their secret affair was a secret to no one in the company.

The couple exchanged a nervous glance. "We're with you," Orisius said, sighing. "Let's get this witch."

"Great," Aric said. "Ergon? Lyra?"

"We're with you, Aric," Lyra said, smiling and grabbing hold of her brother's arm.

Ergon remained quiet, letting his sister tug at his arm as if he was a lifeless doll. He did not contradict her, however, so Aric thanked them with a nod.

"All right," Aric said, smiling. "That leaves you three." He indicated Ashur, Prion, and Jullion.

"Well, that's a surprise," Trissa said.

"What happens if we say no?" Ashur asked, ignoring Trissa's comment.

"To be honest," Aric replied, shrugging, "nothing. The punishment for disobeying orders is the Pilgrimage, but I'm not giving you an order. I'm asking you to come with me voluntarily. I'm asking you for a chance to earn your trust."

"Trust?" Ashur sneered. "You're an idiot, half-prince. But if you want to chase after some imaginary witch, I'll indulge you. Just so you know, though, if we *don't* find any witch, and we *won't*, I'll be requesting that you are removed from command on the grounds that you're insane."

Jullion agreed with a nod while Prion smiled fiendishly.

It was still better than a no, though. Or, at least, Aric hoped it was.

"Fair enough," Aric said. He took a deep breath and looked at Geric still cowering beneath the wooden table. "Geric, come on," he called, slapping his own thigh. The cat, however, refused to move. "Coward... All right, no time to lose. Cloaks off." He removed his own cloak. His dragon scale and glowstone armor shimmered like a frozen lake under the sun. "Single file, heads low, and weapons at the ready. I'm in the lead. Leth has the rear." He walked up to the door and grabbed the knob.

The rest of the company formed behind him quickly and precisely, Saruk's exercises taking over their movements. Looking over his shoulder, Aric approved the formation and tried to steady his breathing.

"Good luck," the old keeper said.

Aric had completely forgotten about him. "Thank you," he said. Then, as if remembering something, he added, "You're the one who first warned me about Eliran. Anything else we should know?"

"Yes," the old man replied, his wrinkled hands shaking. "Dragons aren't the only thing she can control. Give her a chance and she will twirl and shape your mind like a mound of sand."

"Right," Aric said. "No pressure, then." He took a deep breath, swung the door open, and jumped outside.

Flames crackled everywhere. A dark, thick cloud of smoke made it hard to breathe, and a stone bridge connecting two taller buildings had collapsed into the street below, blocking its southern end.

Aric had memorized the way back to the inn, but the landscape had changed so radically, he had to take a moment to recover his bearings. He looked east and saw a massive pillar of black smoke billowing toward the sky a few blocks away. The dark shape of the dragon was swirling around it, jets of fire gushing down at the hopeless city below.

"We should hurry," Clea said.

She was right. Without taking his eyes from the massive beast slashing through the air, Aric agreed with a dull "Yeah."

Could anyone ever get used to a sight such as that?

But there was no time for such thoughts. Springing back to life, Aric spun around and fled north, ordering the company to follow him. They crossed debris-covered streets, dodged smoldering objects, and bumped into panicking civilians. After turning several corners, Aric found the flag-on-shaped plaque.

"The Thirsty Dragon," Leth read from the plaque. "Somebody will be changing the name of his inn later today."

"If he's still alive," Dothea added.

The door was locked. Aric shook the knob violently, but all he got was the rattling sound of wood banging against metal.

"Fire take this!" Aric yelled. "Dothea, can you —"

"Excuse me, Captain," Nahir said, cutting Aric off and pushing him aside.

The tall Cyrinian raised a foot, and it recoiled like a snake getting ready to attack before whipping forward. With a loud *crack*, the lock broke and the door smashed open. No one waited for a signal. The whole company poured inside at once with blades in hand.

It was a sorry excuse for a tavern. The only two tables were overturned, and shards of stoneware littered the floor. Behind a tall, black counter, a middle-aged man covered in soot froze with the handle of a trapdoor in his hand.

"There's no more room," he squeaked, a thick, gray moustache covering his mouth. "Find some other place to hide."

"We're not looking for your basement," Aric told him. "We're looking for a woman."

"There are no women here," the innkeeper said, stepping down the trapdoor hastily. Somewhere down there, a little girl whined and a baby cried.

"One of your customers," Aric said. "With copper hair and flowing white robes. She came in here earlier."

The man stopped, his eyes rolling thoughtfully. "The Samehrian girl?" he asked.

"Of course she's Samehrian," Leth said beneath his breath.

Aric ignored him. "Where is she?" he asked.

"I don't know," the man mumbled. "She paid for a room on the third floor."

"Which one?" Aric demanded, storming toward the staircase.

"There's only the one," the innkeeper replied with a shrug.

Aric was already halfway through to the first floor when the trapdoor closed above the man's head.

Ascending two steps at a time, Aric climbed the narrow staircase with the company in tow.

"Aric," Clea whispered, grabbing his hand and stopping him in his tracks. They were nearly at the top. "If she really is a witch, how do we fight her?"

He had been asking himself the same question for a while.

"She's still human, like you and me," Aric replied, showing her one of his swords. "We can take her."

He looked at the closed door at the top of the flight of stairs. His palms had never felt this sweaty.

"Come on," he urged, addressing the entire company this time.

Steadying his hand, Aric opened the door and stormed in, ready to charge whomever he found.

But there was no one in sight.

Warily, the company walked inside, the wooden floor creaking beneath their boots. The room was so large that all fifteen of them still weren't enough to fill it. Above them stood a skewed ceiling, and several windows surrounded them. If it weren't for the two beds at the other end, the room would have looked like an empty attic instead.

She's not here, Aric thought. *Where could she be?*

Then a spark flashed, too quick for them to realize where it had come from as a wall of flames engulfed the group, besieging them in a circle.

"Who are you?" a thundering voice demanded.

The group shrank into itself, getting away from the flames.

The witch's face jumped out of nowhere, staring at Aric from across the wall of fire, her white robes and hair dancing around her as if a storm was raging at her. "Did he send you?"

Aric's mouth moved, but nothing came out.

He? Who was *he*? What was she talking about?

The witch stepped forward, placing herself so close to the fire, some of the flickering flames licked her clothes. The white garment, however, remained un-scorched, a blue halo pulsing from it as if she were made of glowstone.

"I asked you a question!" she demanded.

Aric was stunned, unable to speak. Her appearance, however... He hadn't expected to find the corpse he had seen in his dreams, but an evil witch wasn't supposed to look this...beautiful.

"We... I know what you are doing," Aric finally managed to say. "We're here to stop you." He aimed his sword at her, hoping it remained steady in his hand.

"Stop me?" she laughed. "Sohtyr sends a bunch of *kids* to stop me? Is this another one of his jokes?"

"Who?"

The witch seemed to grow.

"Don't play games with me!" she warned, her voice climbing and the flames climbing with it. "I will take control of that dragon, I will kill your master, and I will kill all of you if I have to." Bolts of blue lightning snapped from her fingers. "Tell me where he is and I will spare you."

"What are you talking about?!" Aric was at a complete loss. "We're Dragon Hunters of Lamash; no one sent us."

The witch seemed to have a moment of pause; even the furious look on her face appeared to ease slightly.

"Dragon Hunters?" she asked. "What are Dragon Hunters doing here? Why aren't you out there fighting that thing?"

"I…" Aric's entire body was begging him to flee. Instead, he tightened the grip on his sword. "I saw you in the desert. Controlling a dragon. It was you."

"You did?" She sounded perplexed. "I see… So you think *I* am controlling this one as well." The besieging flames she had conjured dimmed slowly but not completely.

"I know you are," Aric said.

The witch shook her head. "I know the stories they tell about me. And yes, I can control dragons. But I am trying to *save* this city, not destroy it." She paused and her eyes wandered for a bit, then she continued. "It's no matter. I need to concentrate, and you are wasting my time."

She turned her back on them and stepped toward one of the windows, spreading her arms.

"You don't fool me," Aric said, taking a step forward. But the wall of flames grew once again, blocking his way.

"I don't care if you believe me or not. I need to focus if I'm going to break Sohtyr's tether to that dragon. So be quiet!"

Eliran's palms faced up and Aric saw something…invisible, yet not really. It pulsed out from her body like hot air escaping a fire.

None of this made any sense. Why had she caged them in that circle of fire instead of fighting them? And who was this Sohtyr?

"Aric," Clea whispered. "We should make a move now." With her chin, she indicated the witch, who now had her back turned to them. She seemed to be in some sort of deep trance.

Is this how she controls dragons? Aric didn't remember any of this from when he had first seen her in the desert.

"We should just run through the flames," Trissa suggested. "It'll be like jumping over a campfire."

Clea and Dothea agreed with a nod. Aric, however, wasn't so sure.

"Who is this Sohtyr?" Aric asked out loud.

Glaring, Clea punched him in the shoulder.

The witch's arms lowered slowly, then after an overlong pause she said, "I need to concentrate!" There was ice in her voice.

"Whoever he is, you can't find him, can you?" Aric said. He received another punch in the shoulder, this time from Trissa.

"What are you talking about?" Clea asked, still in a whisper. "She's obviously controlling the dragon. She's just trying to trick you."

"No, I don't think so," Aric told her, then turned to Eliran. "I'm not sure if you're commanding this dragon or not, but I would bet my cuirass this Sohtyr is the reason you came to Nish. Who is he?"

Clenching a hand, Eliran turned sideways to face Aric. "Not just to Nish. He's the reason I was sent to this goddess-forsaken desert. I've been hunting him for months, and finally, I have him close enough that I can fight him." She took a couple of steps toward Aric. "Which I cannot do unless you're *quiet!*"

"In that case," Aric said, "what I have to know is whose side I'm on. Yours or his?"

"On Sohtyr's side?!" Eliran burst out laughing, her head swinging back so fast, Aric thought her neck would snap. "Oh, that's priceless." She forced herself to stop laughing, gasping from the effort. "No one's on Sohtyr's side, Dragon Hunter. Not even his own damn people. You want to know who he is? Well, he is no one. He doesn't exist. He and his wretched kind are a myth, a secret, and a lie, all wrapped into one fiendish ball of darkness. He's the kind of creature who lets a dragon loose on a city so he can…" She threw her arms up in desperation. "Goddess knows what! And instead of stopping him, here I am entertaining the curiosity of some stupid, useless Dragon Hunter who should be out there fighting the…"

She trailed off, her eyes lost in some faraway place.

"That's it!" She looked Aric in the eyes. "You can help. You all can." She waved a hand and the fire cage vanished. "Your glowstone weapons. You're carrying them, yes?"

"Um, yeah…" Aric replied, confused.

Not everyone was stunned by the witch's sudden change of mood, though. Like lightning, Ashur dashed past everyone in front of him, his sword aimed at Eliran's throat. The attack, however, was fruitless.

With a hand wave similar to the one that had put the fire out, Eliran casually swiped Ashur away, sending him flying across the room and slamming against the wall so hard the wooden planks cracked.

"Anyone else want to try something stupid?" Eliran asked, blue sparks crackling in her hands.

If she was trying to pacify them, it worked terribly. Aric had to hold Prion and Jullion down. Even Nahir was gritting his teeth like a wild beast.

"Everyone calm down," Aric ordered. "No one moves unless I say so. We will not hurt her. Lyra, check Ashur."

Prion spat. "She's a witch," he said as Lyra rushed to check on Ashur. "She should have hung long ago. Let's gut her and get this over with."

Eliran sent Prion a cold, murderous look but refrained from speaking.

"No one's gutting anyone," Aric said.

"My mistake," Eliran said, her eyes on Prion's. "Shouldn't have dropped that firewall." She turned to Aric and her voice softened. "But I do need your help to send that dragon away."

"How?" Aric asked. "What would you need us to do?"

"Aric!" Clea protested.

"Yeah," Leth agreed. "You seem to be forgetting your own plan. Isn't she supposed to be dangerous?"

"I'm not forgetting anything," Aric said calmly. "But I think she's telling the truth. She's not commanding this dragon."

"How can you know that?" Clea asked. "She's a witch, she has...tricks."

"Indeed," Leth said. "She might be manipulating your mind right now, just like the old keeper said."

Aric shook his head. "I don't think so. If she was, we wouldn't even be having this conversation. We would already be on our way to do whatever she's talking about."

That rendered both Leth and Clea speechless.

Eliran smiled. "Smart kid," she said.

"Lyra," Aric called. "How's Ashur?"

"He's bleeding a bit but otherwise just as rude as always."

"Let me go," Ashur grumbled, pushing Lyra away and standing back up.

"How would we help?" Aric asked.

"It's simple," Eliran replied. "Mind-control spells work both ways. That means everything the target feels, the spell caster feels as well. So, if you lot were to attack that dragon with those glowstone weapons of yours, Sohtyr would feel every single inch of your blades as if they were penetrating his own flesh. It won't physically harm him, but it will make him lose his focus. His defenses will drop, and I will be able to cut his mind tether to the dragon and replace it with one of my own, which will allow me to send the wretched creature away. It should also allow me to find Sohtyr so I can deal with him once and for all."

Aric nodded in agreement. "So, we wouldn't have to kill the dragon, just hurt it."

"Exactly," Eliran said.

Behind Aric, several worried looks were exchanged.

"Are you sure about this?" Leth asked him. "For all we know, this Sohtyr doesn't even exist."

"And we've already wasted so much time that half of the city doesn't exist anymore, either," Aric replied. He turned to face the company. "I asked you to come here with me voluntarily, and you did. You wanted me to prove that I had seen the desert witch, and I did. You wanted to know if I could be trusted, or if I was just insane. Well, I gave you a chance to find out, and you got your answer. So, asking is over. This is an order. We are attacking that dragon right now."

He stormed toward the door, his Hunters parting to make way for him.

"Single file; I'm in the lead." As he reached the door, Aric looked behind and saw the whole group staring back at him as if they couldn't believe a single word from his mouth. "I said NOW!"

To Aric's relief, the group snapped from its trance, scurrying to their positions as if Saruk himself was screaming at their heels.

The company sped across smoke-filled streets, jumping over crumbled walls and shattered merchant stalls. The dark shape of the dragon loomed above, letting out spine-chilling growls that echoed between flaming houses. Frightened screams and pained howls surrounded them at every turn. Aric did his best to avoid the lifeless stares of the occasional corpses lying here and there.

"Clea, Orisius, Dothea," Aric called. "Get on the rooftops. Shower that thing with arrows." He drew his glowstone sword. "We need to get that dragon on the ground if we want to really do some damage."

He stopped and looked up, watching the dragon whirl in the air. They were so close, they could feel the heat from its fiery breath.

"Everyone look alive! We have ourselves a dragon to fight."

With steely nods, Aric's orders were obeyed, and he watched his archers climb the nearest house.

"What are we doing here? This is insane!"

The voice belonged to Prion, but the question was aimed at Ashur, not Aric.

After a pause where he received no answer, Prion insisted, "Ashur, let's get out of here!"

It was Jullion who answered. "Are you stupid?!" he asked. "You want to be sent on the Pilgrimage?"

Prion spat. "Fire take the Pilgrimage. And the Guild. We can just run away. Right now." Prion waved toward Aric. "He won't stop us."

Aric was going to say something, but Ashur's cold silence intrigued him.

Prion reached for his friend's arm but never caught it. "Ashur..." he mumbled.

Pulling away, Ashur walked toward Aric. "I'm not a conscript like you, Pri. I'm not gonna run away."

Aric would sooner have expected the dragon to apologize.

"Ashur," Aric said. "I'm making you a squad leader." He indicated both Jullion and Prion. "Those two are your squad. Make sure they don't step out of line. That's an order."

With his back to a fuming Prion, Ashur nodded agreement.

Good, Aric thought.

Leth whispered a "Well played" into Aric's ear, but he ignored it. There was no time to waste.

His three archers had climbed the rooftops and taken positions behind portions of chimneys left standing, their bows aimed at the dragon and ready to fire. Aric needed to get the rest of the company into position in the square the dragon had been punishing for the last few minutes.

"Hey, look who's here," Trissa said. "How does he always find us?"

Aric turned and saw Geric climb down from the wreckage of a fruit stall. The desert lynx did not stay for long, however, and quickly disappeared, sneaking down some dark alley.

"Don't let him fool you," Aric said. "He just likes to pretend that he's helpful. Now come on. Follow me."

Staying low so not to be seen, the group sprinted toward the square and squatted behind a pile of darkened bricks that had once been a wall.

"Clea!" Aric screamed. "Open fire."

He saw the curved shape of three bows appear over the ridgeline of the roofs to his south. The arrows released almost simultaneously, but only one of them hit its target. However, it was more than enough to infuriate the dragon. The glowstone pierced the beast's neck and it reeled in pain, releasing a shriek so powerful, it made the stones the company was hiding behind tremble.

What Aric did not expect, however, was what he saw next. The dragon circled around, slashing through the air. Then it spat a jet of fire aimed precisely at the archers' hiding place.

Aric's heart sank and a scream froze in his throat. Then, to his huge relief, three bows appeared slightly to the southeast and released another volley.

Oh, thank the goddess.

They had been smart enough to move after firing, but Aric chided himself for not having thought of it before and telling them to do exactly that.

This was insane, he thought. They were clearly in way over their heads.

Hunter, a voice rang inside Aric's head. A mix between a hiss and an echo repeated tenfold.

"Wha…" Aric mumbled, baffled.

You do not need to speak. Although distorted and metallic, it was clearly Eliran's voice. *I can hear your thoughts.*

You… You can read my mind?

I can. The voice seemed to vibrate inside his skull. *But I won't dig inside. I'm just listening; don't worry. You are doing a wonderful job. Sohtyr wasn't expecting that. We almost got him from the surprise alone, but it wasn't enough. I'll need you to hit the dragon even harder if I'm going to take that mind tether down.*

Fire take this! Aric thought. *What am I supposed to do?!* The question was for himself, however. Had she heard that as well? *It's very uncomfortable to know you're listening in, you know?*

I'm sure you have worse things to worry about right now. Keep the pressure on and I'll take Sohtyr's spell down in no time. Give that dragon the wrath of Ava, Hunter.

And with that, she was gone. Aric had no idea how he knew she had left. He just…did.

Another barrage of arrows rained down on the dragon. This time, all of them hit their target. The archers were clearly learning the dragon's swift movements, but all it did was make the beast angrier. This time, instead of gushing fire at the source of the arrows, the dragon spread it over a wider area, setting an entire neighborhood on fire.

Aric cursed. Clea and the others wouldn't be able to take this much longer.

"Why won't that thing land?!" Aric hissed.

The plan was clearly not working.

"I have an idea," Aric said. "Ergon, give me your spear."

Sheathing his own sword, Aric grabbed the weapon. Its shaft was taller than Nahir, and its blade was as long as a broadsword's.

"All of you stay here. I'm going to try to get it to present its hind legs to you. The moment he lands, give him Ava's wrath."

Without waiting for a reply, Aric jumped up, but Leth held him down.

"What do you think you're doing?!" Leth demanded.

"What do you think? I'm getting that thing down on the ground," Aric replied.

317

"Are you mad?!" Leth asked.

Aric looked at the spear. The glowstone glistened from the fires surrounding them.

"Remember the Frostbound tunnels?" he asked. "When we found those things attacking Ashur, Orisius, and the others? You and Clea told me to stand back because I didn't know how to fight and you two did."

"Yeah, so what?" Leth said.

"Well," Aric smiled. "I've since learned how to fight." He winked and darted away.

Aric crossed the cobblestones toward the center of the square, limbs of maimed statues littering the way. Once there, he climbed the pile of rubble that once had been a glorious monument to the Empire's might and waved his spear, drawing defiant circles above his head.

"Hey!" he screamed from the top of his lungs. "Down here, you fat lizard!"

It took no time for the dragon's keen senses to notice the tiny human so willingly presenting itself for the kill.

This better work...

As the dragon dove roaring toward him, Aric turned around and fled. He ran faster than he had ever run. Faster than in the Frostbound. Faster than in their training runs across the desert. Faster than he had run inside the Gauntlet to get that red flag out.

The once neatly paved roads tried to trip him with hundreds of scattered stones, forcing Aric to watch where he stepped very carefully while sending quick glances over his shoulder at the incoming dragon.

Aric saw the beast's jaws open and jumped sideways, rolling on the ground just in time to avoid a jet of fire. Feeling a couple of sharp rocks carve into his skin, Aric picked himself up quickly, resuming his flight. He checked over his shoulder again, measuring the distance to the dragon. It was getting terrifyingly closer, but it was also a mere few feet from the ground now.

"Got you, you big, ugly thing," Aric muttered to himself. Then he took a sharp turn and sneaked into a narrow street to his right.

Seeing Aric disappear around a corner, the dragon angled his wings forward, braking so it didn't fly past its prey. The creature lost speed instantaneously, and the ground shook as it lost altitude and landed.

Aric turned around, waiting for the dragon to burst around the corner. He didn't have to wait long.

A colossal black head, studded with horns of every shape and size, exploded between the buildings, roaring under a rain of stone bricks. The nauseating smell of sulfur stung Aric's nostrils, and once again he jumped sideways, this time through a window and into the bowels of some building.

Flattened against the floor, he felt the heat of flames as they flooded through the windows.

Then, as abruptly as they had come in, the flames stopped, replaced by a growl that made Aric's belly turn to water. Expecting the entire creature to burst through the wall, Aric scrambled across the floor as far into the building as possible. The dragon, however, did not come. Instead, wild screaming and yelling echoed from outside.

No, not screaming, nor yelling. Those were battle cries.

Right on time, Aric thought.

He strode toward a window, hurrying back outside, but stopped at the threshold.

Where's the spear?

Aric cursed as his head spun around, searching every corner of the room. The dragon fire had destroyed the furniture inside, and charred pieces of wood smoldered everywhere.

"There you are," he let out, hurrying to pick up the lance.

When he did, however, he found that the pole was broken in half. Dragon Hunter's lances were built to be particularly long so as to give the Hunter some distance from the dragon's deadly talons. Now, all that was left was an arm's length of spear, making it barely safer than a knife.

Well, it'll have to do.

Aric jumped out the window and found the dragon whipping his tail back and forth at the Hunters behind. The narrow street kept it from circling around to face them. It had also become a much easier target. Arrows kept raining down on it, sending it into a blinding fit of rage.

In fact, the creature was so distracted, its neck bent backward, that it did not notice Aric as he emerged from the building.

Taking a deep breath, Aric felt the weight of the spear in his hands and sneaked closer to the dragon. With its long neck stretching back, looking for the attackers harassing his hind legs and tail, the beast had left its chest wide open. It was perfect!

Too bad the spear was now too short to reach that high.

Well, why approach a dragon if you can strike it from afar?

Aric raised his arm and pulled the spear back, then hurled the half-spear, his entire body lending strength to the throw. The weapon flew away. It climbed and climbed until it pierced the base of the dragon's neck.

The whole world shook. Howling and roaring at the same time, the dragon staggered, colliding into nearby buildings, its head whipping around madly.

Walls crumbled all around, and a chimney crashed down right next to Aric. Bricks rained from every side, ricocheting to the ground. He felt a powerful blow between his shoulder blades, stumbled, lost his balance, and fell face first against the ground.

Somewhere in the distance, a deafening roar shook his body. He tasted iron, and a rattle filled his brain as darkness swallowed him whole.

⁀

Aric's ears were ringing.

Hunter!

"Aric!"

His nose and his mouth felt wet. He tried to move, but it was as if his entire body was made of lead.

Hunter!

"Aric!"

A burst of light flooded his eyes and the world came into focus. The first thing he saw was Geric lavishly dragging his tongue across his face.

"Are you all right?" Lyra asked. She was kneeling beside him.

The rest of the company was huddled around him, anxiously waiting for a reply.

"Yeah," Aric said, his voice as hoarse as if he hadn't spoken in days.

Pushing Geric's tongue aside, he sat up, flinching as every bone and muscle in his body complained.

"You are positively insane," Leth told him. "Did you know that?"

"I think you were brilliant," Clea said cheerfully.

Hunter, a voice rang in his head. *Are you all right? Can you hear me?*

Yeah. Yeah. I'm okay. Aric replied.

"It's a miracle you're alive, you know?" Lyra said. She sounded almost angry.

"I'm fine," Aric replied. "Just help me up, okay?"

Leth and Ergon slid their arms under Aric's and hoisted him up.

It seems your plan worked, Aric thought. It still felt very weird to talk with his mind.

I know. I'm in pursuit of Sohtyr as we speak.

Who is he? Aric asked. *Why did he attack the city? I think I deserve to know.*

You're right, Eliran said. *You do deserve to know. But not right now. I can't afford to lose him.*

Do you need help? He's obviously dangerous.

Is that worry, Hunter? Aric felt an amused drumming in his skull that mildly resembled a chuckle. *Don't worry,* Eliran said. *We evil witches can handle ourselves.*

So, when will I see you again? Aric asked, but it was too late. She was already gone.

"Dragon Hunters, I assume."

Aric turned around toward the voice. A tiny man wearing a colorful jacket and the largest golden pendant Aric had ever seen navigated between the wreckage as if he were trying to avoid getting dust on his pointy shoes.

"We are," Aric replied. "Who wants to know?"

The man stopped and gave a flamboyant bow. "I am Kortush, Nish's Master of Keys. His Lordship Narim Parvad, Imperial Governor of the city, demands your presence immediately."

"Really?" Aric asked. He turned to his Hunters, looking impressed. "I guess we get to be rewarded. Nice."

The company smiled, exchanging proud looks.

"I hardly think so!" Kortush said indignantly. "A dragon in the skies of Nish? The whole Guild should drown in shame. His Lordship will see you immediately, and you better have a very good explanation for this."

CHAPTER 17

The Infiltration

Sabium waved Fadan inside with his usual suspicious frown. The old man never really worried himself with making the prince feel welcome.

"Did you burn the book?" Sabium asked, shutting the door behind him.

The prince nodded his confirmation. "It's done," he replied. "I even took the opportunity to practice the fire spell."

"Good." That seemed to relax the old mage a bit. "You never know what sort of magic could be attached to that book."

"There was no glowstone on the book though, Master," Fadan said. "I checked."

"You can't know that. Glowstone can be powdered and hidden just about anywhere." He moved to his desk and sat down.

"Ah, clever," Fadan said. "And fire can destroy glowstone?"

"High temperatures will render the crystals useless, yes," Sabium explained. "If the book has burned, it is no longer a threat."

"I see. But I still don't get what makes these people so dangerous."

"They're fanatics," Sabium replied. "That's what makes them so dangerous."

"So what? Who cares what they worship?"

"You have no idea what you're talking about," Sabium argued, opening one of the books piled in front of him.

"Because you haven't explained it to me!" Fadan said. "I know next to nothing about the Academy. How am I supposed to know anything about their creepy cousins?"

"I don't really have the time right now," Sabium muttered, his eyes scanning the pages in front of him. "You really think you found that book just by chance? It was *planted* for you to find it, and I need to figure out why."

"That doesn't make any sense, Master. Even *I* didn't know I had the Talent when me and Aric stumbled into the book. And even then, I couldn't make any sense of it."

Sabium raised his head from the book. "I find it very hard to believe that a member of the Circle would just 'forget' one of their forbidden books in the Imperial Palace. In fact, what would an Archon even be doing in the Citadel in the first place?"

"A what?" Fadan asked.

"Archon," Sabium repeated, returning to his study. "It's what they call themselves. They despise the term *mage*. For them, it is a synonym for *heretic*."

"It doesn't make sense. How can these…'Archons' be such a big secret?" Fadan asked. "I mean, who else knows about them? Does my father? Because if they're dangerous –"

"He probably does not," Sabium said, cutting Fadan off. "The Circle's existence was a very well-kept secret. By both the Circle *and* the Academy."

"Why would the Academy keep them secret?"

"The Circle was born inside the Academy," Sabium replied. "They were mages who felt magic was a gift from the gods, so they searched for answers among the sacred texts. They were obsessed with excavations of holy sites and relics. They shunned the Academy's scientific pursuit of knowledge. Their vision for the magical community was of a religious order, not a place of learning. There was a divide, and eventually, they were cast out. They became an embarrassment but were not seen as a threat."

"Wait," Fadan said. "Before, you were saying they *are* dangerous. But now you're saying –"

"Because they always *were* a threat!" Sabium interrupted heatedly. "They just weren't seen as one because of their relatively small size. It is always easier to pretend a problem doesn't exist instead of facing it and fixing it. Especially if that problem makes sure to remain out of sight, which is what they did for centuries. The problem, young prince, is that the world has changed. The mages are gone. Your father got rid of them. Which means there's no one left to keep the Circle in check." Sabium massaged his temples, his eyes closed. "It's only a matter of time before their agenda comes crashing down on the rest of us, because believe me. What the Circle of Archons wants involves us all."

"Which is?" Fadan asked.

Sabium sighed, reopening his eyes. "This is a matter for old mages, not young princes. I need to do some research. In the meantime, you can practice."

"You want to me to just stand back here and practice all by myself?"

"No, goddess, not *here*," Sabium said. "You'll distract me. Get back to your palace. Practice there."

"I just came from the palace," Fadan said.

"I know," Sabium told him. "Now go back."

The prince exhaled impatiently, placing his hands on his hips, but eventually turned, cursing beneath his breath, and left for the apartment door.

"And, young prince?" Sabium called.

Fadan turned to his master.

"Try not to lose an arm, please."

⌒⤳

A group of five maids twirled back and forth around the empress like butterflies competing for a flower. A couple of the maids focused on turning Cassia's dark hair into luscious, thick curls. A third maid played with shades of pink on the empress's lips and cheeks. A fourth one fixed every small imperfection of the dress while the fifth and last maid sprayed delicate puffs of perfume around Cassia.

Venia found the ritual almost beautiful. She watched it from across the room, her hands crossed in front of her. Sagun stood beside her, nodding his approval.

"Excellent," he said as the last touches were applied. "The emperor shall be pleased."

Venia saw Cassia inspect herself in the mirror, but she knew the empress was only pretending to care how she looked. If it had been up to her, Cassia would have gone to dinner every night looking like a beggar from the Docks.

"It will do," Cassia said.

Venia had always found it spectacularly impressive how, despite her humiliating condition, the empress always maintained a regal bearing around others. She had seen the empress's mask slip, of course, but that was because Cassia trusted her. In public, however, the woman somehow always found the strength not to falter, especially around her children.

Venia hadn't always been loyal to Cassia, of course. She had originally been placed among the empress's maids to spy on her. However, it hadn't taken Venia long to become a double agent. Cassia hadn't been surprised when Venia revealed herself a spy – the empress had always suspected that her husband would want to know what she did in private – but she did become tremendously grateful. Venia didn't just feed the emperor fake reports; she was also Cassia's eyes and hands, making it possible for the empress to do things Tarsus forbade her to even imagine.

Lately, however, even Venia hadn't been able to maintain what was left of the empress's world from falling apart. As if the poor woman hadn't been through enough as it was.

"I'll be down momentarily," Cassia said. "You may all go. Except Venia. I want you to help me with my shoes."

"Yes, Your Majesty," the spy said, lowering her head.

Cassia received a curtsy from the other maids and a bow from Sagun, after which the castellan shooed the maids out of the room, leaving after them and closing the door behind him.

The empress exhaled with disgust, her whole body deflating slightly. "You have news?" she asked, heading for a chair.

Venia cleared her throat. "I do, Your Majesty."

"What is it?" Cassia asked, sitting down and grabbing a pair of shoes.

"I... I found out who's helping your son," Venia said.

Cassia slipped her foot into a shoe. "Oh, who is it?"

"Lord Fabian Lagon," Venia replied. "I saw them chatting last night. In the Empress's Orchard."

"Fabian?" the empress asked, her other shoe dangling in her fingers. "Are you sure it was him? I don't think he is a spy."

Venia chuckled. "Trust me, Your Majesty. He is."

"If you say so," Cassia replied with a shrug. She slipped on the second shoe and stood up. "Well, let's go." She took a deep breath. "My husband awaits."

The empress started toward the door, but Venia stopped her. "There's more."

Cassia turned. "What is it?"

"I found...something else," Venia replied.

The empress frowned. "You're hesitating... Something bad happened. What is it? Is Fadan all right?"

"He's fine," Venia replied, raising a soothing hand. "But I found out something important. Yesterday, I managed to follow your son to his hiding place, here in the Citadel. He is using one of the abandoned palaces."

"Using it for what?" Cassia asked.

"It took me some time to figure out which palace he was in, so by the time I got to it, the prince was already gone," Venia said. "However, he left something behind. A bucket, with a book burning inside."

"What?!" Cassia was thoroughly confused.

"I didn't bring the book," Venia said. "I decided it was better not to give him any clue that he's been discovered. It would prompt him to change his hiding place. I allowed the book to burn so he could find its ashes upon return, but I did discover what the book was about." Venia took a step forward. "Your Majesty, I believe your son possesses the Talent. He is trying to learn magic."

⌒⟩

It usually took Fadan around an hour to go to Sabium's apartment in the Docks, which meant he spent two hours just *crossing* the city every night he visited his master. Two hours he had completely wasted tonight with his fruitless visit.

He climbed out of the sewage manhole inside the Citadel and studied the night sky. He hadn't exactly left early for Sabium's, which meant it had to be really late. For a moment, he considered calling it a night and taking the opportunity for a few hours of sleep, but he quickly dismissed the thought. He couldn't let an entire night go wasted. Not when he had been making so little progress.

Pushing back a yawn, Fadan started toward the palace. He was going to spend a few hours practicing if he could remain awake. Usually, the empty palace was where he did his practicing sessions, but he felt like his own room was a better idea this time. His plan was to attempt the wall-traversing spell, which wasn't entirely safe to do on his own. Being somewhere where he could cry for help in case something went wrong seemed like a prudent idea. Besides, it was a silent spell that made no noise or flashes of light. It should be safe enough to practice in his bedroom.

Fadan strode through the usual way back to his room, then climbed up to his window. Fabian always kept the way clear of any unwanted eyes. How the old general did it, however, was a complete mystery.

"All right," Fadan said to himself, closing the window and pushing his sleeves up. "Let's work."

The prince lit a couple of oil lamps, then double-checked the lock on his bedroom door. Still not satisfied, Fadan picked up a chair and fitted its back under the door handle, blocking it from being pushed open.

Satisfied with his security measures, he removed his dark cloak and grabbed a vial of runium from one of its inner pockets, then downed the metallic red liquid in a single gulp.

He felt the familiar burning sensation, quickly offset by the transmoga-phon around his neck. Breathing small blue puffs, Fadan tested his powers. It was a small ritual Sabium had taught him that helped him adapt his mindset. The idea was to teach his brain to switch from regular-life rules to magic rules. From that moment on, anything was possible.

"I can do this," he told himself, eyes closed.

Fadan had learned that magic was a tricky business. A single fraction of a moment of doubt and the spell was gone, sometimes literally, up in smoke. The problem was that most spells weren't as intuitive as moving an object. Causing fire, for instance, was more of an intellectual process. He had to imagine objects and substances and what particles they were made of. Then he had to visualize them heating up by friction while providing the right amounts of fuel and oxidizer to maintain the required flame and so on. It was a deeply rational thing that required tremendous amounts of previous study of the physical world, which conflicted with the deeply irrational feat of believing it was possible.

No, not just possible. That it was *actually* happening as he visualized it in his mind. It could be as frustrating as it was overwhelming.

Fadan tried to relax, shaking his arms and steadying his breathing.

This is easy, he thought. *I've done it before. Well, kind of… No, stop it! No doubts.*

"Ah, crap!" he heard himself say, punching his bed's mattress.

It was so hard to fight his own instincts. He did, however, have an idea. It had occurred to him often that he was an overthinker. There was really nothing he could do about it. The solution, then, was probably to do it the radical way. So far, he had just tried to make small objects, like spoons, go through his fingers. What if, instead of risking a few cuts and bruises, he *actually* risked his life? Maybe his mind would focus once and for all.

Maybe it was a genius idea. Maybe it was insane.

No! he thought. *I'm just overthinking it again.*

He gulped, but he had made his decision. He was going to try to cross the wall to the room next door. Provided he survived the crossing itself, it should be completely safe. The room had been empty for decades. It had once been his Aunt Junia's room, until her marriage, and it would have been Aric's room if the emperor hadn't sent him to the servant's wing.

Fadan took a long, deep breath.

I'll have to jump before I dematerialize, he thought. *Otherwise, I'll fall through the floor.*

Which meant he would have to rematerialize before landing on the floor on the other side. What a pity; his spells always worked better with his eyes closed.

Shoving any second thoughts away, and as if he wanted to surprise himself, he darted forward, shooting toward the stone wall opposite his bed. He jumped, visualized himself crossing the wall and-

BAM!

He smashed nose first against the granite and fell flat on his back.

"Goddess damn it!" Fadan groaned.

He rubbed his forehead as if that could somehow make the pain go away. There would be some lumps on his face the next day, but he was not about to give up just yet.

"I can do this," he told himself, taking a couple of steps back and filling his lungs.

I can do this.

Fadan lunged forward, readying his runium reserve to cast the spell, and jumped. The wall came closer and closer. Then, at the last possible moment, he closed his eyes, pushing his fear of failure away.

It all happened in an instant.

He realized he should have collided with the wall and hadn't, so he opened his eyes and saw the other side. It must have been enough to break the spell because his feet connected with the floor and then –

BAM!

He crashed into a tall wooden wardrobe. It was a sturdy old thing, because at his speed, Fadan should have torn the doors to pieces. Instead, he fell flat on his back again, just as he had done with the granite wall moments before.

"Fire take this!" he complained, rubbing the back of head.

Then it dawned on him.

I did it, he thought, his eyes going wide.

Fadan jumped like a cat after a fright. "I *did* it!" He smiled, making a huge effort to contain a celebratory yell.

I have to do it again, he thought.

One successful jump was nothing. He had to make sure it hadn't been pure luck.

Shaking his arms, he braced himself for another jump back into his room. Then, still smiling, he ran toward the wall, but just when he was about to jump, he aborted his own run, stopping before hitting the granite once again.

"No," he said to himself. "Eyes open this time. Eyes open."

Fadan resumed his place at the back of the room, taking quick, deep breaths. He lunged toward the wall leading to his room. He tapped his power and jumped, this time keeping his eyes open, completely ignoring the incoming granite barrier in his way.

It worked beautifully. His vision was blocked for a moment, but his room quickly came into view and Fadan landed as gracefully as if he had just jumped over a puddle of water down in the courtyard.

He had done it. He could cross walls. Just as a precaution, he began inspecting his body to make sure he hadn't somehow hurt himself in the process. He was fine, of course. There was no pain – besides the thumping in his forehead – or blood anywhere, and he began laughing hysterically. His heart was racing so hard, he could hear it.

I can't believe it, he thought, so happy he started jumping as if he couldn't contain his own energy.

It was amazing. He could do it now. He could finally rescue Doric. It was so exciting, he began to tremble slightly. The last time he had felt like this had been months before, and Aric had been by his side. They had nearly done it. They had actually broken Doric out of jail and even left the sewers when…

Fadan didn't remember much. He had never seen them coming. Only Aric had. All Fadan remembered was his brother's hands gripping his collar and shoving him down the manhole. It had been a fall of several feet. Fadan had landed on his shoulder, and the pain had nearly blinded him, at least for a moment. Then he had realized what was happening.

The room seemed to grow darker around him and Fadan sat on his bed as if his legs had decided they didn't want to support him anymore. He looked left and saw himself in the mirror, framed by his bedposts. Just like then, he was alone in the dark.

Fadan could still remember the smell of moss on his face as he had gotten back on his feet. He remembered the screams, the sound changed by having to cross the metal cover of the manhole. The memory wasn't exactly complete. He couldn't remember the exact words, only the soldiers barking threats followed by the thuds and groans of Aric and Doric being hit.

In the mirror, a tear slid down Fadan's cheek.

Hearing the screams, Fadan had climbed the ladder up to the manhole but had stopped halfway up, his hands refusing to move farther, while the rest of his body shook so much, it was a miracle he hadn't tumbled down again.

Aric had screamed the most, and his father had begged the soldiers to stop.

In the mirror, Fadan saw his own hand shoot up to cover his mouth and push down a sob, warm tears collecting around his fingers.

He cursed, jumping up and turning his back to the mirror.

"Goddess damn this," he said, kicking a wooden chest.

Pain shot through his foot, but he ignored it, focusing instead on wiping the tears from his eyes as if they burned.

"I can do this," he said between sniffs. "I can *do* this."

Fadan cleared his throat and steadied his breathing, then looked at his hands. He tapped his power, and even though the transmogaphon didn't allow him to clearly feel how much runium he still had, he knew it was plenty. He tested his powers, using the warm-up ritual Sabium had taught him, and a blue aura shone around his hands and wrists, spreading down his arms.

"I'm going to *do* this!"

⌣⌐

Fadan wasn't planning on springing Doric out of jail that night. He knew that to pull it off, a lot of preparation would be required, and he didn't even have a plan yet. The first step, then, was doing some scouting. Fadan decided to begin right away. He was just too excited to simply go to sleep.

The first problem he had to solve was entering the dungeons. Using the same sewage entrance as the last time was out of the question. The door Aric had shown him required a climb, which would be impossible to do while dematerialized, and Fadan had a feeling that opening it would not be as easy this time. It was, however, still an option for the escape.

The dungeons were located in the underground section of the Legion's headquarters, a large stone building that looked more like a vault than it did a palace.

Fadan left his room, climbing down his window just as he had dozens of times the last couple of months. This time, however, instead of heading for either the sewers or his hideout, Fadan sneaked toward the gigantic rectangle that was the Legion's headquarters.

Getting inside wasn't too hard. The main gate was, of course, guarded, but armed with his new spell, any of the dozens of side and back doors feeding the building would do. He chose one at random and found himself inside a darkened corridor, dozens of nondescript doors flanking him. He penetrated the building, casting a tiny ball of fire, which he kept in the palm of his hand to light the way forward.

The decoration of the building was suitably austere. Occasional statues of great Generals were interspersed with long, hanging banners of famous Legions.

It didn't take long before he found the first patrol. The pair of Legionaries droned across a corridor, far too drowsy to ever notice him hiding behind the hanging banner of the Fifty-seventh Legion of Awam. The deeper he went into the building, however, the more numerous the patrols became. He was forced to patiently inch forward from one shadowed nook to the other, timing his movements to coincide with the Legionaries turning his back on him.

Aric would have loved this, he thought.

He, however, was definitely far more nervous than he was excited. Or maybe *terrified* was a better word.

Fadan eventually found the entrance to the dungeons, a thick wooden door at the bottom of a narrow staircase. Unfortunately, it was being guarded by a sergeant rigidly standing at attention beneath a torch.

In his discussions with Sabium, Fadan had learned about the existence of dozens of spells that would have been useful to him right now: spells that enhanced his hearing and vision, spells that allowed him to detect nearby people no matter what objects stood in the way, spells that created illusions or somehow played with other people's senses, making them hear or see things that weren't really there; the list went on and on. At the time, Fadan had considered the ability to cross walls the only truly essential one for this particular goal. Now, however, he was reconsidering that notion.

The problem was that he had overestimated the advantages of the dematerializing spell. Not knowing what was on the other side of a wall, for example, made it impossible to cross at will, because he never knew if he would land in a clear space or right in the middle of a shelf. He could always not rematerialize if he found himself within a piece of furniture, but that meant he would also fall through the floor, and he had no way of knowing what would be down there, either.

This meant that he had had to abandon his technique of blindly jumping at walls. Therefore, the only safe approach, when he didn't know where he was jumping to, was to only pass through doors, as the likelihood of there being something standing on the other side was minuscule. Unfortunately, as it turned out, passing through doors wasn't a very helpful ability to have when trying to access a prison complex.

There was only one way he was going to get inside. He would have to distract the guard long enough to pass through the door. At least he wouldn't have to come back through there on his way out. He could always drop through to the sewage tunnel Aric had shown him.

Fadan crouched. He was at the top of the stairs, hiding just around the corner that led down to the dungeons. He could see the guard's steel helmet down below, reflecting the torch's light like a fireball.

It gave Fadan an idea. After all, he *did* know a couple other spells.

He tapped his power and ran the usual test, just to make sure he didn't mess the spell up. Then he focused on the flames. He visualized the flames in his head, making sure his mental image perfectly mimicked the real ones. Then he saw them burst upward, as if a bottle of brandy had spilled on them.

The real flames reacted immediately. The explosion of fire wasn't as impressive as the one Fadan had imagined, but the spell did its job and the guard jumped, startled.

Cursing, the sergeant looked up, readjusting his helmet. Fadan had to force himself not to giggle out loud. The man was probably questioning his own sanity. Torches didn't do something like that.

Just as the man seemed to decide he had imagined it, Fadan sent another burst of power, making the flames taller and twice as bright. The Legionary probably felt the heat on his face.

The poor man staggered back, tripped on a step, and fell backward, yelping. Then Fadan made a fist as he visualized the fire burning out. The real flames died as well, sending the staircase into darkness.

"Ava Mother!" the sergeant cried. "Odrian! Odrian, are you there?"

Fadan heard the clanging of the sergeant nervously getting up and climbing the stairs in the darkness.

"Odrian!" the man repeated. "Sergeth? Anyone?! Where are you?"

Making himself as small as he could, Fadan stood still as the sergeant scurried past him in the darkness.

"Odrian? Sergeth?" the soldier kept calling, his voice getting farther away.

The prince did not waste any time. As soon as he knew the sergeant had turned a corner, he raced downstairs, reigniting the torch so that he could see. He jumped toward the door and went right past it, as if it weren't even there, then landed softly on the stone floor on the other side.

He looked back through the bars on the door's tiny window and chuckled, feeling tremendously happy with himself. He sure could get used to these abilities.

He was standing in some sort of main hallway, from which several cell-blocks fed. It looked almost like his father's wine cellar, a succession of low archways where three men would have had a hard time fitting side by side. There were only a couple of torches in sight, their fuel seemingly about to run out, giving the place a cold, grayish light. Echoes of water drops falling into puddles reached him from every direction, and Fadan could swear he heard mice squeaking in a corner. The smell was nearly overwhelming. The last time he had been there, he had assumed the stench from the sewers had followed him, lingering in his nose. It appeared, however, that the two places smelled exactly the same.

The sergeant would surely be back soon, so Fadan walked away. The poor man would have a hard time explaining to his friends what had happened.

Voices alerted him to the presence of guards inside. He had been expecting to find them, so the sound was actually welcome. It was far better to know where they were than to bump into them by accident.

He turned into the first block and walked between the rows of cells, inspecting them. Most were empty. The ones that weren't, though, did a horrible job of housing the inmates.

There was no furniture of any kind. Not even a carpet. Everyone was just lying on the ground, snoring next to foul-looking puddles and rats. At least they weren't too crowded. Usually, prisoners stood in pairs, with the occasional cell holding either three or just one lone prisoner.

It was impossible to see the faces of every single prisoner, as the darkness inside the cells obscured their features. Unfortunately, waking them up to check if any of them was Doric didn't seem like a sensible idea, so Fadan just kept looking.

He had no luck in the first block, so he doubled back, heading for the second.

"Water," a hoarse voice said from one of the cells.

Fadan froze, turning to the source of the sound, a bald man whose bare chest displayed a mess of scars.

"Please," the prisoner continued. "Water."

Where was he even going to find any water in this place?

"I'll…see if I can find some," Fadan replied in a whisper.

"Please," the prisoner begged, rolling and dragging himself across the floor. "Please!"

The man was becoming too loud. Fadan had to rush away. He got back to the main hallway, peeking to make sure it was clear before turning the corner. He could still hear the guards' voices. It sounded like a casual chat.

Fadan tiptoed to the edge of the second block and the voices became louder. Carefully, he took a peek. There were two shapes at the other end of the cellblock, one of them holding a bright torch. They seemed to be discussing the contents of a particular cell.

Well, I hope Doric isn't in this corridor, Fadan thought.

With a hop, the prince skipped across the hallway and headed to the next block. Just like the first, the third block had no guards. It was safe to inspect.

Fadan found no one inside the first couple of cells. The next one was occupied by a pair of mice chewing at something in a corner. Then Fadan saw him.

Doric was lying on the ground, his head resting on what looked like a bag of flour, although that was very unlikely. He was mindlessly playing with a gem tied around his neck, his eyes glued to the ceiling. Dark stains covered his gray linen clothes, as if someone's dirty boots had been walking all over him.

Realizing he had not been noticed, Fadan cleared his throat. Doric jumped, startled, and quickly hid the necklace under his raggedy shirt.

"What do you want?" Doric demanded, raising on his elbows.

"Quiet," Fadan whispered. He took a quick look over his shoulder. "Are you all right? Is there anything you need?"

Doric frowned, suspicious. "Wait," he said. "It's you. What are *you* doing here?"

That had been way too loud.

"Shh!" Fadan whispered. "There are guards nearby."

"Where is Aric?" Doric asked, jumping up and grabbing the bars of his cell. "What happened to him? Is he all right?"

"You don't know?"

Doric shook his head. Now that he was closer, Fadan noticed how feverish he looked. His hair and beard had grown like a wild bush. His skin was pale and hung to his bones like dried leather, dark smudges covering it, and there were deep, dark circles under his blue eyes.

"Aric is… He's gone to Lamash," Fadan replied.

"Lamash?" Doric asked, his shoulders sinking. "Oh, no; what have I done?"

"You didn't do anything," Fadan said reassuringly.

Doric didn't seem to listen. He covered his eyes and began to sob loudly, tears rolling down his dirty cheeks.

"Doric," Fadan pleaded. "Doric, please!"

The prince slid a hand between the metal bars and squeezed Doric's arm. It seemed to do the trick, as the man went silent. His watery blue eyes gave Fadan an empty stare.

"It will be over soon," Fadan told him. "I promise. Just hang in there a little longer."

"Over? What do you mean?"

The prince weighed his words. "I'll help you."

Once again, Doric gave him nothing but an empty stare, but his hand moved up to touch the necklace under his shirt.

"That necklace," Fadan said, trying to sound friendly. "Can I see it?"

"No!" Doric backed away. "They won't take it from me. Not this."

That had been too loud again, and Fadan heard voices coming from the main hallway. He was running out of time.

"Damn it," the prince said beneath his breath, then turned to Doric again. "I'll be back. I promise."

Doric said nothing, his eyes lost somewhere far away.

What did they do to you? Fadan thought.

He left Doric, racing toward the main hallway, but stopped before turning the corner. The voices had become loud enough that he could almost understand what they were saying. And, worst of all, the hallway had become much brighter than before.

They're coming this way, he realized.

Fadan's head spun. The cellblock was a dead end. The only exit was into the main hallway. He had nowhere to go. Excluding, of course, the cells.

Both cells flanking him were empty. He tapped his power, then jumped to his left and landed on the other side of the bars. Outside, two shadows turned the corner. Fadan shrank against the farthest, darkest part of his cell. He began to shake, and his stomach turned upside down.

"As you can see," Fadan heard one of the men say as they walked by his cell, "these cells are smaller, but they could still easily fit five prisoners each."

Those weren't guards. The man who had just spoken was a Paladin commander, and the other one was Chancellor Vigild. What if he recognized Fadan?

The two men kept walking, finally passing him. If any of them noticed Fadan hunching in the corner, they must have assumed he was just another prisoner.

Fadan released the air from his lungs and started panting. How long had he been holding his breath?

"Well, I'd say they'll do," Vigild said, somewhere beyond where Fadan could see. "The prisoners' comfort isn't exactly our first priority, anyway."

"And when can we expect them to arrive?" the Paladin asked.

"The raid is taking place tomorrow," Vigild replied. "Commander Therian is leading it."

Fadan perked up. *Raid?*

"And he is confident that every Augustan rebel will be at the meeting?" the Paladin commander asked.

"Not every one of them, no," Vigild replied. "But our infiltrator has the location of all the other safe houses. I don't expect many of them to slip through our fingers this time. mages or otherwise."

Oh, no, Fadan thought. *Alman.*

CHAPTER 18

The Empty Fortress

"You weren't even close to being prepared!" Saruk yelled. "Have you any idea how lucky you got?"

Aric remained quiet, his eyes avoiding Saruk's and his lips pressed together so hard that they became a white line across his face.

"Let it go, Saruk," Grand-Master Sylene said, getting up from her desk. "It might have been stupid, but at least they aren't cowards. Besides" – she waved the letter in her hands – "we have much bigger problems."

"That bad?" Saruk asked.

"It's worse," Sylene replied, handing him the letter. "See for yourself."

At that moment, the door to the Grand-Master's office creaked open and a man's head peeked in.

"Grand-Master," the man said, "you called?"

"Andraid," Sylene said. "Yes, come in."

The man walked inside, exchanging a nod with Saruk.

"This is Captain Aric Auron," Sylene continued, "of the Twenty-third Company under instruction."

"Ah!" Andraid smiled. "Saruk's sand maggots. I already had the pleasure the other day in the dining hall."

Aric suddenly recognized him. There were always so few Hunters at any given time in Lamash that seeing a familiar face wasn't unusual. This, however, wasn't just any familiar face. It was the same Hunter who had forced Ashur to insult one of the cooks the day before the final challenge for the leadership of the company.

The man ran his leathery fingers through his long, strangely well-kept hair as he stepped inside. "So, why am I here?" he asked.

"Because of that," Sylene replied, indicating the letter in Saruk's hands. "It's from the governor of Nish himself. Captain Auron here just brought it from the city, where his company fought off a dragon."

Saruk handed the parchment to Andraid, whose eyebrows had shot up.

"So it's true?" Andraid said. "I mean, that's all the people are talking about downstairs, but I thought it was hogwash."

"No," Sylene assured him. "It's very true."

"A dragon over Nish…" Andraid mused pensively. "And you kids fought it? Brave!"

"Don't tell him those things," Saruk said. "He's reckless enough without the encouragement."

Andraid concentrated on the governor's letter, reading silently until a whistle escaped his scar-crossed lips. "Man is pissed," he said. "And rightly so, I would say. A dragon attacking a city? When was the last time that happened? Three hundred years ago? Four?"

"We didn't mess up at all," Aric said. He turned to Sylene. "You're not telling him the most important part of my report."

"You're not?" Andraid asked Sylene.

The Grand-Master rolled her eyes. "Captain Auron claims he saw the desert witch herself. That she helped him fight the dragon."

"Oh?" Andraid said, lifting a very doubtful eyebrow.

Aric, however, ignored their skepticism. "The attack is not the Guild's fault. The dragon was under the control of a mage. Eliran didn't tell me much about him, but he must have found a way past our patrols and slipped the dragon into the city."

"Impossible," Andraid told him. "Dragons can't be controlled."

"They can if you're a mage," Aric replied.

"You're not listening," Saruk said. He unfolded his arms and stepped closer to Aric. "Mind-control spells don't work on dragons. The Academy of Mages tried to create a spell such as that for centuries. Why do you think they moved into a whole tower right next to us? They were here to study the dragons. They were obsessed with the idea of taming them, but they failed."

Aric was taken aback. He didn't know what to say. Was that really true?

"Their intentions were good," Sylene told him. "The plan was to turn dragons into a docile, harmless herd that would supply them with the all the blood they needed for their runium. It would also end the dragon threat for good. It was a thousand-year-old dream, really. One they never gave up on, but one that never bore fruit, either. When the Purge came and destroyed the Academy, they weren't any closer to taming a dragon than they were five hundred years ago."

"But... I saw her," Aric mumbled. "We all did."

"You saw a mage," Saruk explained calmly. "Probably scared the life out of her. I mean, just imagine living your whole life being hunted down like a dog, then a group of fifteen armed people barges into your room. What would you have done in her place? She lied her way out of it, of course."

"Scared? She didn't look scared at all," Aric said. "Besides, I saw her in the desert as well. With a dragon."

"You hallucinated," Saruk said. "Just like you hallucinated with the sandstorm. I've told you, it happens. The dehydration, the sun... It messes with our brains."

Aric opened his mouth, rehearsing a retort, but what could he say? He knew what he had seen, knew Eliran was real. Everything else, though... Had she lied?

"It's true," Sylene added. "It happens even to the most seasoned of us."

Silence covered the room while Aric stared at the floor. It was as if his whole life had suddenly stopped making any sense.

"Now, to the pressing matter at hand," Sylene continued, recovering the letter from Andraid. "I will not allow this Guild to be handed to the Paladins. This" – she raised the parchment in front of her head – "is exactly what the emperor has been looking for. An excuse. We *must* do something, and it has to be something drastic. Otherwise, we will find ourselves on the wrong side of a very short leash."

"You have something in mind?" Saruk asked.

"I do," Sylene confirmed with a nod. "A show of force, a demonstration of our capabilities. The largest Hunt the Empire has seen in decades." She got up from her desk and paced fiercely. "We need to prove that we are in control of this desert, so let's drown the bastards in dragon blood."

"And are we?" Andraid ventured. "In control of the desert?"

Sylene stopped her pacing but, instead of replying, shot him a furious look until Andraid raised his hands in surrender.

"All right, all right," Andraid said. "You want a full mobilization and need our support, is that it?"

"What I need is your opinion," Sylene replied. "I did not know your support was in question."

Aric found his head swinging back and forth from the two of them as if he were watching a very fast game of lagaht.

"Sylene, peace," Andraid pleaded. "Of course it isn't. And I agree. A Grand Hunt should appease the capital." He sighed. "I mean, if that doesn't do it, nothing will."

"What about you, Saruk?" Sylene asked.

"I agree as well. My problem is the execution."

"Go on."

Saruk turned and paced along the study. "It'll take a few days to round up the companies in the field, but it *can* be done. Then there are the companies stationed here, none of which are fully rested. However, the situation is dire, and I'm sure they will understand. The problem is the reservists. I mean, we can sort them into reasonably functional companies in a matter of hours, but none of them will be capable of facing a dragon. Not one."

"Then we won't let them fight," Sylene said. "But if we are going to comb this desert from one end to the other, our regulars aren't enough. We need the extra pairs of eyes. They can be our scouts."

"They can, yes," Saruk said, halting. "They won't be fast, but they should be effective enough."

"Excellent," Sylene declared. "It is decided, then. Andraid, please break the news to the regular companies. Saruk, you handle the reservists." She received two nods. "Also, Saruk, I'm reinstating you as captain of the Seventh." She smiled. "Hopefully, your wife won't mind."

"Oh, it'll make her sour as Cyrinian cider," Saruk replied, smiling as well. "Still, better than being stuck here as a babysitter." He turned to Aric. "No offense, kid."

"None taken," Aric replied. "Does that mean I should tell my Hunters to get ready to depart?"

"No," Sylene told him. "We can´t just vacate Lamash. Someone has to stay behind, and your company was the last one to see any action. If anyone deserves some rest, it is definitely the Twenty-third, so…" She stepped closer to Aric and laid a hand on his shoulders. "Captain Auron, you have the fortress."

Aric had read and reread about every recorded war in southern Arkhemia, and this was exactly how he had imagined the armies of the world marching out of their castles. The Guildsmen lacked the shiny steel armors of Augusta's Legionaries or their colorful banners, but it more than made up for it with its wide array of protective gear and weaponry, exuberant hairstyles and tattoos, and what Aric could only describe as the Guild's very own demeanor.

There was no clear order of march, or even any apparent form of hierarchy for that matter, but Aric had been in Lamash long enough to know that everyone down there knew exactly what their place and job was, as well as who would kick their asses if they failed to do so. Guildsmen always looked relaxed, independent even, as if they answered to no one. You never saw anyone bowing or saluting their superiors. A nod was the highest display of respect he had ever witnessed in Lamash. Hunters also seemed to fight all the time. Discussions would erupt during a meal over insignificant matters and end in a bloody fistfight in one of the courtyards. Officers would not only refrain from stopping these fights, they would actually be the first to make a wager on the winner. Yet nothing was regarded higher than efficiency. Not even honor. Some men were downright hated by everyone else in their companies, but no one minded Hunting with them so long as they did their job right. In fact, wasting a couple drops of water was far worse for your reputation than being caught lying.

Not that Aric had grown familiar with these things yet. It was all still extremely outlandish to him. He did not see himself as a Guildsman yet, but at the same time, for reasons he could hardly explain, Aric had to admit that Lamash was growing on him.

Maybe that was why he was feeling so anxious about the idea of being responsible for all of Lamash. The ancient mountain fortress, where count-less thousands of men and women had lived, fought, and died, the Empire's first defense – and nowadays the last – against the great dragon scourge, and it was *his* job to take care of it. It would only be for a few days, a couple of weeks at the most, but still, it was daunting to say the least.

The column of Guildsmen was long gone when the sun touched the ho-rizon, but Aric had still not left the main gate, as if he wanted to personally make sure no intruder got through.

"Grand Master Auron," someone said.

Aric looked over his shoulder to see Leth sauntering toward him.

"Your sentinel rotation scheme works splendidly," Leth continued. "We should maintain good surveillance over all quadrants." He stopped next to Aric, taking a good look over the desert. "Just one problem."

"What is it?" Aric asked.

"You forgot the food, you idiot. The entire kitchen staff is gone. Who in the mother's name is going to cook our meals?"

Aric slapped his own forehead. "Damn it! I knew there was something. You have the rotation schematic with you?"

"Here." Leth handed him the piece of parchment they had created that morning.

"Hmm, everyone's on a pretty tight schedule." Aric scratched his chin. "This is what we'll do. You and me, we're cooking."

Leth did not move. "Don't make me insult you."

"We either unman one of the watch points or remove a couple hours of rest time from someone's schedule. I'm not going to leave us blind in one quadrant, so that leaves option two, in which case, I refuse to ask anyone to rest less than me. So…"

"Leave us blind?! What are you talking about? We're not going to be besieged by a rival neighboring kingdom –"

"There are raiders out there. Thieves, free lances, and smugglers who would love to plunder this fortress. If they find out the whole Guild is out Hunting, what do you think they'll do?" Aric turned around and headed inside. "Come on, it's late. We need to prepare dinner."

"You're being paranoid," Leth said, helping Aric close the main gate. "The dragon-blood stockpiles are empty, remember? We just returned from a Blood Run."

"So what?" Aric asked. "Raiders don't know that. Besides, there are other valuables here. The glowstone stockpiles alone are worth a fortune. Not to mention the conventional weapons, the horses, the cows. Even basic supplies like wood, tools, and candles are worth stealing."

Leth grimaced but otherwise dropped the argument. The two of them found their way into the kitchen and Aric began opening random cabinets.

"I have never so much as walked into a kitchen my whole life," Leth said, twitching his nose as if the place reeked. "If my father saw me now, he would fall into a coma again. I'm a direct descendant of the Ultrarchs of Akham, for goddess's sake."

Aric emerged from a cabinet holding two very large pans. "I didn't know your father was comatose," he said.

Leth shrugged. "Happened long ago. I was six. I can barely remember him healthy."

"I thought comatose people died within days," Aric said.

"It's not truly a coma. He opens his eyes sometimes, even looks at you, but I don't think he's there anymore." Leth shook his head. "The Grand Duke of Nahlwar, the most powerful man in the east, unable to do anything except drool."

"I didn't know," Aric told him. "I'm sorry."

Leth took a deep breath, then exhaled loudly. "So am I," he said. He picked up a pan and looked at it as if it was bottomless. "They say the mages might have been able to help him if they had still been around, but I'm not sure. I think some things just cannot be fixed." He paused. "Sometimes I wonder if the world is not one of them…" Then he snapped out of it with a shake of his head and looked at Aric. "See? This is why I don't like to talk about these things. Now close your mouth and get cooking. What is it exactly that we do?" He held the pan as if it was some kind of indecipherable artifact.

"Well, uh…" Aric decided to drop the subject as well. "Yeah, I used to have all my meals in the Citadel's kitchen, so I watched the cooks every day. It seemed like hard work, but nothing overly complex. Hand me one of those knives, will you? I'm going to chop some of these cabbages."

Aric started out slow and awkward. Apparently, peeling, chopping, and dicing vegetables wasn't as simple as it looked.

"You look like you are trying to dissect a small animal," Leth told him. "It's a cabbage. Just hack away and be done with it."

"You want to do it?" Aric asked, presenting Leth with the knife.

"No, thank you," Leth replied, taking a step back. "You're not doing it wrong enough to turn me into a cook."

Shaking his head, Aric resumed his slicing duty. "How wrong would that be?"

"Well, if you start trying to chop *me* instead of the cabbage, I might take over for you."

Aric raised his head from the counter and looked at Leth. "Don't tempt me."

At that moment, a wailing horn echoed in the distance, startling the two of them.

"What the…?" Leth said.

"Intruders." Aric dropped the knife. "Where is it coming from? East?"

"Oh, come on," Leth protested. "You're not buying this, are you? Someone's obviously messing around."

Aric shot him a stare. "Let's go," he said.

Exhaling loudly, Leth followed Aric out into the main hall. The horn echoed eerily throughout the empty hallways, making it hard to tell where exactly it came from. Aric tried following the corridors leading to the eastern face of the mountain, but the horn's unrelenting howls just grew fainter, so they circled back around.

"Southeast," Aric said, climbing a stairwell two steps at a time. "Irenya's watch point."

"Probably saw a dune lion and panicked," Leth said, chasing after Aric.

The watch point was a tiny balcony on top of a turret. Irenya took the horn out of her mouth as soon as she saw them race toward her. She started panting as if she had been blowing the horn in a single, uninterrupted breath from the start.

"There..." She gasped. "There's..."

"Easy," Aric said. "Just breathe, all right?"

"Raiders," she managed to say, stretching an arm toward the desert. "Dozens of them."

"Where?" Leth asked, looking everywhere.

Aric scanned the vast, golden dunes. There was not a single person in sight. Not even Geric's sneaky shadow. Just the usual rolling sea of dunes.

"I... I don't understand," Irenya grabbed the stone parapet and leaned out. "They were there. Charging across the sand. There were fifty of them, probably more."

"Well," Leth said, "maybe your horn scared them off."

Luckily, Irenya did not pick up the sarcasm, but Aric shot him a stare anyway.

"Have you been drinking enough water?" Aric asked her. "It's really hot out here."

Irenya did not reply. She just kept searching the desert with her mouth half-open. Whatever had happened, she clearly could not explain it.

"Wait, what is that?" Leth asked.

Aric followed his finger but did not see anything.

"Right there," Leth insisted. "A flicker in the sand. Like a mirror."

Squinting, Aric tried to focus on the spot Leth was indicating.

He was right. There *was* something in the sand. At first, it was just a sparkle, then…

"Are those white robes?" Irenya asked.

Eliran… Aric thought. He turned and left. "It's her," he said. "It's Eliran."

"What? Where are you going?" Leth asked. He was forced to race after Aric across the whole fortress, crashing into the main gate just as Aric was opening it and forcing it closed once again. "Will you listen to me?" he said, his shoulder locking the gate in place. "We can't know if we can trust her."

"I think she needs help," Aric said.

"How do you know?"

"She was clearly lying on the ground, fallen. She probably can't walk. I'm guessing she used a spell to cause Irenya to hallucinate and sound the alarm. It was a call for help."

Footsteps echoed through the hall. It was Clea, Ergon, and Ashur.

"What's happening?" Ashur asked. "What was all that fuss about?"

Instead of answering, Aric turned to Leth. "You want to stay here? Fine," he said. "But let me out."

"It might be a trick," Leth insisted, but he still stepped away from the door. "Remember all the valuable stuff in the fortress?"

"I doubt a sorceress has any interest in goats and hammers," Aric replied, stepping out the door.

"Will someone please explain?" Clea said.

"Leth will fill you in," Aric said.

"Wait!" Leth grabbed Aric's arm. "At least take a horse. You'll waste the better part of an hour just getting up and down the mountain."

Aric agreed with a nod, and moments later, he was galloping down the mountain, a cloud of dust and sand trailing in his path. He found Eliran about two hundred yards south of the foothold of Lamash, her white robes spread across the sand like a puddle of milk.

With a jump, Aric got off the horse and knelt beside her. She did not look in very good shape. Her robes were torn to shreds, three crimson slashes crossed the pale flesh of her face, and one of her hands looked like it had been burnt to a crisp.

Exactly like the corpse in my dreams...

"Eliran?" he called, grabbing one of her shoulders.

Aric shook her, slowly at first, then more vigorously, but she did not respond. He placed an ear on her chest and felt it rise before hearing a faint heartbeat. She was alive.

"What happened to you?"

Having run out of options, Aric decided to lift her to his horse, then galloped back to the fortress.

He raced up the mountain and stormed straight into the fortress's main hall, the horse's hooves clopping wildly on the stone floor.

"What happened?" Clea asked.

"I don't know," Aric replied, taking Eliran's body off the horse as gently as possible. "But I bet it was the other mage. Help me get her into a bed. Ergon, get your sister, please. She might be able to help."

"The other mage," Leth said, locking the great wooden gate. "You mean the one we don't even know for sure exists?"

"She's unconscious, Leth," Aric said. "Just look at her wounds. We need to help her."

"Sure," Leth said. "She was probably not unconscious when she made Irenya hallucinate with dozens of raiders, though."

"Yeah, she's probably playing with our heads," Ashur said, stepping closer to Eliran's body. "I bet those wounds are fake."

Aric looked from Leth to Ashur. "Well, she made the two of you agree. That's powerful magic indeed."

⌒

They placed Eliran right across from the company's quarters, in a room Aric guessed had once been the private chamber of some captain or lieutenant. Lyra washed the witch's wounds the best she could, but everything else was beyond her knowledge. The burn on Eliran's left hand, for example, was nothing like anything she had ever seen. All Lyra could do was treat it like any other burn and hope for the best.

Aric, Leth, and Clea were standing by the door, watching quietly as Lyra changed the wet towel on Eliran's forehead.

"You know there's no point in you three standing there, right?" Lyra said. "She won't get any better just 'cause you're staring."

"I want to be here when she wakes up," Aric said. "I'm the one who brought her in. I want to make sure I don't regret that decision."

"So you're just going to stand there night and day until she does?" Lyra asked. "What if she never wakes up?" She turned and placed two fingers on her patient's neck. "Her pulse is weak and uneven, she might never –"

A hand jumped from the bed and grabbed Lyra's arm, making her squeak.

"What are you doing? Who are you?" the witch said, her eyes bulging, suddenly awake.

"I... I'm..." Lyra mumbled.

"She's one of my people," Aric said, stepping forward and releasing Lyra from Eliran's grasp. "And she's trying to help you."

There was a flicker in the witch's eyes, and she seemed to relax, but only a little.

"What is this?" she asked, raising her charred hand. "What did you put on my skin?"

"It... It's just an ointment," Lyra replied, standing up from the bed and taking a step back.

"Of *what?*" Eliran demanded.

"Blonde grass," Lyra replied. "And... and blood parsley... I think."

"You *think*?!" Eliran smelled her hand and sat up on the bed.

"Hey!" Aric snapped. "She probably saved your life. The least you can do is show a little respect."

Once again, Eliran seemed to calm down. "My life wasn't in danger," she said, then turned to Lyra. "Where did you learn how to heal?"

Lyra was going to reply, but Aric cut her off. "She doesn't owe you an explanation!" he said.

"I'm a mage, you fool!" Eliran stood up, her raggedy white robes flowing around her. "And I was under a heavy dose of runium. My body responds differently from regular people's." She looked at Lyra. "The ointment seems harmless enough, but I need to know what else you gave me." She moved her tongue as if she was savoring something. "You gave me something to eat? What's this taste?"

"Just an infusion," Lyra replied. "Galennia petals and white bark leaf."

"Anything else?" The witch received a vigorous shake of the head. "Hmm, let me guess: temple healer?"

"Yes. I used to help the healer in my orphanage. She taught me."

"See?" Eliran told Aric. "If she had told me sooner, there would have been no need to worry. The temple specializes in pointlessness." She turned to the bed and fumbled around the sheets. "Where are my things? I had a satchel with me."

"Your possessions are under my custody for now," Aric replied.

An eyebrow climbed Eliran's forehead. "What is that supposed to mean?" she asked.

"Why are you here?" Aric demanded.

The witch did not reply right away. "My battle with Sohtyr did not…go according to plan," she eventually said. "I needed a place to rest."

"This Sohtyr you keep talking about," Aric said, "I'm still unsure he really exists."

"You think I would do this to myself?" Eliran asked, showing him her charred hand.

"I don't even know what that is," Aric replied.

"There's also the matter of you being able to mess with our minds," Leth intervened. "As you did to our sentinel."

"Yes, I did that," Eliran admitted. "Had to. I was spent. Couldn't walk any further. Under the circumstances, it was the best I could come up with. Apologies for that. However, the runium has worn off now. I couldn't cast a spell if I wanted to." She showed her hand again. "I can assure you that this is no hallucination."

"What about that mysterious mage?" Clea asked. "We believed you back in the city, did what you asked —"

"And the dragon flew away," Eliran cut her off. "Just as I said it would."

"How?" Aric asked. "How did you know that the dragon would fly away if we attacked it?"

"Because I would take control of it and make it go," Eliran said.

"Lies!" Aric snapped. "I know you were lying. I know you can't control dragons; no one can. It's impossible."

"Yes," Eliran replied, "that's what I was taught as well. In fact, that's what every student of the Academy is taught. So you can imagine my surprise when, shortly after arriving in the desert, I saw with my own two eyes that this evil mage I had been sent to kill was actually able to do it." She paced along the room. "The bastard or some of his twisted friends figured it out. They cracked the secret. A thousand years' worth of research, piles of resources invested, some of the greatest minds of the Academy dedicated exclusively to this effort, and who gets to achieve it? That wretched creature! Ava must have really forsaken us for good." She looked straight into Aric's eyes. "The problem was never the spells. It was the runium. Apparently, you can't control a dragon if the runium fueling your spells is made from dragon blood."

"I thought runium could *only* be made from dragon blood?" Clea questioned.

"And so did everyone else," Eliran said. "Except they broke that myth as well. The bastard managed to create runium from human blood. *Human* blood! Even destroyed the brewing chamber of Nish in the process. They will have to come up with a safer process, of course. There aren't that many Bloodhouses in the world. They can't just destroy one each time they brew their potion. But still, it's remarkable. Scary, but remarkable."

"They?" Aric asked. "It used to be about this Sohtyr; now there is a *'they'*?"

"Sohtyr obviously did not accomplish all this on his own. He is part of a larger organization. A splinter group of the Academy. Its younger, creepier sibling, you could say. They call themselves the Circle of Archons. Yes, I know, you've never heard of them. That's mostly because they prefer to lurk in the shadows, but it's also our fault."

"*Our* fault?" Leth asked.

"No, not *yours*," Eliran said. "*Ours*, the Academy's. We've known about the Circle since its inception. However, the council of Arch-Mages always thought it better to keep the Circle's existence a secret. They feared that if the Circle's existence was revealed to the public, the image of every mage would be negatively affected. They also had absolute trust in the Academy's ability to maintain the Circle under control. That's why we have people like me. Archon Hunters. It's a bit like what you do, except my prey is far less agreeable than yours."

"Wait," Aric said, "you talk as if the Academy still exists. As if you are still a part of it."

"Yes, try not to faint, but some of us did survive the Purge." Eliran sneered. "We're a much smaller organization now, sure. And we have had to adapt to...our new circumstances, but there is still plenty of runium in the black market to keep us afloat."

Aric, Leth, and Clea exchanged a confused look.

"Any more questions?" Eliran asked. "Go ahead. You wanted to know everything. Ask."

"Why?" Aric asked.

"Why what?" Eliran was confused.

"Why do you hunt them?" Aric clarified. "What makes them so dangerous?"

"Are you kidding? Did you not see what Sohtyr did to Nish?"

"Assuming he exists, yes, of course. That's not what I meant, though. Why did he attack the city? There has to be a larger move at play here. Or is that what Archons do? Go around the Empire, attacking random cities?"

Eliran sighed and let herself fall back into a chair.

"I'm not sure," she said. "When I first arrived in the desert, months ago, I thought this was just another mission. Track a random Archon down, follow his trail of magic, force him into a fight, and kill the bastard. But this one was different. His trail of magic was...random, experimental.

"Then I discovered people were talking about me. *Me!* All across the edge of the desert, townspeople were muttering my name. Eliran, the evil desert witch who would come at night and steal your children. I figured it had to be Sohtyr. It had to be his way of letting me know he was on to me. I was impressed, to be honest. If nothing else, it showed the man has a sense of humor, despite everything. Not bad. Then came the human runium. He killed a couple of Paladins guarding the Bloodhouse, brewed himself a few casks of his special recipe, and destroyed the chamber in the process. Guess who was blamed for *that?*

"Anyway, that's when I knew for sure this was no ordinary Archon I was chasing. This one was up to something big. I had to end him quick. Sohtyr covered his tracks well, but not well enough. I found his hiding place and witnessed him taming a dragon. I thought I had lost my mind, even considered returning home to have my mind inspected. But it was true, all right. So, I decided to experiment and stole some of his vials. Made me sick to my stomach, but I drank the human runium. Had to be done. That was when you saw me." She indicated Aric. "I used a simple mind-control spell on a Mahari Black Dread. Worked perfectly. Finally, I tracked him back to Nish. I was hoping to finally corner him and force him into a fight. I wasn't expecting the dragon, however. Wasn't prepared for it. Luckily, you showed up, and I still had some human runium. So I got my chance to fight the bastard."

She paused for a moment and shook her head before continuing.

"Damn, what a fight... I tried everything, gave him the wrath of Ava, but nothing got through his defenses. He, on the other hand, got me good a couple of times." Eliran lifted her charred hand as evidence. "As we fought, however, I also tried to peek into his mind. It wasn't exactly easy, but you could say that mind spells are my area of expertise. I did glimpse a few things. Not much, unfortunately."

"Go on," Aric said.

Eliran took a deep breath. "Well, it's something about the Frostbound. That much I know. There's something trapped in there. No, *frozen*. Frozen is

356

a better word. Whatever it is, though, Sohtyr wants to release it, so it can't be good. I also know that the power to tame a dragon is key to what he aims to achieve. But that is all. I was unable to discover anything else."

"That's it?" Aric asked. "It's not much to go with. I mean, what is your plan? Search the Frostbound tunnels for whatever this thing is?"

Eliran limited herself to staring silently at Aric for an overlong moment. It was obvious she had no idea how to proceed.

"Well," she finally said, "I am in the right place to find my answer, just not in the right time."

"What does that mean?" Leth asked.

"The Mages' Tower of Lamash," she said. "If there is one place in the world where I could find the answers to my questions, it would definitely be the library in there. Unfortunately, the Paladins destroyed it ten years ago."

"Not all of it," Leth said. He looked at Aric. "There's that walled-off section we never managed to get access to."

"So, you believe her now?" Aric asked.

"What walled-off section?" Eliran echoed, a sparkle returning to her eyes.

"The library in the Mages' Tower," Aric explained. "It has a walled-off section protected by a glowstone lock. Our guess is that it was created to save the most important books from the Paladins."

Eliran jumped to her feet. "Take me there. Now!"

"Well," Aric said, "since you're asking so nicely..."

CHAPTER 19

The Raid

Fadan raced across the city as dawn crept up the sky. He ran through streets, avenues, plazas, crossed all three walls between Mount Capitol and the Docks, and only slowed down when he finally reached Sabium's apartment, feeling as though his lungs were about to explode. He banged on the door weakly, gasping for air. His arms were limp and his legs were shaking.

"Master," he called, knocking once more. "Open up."

The door opened with a creak and a suspicious Sabium peeked outside. "Oh, it's you," the old mage said. "Come in, come in. I found something."

Sabium waved him inside with one hand while the other held a large, opened book.

The prince obeyed, closing the door behind him. "Master," he said. "There's something –"

"Here, look at this," Sabium interrupted, sitting down at his desk and sticking a finger on the page in front of him. "It's all in Orelianus's work. The man was a genius."

"Master," Fadan insisted, finally steadying his breath. "You need to *listen* to me. I have very bad news."

"What?" Sabium asked, turning to Fadan as if he had only now realized the prince was there. "What's wrong with you? Why are you so pale? Is your transmogaphon charged?"

"What? Yes. Just listen to me, please. I went to the dungeons, in the Citadel, where Doric and the others are being kept."

Sabium's familiar frown wrinkled his forehead further. "How in Ava's mercy did you do that?"

"I was practicing dematerializing," Fadan replied, waving a dismissive hand. "Doesn't matter. Inside –"

"What do you mean, 'it doesn't matter'?" Sabium interrupted. "You managed to do it? A full-body dematerialization?"

"MASTER!" Fadan cried, startling the old man and gaining his attention. "This is *important.* I overheard a conversation between the chancellor and a Paladin commander. They are gearing up for a large-scale raid on all rebel hideouts here in the city. We need to warn your brother."

Sabium let go of his book. "What? When?"

"Today," Fadan replied. "I can't know the time, but it'll be today."

"Today..." Sabium echoed, his eyes wandering out the tiny window next to his desk. "What time is it?"

"Early morning. The sun should be up any moment."

"Goddess damn this," Sabium muttered, heaving himself off the chair. "I told that fool this would happen one day." He stormed over to a corner, kneeled, and lifted one of the floorboards.

"I came as fast as I could," the prince said. "We should have plenty of time."

"Plenty of time," Sabium snorted as he stuck a hand into the hidden cache and retrieved two vials of runium. "Paladins always strike at dawn." He allowed the floorboard to fall back into its place with a thump. "They prefer us when we're sleepy."

⌒

For a moment, Cassia felt transported to her father's castle during the civil war of her youth. Doors flew open and slammed closed as officers marched in and out. Paladins frenzied up and down the corridors and staircases, barking orders and relaying messages. The Palace seemed to have been turned into the makeshift headquarters of some major operation.

It was still early. In fact, if it hadn't been for all the ruckus outside her room, Cassia would probably still be in her bed.

She walked slowly to the great stairwell leading down to the main hall, listening to the fleeting Paladins around her.

"Tell Captain Sorba he has enough men," a tall major told a sergeant, pushing him down the stairs.

"I don't care," a colonel yelled from farther down the hall. "Start rolling those prison wagons right now." A group of Paladins surrounding him acquiesced with a salute and darted away.

What is going on? Cassia wondered.

A few feet behind her, the door to Tarsus's study burst open. The emperor emerged with a small battalion of officers in tow.

"We're going to need reinforcements near the fish market," one of the Paladins said, placing a finger on a report in the emperor's hands. "There's also some more resistance than expected out near the Maginus Bridge."

Tarsus nodded. "Send the reserve squads to the southern edge of the district," he said, lifting his head from the document. "Ah, good morning, my love." He looked unusually pleased with himself. He paused to kiss Cassia's hand and the entire column halted behind him. "You'll have to forgive me, but I won't be joining you for breakfast today. Busy morning, I'm afraid."

"I can see that, husband," the empress replied, doing her best to sound casual. "What exactly is going on?"

"We'll speak later, my dear," Tarsus said, giving her hand an extra kiss. "I am needed at the moment."

Cassia curtsied slightly and the emperor marched away with his escort, resuming his instructions. A pale, silver-haired maid crossed the group with her head low, quickstepping toward the empress.

"What's going on, Venia?" Cassia asked her.

The spy checked their surroundings. "Some sort of raid down in the Docks."

"A runium grab?" the empress asked, doubtful. "They wouldn't go to this much trouble for a bunch of smugglers."

"I still don't know who the target is. But there's something else, Your Majesty," Venia said, pausing for a moment before revealing, "The prince did not return this morning."

Cassia's head jolted toward the spy, yanking her attention from the buzzing Paladins.

"There's probably no reason to worry," Venia offered. "He's almost certainly in his hideout. I'll look for him there."

The empress nodded stiffly but said nothing. Something felt terribly wrong.

⌒⌒

Alman's house stood across the corner. Fadan and Sabium huddled behind the remains of a rotting chest of drawers and checked to make sure the way was clear. The streets were still mostly empty, with only occasional early risers here and there. Above them, the stars were long gone and the sky had become a slab of gray metal.

"I don't see any Paladins," Fadan whispered.

"We might have gotten lucky," Sabium grumbled. "Come on." The mage took off from their hiding place, striding toward his brother's house, but his head kept swinging from one side to the other, checking for any unwanted presences.

Fadan hurried behind his master and stood guard as he knocked on the door.

"Alman," Sabium called, keeping his voice low. "Alman?"

Fadan's head moved slowly as he scanned around them, looking for signs of any Patrols.

"*Alman,*" Sabium insisted, raising his voice and knocking harder.

"You think we're too late?" Fadan asked.

"I don't know," Sabium replied, turning away from the door. Then, out of nowhere, he kicked the door in frustration. "Goddess damn you, Alman!"

Fadan jumped, startled at the burst of sound.

"This is why I didn't want that fool to join the rebellion," Sabium muttered in irritation. "How was this going to end any differently?"

"Maybe he's not back yet," Fadan suggested. "He might be on his way home right now. We should just wait."

"For what, the Paladins?" Sabium shook his head vigorously. "No. Come on. Let's get out of here."

Hesitantly, Fadan followed the old mage as he turned a corner and headed south toward the riverfront.

"Where are we going?" Fadan asked, having to speed up to keep pace.

"Remember when my brother said he worked for a ship owner?"

Fadan nodded.

"It's a lie," Sabium said. "The ship owner is a just a front, a cover-up for a runium smuggling operation. Why do you think we are always so well supplied? Anyway, they have a warehouse and a dry dock near pier twenty-one. If he hasn't been taken yet, that's where we'll find him."

Fadan gave his master a look. "Or the Paladins."

"Or both."

They turned into a wide plaza packed full of merchant stalls, still closed for the night. A tang of fish lingered in the air, and a large flock of gray river gulls covered the wooden scaffolds of an adjacent dock. The birds' occasional cries sliced through the lapping sound of the river waves against the shore.

The warehouse stood just a couple hundred feet downriver, an enormous wooden rectangle surrounded by a sea of seemingly discarded objects including rows, rope, fishnets, and barrels. Above a vast, sliding door hung a tablet with a burnt inscription bearing the name Boarhead's Saffyan Shipping Company. It, just like the rest of the building, looked about to tumble to the ground.

Sabium knocked on the door loudly. "Alman," he called. "Alman, are you there?"

"Shh!" Fadan begged. "You want every Paladin in the empire to hear you?!"

"You said they're hitting every rebel hideout, correct? Then they already know about this place and are on their way. What difference does it make?" He resumed his pounding on the door. "Alman!"

The door slid out of the way and a frowning Alman greeted them on the other side, a lantern in his other hand.

"What in the mother's name are you doing?!" Alman protested. He peeked outside, inspecting the street. "You shouldn't be here."

"Trust me, I know," Sabium retorted, shoving his brother inside. Fadan followed them, closing the warehouse door behind him.

"And you brought *him*, too?" Alman asked. "You can't just barge in here like that."

"For once in your life, just listen," Sabium said, then turned to the prince. "Tell him what you told me."

"I overheard a conversation between Chancellor Vigild and a Paladin commander," Fadan explained. "There will be a raid today. They were discussing how the dungeons wouldn't be enough to hold all the prisoners. It will be big."

"Morning is already here," Sabium added. "I assume Paladins will be storming this place within the hour."

Alman's expression melted into one of dread. "You're sure of this?" he asked gravely.

Fadan nodded. "I am."

Alman wiped his forehead. "I have to warn the others."

"I knew he would say something stupid like this," Sabium sighed, flinging his arms up in desperation. "Did you *hear* us? There's no time!"

"You don't understand," Alman said. "This isn't just another day. There's a high-level meeting scheduled for this morning. rebellion leadership from all across the Empire are here in Augusta right now."

"Well, that's certainly very stupid," Sabium said. "Why would they schedule something like that right under the emperor's nose? More importantly, why do *you* care? You owe these people nothing. If anything, *they* owe you."

Alman circled them, his fingers clasping his milky hair. "They came under the guise of the petitioning," he muttered, then halted, straightening up. "I have to warn them. You two get out of here. Stay *out* of the apartment. In fact, leave the city."

Sabium cursed beneath his breath but turned to Fadan and pushed him toward the door. "Come on," he said.

"Wait, we're just going to leave him?" Fadan asked.

"Well, what do you want us to do, drag the idiot behind us?" Sabium snapped. "We did our part. If he wants to get himself killed, there's nothing we can do to stop him."

"I'm not about to just –"

Sabium's hand abruptly moved to cover his mouth, muffling his words.

"No one makes a sound," the mage whispered. He sent his brother a worried look. "They're here."

A crash came from the door, the wood cracking as splinters flew inward, peppering over them.

"In the name of Tarsus the Fifth," a voice yelled, "lay down on the ground!"

Fadan forgot how to breathe. The goat-shaped tip of a battering ram was sticking in through the warehouse's front door. He saw it retreating, readying to be swung for another hit. Before it had time to do so, a powerful blue glow shimmered around Sabium as he let go of Fadan. The mage raised his palms as if he were lifting something very heavy, and as he did, the entire wall containing the front door burst into flames.

Screams from outside filled the air.

Sabium turned to his brother. "Get us out of here," he yelled.

Alman was staring at the fire, his eyes wide. "This way," he finally said, fleeing behind a pile of containers, Fadan and Sabium fast on his heels.

⌣⟶

Venia hurried into the large, abandoned manor, closing the door behind her without a sound. With the scarce light of day coming through the cracks of boarded windows, the mansion's state of decay was even more obvious. Dark blotches of mildew covered the ceiling while loose floorboards were spread across the corridors like booby traps.

The floor was covered in a blanket of dust that lifted around her in tiny puffs with her every step. Whistles of wind crisscrossed the hallways, highlighting the eerie silence of the place. If the prince was here, he was being very quiet.

Just like the previous time, when she had discovered the burning book, Venia climbed the steps to the attic, making sure the creaky floor did not give away her presence. Once again, the room was empty. The bucket was still in the same place, but the burning smell was gone.

Where are you, Your Majesty? Venia wondered.

This wasn't a good sign, but in all honesty, Venia had not really expected to find Fadan here. If the prince *was* a mage, as she suspected, his nightly activities probably involved visits to the Docks. He had to have a runium supplier, and those were usually working out of the Docks. With the Paladins raiding the district now, the most likely scenario involved the prince being caught by one the patrols.

That will be a hard one to solve.

"Looking for someone?"

Venia jumped, circling toward the voice, her dagger sliding into her hand. It was Lord Fabian.

How did I not hear him? she thought, her heart racing.

"Well, you know me, boss," Venia said. "It's what I do."

The old general stepped slowly into the room, inspecting it as if for the first time. "Looks like you didn't find him, though. That's…disappointing."

Venia studied the man from head to toe. He had clearly followed her, but why? Which prompted another question – could she beat him in a fight? His technique was probably still flawless, but at his age, how strong and quick could he really be?

"Is this a performance review?" Venia asked. "Because I promise you my next report *will* be ready on time."

Fabian shook his head. "I'm not amused, Venia," he said. "Where is he?"

"Where is who?"

The man snapped forward. He lunged at her, grabbing the wrist of her knife arm. Without even realizing what had happened, Venia felt herself spin. The old man had her pinned in a neck lock, her knife arm twisted so hard, she couldn't even twitch it.

Goddess damn it, she fumed, admonishing herself.

"This isn't a game, Venia," Fabian said. "I don't care about your fake reports. I just want to know where the prince is."

"I really wish I could tell you," Venia struggled to say. "You know, since you're asking so nicely."

Fabian tightened his grip. "What is this place?" he asked.

What?

"Are you serious?" Venia asked. "Shouldn't you, of all people, know that?"

"The prince didn't want me to know about it, so I respected his privacy," Fabian replied. He sounded almost apologetic.

"Oh, well, that's certainly helpful right now." She felt the grip around her neck loosen and managed to push herself free, gasping for air.

"He's clearly not here. What other leads do you have?" he asked. "Where were you going to look next?"

"I actually hadn't planned that far yet," Venia replied, massaging at her neck. "But, just to clarify, if you *didn't* know about this place, does that mean you don't know what the prince was doing here? What he…*is*?"

"No, I do not. Whatever the prince does – or *is* – is none of my concern. Or yours, for that matter. Right now, however, I do care if that knowledge can help us locate him."

Venia smiled, sheathing her dagger. "If I had to guess, yeah, that knowledge probably can help. What do you know about the Paladins' raid taking place as we speak?"

"I know that it's going to go down fast, and I know that it has already started," Fabian replied.

"In that case, you'd better get the entire Scriptorium to work, boss. Because I'm pretty sure the prince is about to be arrested."

⌣⟶

Alman led them out through a hidden tunnel beneath the hull of a ship standing up for repairs on a dry dock's scaffolding. It was a narrow, short underpass, and they were forced to crawl their way through in complete darkness before emerging about a hundred feet east of the burning warehouse.

Sabium's fire had spread quickly. Bells rang and people were pouring into the street, holding buckets and rushing to haul water from the river to the growing inferno. Rugged sailors and fishwives cursed the gods, sweating as they hurried from the fire to the river.

The tunnel's exit was hidden by a wall of wooden containers, probably ready to be shipped out of the city.

Breathing heavily, Alman peeked out into the main street. "The Paladins are spreading out," he said. "They're looking for us."

"I say we run for the gates," Sabium suggested. "Get out of the city."

"No," Alman argued. "Always avoid the main exits. That's where they expect you to go." He wiped sweat from his temples and moved away from the edge of the crate wall. "Listen to me. The rebellion has a contingency plan in place for situations such as these."

"Contingency?" Sabium echoed. "Alman, the entire rebellion in Augusta is being arrested as we speak."

"We're not that easy to catch," Alman assured him. "Every safe house and hideout has its precautions. Fake walls and hidden tunnels just like this one. Some of us *will* make it."

"What exactly is the contingency plan?" Fadan asked.

"A rotating safe house," Alman explained. "A place to fall back to and regroup. Its location is only known by lieutenants, and it changes every other day."

"Alman…" Sabium shook his head. "They are raiding the *entire* rebellion in Augusta on the very day when you had scheduled an Empire-wide leadership meeting. The Paladins have obviously infiltrated your organization."

"I understand that, but they would have to be infiltrated pretty deep to know about something like this. It's very unlikely." He took another peek out to the street. "We'll walk out of here casually, all right? There's no reason for them to suspect us. The Paladins don't know what we look like. The crowd will be our cover."

"Wait," Fadan said. "There's one little detail. How are we going to find one of your lieutenants now?"

"Oh, that's easy," Alman replied. He opened his arms. "Ta-da!"

"What?! I thought you just helped with supplies."

"That was just part of his scheme to get you to join the rebellion," Sabium said, a finger aimed at his brother's nose.

"What does it matter what my rank in the rebellion is?" Alman asked. "Now come on, before they come sniffing around this way."

"Before *who* comes sniffing around?" an unfamiliar voice asked.

All three of them turned at the same time to see four Paladins, two of them with swords aimed high and two holding rectangular, man-sized shields, blocking the way out of the small nook of wooden crates.

A cold hand squeezed Fadan's stomach. He instinctively went for his sword, but he was carrying none.

"Get down!" Sabium thundered, opening his arms.

Alman and Fadan dove to the ground just in time to avoid a wall of crates flying toward the Paladin squad. With remarkable precision, the shield-bearing Paladins stepped forward to protect their comrades. The massive crates exploded everywhere, shattering on impact with either the ground or the Paladin shields.

"MAGE!" one of the Paladins yelled.

Somewhere near, a horn wailed, and shouts of alarm erupted from every direction.

"We have to go," Sabium cried. "Run!"

The prince jumped up and lunged toward the huddling Paladins.

"No!" he heard Alman yell. "This way."

But Fadan knew exactly what he was doing. With a quick slide, he grabbed the fallen sword of a Paladin, then raced back after Alman and Sabium.

They jumped over the remains of the wall of crates that had formed their hiding place up until moments before, only to find another one just as tall beyond it. They looked left and right. All they could see were containers and more containers. It felt like being inside a maze, the echoes of their pursuers seeming to come from everywhere.

Alman made a decision. "This way," he said, running left.

Fadan and Sabium followed him, glancing backward in search of their pursuers. They turned left again, and then right. Some of the piles of crates were taller than others, but none were short enough that they could climb over. They would have to find a way out of the labyrinth.

After another turn to the right, the three of them were forced to skid to a halt. They were at a dead end.

"Goddess damn this!" Sabium cursed.

Fadan turned back to the way they had come, lifting his sword into a guard position. "I can hear them coming," he said. Neither of the two brothers seemed to hear him, though.

"You're a goddess-damned *Mage,*" Alman said. "Just carve a path for us already!"

Sabium closed his eyes, whispering a curse, but obeyed nonetheless. There was a loud, thundering sound and the crates began to slowly slide, half to one side, half to the other, slowly parting like the gates of a great hall.

"There they are!"

Three Paladins had just turned a corner and charged toward them.

"Here they come!" the prince said, testing the weight of his sword.

"Don't use magic on them," Alman told him.

"*What?*"

"I said don't use magic on them!"

"Quick, go," Sabium said, sweat breaking out on his temples. "I'll hold it."

The crates had parted enough to create a narrow opening, but only the ones stacking up to a few feet high, which meant the crates stacked above were teetering on the brink of collapsing through the gap.

"Quick!" Sabium repeated.

Alman hesitated for a moment, then jumped through the precarious opening.

"Now you," Sabium ground out.

Fadan looked over his shoulder at the opening Sabium had created, then back at the Paladins lunging toward him like a pack of starving wolves. The last time he had faced several opponents in a real fight, he had woken up hours later in Alman's house. A magically hanging tunnel of crates was certainly the wiser choice. He spun and raced through the makeshift archway, then turned back again in case any of their pursuers had followed him through. None of them had the chance.

Sabium lunged after Fadan, and just as he crossed the threshold, the passageway collapsed, blocking the Paladins on the other side.

Screams and curses echoed from the other side and Sabium wiped sweat from his forehead, panting heavily.

"That was great," Fadan said, his heart pounding in his chest.

"We're not out of this yet," Sabium told him. "Alman, where to?"

"This way," Alman replied.

The distant sound of the fire still raged, and they could hear the shouts and yells of the collective effort to put it out. Their pursuers weren't exactly silent either. Echoes of officers trying to coordinate their squads reached them from everywhere.

"East side is clear."

"Circle back toward the warehouse. Block the exits."

"They're moving south!"

With silent gestures, Alman led them through the labyrinth of cargo, taking prudent peeks around each corner before turning. On a couple of occasions, they heard the footsteps of patrols skittering down adjacent corridors, freezing with their backs to the wooden containers.

"There," Alman said, kneeling behind two barrels oozing with the delightfully woody smell of brandy. He was pointing at an opening between two stacks of crates, beyond which stood the main street. Civilians raced from one side to the other, carrying buckets to and from the fire.

"So we make a run for it?" Fadan asked. "Seems like an obvious exit. Won't the Paladins be covering it?"

"Yes," Alman confirmed.

"*Where are* they, though?" Fadan wondered. "I can't see them."

"They are there, believe me," Sabium muttered.

"Our only option is fighting our way out of here," Alman said. "They are covering multiple exits while chasing us in here, which means they're spread out thin. That should be enough of an advantage. Besides, we do have two mages."

"Why did you tell me not to use magic on them?" Fadan asked. "Back there, when they had us cornered?"

"Because it wouldn't have worked," Sabium explained. "Paladins wear syphons. It's a glowstone device that absorbs any spell. Pretty ingenious, actually. It uses the energy of the absorbed spells to recharge, which means once built, a syphon lasts forever."

"I see..." Fadan let out a sigh. "So that's how they defeated the Academy during the Purge."

Sabium nodded. "It still cost them. If you keep your distance from them, you can still cast spells. They just won't work if they're aimed at the Paladins themselves. The trick is using indirect attacks."

"What does that mean?" Fadan asked.

"Use spells on other things," Sabium explained. "Hurl a heavy object at them, or block their path with fire. After an object is in motion or a fire is burning, there's no more magic at work. There's nothing for the syphon to absorb."

"But if you try to set their clothes on fire, for example," Alman added, "it won't work."

Fadan nodded. "I get it." He took a deep breath and adjusted his grip on the sword. "Okay. I'm ready."

The two brothers exchanged a look, then nodded at each other.

"I'll create a distraction," Sabium said. "On my signal, run."

The old mage stood up, a blue aura thrumming around him. He raised his hands as if pushing an invisible wall in front of him, and the tall stacks of crates began to tilt outward and into the street.

"Watch out!" someone yelled from the other side. "It's going to fall."

There was the high-pitched scream of a woman and what seemed like a dozen yelps and gasps as the large containers tumbled and fell down to the street.

Fadan grabbed his master's robe. "What are you doing?!" he demanded. "You'll crush those people."

But the mage wasn't listening. His arms swung down into an upward hook as if holding an invisible baby and...

Silence.

None of the crates ever even touched the ground. The massive wall blocking the street from view had disappeared, but the containers that it had been made of were now floating in the air about three feet above the ground, held in place by Sabium's magic.

"Quick!" Sabium said, his face red and every vein in his neck and forehead standing out. "Before they recover."

The prince was dumbstruck by the sight. It was Alman who snapped him out of it, rushing past him and hauling him by the arm. They raced out through a corridor made of magically flying wooden boxes. Dozens of people, Paladins included, crouched beneath them with hands over their heads. It took them all a moment to come to grips with what was happening, long enough to allow Fadan and Alman to run through and disappear into the shadow of a back alley.

Alman kneeled behind a pile of trash, panting, and Fadan skidded next to him, squatting low to stay out of sight.

"That was amazing," the prince said. He wasn't breathing as heavily as Alman, but he was panting as well.

Alman punched the ground. "It was stupid!"

"Are you kidding? It was the most incredible thing I've ever seen. Where is he, though?"

The reply didn't come right away.

"He's not coming," Alman replied flatly.

"What?!"

There was a crashing sound from outside the alley, followed by the echoes of a commanding voice.

"On your knees, mage! Hands where we can see them."

"He's been syphoned," Alman said, covering his eyes. "They got him."

⌒⌐

They entered the finely cobbled streets of the Palatine District. Far behind them was the commotion of the besieged Docks. Every now and then, a squad of Paladins rushed by, headed toward the river, but that didn't concern them. They were now two mere citizens on their way to their own affairs.

Beneath the gray morning sky, the streets were teeming with people. Merchants finished opening their stalls, crying the merits of their wares to all passers-by. The smell of warm, freshly baked bread flooded their noses, and Fadan felt his stomach wake up with a roar.

"Alman?" Fadan called.

"Yes?"

It was the first time any of them said anything since Sabium's arrest.

"The rebels…do they know about me?"

Alman glanced back at the prince. "No," he replied. "To be honest, I was afraid of what the leadership might decide to do if they found out."

Fadan nodded. "Can we please keep it that way?"

"Sure. Don't say anything. Let me do the talking." With trembling fingers, he massaged his baggy eyes. "I'll still need your help to enter the dungeons."

"You'll have it; don't worry. We're getting Sabium out today." Fadan sighed. "I'm pretty sure that's all the time he has."

"What about the others?" Alman asked. "There will be dozens, maybe hundreds of prisoners from today's raid alone. The rebellion will want to rescue as many as possible."

"I've told you before. I'm not comfortable betraying my father." Fadan paused. "But I'm not sure I can rescue your brother alone, so…if that is the price of saving him, then I accept. Besides, I was planning on rescuing Doric and his friends sooner or later. Might as well do it today."

Alman nodded and the conversation died.

They stopped at a carpenter's shop. A small counter, packed full of wooden tableware, separated the store from the street. The shop itself was small and rectangular, carpeted with wood shavings. Benches and small tables, stacked upon each other, lined one of the walls, while an unfinished wardrobe occupied most of the remaining space.

Alman grabbed a spoon and started hammering on the counter with it. "Anyone there?" he shouted.

A man emerged from somewhere at the back of the store. He wore a simple brown tunic and seemed to be as large as the wardrobe he was building.

"Morning. Anything I can do for you?" he asked, joining them at the storefront.

"Good morning, sir," Alman greeted. "You wouldn't by any chance have anything in alabaster, would you?"

The carpenter was carrying a chisel, and he was squeezing it so hard, his knuckles had turned white. He studied both Alman and Fadan from head to toe. "Maybe," he said. "Why don't you come in? We can check the storeroom out back."

Alman nodded and the carpenter lifted a section of the counter so they could step inside. They followed the man into a narrow corridor and down a staircase leading into a basement. A locked wooden door stood downstairs, and the carpenter knocked. First once, then three times, then once again.

Something clicked, and a rectangular slot opened in the door, revealing a set of eyes.

"I have visitors," the carpenter said, motioning toward Fadan and Alman.

The peephole closed and the door opened.

"In you go," the carpenter told them.

Alman motioned for Fadan to follow. "Come on."

On the other side of the door, whoever had opened it was holding a lantern that barely lit the way. The basement had an old, dusty smell that somewhat resembled the dampness of the dungeons, even if it wasn't nearly as bad. It was a cramped space, full of sacks, barrels, and chests. Three more doors led to what Fadan assumed were storage rooms.

Besides the man that had opened the door, there were two women inside, both staring intensely at Fadan, their hands resting on the pommels of swords at their waists. They weren't making him feel very welcome.

The door slammed shut, its lock clicking into place, and Fadan realized the carpenter had not followed them inside.

"Who's this?" one of the women asked. She had thick, dark hair tied back by a blue bandana on her forehead. Fadan guessed she had to be about his mother's age, and she was giving him what was probably the least friendly stare he had ever received.

"He's with me," Alman replied.

"That's not a very good answer," the other woman said. She had shaved her hair and wore full body armor resembling that of a Legionary.

"As we speak, hundreds of our people are being taken by the Paladins, Alman," the woman with the bandana said. "And you come in here with a stranger?"

"Calm down, Shayna," Alman replied calmly, as if trying to soothe a wild animal.

The woman with the shaved head drew her sword. "Don't tell her to calm down," she snapped. "We have a traitor in the ranks. Who is this?"

"Yes, we do," Alman agreed. "We've had a traitor in our midst for a long time. Probably more than one. That's why Doric, Hagon, and the others got arrested in the first place. But believe me, that traitor will be someone we know." He waved toward Fadan. "Not some stranger."

"I agree," Shayna replied, then drew out her knife and pinned Alman against the wall, her blade pushing at his throat. "The traitor is definitely someone we know."

"Wait!" Fadan cried, but as soon as the sound came out of his mouth, the man who had opened the door grabbed him from behind and locked his arms behind him.

"Easy," Alman begged.

"Who *is* he?" Shayna repeated.

Alman sent Fadan an apologetic glance.

Please don't tell them, the prince thought.

"He's…"

Please…

"He's my brother's apprentice."

Both women turned to Fadan.

"He's a *mage*?" the shaved-headed woman asked.

Good idea, Alman, Fadan thought. He tapped his power, jumped, and dematerialized. By the time his feet fell back to the floor, he was free from his captor and spun away from him.

The man did not pursue him, and both women lowered their weapons.

"Well, you could have said so sooner," Shayna told Alman.

"I was trying," Alman replied, indicating the other woman's knife.

"So what's your name, boy?" Shayna asked.

Fadan opened his mouth but said nothing for an awkwardly long time. "I… I'm Aric," he finally managed to get out.

Stupid!

Alman glared at him, but Fadan pretended not to see it. The other two introduced themselves as well. The man was called Theudis, and the other woman was Lucilla.

"Aric, huh?" Lucilla said thoughtfully. "A friend of mine has a son called Aric."

"That's not Aric," another voice said.

Fadan turned to the sound and his heart sank. Coming from one of the other rooms, an olive-skinned woman wearing a flawless white uniform stepped up to him.

"Aric is his brother."

"Lady Margeth?" Fadan mumbled.

The Archduchess bowed deeply beneath the confused stares of her associates. "Your Majesty," she said, then stood back up. "Shayna?"

"Yes, mistress?"

"Syphon him."

⌒⟶

Intila's office was as spacious as it was austere. A plain slab of obsidian served as a desk, standing atop square iron legs. Behind it, a large window overlooked the gray wall of the Legion's headquarters. It was remarkable how the architect had managed to find such a drab view in a place like the Citadel, where there were more gardens than actual buildings.

A file of busts representing each of Intila's predecessors lined one of the walls as if awaiting inspection. There wasn't a single carpet warming the cold, stone floor, only a banner draping the wall opposite the dead High

Marshals. It was a washed-out blue and had a fading yellow inscription that read: Fifth Expeditionary Legion – North Aletia. It wasn't completely tattering yet, but it did have a couple of tears here and there, not to mention a handful of dark stains that Cassia guessed had to have been caused by blood.

The empress had been sitting in that awful chair so long, she had memorized the shape and position of every mold stain on the Legion's headquarters' wall outside the window. Where was Intila? It wasn't like him to make her wait this long.

The door opened and a Legionary tipped his head inside. "Your Majesty," he said, "is there anything we can bring you? A drink, perhaps?"

Cassia made to respond but heard someone else reply, "That's all right, Barca." She recognized Intila's voice. "I'm here."

The Legionary opened the door wider, making way for the High Marshal while slamming a fist against his heart.

"Sorry to keep you waiting, Majesty," Intila said to Cassia. Behind him, the door closed. "It's been a…busy day."

"I've noticed," Cassia replied.

Intila acknowledged that with a nod and headed for the chair behind his desk. "What is it you wanted?"

"To ask you about Doric," she replied nonchalantly. "How is he doing? Is he being well treated?"

"I wouldn't know," Intila replied, sitting back in his chair. "I handed control of those prisoners to Vigild weeks ago."

"I see. Has Vigild replaced you at everything else as well? He seems to have jurisdiction over the rebels now; maybe he will get the Legions, too."

Intila frowned as his fingers played with the sharp end of a quill. "Vigild argued that since the rebellion harbors most of the fugitive mages, they should be under his Paladins' jurisdiction. The Scriptorium has not lost its authority on this matter, but the Chancellor promised the emperor some… eye-catching results. Despite my guarantees that the Scriptorium's approach would provide a more definitive solution to the problem, my methods were considered too slow, and Vigild received the go-ahead."

"So, this is what it's been all about?" the empress asked. "Is this why my husband…my former husband is rotting in a dungeon while my eldest son is made into dragon bait? So that Vigild can replace you as Tarsus's favorite?"

Intila's index finger tapped the dried tip of the quill. "It would appear so," he replied after a while. "What was I supposed to do?"

"Are you sure you want me to answer that question?"

The quill flew from Intila's hands as he tossed it away. "Will you please stop beating around the bush already? What is it you want?"

Cassia held Intila's stare for a while, then sighed, as if giving up. "Actually, I came to thank you. It's true, I did. I know about Fabian," she explained. "I assume you know about Venia?"

"Of course I know about her. Who do you think chose her to be stationed with you?"

"Then all the more reason for me to thank you," Cassia said. "Fadan shut me out when Aric was sent away. Thank you for keeping an eye on him."

The High Marshal told her it was nothing with a wave of a hand. "It was as much Fabian's idea as it was mine," he said. "A prince should not be alone."

"Oh, I'm pretty sure he is not alone. I think he has found a different kind of friend outside the Citadel, Intila. That's what worries me."

"You have nothing to worry about. I am mobilizing every resource available to me. If the prince is among the prisoners, we will find him and we will release him. The emperor will be none the wiser. I guarantee that."

Cassia studied the High Marshal. Was that display of confidence simply for her benefit? It wouldn't be besides Intila to do so. He had always thought of her as some fragile, helpless little girl.

"I know you'll do everything you can," the empress replied. "Just tell me one thing, and please be honest."

"I'm always honest with you, Cassia."

She nodded. "What will Tarsus do if he finds out about Fadan's…abilities?"

"He's your husband," Intila replied. "I would hope you, of all people, would know the answer to that."

"That's the problem," Cassia said, getting up. "I really don't."

"Margeth, what in mother's name are you doing?" Alman demanded, struggling with his shackles. "He's a *friend!*"

The Archduchess paced along the small basement, her eyes locked on Fadan. The prince returned her stare, trying to look as calm as he could. He wasn't going to give her the satisfaction of wriggling uselessly against his restraints.

"How many of my people do you think your father would be willing to trade for you?" Margeth asked, ignoring Alman's pleas.

"You'll have to ask him," Fadan replied. "I'm sure it'll be an interesting conversation."

"Margeth! This is insane!" Alman insisted. "He came here with *me* out of his own will."

The archduchess raised a finger at him. "You will address me as 'my lady' or 'Archduchess'," she warned him. "You may have lost your title, but I have not."

"Not yet, at least," Fadan muttered.

"Ah!" Margeth returned her attention to the prince. "Spoken as a true Patros. There's just one problem. Without his Legionaries, even an emperor is as harmless as steel to a dragon. You're not in your Citadel anymore, young prince."

"If you really believe that," Fadan replied, "why don't you take this syphon off of me?" He showed his hands and the glowstone-encrusted handcuffs binding them.

Margeth chuckled. "Please." She stepped toward the prince, reached into his shirt, and pulled the transmogaphon around his neck out from under his clothes. "You are a Novice. Theudis over here could probably take you on his own."

Fadan inspected the man. He was wearing a studded coat, much like the ones the weapons instructor always made him wear during practice. There was a long scar that split his face in two. It was evidence enough that this man knew how to use the sword hanging from his hip.

"So, explain this me." Margeth looked to Alman. "The prince lands in your lap, tells you he's a mage, and you send him to your brother for some lessons. You even supply him with all the runium he needs, but you never thought about mentioning this to us?"

"I wanted him to join the rebellion out of his own free will," Alman explained. "It had to be *his* decision. He couldn't be coerced." His chin indicated Fadan's shackles. "Don't you see? It could change everything if he became one of us. Even some of the Legions could come to our side."

Margeth shook her head. "You're a good man, Alman Larsa, but you are also naïve. Do you honestly believe he would betray his father? You think the prince would join the losing side of a civil war? For what? The throne? It's his anyway. All he has to do is wait."

"I might be naïve, Archduchess," Alman spat back at her as if the words tasted bitter. "But at least *I* know what I stand for. The prince is a friend and *this* is not how the rebellion should treat its friends. Do you want to know why the prince came here?"

"As a matter of fact," Margeth said. "Yes, I do."

"To tell us how he plans on infiltrating the dungeons and helping us release our friends."

Fadan caught Shayna and Lucilla exchanging a look.

"Is that so?" the archduchess asked. "Well, you'll have to forgive me if I'm skeptical. Besides, there's so much we can achieve simply by threatening the emperor that we'll kill his precious heir. To me, that sounds a lot smarter than a suicide mission into the Citadel dungeons."

"Wait," Lucilla said. Everyone turned to face her. "If the prince truly has a plan, I want to hear it."

Margeth snorted. "You're kidding, right?" she said. "I already made a decision."

"You're not in charge here," Lucilla replied. "You might be an archduchess in Pharyzah, but here, in Augusta, you are a guest." She turned to the prince. "What was the plan?"

"There's an access into the dungeons from the sewers," Fadan explained.

"Unfortunately, after my brother and I tried to release Doric from prison a few months back, that access was blocked. However, I can enter the dungeons from the Legion's headquarters using a spell. I've done it before. It shouldn't be a problem. From there, I can open the sewer access and get your people into the dungeon."

"I am aware of your attempt to break Doric out of jail," Lucilla said. "It was brave, a bit foolish too, and this plan of yours sounds awfully similar to your previous attempt. We all know how *that* turned out."

"We just have to make sure no one sounds the alarm," Fadan replied. "But if it happens" – he looked at Alman – "we hide in one of the empty palaces instead of going for the exits."

Alman smiled and gave the prince a nod.

"Hide about three hundred people *inside* the Citadel?" Lucilla asked. "I think not. Shayna, what do you think? Can it be done?"

The woman in the blue bandana shrugged. "Hard to say. It's as the prince says. We'd need to neutralize every guard inside the dungeon before any of them sounded the alarm. The problem is, how many guards are we talking about? Our intel of the dungeon is good, but with today's raid, I think it's safe to say that they'll have changed things up a bit. My guess is they'll have at least tripled the guard."

Lucilla nodded thoughtfully. "And you?" she asked Fadan. "Are you truly willing to help do this?"

"Yes," Fadan replied. "I owe Sabium that much."

"Very well, then."

"You can't be serious," Margeth said. "This is a horrible plan!"

"Margeth," Lucilla sighed. "I'm sorry, my lady. I'm sure your bureaucratic strategy to overthrow the emperor is absolutely brilliant, but horrible plans are what we've been doing for the past ten years. Believe me, we've become rather good at it. Theudis, release Alman and the prince. Shayna, gather a strike team. We're hitting the Citadel dungeons."

The sloshing footsteps of the group echoed through the sewer. Fadan found it was remarkable how easy it had become for him to navigate the dark tunnels.

Archduchess Margeth had stayed behind. The strike team, as Lucilla called it, was comprised of seven men and five women, all wearing simple studded jackets. However, none had brought swords. Instead, they had knives. The logic seemed obvious to Fadan: they weren't planning on actually fighting, just killing, because if any of the guards saw them coming, the mission was already over.

"I have to apologize for Margeth," Alman told Fadan. They were walking a few paces ahead of the group, and he was talking in a voice that was low enough that he wouldn't be heard. "She was completely out of line."

"Well," Fadan replied, "you *did* tell me you were afraid of what the rebellion might do if they found out about me."

Alman sighed. "Yes, well... The truth is, we can't afford to refuse anyone's support. That has made the rebellion into a...disparate group. For example, there are those, like Margeth, who envision the end of the Empire and a return to the city-states and kingdoms of old."

"Which would make Margeth a Queen," Fadan said. "No wonder she didn't like your idea."

"Exactly. But people like her are a minority. Unfortunately, that is because there are plenty of other factions." He paused. "Which is why it would be so important for you to join us. You would give the rebellion a purpose. A path. A leader for us to rally behind."

"Alman..."

"I know, I know. I won't insist; don't worry. But I won't lose hope, either. Try not to hate me for that."

"Hate you?" the prince echoed. "Alman, whatever happens today, I don't think we'll ever see each other again."

They exchanged a glance.

"Well," Alman said, "I sincerely hope not."

Fadan didn't really have anything to reply to that, so instead, he looked over his shoulder. "So, who's she?" he asked, indicating Lucilla. The fire of her torch gleamed on her shaved head.

Alman looked back to confirm who the prince meant. "Lucilla? Well, she's un-landed nobility," he replied. "She's been with the rebellion even longer than I. The soldiers respect her deeply, which is why she's one of the people in charge of the Augusta cell."

"Soldiers?" Fadan asked. "You talk as if you have a standing army."

Alman smiled. "That's because we do. We've been fighting a guerrilla war for all these years, but that will change sooner or later. When it does, we'll be ready."

Fadan shook his head. "I don't even need to ask to know you'll be heavily outnumbered," he said. "Even if you weren't, it's not any army that can defeat the Legions."

"You're right," Alman agreed. "Our men are well trained, but probably not as well as a professional Legion. Which is just one more reason why we need you so badly."

The prince sent Alman an angry glare. "I thought you said you weren't going to insist."

Alman raised his arms in an apology. "You're right. I'll shut up."

They arrived at a junction and Fadan stopped. When the rest of the group caught up with them, he said, "This is where we split. Keep going in this direction." He aimed along the dark river of sludge. "Within a couple hundred feet, you will find a trapdoor above your head in the upper wall. Wait there. I'll open it from the other side."

The prince received a few nods, and Lucilla even wished him luck.

Hours had passed since Sabium had been arrested during their escape down at the Docks. Not only the morning but also the afternoon were long gone. At least it meant he would have the cover of night as he crawled out of the sewers, a maneuver he was now fairly experienced in.

An empty garden met him as he emerged at the surface, and whispers of conversation reached him as the prince carefully closed the manhole behind him so as not to make a sound.

A full moon glistened on the blocks of marble paving the streets. Around him, the silhouettes of towering estates displayed occasional lights shining from lonely windows. He caught the pleasant scent of burning pine coming from a nearby chimney. It reminded him of winter meals eaten in front of the warm fireplace in the great hall, and his stomach growled over the sound of the wind rustling through leaves.

The prince swung around, getting his bearing in the night, and quickly discovered the way to the Legion's headquarters. If he was lucky, infiltrating the dungeons wouldn't be any harder than the last time. Lucilla had given him a brand-new vial of runium, which he had downed shortly after entering the sewers. He didn't exactly have a wide variety of spells to resort to, but at least he didn't have to worry about running out of magic.

Squatting and keeping to the shadows, Fadan skirted the garden of the Strada estate. Beyond it, House Axia's palace rose like a cliff. It was the only one in the Citadel without so much as a lawn around it. All the more shadow for Fadan to hide in – the shadow of the gigantic building itself.

As a contrast, the relatively small mansion sitting right next to it, which the up-and-coming House Novara had recently acquired, was surrounded by what could only be described as a thick forest of cedar and pine trees. It was the perfect shortcut to the Legion's Headquarters.

Dead pine needles crunched beneath his feet, and Fadan slowed to almost a crawl, approaching the edge of the garden one careful foot after the other. As he did, his goal finally came into view.

A pair of Legionaries stood guard at the main gate while another pair circled the building in a steady but slow march.

Fadan ran along the line of trees until he was at too much of an angle for the pair at the main gate to see him, then waited for the other two to circle behind the building.

Come on, come on…

The Legionaries disappeared behind the wall and Fadan raced out of his hiding place. Just as he cleared the tree line, one of his feet skidded on the slick surface of fallen leaves, sending him flat on his back with a *thud*.

All air abandoned his lungs, and Fadan wasn't sure if that was due to the fall or the explosion in his heart as it began to pound in his chest.

He sprang up like a frightened cat and squatted low. At the Legion headquarters' main gate, both guards still stood at attention, apparently oblivious to his presence.

Fire take me!

There was no point in hanging around. He jumped up and raced to the side wall of the blocky building. In his mind, he visualized the last time he had done this, remembering which door he had used to enter the building. They all looked the same, especially in the dark.

It was the third from left, he remembered. *Yes, third from the left.*

Tapping his power, Fadan jumped through the door and landed inside. He was happy to be greeted by a familiar sight. This was definitely where he had come in the last time.

Okay, almost there.

He slipped down the corridors, trying to keep to every shadowed nook he found. Surprisingly, he didn't bump into any patrols inside. Every hall-way was empty, and there wasn't the slightest sound to be heard.

His back to the wall, Fadan arrived at the corridor where the entrance to the dungeons stood. It was pitch-black, with not a single light to guide him forward. It made no sense. Fadan remembered quite vividly the torch above the dungeon's entrance. He had used it to trick the guard and slip past him.

One thing was sure, Fadan was not going to make any light.

His heart was pounding ever harder, and the prince struggled to control and steady his breathing. For a moment, he considered checking his trans-mogaphon. Was it malfunctioning?

He slithered across the wall, his hands feeling the way ahead. With every step, he expected a guard waiting for him in the dark.

The wall ended, and tapping his foot, Fadan felt the steps leading down to the dungeons. He turned the corner. Something glowed in the dark before him. Not a torch, not even an oil lamp, but moonlight, a sliver of it shining around the edge of the door. It was open. Just a tiny bit, but it was.

Something's not right...

Fadan took a step back and considered running away. This felt too much like a trap.

I'm the prince, he thought, trying to shove the fear away. *They can't hurt me.*

He stepped toward the door, guided by the trim of moonlight, and pushed the other open. It creaked and Fadan jumped, but there was no one on the other side.

What is going on here?

Everything in his body commanded him to turn back and flee, but he steeled himself and forced his feet to move ahead. It was too quiet. There was no sound at all. None of the wailing, coughing, or snoring he had heard the last time. It was almost as if…

Fadan's eyes grew wide. He lunged forward and turned the corner to the first cellblock.

All jail doors were open. There was no one inside. Not a single prisoner.

What in the name of —

"Kind of blows your mind, doesn't it?"

Fadan caught such a fright, he thought he would faint.

Twisting toward the voice, he managed to say, "Stay right there," a fireball burning in his hand, somehow not nearly as hot as whatever he was feeling in his chest.

"Sorry," the voice replied softly. It was a woman. She was standing at the entrance of the cellblock as if she had just trailed his steps. A gray cloak fell over her slim frame, and long silver hair covered her shoulders. "I stood here a while, trying to figure out what to say so as not to startle you." She shrugged. "Concluded there was really no way to avoid it."

"Wait," Fadan said, looking closer at the woman in the flicker of moonlight. "You're one of my mother's maids."

"Yep," the woman confirmed. "That's exactly what I am."

"What in Ava's mercy are you doing here?" Fadan asked. His heart felt like it had slowed down somewhat, but he still had his fireball burning at the ready.

"Looking for you," she replied. "I would have waged three weeks of salary that you had been arrested today. You know, when you didn't show up this morning?" She inspected one of the empty cells at her side. "They're all gone. Today's prisoners and the ones who were already here." She returned her gaze to Fadan. "Including your brother's father."

"I can see that," Fadan said. "Now, how does a maid follow me into the dungeons?"

"Oh, no," the woman chuckled. "I didn't follow you. Fabian's spies assured me you were not among the prisoners. You weren't back home either, so I figured you were probably planning one of your famous rescue missions. I was waiting for you."

Fadan's mouth moved but produced no sound. This woman was no mere maid. Who was she, then? How did she know all these things?

"I'll be honest with you," she said. "Your mother is in a bit of an emotional breakdown as we speak. I wouldn't mind hauling you back to her." She motioned toward Fadan's fireball. "I would, however, prefer not to get scorched in the process."

"Stay right where you are," Fadan warned. "You said Fabian's spies knew I hadn't been arrested. Does that mean they also know where the prisoners have been taken?"

The woman nodded and jerked her thumb toward somewhere at her back. "Transferred. They were taken aboard a prison barge hours ago. They're probably halfway to Capra by now."

"Goddess damn it!" Fadan punched a wall and the fireball in his hand exploded, making the woman jump, startled. "Listen," he said, trying to regain some composure, "I don't know who you are, or who you're working for, but if you really *do* work for my mother, please just...just tell her I'm okay. All right?"

"So...not coming with me, then?" She raised a finger. "Question. How do you plan on finding this prison barge? You're not going to catch it before it reaches the ocean."

That gave Fadan pause.

"Do you remember that necklace your brother gave to you and you gave to your mother?" she asked

Fadan frowned. "Yes."

"What if I told you that was not just an ordinary necklace?"

Not an ordinary necklace?

"The jewel *was* glowstone…" Fadan mumbled.

"Exactly," the woman said, taking a step forward. "Have you ever heard of tracker-seekers?"

CHAPTER 20

The Secret

Eliran halted as they crossed the stone bridge to the Mages' Tower. The narrow mountain peak rose above them like the fang of a beast. Eliran sighed and walked inside, Aric, Leth, and Clea following her without a word. A gust of air wiped the sand off the floor in front of her. She swung her head from one side to the other, reverently drinking in each detail of the abandoned tower.

With delicate hands, she brushed over the dusty statues flanking the hallways and the ribbon-like thresholds of doors. Then one door caught her attention. She turned, moving one step into the room but refusing to go any farther.

"This was a classroom," she said.

Aric looked inside. There was nothing there. No furniture, nothing adorning the walls, it was just an empty room.

"How do you know?" Aric asked.

Eliran casually motioned toward the floor. "The markings," she said. "They count the passage of time. We used to do the same thing at my school when a tutor was very boring."

She was right. Half of the room's floor was riddled with strange stripes and circles engraved in the stone slabs. It had obviously been done using magic. Aric couldn't picture anyone being bold enough to start chiseling away at the floor during a class, no matter how boring a tutor was.

"I didn't know there was a school here," Clea said. "I thought it was just a research center."

Eliran turned around and left the room. "Every facility of the Academy was a school. There were some exceptions, but you could count them on your fingers. Come on. Show me the library."

Aric, Leth, and Clea took her through corridors and staircases leading to the abandoned library, but this time, the Witch avoided so much as glancing at her surroundings.

"So, as you can see," Leth said as they walked into the library, "the painting on the floor ends abruptly, as if the wall was originally not here. And" – he placed himself next to the protruding archway and dug a couple of fingers between the stone blocks – "you can feel air coming through the fringes. Also, if you look closely –"

"I know," Eliran said, pushing him aside. "You can see the glowstone." She inspected the mechanism briefly, then grabbed a small vial containing a silvery liquid from the satchel Aric had returned to her.

"Wait!" Leth said, grabbing Eliran's arm. "How can we know you won't just –"

"Just what?" Eliran asked. "What am I going to do?" She shook her arm free. "Your tower is across the bridge. This place belongs to me. Belongs to mages."

In a single shot, Eliran drank the entire content of the vial and her face grimaced horribly. As if the air had suddenly turned cold, she began exhaling a small cloud, but the mist was as blue as her eyes.

"Are you all right?" Aric asked, stepping closer to her.

"I'm fine," Eliran replied, shoving him away.

After taking a couple of deep breaths, she turned to the stone door and spread out her arms. A blue halo engulfed her and sparks began flying off her fingers.

A rumbling sound filled the room as if a herd of wild animals was stampeding toward them. The entire wall began to shake. Then –

BOOM!

Eliran was kicked back and sent flying away from the door. She slid across the floor for several feet until coming to a stop.

Clea jumped with a squeak, and Aric sprinted after the sorceress.

"I'm fine, I'm fine," Eliran assured, her voice pained.

"First Sohtyr, now a door," Leth said. "This is definitely not your week."

"Apparently not," Eliran said, standing back up. "Since I don't know the counterspell to that glowstone lock, I tried to force it open, but whoever built that door clearly knew what they were doing. I don't think I can get inside."

"Are you sure?" Aric asked. "You're giving up after just one try?"

"There isn't anything else to try," Eliran replied.

"Can't you…I don't know, tear the wall down or something?" Clea asked.

"What do you think I was trying to do?" Eliran snapped. "We'll have an easier time figuring out the counterspell." She crossed her arms. "If only I hadn't lost my visor… I'd bet my Talent Persea knows how to open this."

"Who's Persea?" Leth asked.

"Arch-Mage Persea," Eliran replied. "She's my…boss, you could say."

"You said visor," Aric said. "Do you mean *hyper*visor?"

"Aric!" Leth warned.

"Oh, just give it a rest," Aric told him. "We've come this far. We're seeing this through."

"There's a hypervisor here?" Eliran guessed.

"Yes, downstairs," Aric said. "Follow me."

A pile of sand had collected behind the door to the room with the hypervisor, forcing Aric and Leth to push it open with their shoulders. A strong wind blew from the only window inside, and Clea rushed to close it.

"This is it," Aric told Eliran, indicating the massive glowstone artifact. "Stupid Paladins probably mistook it for a simple mirror."

"It's magnificent," the sorceress said in a low voice. Placing a gentle hand on one of the statues holding it upright, Eliran admired the artifact. "There were a few of these on the conference rooms of my school in Niveh. But none were this beautiful." She raised a finger and did a weird gesture, making every glowstone shard in the device come to life with a powerful glow.

"Are you turning it on?" Clea asked.

"The crystals are spent," Eliran replied. "I'm recharging their spells. All right, stand back. I'm going to contact my boss."

The three Dragon Hunters exchanged a look.

"Why do we have to stand back?" Aric asked. "Is it dangerous?"

"Might be," Eliran replied. "If Persea doesn't like you."

Again, the Dragon Hunters exchanged a look but decided it was better to stand aside.

The mirror-like surface of the device rippled like a pond under soft rain, but otherwise, nothing else happened.

"What if your boss isn't watching her own hypervisor?" Leth asked. "She might be somewhere else."

Eliran looked over her shoulder at Leth. "Persea is *always* watching, believe me," she said. And, as if to prove her point, the blurry image of a woman appeared in the hypervisor, the water-like ripples slowly bringing her into focus.

"Eliran?" the woman asked in a muffled, metallic voice. "Is that you? Where have you been? You haven't reported in weeks. I was about to send a search party after you."

Her tone was angry, but nothing in her tall, slender features gave any impression of it. She had her long, delicate fingers peacefully entwined at her belly over a simple yellow tunic. Her hair, tied in one single braid and as white as Eliran's robes, fell over the left side of her chest and would have tumbled over her shoulder if she had so much as twitched her head. There wasn't a single wrinkle on her glowing face, despite the obvious age of her voice. It was unsettling, like looking at two people that shared the same body – an angry old woman and a quiet young damsel.

"Mistress," Eliran said, bowing ever so slightly. "Your concern is touching."

"And your quip is tedious," Persea retorted. "What have you been doing? Is your mission complete? And who is that with you? Yes, you three. No point hiding in the back. I can see you quite clearly."

"They are Dragon Hunters, mistress," Eliran replied. "They are helping me."

"Helping you?" Persea asked. "How are they helping you? Wait…" She seemed to take a look around Eliran. "Are you in Lamash? What in the goddess's name are doing you there?"

"That is a long story, mistress," Eliran replied. "I need your assistance."

"I imagine it is a long story," Persea said. "With you, it always is. What do you need?"

"Access," Eliran explained. "Access to a walled off-section of the library. Here, in Lamash."

The Arch-Mage sent Eliran a long, stern look. "You *found* it?" she asked.

"Actually," Leth intervened. "That was me."

Persea's stern look shifted toward Leth. "Congratulations," she told him. "You are smarter than the average Paladin."

"Thank you," Leth replied. "I'm glad you were around to let me know."

In exchange, he received an even harsher stare.

"Mistress," Eliran called. "Can you help me?"

Calmly, Persea returned her gaze to her subordinate. "No," she replied.

"Are you trying to tell me you don't know how to open that door?" Eliran asked.

"Of course not. I'm trying to tell you that there is no way I will let you inside that vault. It was closed for a very good reason."

"Mistress," Eliran fumed. "*This* is important!"

The Arch-Mage finally lost her composure. "All the more reason to let me in on every detail instead of telling me you're too busy to report!" she yelled.

Aric almost expected the hypervisor to shatter into a thousand pieces. He looked at Eliran and saw her fists clench, small sparkles flying off of them.

"Very well," Eliran said coldly. "You want a report? How about this for a report: You didn't send me after just any random Archon, did you? You sent me after one of their leaders. That's what Sohtyr is, isn't it? One of the head Archons!"

"You fought him, then," Persea concluded. "How was it? How strong is he?"

"You could have gotten me killed!" Eliran screeched.

"Calm down," Persea commanded. "You are being childish. I had complete confidence in your ability to survive. I would not have sent someone that would not have been able to report back."

"Why not at least warn me?" Eliran demanded.

"Because I don't know how strong a mind-reader he is, of course," Persea replied. "Had he discovered that we possess that sort of knowledge, it could have raised suspicions. The less you know, the better. So tell me, what is he capable of?"

"What is he capable of?" Eliran echoed. "He is capable of controlling a dragon, that's what. I saw it with my own eyes."

Persea's eyes grew. "He's done it?"

"Did you know that this is what he was after?"

"It's what we are all after, silly girl. What else have you found? You fought him; you must have pried into his mind."

Eliran didn't reply right away. She stared angrily at Persea with her arms crossed before saying, "There's something frozen in the Frostbound tunnels. He intends to use the dragon-controlling spell on whatever it is. That's all I know."

A serious frown grew on the Arch-Mage's face. "Are you certain?" she asked, but didn't even wait for a reply. Instead, her eyes drifted. "Would it even work? He obviously thinks so…"

"What are you babbling, mistress?" Eliran asked.

Persea twitched and covered her mouth with one hand. "I cannot speak of it," she said. "Not unless those three leave."

Looking over her shoulder at Aric, Leth, and Clea, Eliran smiled. "Suit yourself," she said, returning her gaze to Persea. "But I'll tell them everything anyway."

"Insolent girl!" the Arch-Mage yelled.

"I need their help!" Eliran retorted. "I told you, Sohtyr is stronger than me. So, unless you can send me any reinforcements, don't ask me to keep secrets from them."

Persea squeezed her own hands until they became as white as her hair. "You know as well as I do that it would take me weeks to send someone down there."

"Then why are we wasting time?"

Eliran's question was left unanswered. Persea shifted her weight as she briefly inspected the three Dragon Hunters.

"What are you so afraid of?" Eliran asked. "What has the Academy done this time?"

"We have done what we always do," Persea replied. "We protect the world from the things it doesn't even believe in. We make sure the legends and myths and scary bedtime stories remain just that – stories. But our influence is diminished. Our watchfulness impaired. With the resources at our disposal, there is little more we can do beyond trusting that the knowledge we buried *stays* buried. Unfortunately, it would seem the Circle has discovered at least a good portion of it."

"Please, mistress, get to the point," Eliran pleaded.

Persea sighed. "Arkhemia wasn't always as it is today. There was a time, long, long ago, when the most magnificent things took place. We know it happened because some vestiges of those times survived to our days. Vestiges like Bloodhouses and other places of power. We cannot know who built the Bloodhouses, what their runes actually mean, or how their brewing chambers turn dragon blood into runium. What little information we have about these times got to us in the form of religious texts and beliefs. All mention some kind of war between our gods and the gods of dragons. But the accounts vary.

"According to the Arreline cult of Ava, today known only as the Temple, we won. On the other hand, some Akhami sacred tablets seem to indicate that the dragons won the war instead. In any case, for centuries, all our historians and archeologists had for evidence of this divine war that took place in our world were vague, dubious, and conflicting religious texts. That was, until we found the Frostbound.

"I'm not going to go into too many details about the discovery, but suffice it to say that the place left everyone in the Academy extremely intrigued. It looked to have been built by the same people who built the Bloodhouses, and dating spells suggested it was just as old. Not to mention it was completely frozen despite being right in the middle of the desert. These were the golden days of the Academy, when the Empire was still young and prosperous, and we were its most influential and rich institution. After the Imperial House, of course.

"Piles of resources were dumped on the Frostbound. Studying it became our biggest priority. What we found, however, made us forever regret this decision. Our archeologists dug through hundreds of feet of ice as hard as steel, and beneath it, they found a frozen, dragon-shaped body as large as a mountain. We found the corpse of a god."

A chill crept up Aric's spine and he shared a look with Leth and Clea. They seemed even more incredulous than he felt.

"What?!" Eliran cried.

"We don't know much about the creature," Persea continued, ignoring her audience's shock. "There were some who believed we should have studied it further, but the majority of the Academy was far too frightened. The preliminary analyses indicated that the creature was not entirely dead. Instead, it was being kept frozen by a remarkably powerful spell stored inside the glowstone blade of a sword buried in its chest. The Council of Arch-Mages decided to leave it alone. A massive steel crypt was built around it, and several protective spells were cast to make sure no one else found it. The entire affair was made a secret. Some of the lower echelons involved in the excavations even had their memories erased out of precaution."

"Wait!" Aric said. "You're saying Sohtyr wants to control a god in the same way that he can control a dragon? That can't be possible."

"It doesn't matter if it's possible," Persea told him. "If Sohtyr is allowed to wake the creature up, the consequences will be cataclysmic, whether the mind-control spell works or not."

"You keep referring to it as 'creature'," Clea said. "This is a god we're talking about —"

Persea cut her off. "It *was* a god. We don't know what it is now."

"You mentioned protective spells," Leth said. "What exactly are we talking about? Because if you mean those blue creatures, there's no way they can stop Sohtyr. They're barely a challenge for the Guild's trainees."

"That's a just a low-level security measure," Persea explained. "Aimed at scaring away random adventurers. There are other, more sophisticated defenses in place."

"You arrogant fools!" Eliran accused. "That's why you won't let me inside the vault upstairs?"

"Eliran!" Persea warned.

"You locked the creature up, but instead of throwing out the key, you kept it here, in Lamash."

The Arch-Mage looked like she was about to burst with rage. They saw her open her mouth and began to scream at the top of her lungs, but all they heard was a garbled, unintelligible mess.

"What?" Eliran asked. "Mistress, you're breaking off." She stepped toward the hypervisor and waved her hand. "Stupid old thing…"

Then a horn blew somewhere near, echoing between the mountain peaks.

Aric cursed. "Raiders," he said.

Eliran looked from Aric to the scrambling image in the hypervisor. "No, not raiders," she said. "Sohtyr."

⌐⌐

The sun was hanging low, reddening the sky as if it were ablaze. Lyra watched it quietly with one leg dangling outside the stone railing. Beside her, Nahir slid a whetstone along the steel blade of his sword.

"Must you keep doing that?" Lyra asked. "It can't possibly get any sharper beyond a certain point, you know?"

"I know how to sharpen a blade, Lyra of Awam," Nahir told her without taking his eyes from the sword.

"Right. You're an Honor Guard," Lyra said. "I bet they gave you your first sword when you were six or something."

"Five," Nahir corrected. "I was five at the time. I remember being very happy."

"*Five?*" Lyra couldn't believe it. She shook her head. "Did you have any toys at all?"

This time, Nahir raised his head. "Why would I need a toy when I had the real thing?" he asked.

"Hey!" Tharius burst into the small balcony, gasping. "Have you guys seen Aric?"

"He's in the Mages' Tower, I think," Lyra replied. "With the witch."

"Oh, damn it," Tharius let his head fall to his chest.

"What's the matter?" Lyra asked

"Ashur is complaining that his shift is over and no one has shown up to replace him," Tharius replied. "He's threatening to leave the watch point."

"So?" Lyra asked.

"What do you mean, *so?*" Tharius asked. "We can't leave a watch point vacant."

"All right, then replace him," Lyra suggested.

"I just finished an eight-hour shift," Tharius said. "Can't you please go?"

"Me?" Lyra asked, pretending to feel offended. "I'm responsible for healing the witch. It's not my fault she left the infirmary."

"What infirmary?!" Tharius argued. "You're not healing anyone; you're right here. What difference does it make if you just move to the eastern wing?"

"I'm spending time with my good friend here," Lyra said. "And we're having a great time, aren't we, Nahir?"

The Cyrinian glanced from his blade to Lyra and then back to his sword but didn't really say anything.

Tharius exhaled loudly. "You're going to make me go all the way to the Mages' Tower?" he asked.

Lyra shrugged. "I'm not *making* you do anything." She turned to the desert so Tharius couldn't see her smile.

"And what about you?" Tharius asked Nahir. "This is your watch, but you're not even looking out."

The grinding sound of Nahir's blade stopped.

"No need," Nahir said. "She's doing it for me."

Tharius gritted his teeth. He felt like growling.

"Calm down, Tharius," Lyra told him. "Just breathe and enjoy the view.

Look at this gorgeous sunset over the dunes. Look at that beautiful eagle over there, soaring in the sky. When was the last time we had the chance to just relax?"

"Eagle?" Tharius asked, then his jaw dropped. "Merciful Ava…"

"What?" Lyra asked.

The metallic singing of Nahir's whetstone stopped.

"That's no eagle," Tharius said.

"Get inside," Nahir commanded, standing up. He took the horn across his shoulders to his mouth and blew as hard as he possibly could.

⌒⟶

Clea ran toward the window and opened it, flooding the room with light and making the sounding horn even louder.

"It's coming from the main tower," she said. "From the south, I think."

"We have to go," Aric said. "*Now.*" He turned and stormed out of the room.

Without a word, Clea and Leth turned and followed him. Eliran, however, did not move.

"I can't," the sorceress said.

"*Can't?*" Aric asked. "We need your help. You're probably the reason he's here in the first place."

Eliran shook her head. "No," she said. "He's here for that vault. I have to stay. I can't let him get inside."

Leth and Aric exchanged a look.

"You think he can get in?" Leth asked. "I thought you said that wasn't possible without the counterspell?"

"I also thought I could defeat him before I faced him," Eliran said. "You should go. Help your friends. But I have to protect that door."

Aric hesitated. "All right, they will stay and help you," he said, indicating Leth and Clea.

"Out of the question," Eliran told him. "I can't let you risk your lives for matters of the Academy. Besides, you don't even know *what* is attacking the main tower. My guess is you'll need as much help as you can get."

"Matters of the Academy?" Aric asked. "I heard your boss. If Sohtyr wakes that thing up, it'll be everyone's concern."

"I'm not fond of the idea," Leth said, "but I agree with Aric. By your own account, you are weaker than this Sohtyr. What chance do you have against him?"

"I'll know what to expect this time," Eliran replied. "Also, I don't need to defeat him, just make sure he doesn't get into the vault before his runium wears off. And I'll have the protective spells of the vault to assist me." She stepped closer to Aric and looked him in the eye. "You'll have to trust me on this one. I know what I'm doing."

Aric took a deep breath. This didn't sound right, but across the stone bridge, the alarm kept sounding eerily. Whatever it was, it was dangerous, and his Hunters needed him.

"Fire take this!" Aric let out. "All right, we'll deal with whatever it is and get back here as quickly as possible."

Eliran nodded. "Agreed."

With a sigh, Aric turned and fled toward the stone bridge, followed by Leth and Clea. They swung the door open and sand swirled around them, forcing them to cover their eyes. The stone railing was searing hot, but the winds at that height were too strong, and they were forced to hold on as they sped across the bridge. The horn suddenly went quiet and was replaced by the whistling of the wind.

Then, a roar thundered right above them, and Aric felt his stomach sink.

Grimacing, the three of them looked up and saw the massive shape of a red dragon. The beast opened its mouth and spewed forth a jet of fire.

"Run!" Aric yelled, racing across the bridge.

A wave of fire pursued them as they ran, and Aric rammed the door to the main tower open, bursting through it just in time to escape the blaze. Leth and Clea rolled into a ball, crashing in right next to Aric, the edges of their clothes smoldering and smoking.

"Merciful Ava!" Clea said, gasping.

Aric tried to stand up but fell back down, screaming and holding his shoulder. He cursed and his eyes welled.

"What is it?" Leth asked, rushing to his side. He helped Aric stand up straight.

"I think I dislocated my shoulder," Aric managed to say. "Do you know how to –"

He finished the question with a frightening howl of pain. Leth had just pulled Aric's arm back into place. "Yes," he replied.

Aric closed his eyes and gritted his teeth, then gasped as a tear rolled down his face. "Thank you," he ended up saying. He looked as pale as Eliran's robes.

"What do we do?" Clea asked. She was trying to look outside, to see where the dragon was.

"We should be safe as long as we stay inside," Leth replied, helping Aric back up. "This fortress was designed to be dragon-proof."

"The lower levels, maybe," Aric said. "But if that thing wants to burst through the balconies, it can."

"There's a lot of fortress to hide in," Clea added. "And not that many of us."

"And let a dragon destroy Lamash?" Aric argued. "No way."

"What do you suggest?" Leth asked.

"I suggest we kill it," Aric replied.

When Aric, Leth, and Clea got to the entrance hallway of the fortress, most of the company was already there. The young Hunters were huddled behind the slanted, tendon-like columns, their heads low, as if they were afraid the ceiling might collapse at any moment. Somewhere outside, the dragon roared fiercely.

"You're all here. Good," Aric said, kneeling next to them.

"I gathered as many as I could find," Tharius said. "I knew you'd want the company together."

"Yeah," Ashur added. "He even made Orisius and Irenya race to the armory. He seems to think we're about to fight that thing out there."

"Good," Aric said. "Because that's exactly what we're going to do. Who's missing?"

"Just Prion," Tharius replied. "I couldn't find him."

"Fine," Aric said. "We don't want to be fighting next to anyone who doesn't have our back." He paused, then looked straight into Ashur's eyes. "In case you didn't get that, I was saying –"

"I'm staying," Ashur cut him off. "If you're fighting a dragon, then so am I."

Ashur stared at Aric with a defiant look. It was almost as if this was just another one of Saruk's challenges.

"Good," Aric said, smiling. "Okay, here's the plan. This is the largest place in Lamash. It's big enough to fit a dragon *and* should give us enough room to fight it. So we're going to lure that thing in here."

There was a sudden look of apprehension on everyone's face, but Aric ignored it.

"Lyra, you'll stay in the rear. If anyone falls or gets hurt bad enough, you step in and get them out."

"Understood," Lyra replied with a nod.

"Clea, Orisius, Dothea, the same as in Nish." Aric pointed at the stone platforms around where the columns met the ceiling. "Get yourselves up there and harass the dragon with arrows."

"Up there?" Dothea asked. "How are we supposed to climb up there?"

"I brought ropes from the armory," Orisius replied, showing them a large bundle of thick, strong rope. "I was thinking we could tie the dragon down."

"And I told him that was a stupid idea," Irenya said.

"It's not stupid," Orisius retorted, then turned to the rest of the group. "Someone tell her it's not stupid, please?"

"Yeah," Clea said, taking the rope. "It's pretty stupid. But it'll get us up there."

"Good," Aric said. "Then start climbing. We need to hurry."

Clea gave him a nod and the three archers left the huddle.

"Leth, Tharius, and Nahir," Aric continued, "you're with me. We'll be the bait." He received three serious nods. "Everyone else, find cover around the hallway and keep out of sight until I give the signal to attack." He inhaled deeply and glanced around at each one of his Hunters. "Get ready. We're about to slay our first dragon."

It took the company a moment to digest that thought. Feet shifted, and there were a couple of loud sighs, but no one said anything. Then, with a final nod from Aric, everyone hurried to their positions.

The main gate was fastened shut by a thick wooden bar, which Nahir's powerful arms removed. With the gate opened, Leth sneaked out, followed by Tharius. The two of them inspected the sky, looking for the dragon. Aric stayed behind, collecting torches from the lobby's walls. He made one last survey of the hallway, making sure the company was ready for the fight. He saw the shapes of his Hunters hiding behind the hallway's columns, their glowstone lances firmly in their hands. Up near ceiling, his three archers dangled from the ropes, only a couple of feet left to climb. They were as ready as they would ever be.

"There it is," Tharius warned.

Aric stepped outside and followed Tharius's arm.

There it was, a jagged, dark red gash in the twilight sky. To the west, black smoke billowed from the side of the mountain. Clearly, the beast had been busy destroying that flank of the fortress.

"Are we sure about this?" Leth asked. "We could just hide in the lower levels. There would be no shame in that. We're not graduated yet."

Instead of replying, Aric simply handed a burning torch to each of them. "Here," he said. "This ought to get its attention."

Leth shook his head with an amused smile. "Damned crazy Aurons."

It didn't take very long for the dragon to notice them as they began to wave the torches above their heads. The dragon shrieked and turned, drawing three quarters of a circle in the air. Furling its wings, the monster plunged toward them, letting out another roar.

"Ava Mother…" Tharius mumbled.

"Brace yourselves," Aric said.

The dragon grew larger and larger, flames coming out from the corners of its mouth as if it were a furnace.

"This might not be the ideal moment to point out a flaw in your plan," Leth told Aric, "but what now?"

"What do you think?" Aric asked, turning around. "*Run!*"

He didn't have to give that order twice. All four of them turned tail and fled back into the fortress, the massive dragon darting after them so fast that they could hear it zooming through the air. At the last possible moment, the beast opened its wings, braking and touching down right in front of the main gate with an earth-shaking *thump.*

"Dive!" Aric screamed.

The four Hunters jumped sideways, landing flat on the ground just in time to avoid a gush of fire. They picked themselves up quickly, resuming their flight deeper into the hallway, hoping the beast would fall into their trap. Lurking in the shadows of the columns on both sides were the rest of Aric's Hunters, ready for their moment to strike.

The dragon, however, did not seem ready to cooperate yet. Maybe something about that hollow did not feel right.

"It's not coming," Tharius said. "It's not falling for it."

"Leave this up to me, Captain," Nahir said, drawing a glowstone axe from his back.

"What? What are you going to do?" Aric asked, feeling unsure.

"What I can," Nahir replied. "Get ready to strike." And with that, he plunged forward, screaming like a madman with his axe swinging above his head.

The dragon roared.

"Fire take this!" Aric complained, regretting not having stopped Nahir. "All right. Leth, Tharius, spread out. Join the ambush."

He rushed behind one of the columns and watched Nahir duck beneath a jet of fire, rolling forward and standing right back up without so much as slowing down, even though part of his jacket had caught on fire.

To Aric's great relief, Nahir wasn't about to commit suicide. At the last moment, the Cyrinian turned and hid behind the open gate, disappearing from the dragon's sight. But the beast wasn't about to let him escape that easily. Shrieking, the dragon stormed into the fortress, its paws shattering the stone slabs beneath them.

"*Now!*" Aric screamed. "*Attack!*"

Arrows rained from above at the same time a swarm of Hunters charged at the beast. The dragon was momentarily overwhelmed by the sudden attack. It sent its head lurching backward, screeching in pain. Aric saw Trissa drive a spear into the monster's ribcage, and next to her, Ergon slashed one of its massive heels.

Then, rage took over the dragon. With swords, arrows, and spears sticking out from its body, the monster crashed against the columns on his sides as if it was a cage he was trying to escape from.

The onslaught came to a halt as the Hunters tried to protect themselves. Jullion was knocked down by the dragon's tail, and Ashur screamed for Lyra.

"It's going to tear the place down!" Leth screamed, taking cover from the falling debris.

It certainly seemed that way. Aric stepped back from the beast. The entire fortress was shaking. Huge blocks of stone fell from the walls and ceiling. It looked like the hallway was about to cave in.

This was a bad idea.

"Everyone back off!" Aric screamed over the chaos. "Retreat!"

However, it was useless. There was nowhere to hide.

Aric looked up at the stone platforms above the dragon and saw the shape of one of his archers. It was impossible to tell exactly who it was, but he or she was holding on for his life up there. The pillar was about to fall down.

Aric cursed. He looked at the rope dangling from where his archer was about to fall, then gritted his teeth.

"Oh, screw this!" Aric said. He raced toward the rope and began to climb it as fast as he could. "Leth!" he called. "Leth, swing me!"

"What?" Leth asked.

"Swing me, damn you!" Aric insisted.

Leth obeyed, confused. Around them, the company was in full retreat, some running toward the great staircase, others fleeing the other way, trying to get outside.

"No, not that way," Aric told Leth. "Toward the head. Swing me toward the head."

Leth was going to protest but figured this was not the best moment. Holding the rope, he ran away from the beast's head, pulling Aric along above him, then released.

Aric soared across the hallway, describing an arc that carried him over the dragon. When the rope was coming to a stop, getting ready to swing back around, Aric unsheathed his sword and let go. He fell, screaming, sword first on top of the dragon's head, and the glowstone blade buried itself in the beast's skull.

There was a squelching, and a gush of warm blood sprayed Aric's face. The beast released a guttural sound that lasted no more than a moment, then its head fell lifelessly to the floor. The impact was such that the handle of Aric's sword broke from the blade, and he came tumbling down, crashing to the floor.

A burst of pain flooded his torso, and for a moment, there was only silence as Aric saw the world dance above his head, a thousand stars blotting out his vision.

"Fire take us all," he heard Tharius mumble.

Then, Leth's face came into focus above him and the world became slightly more recognizable.

"Are you all right?" Leth asked.

Other people gathered around. Everyone was staring at him with astonished looks on their faces.

"Are you insane?!" It was Lyra. She knelt beside him and began inspecting his body from head to toe. "You could have been impaled by one of the horns."

Aric moved his mouth, but the pain in his chest made it hard to speak.

"What is it?" Leth asked. "You can't talk?"

"Eliran…" Aric gasped.

"Oh, forget about the damn witch," Lyra grumbled.

"No," Leth said. "He's right. We need to go back to the Mages' Tower."

"Help me up," Aric asked, cringing from the pain.

"You can't move," Lyra said, impotently. "You might have a broken rib or something."

"I'm fine," Aric replied, but the fact that he was still leaning on Leth for support betrayed him.

Lyra protested further, but Aric ignored her.

"Is everyone okay?" Aric asked.

"Jullion broke an arm," Lyra replied, giving up. "Trissa, Nahir, and Athan have some burns, but nothing serious. All in all, I think we got lucky."

"Lucky?" Tharius asked. "That's not luck." He pointed at the dragon's massive carcass. "We got badass; that's what we got."

There were immediate cheers and whistles.

"Damn right," Trissa agreed, holding on to her arm.

"Stop celebrating," Leth said. "This isn't over yet."

"Everyone who's not hurt, follow me," Aric said, limping away. "And be ready."

Despite her complaints, Lyra stayed behind, taking care of Jullion. Everyone else went with Aric.

The group tried to speed across the fortress, but the truth was that they weren't in very good shape either. Still, they pushed ahead.

There was barely any light left when they crossed the bridge to the Mages' Tower, but the damage from the dragon's fiery breath was still visible. Large portions of stone had turned charcoal black, and it was possible that the structure had been affected, but it did not deter them. Carefully, the group crossed and penetrated the abandoned tower, following through the corridors that led to the library.

"I don't like this," Leth said. "It's too quiet."

Aric shushed him. He didn't like the silence any better than Leth. He had been expecting to come into a fight, and if there wasn't one, then it probably meant Eliran had already been defeated. However, if Sohtyr was there, the element of surprise was probably the only thing they could count on.

The group put away their glowstone blades and drew their steel weapons as they tiptoed up the staircase. The great door to the library was shut, and Aric counted to three with his fingers before opening the door and bursting through it.

They halted immediately, jaws dropped. Every bookcase, table, and chair had been smashed to pieces, and there was no one in sight. No sign of Eliran or anyone else met them, not even their bodies. Instead, there was a massive hole in the wall where the secret door had once been, and beyond it, an altar of sorts where a purple cushion no longer held anything.

Aric lowered his sword and looked around. Had there been a fight, or was that destruction just the consequence of cracking the glowstone lock?

"Well, I finally got inside," Leth said, stepping into the now opened vault. "Too bad I still have no idea what this was all about."

CHAPTER 21

The Rescue

"You've brought us into a trap!" Lucilla cried, a threatening sword in her hand.

Fadan gave her a cold stare. "If this was a trap, you would have all been arrested by now," he hissed.

It was the truth. Fadan had no idea what was going on, but he had been at the wrong end of one of his father's ambushes once. This was not one of those, but then, what *was* it?

"The prince is right," Alman said, pacing along a row of empty cells. "They seem to have just packed up and abandoned this place."

Lucilla lowered her sword hesitantly. "Then they want us to follow the prison boat," she concluded. "That's where the ambush will be."

"Why go to that much trouble?" Fadan asked. "If my father is expecting a rescue" – he opened his arms – "this is the best place to spring a trap."

The group exchanged a series of glances. They could obviously see he had a point, but that just made the enigma all the more puzzling.

"Do we have a choice?" Shayna asked. "I mean, we can't just abandon our people. Wherever they're going, they'll be executed upon arrival."

Silence filled the prison hallway, water droplets echoing from the hollow cells.

Fadan clenched his fists. Little flames escaped from between his fingers as he turned around and stomped away from the group.

"Hey!" Lucilla shouted. "Where do you think you're –?"

Alman raised a hand, begging her to calm down. "Let me," he said.

The group of rebels closed into a tighter circle, frustration seeping into their whispers. Alman followed Fadan around a corner and into one of the cellblocks. The prince was standing in front of a cell. Inside,

Alman saw a rat squeaking in a corner, trying to dig himself into what looked like a bag of flour.

"Looking for something?" Alman asked.

Fadan did not reply right away.

"I've arranged with the spy to get my mother's necklace," he said at length. "I can get it for you. It'll lead you straight to the prison barge."

"Is this where Doric was jailed?" Alman asked, motioning toward the cell with his chin.

Fadan nodded.

"Before, in the sewers, you asked me about Lucilla. You want to know why she joined the rebellion?"

The prince looked at him suspiciously but did not reply.

"We all have our reasons," Alman said. "I joined because I lost everything I had. My title, my lands, everything... Shayna joined because she and her husband were caught harboring mages. Lucilla's reason is her daughter. Her name was Claura. It had been two months since she had been accepted into the Mages' School of Augusta when the Purge began. She was only nine. Couldn't cast a spell if she wanted, had never so much as tasted runium, but she did have the Talent. It was enough for Tarsus's Paladins."

Alman saw Fadan grow pale.

"Claura was captured along with the rest of her class and hung at the gallows five days later. Lucilla and her husband tried to stop it. The last thing little Claura saw was her parents being cut down by Legionaries. Lucilla survived her injuries and was rescued from prison by what would eventually become the rebellion. She has shaved her head every day since."

"Why are you telling me this?" Fadan snapped.

"Because that's why you are so angry," Alman said. "You're not just frustrated we've hit a wall. That happens. You've hit tougher ones. But you thought this was it. That Doric and the others would be free and you could finally stop this little war against your father." Alman shook his head. "But you know better than that. Deep down, you know you've been fooling yourself. You know what you have to do, and just helping with these prisoners isn't enough."

Fadan's eyes flickered and his chin trembled slightly. "What kind of person fights his own father?" he asked.

Alman grabbed the prince's arms, looking deep into his eyes. "I'm sorry to say this, but considering what your father is, what kind of person wouldn't?"

Fadan tried to say something. His lips moved, but no sound came out.

"The rebellion is hopeless, Your Majesty," Alman continued. "We all know it. We keep fighting because, honestly, there's nothing left for us to do. But with you... With you, we wouldn't even *be* a rebellion anymore. We'd be the people of the Empire, stomping their feet and saying 'No more!'"

"I'm just a kid, Alman."

"You are the prince, and you are a mage. You are brave enough to challenge your all-powerful father. You'll be a beacon of hope, a banner waving proudly in the wind, telling the people they don't have to cower in fear anymore. Every army needs someone to rally behind. You're the person we've been waiting for, except you're much better than any of us could have hoped for."

Fadan shook his head. "You're delusional. You're seeing what you want to see."

"Maybe," Alman agreed. "What about you? What do *you* want to see?"

⌒

Cassia strolled around the dry fountain in the middle of the patio, her fingers unable to stay still as they plucked at each other. "Are you sure Fadan knows where this is?" she asked.

Venia nodded. She was standing in a corner by a large staircase that went up to the veranda surrounding the courtyard. The spy, Cassia had noted, always made sure she had her back to a wall, even when the two of them were alone.

Wind played through the archway leading out of the courtyard, whistling and howling. Cassia hugged herself, fighting off a shiver.

"It's been years since the last time I was here," Cassia noted, inspecting the vines tumbling from the arches of the veranda. They had grown much longer than she remembered.

"You used to come here?" Venia asked.

"Before Doric and I got married," Cassia explained. "We usually sneaked out of the Citadel when we wanted to be alone, but sometimes we just found an empty palace. This was my favorite."

The spy glanced around at the shutters hanging from their hinges. "I thought you and Doric were from Fausta," she said.

"We are. But for a few years, Doric lived here. When his father was High Marshal." She adjusted her cloak. "I hated it. The distance. Never knowing when I would see him next. My father usually visited Augusta once a month. Because he had been the first of the Revolt's nobles to surrender, he got to keep his duchy, but his relationship with the emperor was fragile. But my father always had a plan. He realized Tarsus liked me, so he planned to marry me to him. I didn't mind, because it was the only way I got to be with Doric."

She chuckled. "I always cried when it was time to return to Fausta. I remember spending sleepless nights rolling in bed, picturing Doric surrounded by the Lagon and Strada girls." She shook her head. "One day, I must have been feeling rather vulnerable, I'm not sure, but I told him. The next day, he gave me this." Cassia reached into her dress and pulled her glowstone pendant out. "'This way, we'll always be connected,' he said." She chuckled again. "I know it sounds ridiculous, but…at the time, it felt like the most beautiful thing anyone could possibly say." She glanced at Venia smilingly. "Earned him a very decent kissing session."

The spy chuckled. "I guess loving a poet does have its perks. Weren't you worried the emperor would eventually agree to marry you to Tarsus, though? Wasn't Doric?"

Cassia nodded. "I was, yes. Especially because I knew Tarsus was trying to persuade his father to accept. Doric, however, wasn't worried at all."

"Really? He wasn't jealous?"

"Jealous?" Cassia threw her head back, laughing. "You clearly don't know Doric. He was jealous of Ambrosian Astal or Dionesia Mantara, anyone who could write better than him. My suitors didn't worry him. I think that was one of the things I loved most about him. Besides, his father knew the emperor well. Doric always assured me Tassan had no intention of marrying his son to one of his enemies' daughters. According to Faric, my father was a fool for even trying. There was only one other person Doric was truly jealous of. Intila."

"I'm pretty sure that was mutual, though."

"Maybe," Cassia said with a shrug. "You know, when we were little, those two were actually inseparable." She paused, her eyes set somewhere among the stars. "It's incredible how people can grow apart..."

"It takes a very special kind of bravery to remain friends with someone who has everything you ever wanted."

The empress turned to her spy but said nothing for a while. "Now, there's something neither of them would ever admit."

An owl cooed and Venia perked up, her eyes shooting toward the patio's entrance. "Your son is coming."

"You can hear him?" Cassia asked, searching the darkness beyond the gate. "Is he alone?"

The answer came shortly as Fadan's silhouette crossed into the courtyard. The empress would have recognized his walk if it was foggy and she was half-blind. A dark cloak flowed around the prince, and when his features finally became visible, he looked...older, somehow.

When had she seen him the last time? It couldn't possibly have been that long...

"Sweetie," Cassia said, taking her son into her arms. "Are you all right?"

"I'm all right, Mother," Fadan replied.

It was a silly, empty question. What else would he reply?

But he was not all right. She looked into his deep, dark eyes and what she saw was pain. It wouldn't have been more obvious if he was sobbing while tugging at her skirt, except he didn't do that now.

Cassia ran a delicate finger along his cheek, where his fair skin turned slightly pink. It was so easy for a mother to miss it when her little boy turned into a man. Had she really missed it, or was she just pretending like she had?

"I wish you had told me," Cassia said. "About your abilities."

"Mother, I know there is a lot to talk about, but time is against us. Every moment we waste is —"

"I know," Cassia interrupted. "Your friends can have the damn necklace. I just want you to be safe."

"Mother…" Fadan looked down, then quickly back up and into her eyes. "I'm going with them."

"*What?*"

"I'm sorry," Fadan said. "This is something I *must* do."

"You can't," the empress almost screamed. "I'll gladly give your friends the necklace; I don't care. But you can't —"

"I'm not asking for your permission," Fadan told her. He grabbed her hand. "Mother, I've had enough. I won't be a part of it anymore."

Cassia frowned. "What are you talking about? A part of what?"

"Father's schemes," Fadan replied. "The arrests, the lies, the persecutions. I can't take it anymore."

"Son…" Cassia shook her head. "You have *nothing* to do with any of it. It's not your responsibility."

"Yes, it is!" Fadan snapped, then regained his composure. "I'm the prince. The heir. What I do matters, and what I don't do matters just as much." He let go of Cassia's hands. "Mother, I'm going, and I'm not coming back."

That was not something Cassia was prepared for. She mumbled something incoherently until Fadan spoke.

"Mother, you have to understand what this means. I'm setting you free as well. There'll be no more reason for you to stay. Aric is out of Father's reach. Soon, Doric will be as well. You can leave. Escape."

Cassia's expression was paralyzed in shock. She glanced at Venia, then back to her son. "I… Your father… He will…"

"Fire take my father!" Fadan shouted. "He can't keep doing this to people. You included. This ends now."

"Son… Let's think about this, please."

Fadan shook his head in such a calm, definitive way that Cassia's stomach went cold.

"I've thought about it for too long already," the prince said. "But I've only been delaying it. My decision has been made. I'm sorry I won't be here to help you escape" – he looked at Venia – "but I'm sure you will be fine."

"No," Cassia said, her hands joining in a plea. "If you're going, then I'm going with you. I won't let you fight Paladins on your own."

"I won't be alone," Fadan replied. "Besides" – he showed his mother a hand and it burst into flames, startling her – "I can defend myself." He looked at Venia. "Can you get my mother out of Augusta?"

"I can," the spy replied.

Cassia's head swung from Fadan to Venia then back again, her lips attempting to form words. "I... Where will we go? How will I find you?"

"We'll find a way, Your Majesty," Venia replied. "Leave that to me."

Cassia swallowed through the constriction in her throat, then sighed. She slowly removed her glowstone pendant from her neck. "The enchantment is weak, but it still works," she said.

The thin blue shard swung around like a pendulum until it stopped, obliquely, as if a magnet was pulling it sideways.

Fadan grabbed the necklace, but Cassia clenched her fingers.

"Please, be careful."

With a smile, Fadan hugged his mother. "You too."

⌒

The cry of a seagull woke Fadan. He felt sweaty, despite the cold breeze, and his arm flattened against the wooden deck, itched with numbness. He sat up, leaning on the ship's bulwark, the Saffya's tame undulation sprinkling water on his arms and face.

A single tall mast dominated the seventy-foot-long river barge. It creaked as the boat swung from one side to other.

"Good morning," Lucilla said. She was standing next to Fadan, holding on to the eagle's head on the ship's bow. "Not the most comfortable place you've slept in, I imagine."

"Yes, one would imagine that, wouldn't they?" Fadan said, rubbing at his eyes.

Besides Lucilla and the sailors working the ship, everyone else seemed to still be asleep, wrapped in cloaks and spread around the dummy cargo occupying most of the deck.

Fadan stood, the freezing wind cutting across his cheeks. "Is that Capra?" he asked.

The silhouettes of buildings grew on the horizon, spreading north and south like a mountain range.

"We should be docking within the hour," Lucilla replied.

The prince reached into his shirt. He had both his mother's necklace and the transmogaphon around his neck.

"I'm wearing more glowstone than most people have seen their whole lives," he said, taking the artifacts out. He held his mother's pendant up and the tiny blue shard stretched westward. "I suppose we're still headed in the right direction. How far behind do you reckon we are?"

"Hard to say, but we should know more as soon as we dock. Our people in Capra will have taken notice of a prisoner shipment that large. Most importantly, they'll need to move the prisoners into a seaworthy vessel. It should delay them at least an hour."

"We'll need to have a faster ship than theirs," Fadan said.

Lucilla nodded. "Most of our ships are fast. We can't afford to be boarded very often, and we'll be travelling much lighter. I think our chances are good."

Another taller, wider ship, travelling upriver, passed by them, a couple hundred feet off their port side. It left a trail of tall waves in its wake, which sent their own ship into a series of steep climbs and falls. The turbulence woke several of the sleeping crewmembers with startled noises as waves showered over the deck.

Lucilla closed her eyes, water pouring over her. As the river calmed down, she reopened her eyes, wiping water off her shaved skull. "What does trouble me, though, is how many guards we will be facing," she said. "I think it's pretty likely we'll be heavily outnumbered. Which means we will be counting on your magic."

The prince was now soaked and shivering. He sent Lucilla a resentful look. "Yeah, thanks. I definitely needed to hear that."

In her years in the Citadel, Cassia had had few pleasures. Watching both her sons chasing each other in the gardens around the Core Palace, taking a warm bath in the Citadel thermae all by herself, and, of course, humiliating Tarsus over a game of lagaht.

The emperor wasn't a terribly bad player, but he was predictable. No matter what was happening in the game, he would always attack any vulnerable piece he spotted. Every time Cassia laid out a trap, she had a feeling that her luck had finally run out, that there was no chance Tarsus would fall for it again. And yet he would do exactly that. That wasn't the sole reason she almost always managed to defeat him, but it certainly helped.

The board they were using today was Tarsus's favorite; an alabaster hexagon with a mountain range occupying most of its center, which forced the battles to take place on the edges of the map. It made for interesting choices.

A fire warmed Cassia's legs and glared on the polished surface of the miniature armies. The emperor's lines were in shambles. His right flank had all but fallen, which meant it was a matter of time before Cassia's silver cavalry trampled over his reserves.

What an odd way to say goodbye, she thought, glancing over the golden leftovers of her husband's forces.

Tarsus bent forward and moved a horseman, taking one of Cassia's swords but in turn exposing itself to one of her spears. He was getting desperate, sacrificing pieces he could no longer afford to lose. How wonderfully ironic.

Cassia didn't need much time to think about her next move. All that was left for her to do was bring her cavalry across from Tarsus's defeated right flank and mop up his survivors. Her horse clinked on the alabaster board like a Legionary's boot on the marble steps of the palace, and she leaned back in her chair.

One of the reasons she truly loved these games was how little they talked. There was no need to weigh her answers, disguise her contempt, or restrain herself from snapping at him. She could just enjoy beating him at something he considered himself superior.

Come to think of it, this is the perfect way to say goodbye.

Venia wouldn't need more than a couple of hours to arrange their escape. As soon as this game was over, the two of them would be on their way.

There was a crackle in the fireplace, and a log tumbled and rolled across the hearth. Tarsus glanced at it.

"That seems like a bad omen," he said.

Cassia looked at her husband, the fire's orange hue trembling over the wrinkles of his face. "Since when are you superstitious?"

"It's not superstition if it involves fire, my dear," Tarsus replied. He leaned over the board, scanned his few remaining pieces, and pulled a spear back from his main force.

"Is there anything you regret, Tarsus?" Cassia heard herself ask. She regretted those words as soon as they left her mouth. She couldn't afford to act suspiciously.

The emperor stared at her, contemplating the question with absolute seriousness. "Yes," he replied as Cassia moved another one of her horses, closing the jaws of her army around Tarsus's vulnerable forces.

"Care to be a little more specific?" she asked, leaning back with a satisfied smile on her face.

Tarsus ignored the lagaht board for a while and glanced outside. A heavy downpour rattled the wide windows of the room.

"I regret..." He paused, considering his words. "I regret bringing your other son to the Citadel." He looked into her eyes. "He should have stayed with his father. I think it would have saved us all a lot of bitterness." Tarsus focused on the game again. "Besides, a boy should be with his father."

Cassia shifted on her chair, struggling to keep her mouth closed. What bothered her the most about what he had just said was how much sense it made.

There was a knock on the door.

"Come in," Cassia said far too quickly.

Venia padded inside. "I have completed my chores, Your Majesty," she said, her head low.

The empress was forced to hold down a smile. "You should rest, then. Come, warm yourself by the fire."

Venia quietly obeyed while the emperor moved one of his pieces. He was trying to rearrange his troops into a more defensible formation.

It was time to finish him off. Cassia consulted her hand. She still had one last spell card. One of the best in this board's entire deck. She laid it down, showing Tarsus its content: *Choose and destroy an enemy piece for every enemy piece you take during the next three turns.*

Tarsus's eyebrows jumped. "I guess this is it," he said.

A chuckle escaped Cassia. "I guess so."

Before Tarsus could make his move, however, there was another knock. The door opened to let Sagun inside. The castellan strode toward the emperor without a word and leaned into his ear. Cassia watched him whisper, trying to read her husband's blank expression.

The emperor nodded and waved Sagun out of the room. "I still have one spell card left as well," he told Cassia.

The door of the study clicked shut behind Sagun and Cassia sat up straighter.

"I am a firm believer in patience," Tarsus added, showing her his last card. It read: *Take control of every active enemy spell.* He stood up, throwing the card onto the alabaster board. "You're still able to take some of my pieces, but in the next three turns, I'll destroy half of your army. By then, you'll be the outnumbered one. You may want to see this game through to the very end, but as far as I'm concerned, it is over." He stepped away from the table and yelled toward the door. "Send him in."

The study's double doors burst open and a bloodied Lord Fabian stumbled inside, crashing to the floor, flanked by a pair of Paladins.

⌒

Augusta's Docks could be the Empire's commercial heart, but this was its brain, and it was busy.

Capra was the gateway to the Saffyan route, a sprawling metropolis surrounding its magnificent port. Or, better yet, ports, as there were two of them, the riverside port and the seaside port, connected by a large canal. Both were magnificent feats of engineering, consisting of artificial bays capable of docking hundreds of ships at the same time. A network of towers, some surrounding the two ports, others erupting from the water, stood watch over the ceaseless comings and goings of ships.

At the center of the riverside port stood a circular fortification, connected to the shore by a single stone bridge. The island fort had its own docking piers around its outer wall, and, docked to them, Fadan recognized the third flotilla of the Western Fleet. One hundred Imperial war galleys, each bristling with ballistae like a wild beast baring its fangs.

After mooring the river barge, the group proceeded to the seaside port, where Lucilla assured them a ship had been prepared and was waiting for them.

Bells rang every once in a while, signaling the arrival and departure of more vessels. Captains and local merchants haggled over imports and exports so loudly, they deafened the cries of the seagulls littering the sky.

Everywhere Fadan looked, throngs of workers pushed wooden containers to and from ships and warehouses. The crowd was so thick, they were forced into a single file, meandering as they carved a path to the seaside port.

"This is it," Lucilla finally indicated, waving toward the dark hull of a two-masted ship.

It was small for an oceangoing vessel. So small it had no castle, aft or fore.

Fadan halted in front of the boat's nearly vertical keel. "*This?*" he asked. "You said it would be a fast ship."

"It is fast!"

The voice did not come from anyone in the group but from someone up on the ship's deck. Fadan looked up, shielding his eyes from the bright, morning sun. There was a man perched upon the ship, his feet atop the bulwark while his hands wrapped around a thick rope tying one of the sails to the bow.

"It's a tiny old caravel," Fadan told the man.

"Which makes it fast and maneuverable," the man replied, scratching his dark beard. "Lucilla, Shayna."

Both women greeted him with a simple "Drusus."

"I was expecting something a bit more modern," Fadan insisted, following the others into the boat. "Like a Thepian frigate, for example."

The captain jumped from the bulwark and landed on the main deck just as they climbed onto it. "I guarantee *Blessed Marian* is as fast as any frigate," he said, kissing Lucilla's hand.

"This is Captain Drusus," Lucilla told Fadan, then turned to the captain. "I suppose you know who this is?"

Drusus nodded. "Your bird reached us, yes," he said. "Still a bit hard to believe. Even if he *is* standing right here."

"Well," Shayna said, climbing onboard, "we're the ones who brought him, and I'm still struggling with it."

"Alman!" the captain yelled. "Alman Larsa, you beautiful sack of bones."

"Drusus," Alman greeted him as the two embraced each other. "I'm sure we have a lot of catching-up to do, but we should be going."

The captain nodded in agreement, then stuck two fingers in his mouth and whistled so loud, Fadan lost his hearing for a moment.

"Wake up, you lazy mutts," Drusus barked at his crew. "Let's get the girl back in her waters."

A small crowd of olive-skinned, bare-chested men and scantily clad women came alive across the entire boat, tying knots here, untying knots there, and getting to their respective positions.

"Make yourselves comfortable in my cabin," Drusus told Lucilla, pointing at a door aft of the ship. "I'll meet you shortly. Just want to make sure we don't sail into the customs building."

Around them, sails unfurled and swelled as the crew got the ship in motion. The soldiers who had accompanied them from Augusta were led belowdecks through a trapdoor while Fadan followed Lucilla, Shayna, and Alman to the captain's cabin.

It was a narrow, dark room, lit only by a small window behind a desk. It smelled like an empty wine barrel and looked slightly less clean than one. Besides the desk, the only other furnishings were a wardrobe and a narrow bed that had been nailed to the floor and wall.

Fadan walked to the tiny window and looked outside, the city slowly drifting farther away as they picked up speed.

"If Drusus says this ship is fast, it's because it is," Lucilla said.

"Then my question is: is it fast enough?" Fadan muttered.

"And the answer is the same," Drusus replied, surging through the door. "Yes, it is." He walked to the wardrobe and opened it.

Fadan's eyebrows jumped. Instead of clothes, the wardrobe was packed full of bottles. Drusus selected one and poured himself a cup of its contents.

"How can you be sure?" Fadan asked. "Any frigate will be faster than this ship."

"That's not true," the captain retorted. His expression softened and he raised the bottle. "A sip, anyone?" They all passed. "Besides, we're not chasing a frigate. They moved the prisoners to a big, fat carrack called *The Faint Star.*"

"You are sure of this?" Lucilla asked.

Drusus swallowed a mouthful of his drink. Golden droplets spilled into his beard. "Nothing happens in our port that we don't know about," he replied. "And that's not all we found out. We have all the details of His Imperial Vileness's plan." He turned to Fadan. "No offense."

"Go on," the prince said.

"Well, it's devilishly simple. *The Faint Star*'s entire water supply has been poisoned. The crew will die and the ship will be left adrift. There will be a search, of course, but ultimately, the investigators will conclude that the carrack sank somewhere along its route. For all intents and purposes, everyone on board will be the victim of an unfortunate, unknown accident. Including those the empress has been guaranteed will be kept alive."

"Like Doric," Fadan muttered. "And all those people will die, even the Paladins and the crew members," He looked down. "Just because he's jealous."

"Hey, this is great for us," Drusus said, his arms wide. "Think about it. The crew will be dead. There will be no one left to guard the prisoners. It'll be easier than bribing an Akhami."

The captain's enthusiasm met little echo as Alman, Lucilla, and Shayna sent concerned glances at Fadan, who didn't even look like he was listening.

"Did you hear me?" Drusus asked. "The emperor won't even know we rescued his prisoners. He doesn't expect anyone on that ship to return. There won't be a report. He'll be none the wiser."

"Yes, we get it, Drusus," Alman said. "What about... What if the ship ends up washing up on some beach or something? I mean, if there's no one to steer it..."

"Not in the Western Sea, old friend," the captain replied.

"If they're adrift," Fadan told Alman, "the current will drag them southwest, to the Broken Sea."

"All we have to do is find them before they get that far," Drusus said.

"Yes," Fadan agreed, narrowing his eyes toward the captain. "As long as your ship is fast enough."

⌒⌐

Cassia jumped from the chair, her heart hammering in her chest. She didn't even notice the emperor striding past her until he was on top of the old general.

"Traitor!" Tarsus screamed.

Fabian tried to hoist himself from the floor, but one of his arms failed him and he fell again. The guards had beat him into a pulp. His left eye was so swollen, the man couldn't even open it.

"Majesty..." he mumbled through the bloody swell of his lips. "I never –"

"Liar!" The emperor shouted. "I know everything, you scum."

Cassia found her hands grasping at the neckline of her dress, but her pendant wasn't there anymore. Beside her, Venia shifted sideways, edging slowly toward one of the windows.

"Did you think I wouldn't find out?" Tarsus asked, beginning to pace around Fabian's defeated body. "Did you think you could betray me in my *own* palace?"

The empress opened her mouth to say something, but nothing came out. She felt like something was reaching inside her guts and tearing her apart.

He knows.

Tarsus knelt beside Fabian, grabbed his hair, and pulled the man's head back. "You will not die quickly, Fabian." He dropped the man's head and stood back up, facing his guards. "Escort the empress to her quarters."

For a moment, Cassia was sure she was about to vomit.

"And the maid?" one of the Paladins asked.

Venia stiffened and the emperor looked at her, disgust twisting the corners of his mouth.

"Take her as well."

⌒

Thunder crackled in the sky just as the ship reached the crest of a wave, leveling out and tumbling forward, falling down the other side as if they were sliding down a steep hill. The sky was so dark it felt like night had already fallen. Around them, the ocean had turned into mountainous black swells, rising and falling furiously. Sprinkles of foam spun in the air, dissolving into the swathes of rain blowing sideways.

"All hands to the windward rail, lads!" the captain ordered, a wave washing over him. "We'll be upon them soon." The man was standing on the bulwark, holding onto a rope above his head while his body dangled outside the ship.

"You heard the captain!" an ensign barked. "Man the starboard rail!" A sailor ran past him, skidded on the slippery deck, and fell. "On your feet, Holsen." The ensign hoisted the sailor up by his collar. "Man your station."

Fadan could barely see far enough to witness the crew obeying their orders, but he could hear their shouts over the raging gusts of wind. He was tightly gripping the bulwark right beside the standing Captain. "We should have caught them by now," he yelled.

"The prince is right," Lucilla agreed, her arms around the upright keel. "We can't keep sailing into the Broken Sea."

Drusus's head swung back as he burst out laughing. "This isn't the Broken Sea yet, my girl," he said. "We've barely reached its edges."

Lucilla glared up at him.

"He's right," Fadan told her, wiping water from his face. "This storm is nothing. In the Broken Sea, waves can get as tall as towers, and the wind is strong enough to send ships flying into the air."

"How would you know that?" Lucilla asked.

Fadan shrugged. "Technically, the Broken Sea is part of my Empire too."

"This is insane!" Shayna cried. "We can't keep going like this. We have to turn back."

Just as she finished her sentence, the ship swung downward and hit the base of a wave, and a massive wall of water crashed down onto the deck.

Fadan's feet were swept from beneath him, and he felt himself slide across the deck until his head struck something. The world seemed to disappear for an instant, then, as everything returned to focus, Fadan coughed water, gasping for air.

"Are you all right?" Lucilla asked, helping the prince up.

Fadan nodded and looked up at where the captain had been standing, positively sure that the man had been swept away by the water. Drusus, however, was still there, laughing madly.

"Captain," a crewmember called, stumbling near them. "Captain, the foremast is cracking. It can't take this much longer. We *have* to slow down."

"Nonsense, Calban. She can take it. Steady as she goes."

"But Captain —"

"Calban, man your station before I have you flogged!"

The crewman mumbled something beneath his breath but obeyed.

"Drusus, where is that prison ship?" Lucilla asked.

"Dead ahead," the captain replied. "If the prince's pendant is to be trusted."

"Yes, I know they're dead ahead, but how far?"

"We've been at this for an entire day, Captain," Fadan chimed in. "They'll be at the bottom of the sea if we don't find them soon."

"And we'll be joining them pretty quick," Lucilla added.

"Faith and patience," the captain said. "Faith and patience. They had a five-hour head start on us. We've been catching up on them ever since we left Capra. It won't be long now."

Fadan wasn't so sure. He gritted his teeth and turned to Lucilla. "We should have brought a faster ship."

"SHIP AHOY!"

They all simultaneously turned toward the voice. A sailor, perched atop the aft mast, lowered a spyglass and stretched an arm to the southwest.

"Three-masted ship," the watchman shouted. "Two points off larboard."

"Ha! What did I tell ya?" the captain cried, swinging and jumping onto the deck. "Faith and patience!" He turned to address his crew, his hands at his waist as if the ship was standing perfectly still. "We've got them in our sights now, boys and girls. Keep her going. Pasheen."

"Yes, Captain."

"Rouse everyone belowdecks. Prepare boarding parties. Fast and springy."

"Aye, aye, sir."

Fadan searched the distance. The horizon was a shifting mess of waves surging and plunging from the deep. From the fog to the curtain of rain, not to mention the overall darkness caused by the thick layer of clouds up above, everything seemed to conspire to keep the prison ship hidden. It took at least half an hour until their goal became clearly visible.

It was indeed, as Drusus had put it, a big, fat carrack. A ship designed to haul as much cargo as possible, much bigger than their own caravel.

Behind Fadan, a crowd filled the deck. About fifty men and women gathered, all armed to the teeth and salivating for battle.

"Grappling hooks at the ready!" an ensign shouted.

"Those Paladins are thanking the goddess for the rain right now," another one said. "This way, no one will see them wet their pants."

The men and women laughed obscenely, waving their blades in the air. Fadan had some trouble sharing their enthusiasm. Drusus must have noticed it, because he knelt beside him, spyglass to one eye, and said, "Don't worry, young prince. There probably won't be any violence today."

He handed Fadan the spyglass and the prince looked through it. It took some getting used to. Every small twitch of his arm made him lose sight of the ship, and their own caravel wasn't exactly standing still.

Fadan eventually managed to get a good glimpse of their target. The lenses of the spyglass made it seem like the carrack was right next to him. Its main deck was big enough to fit their caravel and was jammed between a tall forecastle and a wide aftcastle. But it wasn't the construction of the vessel that caught Fadan's attention.

He lowered the spyglass.

"It's empty. There's no one on board."

"I told you," Drusus said. "The water was poisoned. The crew is dead."

"What... What about the prisoners?"

Drusus shrugged. "Hopefully, they didn't drink any of it. Paladins aren't famous for their hospitality."

Slowly but steadily, they approached the carrack until it was close enough that everyone could see its empty deck. The crew's thirst for battle seemed to wilt away, and their brave cries became whispers and mutters. Fadan heard the words "ghost ship" twice.

"Wake up, you loafers. Time to earn your coin."

"Hooks away!"

"Lively now, boarding planks out!"

At the spurs of their superiors, the sailors sprang up a little and rushed to their duties. Grappling hooks were hurled and the prison ship was harnessed to theirs.

Drusus jumped to the bulwark, holding onto a rope that dangled from above.

"All right, sailors, let's get our brothers back to safety. For Arrel! For the rebellion!"

"For the rebellion!" came a collective shout.

Fadan felt a hand on his shoulder and looked up. Alman gave him a nod. "Ready?" the old man asked.

"Ready," the prince replied, instinctively tapping his power.

Wave after wave, the crew crossed onto the main deck of the prison ship. On the other side, no one was there to meet them except for sailing paraphernalia, creaking and swinging in the storm.

Fadan swung himself on a rope and landed next to Alman, skidding on the wet boards. The boarding party formed a compact group, their blades at the ready. One step at a time, they spread across the deck, the pouring rain making it hard to see more than a couple of feet ahead.

Lightning flashed, bringing the entire ship into view for a brief moment.

"I don't get it," Fadan yelled over the howling wind. "If the crew was poisoned, where are their bodies?"

Thunder roared, this one so loud that most in the group jumped with fright. As if on cue, the doors to the aft and fore castles slammed open. A stream of Paladins flooded the deck, yelling a war cry.

The boarding party closed in on itself, forming a nearly perfect circle. The Paladins besieged them, their numbers growing as more and more kept coming, their swords and lances at the ready.

"Drop your weapons!" a Paladin commander ordered.

"Fire take you all!" Lucilla cursed. "We'll sink you lot with us."

"Easy, there," Drusus said from the other side of their circle. "There's no need for useless bloodshed."

"Silence!" Lucilla ordered. "There will be no surrender."

"We're heavily outnumbered," Drusus offered. "It's done; we lost. Sailors, put your weapons down."

Drusus's crew didn't need much encouragement to obey, and slowly began to lower their swords.

"Stand up and fight, goddess damn you all!" Lucilla yelled. "Pick up your weapons or Ava be my witness, I will kill you all myself!"

"Lucilla..." Fadan said, grabbing her arm. "He's right. Stand down."

She shook herself free, ignoring the prince. "Did you *hear* me, you cowards? Grab your weapons!"

"LUCILLA!" Fadan yelled. That got her attention. "I said. Stand. Down." The prince turned to the rest of the group. "Everyone throw your weapons to the deck."

Alman obeyed, followed by Drusus, his sailors, and then the Augustan soldiers. The swords and daggers hit the wooden deck in a clanking chorus.

"We can't win this fight," Fadan told Lucilla. Only she and Shayna still held their weapons in defiance. "There's no point in wasting all this life here. Stand down."

Lucilla's mouth opened, but her arm finally went limp and her sword fell to the deck, followed by Shayna's.

⌒

The bedroom door closed and its lock clicked, leaving Cassia and Venia staring at each other in silence.

"What in the name of Ava has just happened?" the empress asked.

"The emperor knows," Venia replied.

"What? *What* does he know?"

Venia swallowed. "I think he knows everything."

"What does that mean?" Cassia asked, her hands on her head. "Does he know about Fadan?"

The spy strode to a window. "For the moment, we should assume the worst," she replied, scanning the gardens outside.

"Oh, goddess, if Tarsus has found out that Fadan possesses the Talent..." Cassia trailed off as if she didn't have the courage to finish the sentence.

"I might be able to get us out through the window," Venia said. She tried the window's handle, but it was locked. She reached into her sleeve, removed a pin, and started working on the lock.

"In broad daylight?" Cassia asked.

Venia looked at the empress. "Considering our circumstances, I think it's our best shot, yes?"

Cassia pondered that for a moment, then nodded. Venia resumed her work.

"You should change into something less conspicuous," the spy said. "Choose something dark that doesn't restrict your movements."

Without a word, Cassia darted to a wardrobe and swung its double door open, revealing a wall of colorful dresses. She began fiddling inside, searching for something suitable, but before she could, the bedroom's door clicked and swung open.

Both women jumped away from where they were, looking far less innocent than they would have liked. Two Legionaries stepped inside, their armor clanking with their every move.

"Your Majesty," one of them said. "We have orders to escort you."

"Orders to escort me where?"

"We're not authorized to divulge that," the soldier replied. Just as he did, the man grabbed Cassia's arm and pushed her toward the door.

Venia's eyes went wide.

"Venia, that will be all!" the empress said.

The spy froze, one arm deep into the other's sleeve.

"You are dismissed for the day," Cassia added.

"No," the second soldier said. "We have orders to take the maid as well." He pounded across the room and pushed Venia after the empress.

The Legionaries marched through the corridors, shoving both Cassia and Venia in front of them.

"What in the name of Ava do you think you're doing?" Venia demanded. "You can't touch the empress like that."

If either of the two soldiers heard her beneath their steel helms, neither gave any sign of it. They simply kept marching. But they were not using any familiar route. Instead of taking them through the great staircase that led down to the main hall, the soldiers forced them through one of the narrower side corridors. Cassia found herself going down barely lit hallways and darkened stairwells she didn't even know existed.

"Where are you taking us?" the empress asked, her heart pounding heavily.

They arrived at a corridor where no window was in sight. Only torches lit the way forward, their orange glow casting trembling shadows.

"Move," one of the Legionaries said, pushing at Cassia's back and shoving her forward.

The empress felt the air momentarily leave her lungs. Something twisted in her stomach.

"What is this place?" she asked, obeying and stepping forward nonetheless. "You can't just treat us like this."

As the words left her mouth, the ridiculousness of them dawned on her.

Of course they could. She was powerless, as she had always been. Tarsus could do with her as he wished, and there was nothing she could do about it.

Having Venia at her side these last few years had numbed the sense of humiliation, but it had been a lie. A lie she had been telling herself. She was simply something the emperor owned. There was nothing even Venia could do about it.

No, not anymore.

She stumbled and nearly fell. Her whole body was shaking.

"Enough!" she yelled, turning on her heels and grabbing the sword at the waist of the Legionary marching behind her.

The blade sang as she unsheathed the sword and aimed it at the soldier's throat. Venia moved like a cat, jumping to cover Cassia's side, a knife appearing in her hand as if out of thin air.

"Cassia!"

The Legionaries stood still, neither making a move to attack. The voice had come from the empress's back and echoed through the dark hall. She turned toward it.

"Intila?"

"Will you please return my soldier's sword?" the High Marshal asked.

"You will not be needing it, I hope." He was standing at a small door and moved aside, motioning for her to come in.

Hesitantly, Cassia lowered the sword but kept it. She exchanged a look with Venia, then followed Intila through the tiny door.

The tang of manure flooded her nose and she quickly realized why. They were in some kind of underground stable. Horses and hay were everywhere. A carriage waited in the center, surrounded by what looked like an entire Maniple of Legionaries.

"This is an old, secret exit of the Palace," Intila explained. "Designed for emergency evacuations of the Imperial family." He looked around as if inspecting the facility. "It's been centuries since it was last considered necessary, so it has become…forgotten. At least by most."

"What… What do you mean?" Cassia asked.

"This carriage will take you out of the city," Intila said. "These Legionaries will obey you and only you. They will protect you against the emperor himself if need be."

Cassia looked at the soldiers, and her mouth dropped. She almost expected them to deny what the High Marshal had just said. Instead, they simply stood at attention like silver statues.

"Intila… I don't know what to say," Cassia murmured. "How will you… If Tarsus finds out…"

"He won't."

"Intila, he knows about Fabian."

"Yes." The High Marshal's head sank slightly, but he quickly straightened back up. "That, unfortunately, could not be avoided. Vigild has infiltrated the rebellion *and* the Scriptorium. We knew that, but when we were forced to look for the prince among the prisoners… Well, Fabian exposed himself. There was no other way. He was aware of that."

"Oh, goddess," Cassia said, covering her mouth. "Can't you do anything? Can't you *help* him?"

Intila shook his head. "That would only serve to incriminate me as well," he replied. "The emperor still needs me."

"*Needs* you?" Cassia could not believe it. "After all this, you're *still* remaining loyal? After helping me and Fadan?"

"Cassia, my loyalty to the throne is absolute," Intila said.

"No, it's not. If it was, I would still be up in my room. Or goddess knows where…"

"That's different."

"Different?" Cassia asked. "What about Fadan? You know where he is, what he's doing."

A smile grew at the corner of his mouth. "I said my loyalty is to the *throne*, not the emperor."

Cassia sighed, exasperated.

"I know you will never understand, but I'm the High Marshal of the Legions," Intila explained. "I will not abandon my oath. Now, enough talk. You must hurry before your absence is noted." He turned to the soldiers around the carriage. "Empress's Own, you know your orders."

There was a loud clank as every one of the soldiers smashed their fists against their breastplates.

"Empress's Own?" Cassia echoed.

"A longstanding Imperial tradition," Intila replied. "One only Tarsus is known to have broken. These are your soldiers now. They will die for you if they have to." He looked at the troops. "But they're supposed to stay alive. Understood?"

"YES, SIR!"

"Now go," Intila insisted, taking the sword from Cassia's hand.

"The High Marshal is right," Venia said. "We should hurry."

The empress stood motionless for a moment, then lunged into Intila's arms.

"Thank you!" she said. "I owe you everything."

Intila waved dismissively as they stepped apart, but did not really say anything. Instead, he turned to the soldiers once again, and Cassia had the feeling he was hiding his eyes from her.

"Empress's Own, mount up!" Intila said, his voice as firm as always.

CHAPTER 22

The Sleeping God

Aric's cloak flapped around him as he stared at the desert below. The dragon had carved a gaping hole in the mountain, exposing five floors of the fortress's inner structure. That corridor, for example, used to stretch for at least another dozen paces. Now, instead of shining through the window, moonlight was pouring through the whole width of the passage.

"You called?" Leth said, stepping to his side.

Aric nodded absently. "How's the work going downstairs?" he asked.

Leth inspected the wreckage around him. From where they were standing, it was possible to peer down into the two floors below them. Tapestries, banners, and pieces of furniture still smoldered everywhere.

"It's going," Leth replied. "We already filled two crates, but the blood just keeps pouring."

"It's a big dragon," Aric noted.

"It was," Leth said. "And it had a lot of fun in here."

Aric confirmed that with a nod, then stretched an arm toward a room to their right that was missing half of its walls, ceiling, and floor. "That's where Eliran recovered," he said.

"I know," Leth replied.

"Think that's a coincidence?" Aric asked.

Leth shrugged. "That cleaning cupboard over there got smashed as well. So did everything else two floors above and below us."

"Sure," Aric said, "but this is a very big mountain."

"Can't argue with that." There was a silence before Leth added, "I know what you're thinking. You want to go after her."

"You disapprove?"

"I'm not sure," Leth replied. "I don't even know what she took."

"You don't even know if she's the one who took it."

"You're right, I don't," Leth said. "But it is the likelier scenario. What evidence do we have this Sohtyr isn't just fiction?"

"We don't have any," Aric sighed. "But I have something else. I... I've been having these dreams ever since I got here. And most of them ended up happening. Not really, but kinda..." He shook his head as if it sounded silly even to him. "I dreamt of seeing Eliran in the desert, and then I did. The night you showed me the secret door, I dreamt of her opening it. Which we know also happened. Or at least kind of. A few weeks back, I even dreamt I was with her in this same corridor, and guess what happened in the dream." He gestured at the gaping hole in front of them.

"I see," Leth murmured.

"Even the color of the dragon was the same! Red, just like the one downstairs."

"A Cyrinian Crimson-back," Leth said, lost in thought. "According to Tharius."

Aric exhaled forcefully. "I can't know if she lied about Sohtyr or not. Maybe she did trick us; I don't know. But what I *do* know is that I have to go after her."

"Damn," Leth said. "It must be so confusing to be you."

⌒⁀

Aric had everyone in the company before him. Even Geric had decided to show up. The only exception was Prion, who was still missing.

The Hunters were packed into a group, some standing, others sitting on the five crates they had just filled with dragon blood. Behind them, the gigantic corpse of their fallen prey still loomed in the middle of the main hall, taking up nearly half of the cavernous space.

"What does Leth think of this?" Ashur demanded when Aric had finished talking.

"I think our captain is insane," Leth replied. He was sitting on the great staircase behind Aric, leaning back on his shoulders. "But he's not a liar. If he says he had these dreams, it's because he did."

"But those could be just more of his hallucinations," Ashur argued.

"The thing is, though, that he wasn't hallucinating before," Leth said. "The witch exists, and she confirmed everything Aric said he saw."

"Wait," Irenya said. "Did Ashur just ask for Leth's opinion?"

"Yeah," Trissa mused. "I think we're all hallucinating."

There were chuckles and giggles.

"Settle down!" Aric called out, raising a hand. "This is serious, and we don't have much time. If we are to believe the conversation between Eliran and her boss, then this Sohtyr is about to unleash something terrible into the world, and I will not allow it. However" – he paused, indicating his lieutenant behind him – "Leth believes that conversation was just a little theater for our benefit. Although, to be honest, I can't find a good reason for them to do such a thing."

"To throw us off, maybe?" Dothea suggested.

"Then we'll just find the Frostbound empty, save for its usual inhabitants," Trissa said. "Doesn't seem like much of a reason not to go."

Dothea didn't have an answer for that. Neither did anyone else, for that matter.

"Clea," Aric continued. "You were there as well. What do you think?"

Clea did not reply right away. "I think it's impossible to know for sure if we were tricked or not. Doesn't matter what I believe," she said at last. "However, I also think we can't risk just standing here if there is even a remote chance that a dragon god is about to be awoken."

Aric agreed with a solemn nod.

"Okay, sure," Ashur told Clea. "But can we actually *do* anything about it?"

"Oh, stop being a coward, will you?" Trissa said.

"What did you say?!" Ashur tried forcing his way through the group, but the others held him back.

"You didn't hear me?" Trissa asked provokingly. "Come on over. I'll whisper it into your ear."

"Trissa, please," Aric pleaded. "Ashur makes a good point. There's no way to know if we can stop this from happening, even if we try. For all we know, this could be a one-way trip. If anyone wishes to join me, they have to understand that."

"I'm sure none of you care," Leth said, standing up, "but I already agreed to go."

"I'm going too," Clea said, lifting a finger.

"Me too," Tharius added.

Nahir and Trissa piled on. Then Athan, Dothea, Irenya, and Orisius. It was flattering that so many of them had grown to trust him this much. Still, Aric couldn't help but wonder if they realized what they were signing up for. Or even himself, for that matter.

"All right," Aric said. "All those not going can —"

Lyra cut him off. "Oh, goddess damn you all," she said. "I can't just stay here. I'm in too."

"You should stay, Lyra," Aric said. "Take care of Jullion."

"Oh, he's fine," Lyra said, waving a dismissive hand. "There's no sign of infection and the splint will keep his stupid arm in place."

"If you're going, then I'm going too," Ergon told her.

"You know what?" Ashur said. "You're all a bunch of idiots. You'll either take a huge trip for nothing or get yourselves killed for nothing. No, thanks." He crossed his arms stubbornly, waiting for some retort, but none came.

"Fair enough," Aric said after a small silence. "Ashur and Jullion will stay and watch over the fortress. The rest of you get ready. We leave right away."

⌣⟶

To make sure they didn't get lost, Aric borrowed one of the maps from Sylene's study. All of Lamash's horses had been taken, forcing them to take the whole trip on foot. It was a harsh desert run. Pressed for time, Aric decided to skip sleep altogether, and they spent the whole night sprinting across the dunes beneath the silvery moonlight. At least the air was fresh.

As dawn came and the dunes turned gold, temperatures quickly spiked. They stopped to rest beneath the shadow of a large brown rock formation. Lyra looked like she was about to faint, and Athan didn't look much better. They swallowed a few bites of bread and washed it down with some water, but didn't rest for long. As soon as no one was gasping for air, Aric ordered them to resume their journey.

The sun climbed steadily across the sky, bringing back the familiar, searing temperatures of the Mahar.

The jagged edges of the Frostbound valley appeared in the distance around an hour after midday, and the wind began to slowly cool down. At first, it felt like a fresh morning breeze, but it quickly became a frigid blizzard. The company was still warm from the long run, but it didn't take long before everyone started shaking, steam forming before them, billowing out with their every breath. Spots of white snow began to blotch the yellow dunes, and the sound of their footsteps became a crunch as ice-covered rocks gradually replaced the sand.

Occasional rock formations were common in the Mahar, but in some regions, sand was as rare as water, and the dunes gave way to sprawling mountain ranges and plateaus. The Frostbound was one such region, where sand could only be found in the deep end of ravines.

Aric ordered the company to slow down as they entered a narrow chasm. Shadows engulfed them, and the wind howled between the massive walls around them. Slowly, quietly, they pushed through the ravine. The hairs on the back of their necks prickled, and they swung their eyes from one side to the other. Was someone watching them?

"I have a bad feeling about this," Tharius said, shivering.

"Be quiet, you fool!" Trissa whispered urgently.

Aric had been confident that he could find the entrance to the tunnels up until that moment. Everything around him looked unfamiliar, alien even. Not only that, but it had also been far less scary the last time around. Of course, at the time, they hadn't been aware of the frozen dragon god buried deep beneath the surface.

On the other side of the ravine stood a small plateau of sorts, surrounded by several peaks as sharp as a dragon's teeth. Aric climbed onto a rock, trying to get a better view of their surroundings. Covering his eyes, he studied the snow-covered landscape. It was as if they had just climbed the Shamissai Mountains.

"Over there," Clea told Aric, aiming south. "We came through that way the last time."

"Are you sure?" Aric asked. "How can you remember?"

Clea shrugged. "I just can."

It wasn't much of an answer, but it was the only one he had.

"All right, south it is, then." Aric jumped down from the rock. "Clea, you have the lead. Get us there."

Clea nodded and, without another word, sprinted ahead. The young Hunters followed her across the craggy terrain, trying their best to keep up with her fast pace without making any sound or tripping on the slippery ice. Clea's relentless advance finally came to a stop when she reached the edge of a massive crater.

"It's over there," Clea said as Aric reached her side. "The tunnel's entrance."

Aric remembered the large crater they had emerged into after their trial in the tunnels. Right in its middle stood the entrance itself.

However, the stone slab that once had covered it had been smashed to pieces, leaving a gaping black hole in the middle of the snow-covered sand of the crater.

"We clearly did not get here first," Aric noted.

Leth came to his side, thin white clouds forming with his breath. "She's in a hurry."

Aric glanced sideways at him. "Or he."

"Or they," Clea added. "Doesn't matter. Shall we?"

Aric looked over his shoulder. Everyone was accounted for, even Geric, but something was wrong with the cat. His body was tense, his ears flattened and his head low.

"What's the matter with you?" Aric asked.

Everyone jumped as a few rocks and pebbles skittered down the ravine to their left, startling them. Then, a shadow covered them and a dragon swooshed by, screeching.

The company scrambled to hide between the crevices around them. Only Geric stayed put.

"Damn stupid cat," Aric said, leaving his hiding place and pushing Geric out of sight. He practically had to drag the cat across the ground.

The dragon swirled above the valley's crater, roaring.

Aric cursed. "I should've seen this coming," he said.

"It's an Eastern Short-tail," Tharius noted.

"Oh, shut up, Tharius," Trissa snapped. "No one cares."

"We have to know what we're fighting," Tharius retorted angrily.

"We're not fighting it," Aric said.

"Why not?" Tharius asked. "We've killed a dragon before."

"Will you listen to him?" Dothea pressed. "We killed *one* dragon. Probably because we got lucky —"

"And we didn't do it out in the open," Aric added.

"What do we do, then?" Clea asked.

Aric thought about it for a moment. "We need to send it away," he said, then looked at his Hunters. "I need you guys to lure it away from the crater so that I can enter the tunnels."

There were no odd looks, nervous glances, or shifting feet. Only a couple of nods.

"All right," Trissa said. "But I don't think you should go in alone."

"I agree," Leth said. "It's probably safer up here with the dragon than in there with…whomever."

Aric took a little while but ended up nodding. "All right," he relented. "Leth and Clea will come with me, then. Everyone else will be bait, but I need you to stay away from it. Show yourselves, then hide. Whatever happens, *don't engage that dragon.*"

Once again, there were several nods, and even a couple of *Yes, Captains.*

Aric took another deep breath. "Let's do this."

The diversion worked like a charm. With the help of some arrows, the bait group led the dragon away from the crater, screaming and shouting. Still, Aric, Leth, and Clea couldn't help but keep looking over their shoulders as they raced toward the tunnel's entrance. They jumped in, and the glowstones on Aric's armor immediately lit up, the same happening with the shards in the corridor's wall.

Aric drew the glowstone sword from across his back with one hand and a steel sword at his hip with another. "Let's go," he ordered.

"Wait," Clea said. "Shouldn't we light a torch? You know, in case those blue things come after us."

"No need," Aric replied, marching away. "We're carrying enough glowstone to keep them away."

"All right," Clea said with a sigh. "Here we go." She drew one of her daggers and followed after Aric.

"I think it's fairly safe to assume that what we're looking for is that large hallway with the statues," Leth said. He was the only one of the three who hadn't drawn any of his weapons. "You remember? Where we found the blue creatures attacking Orisius and the others?"

Aric nodded. "There was that huge steel gate with the engraved runes."

"I bet you my land and titles that's the crypt the mages built for the dragon god," Leth said. "Oh, wait… I already lost those when I joined the Guild." He shrugged. "Well, it's the intention that counts."

Clea shot him a serious frown. "Please don't be cheeky," she said.

"I thought you liked my cheekiness," Leth shot back.

"I do," Clea replied, checking the shadows around her with a nervous look. "But right now, I hate it."

Leth was going to reply but was silenced as Aric raised a hand, cutting him off.

"You hear that?" Aric asked. He pointed toward a corridor to their left. "That way."

As they crossed the threshold, a faint female voice echoed around them. She was mumbling something, but it was impossible to understand a word.

Aric signaled Leth and Clea to follow him, then tiptoed down a stairwell. They spiraled downward for what felt like an age, the gloomy blue lights from the glowstone shards in the walls lighting the way. The female voice gradually became louder and louder, but the words remained indecipherable.

"Eliran," Aric whispered as he exchanged a look with the others.

The stairwell turned and kept turning until it felt like they were stuck in a bottomless well. Eliran's voice became louder with every step, and suddenly the great hall jumped out to meet them. They shrank against themselves, trying to remain out of sight. Eliran stood at the very center of the hall, surrounded by the army of statues that lined the hall's floor like a lagaht board. She had her palms facing the gargantuan steel gate and seemed to be chanting something in a foreign language.

Aric gritted his teeth. "She tricked us!"

The three of them exchanged another look, and Aric signaled for them to follow him. Keeping to the shadows, they lurched from statue to statue, sneaking closer and closer to Eliran. The witch showed no sign of noticing their presence as she continued her chant, almost as though she were in some sort of deep trance.

Aric reached the statue closest to her and tried to lower his breath, tiptoeing as carefully as he possibly could. He readied his blades. Behind the two statues adjacent to his, Leth and Clea steeled themselves as well. Eliran was surrounded.

A blue halo pulsed from the witch like a wave of heat, and in front of her, the runes etched upon the massive gate began to gleam like blue flames.

Leth and Clea had their eyes fixed on Aric, ready to jump at his slightest movement. He made a countdown with his fingers, and as he reached zero, the three of them jumped, a total of four blades descending on Eliran –

BOOM!

They were sent flying backward across the hall and crashed into the forest of statues.

Aric felt a sharp pain on the back of his head. He reached to brush his hand against the back of his head, and his fingers came back bloody. He made to stand back up as fast as he could, searching for his swords. Stumbling, he found only the one made of glowstone, but the crystal had shattered.

He looked at Eliran as he drew a glowstone dagger from a sheath on his arm. The witch was unperturbed. She kept up her trance-like chant as if their attack hadn't even happened. Aric tried to look for his friends among the shadows and saw Leth using a steel sword as a cane to help him back up. He had blood dripping from his mouth. A few feet away from him, Clea was already standing straight. She drew out her bow and fired an arrow.

Then, at the last possible moment, a shadow – no, a hooded figure – came out of nowhere and deflected the arrow away as if it was no more than an annoying mosquito.

"Now, now," the hooded man said in a deep, thundering voice, "that is most impolite. Our sorceress here is in the middle of an important task. We mustn't bother her."

He wore robes as black as night, its shadows making it impossible to see his face. It sent a shiver down Aric's spine.

Then, without another word, the hooded man gave a flick of a hand, and all three Hunters were sent flying upward. Aric felt his throat tighten and burn. He tried to breathe in, opened his mouth as wide as he could, but found no air would come. Legs dangling three feet above the ground, he grabbed at his throat, instinctively searching for whatever was squeezing it, but there was nothing.

In the meantime, Eliran kept intoning her spell as if nothing at all was happening around her. In front of her, the great steel gates screeched, and a slither of light poured between them as they parted open.

The dark mage chuckled.

Aric tried to scream, but his throat couldn't produce a sound. His lungs began to burn, and the world became blurry. He felt as though he was going to pass out at any moment, when all of a sudden there was a growl followed by a scream. The grip around Aric's neck loosened, letting him fall to the floor. Gasping for air, he raised his head and saw some wild beast standing over the hooded man, gnawing at his neck.

It was Geric.

Only then did Aric realize Eliran's chant had died out, and the gates had stopped opening. Aric looked at the witch and saw her lower her arms with an extremely confused look.

"What…" she muttered.

A whimper echoed across the hall and Geric flew into the air, disappearing into the shadows. The hooded mage stood back up, growling.

"Fire take you!" Eliran screamed, furious. She flung her palms at him, and a wave of blue power came pouring out from them.

The dark mage casually raised a hand, absorbing Eliran's attack. It sounded like a piece of meat searing in a pan, but he gave no sign of feeling any pain.

"Don't just stand there!" Eliran yelled. "Help me, you fools!"

Aric snapped back to himself and lunged forward, screaming, with his dagger in hand. Leth and Clea did the same. Their charge never reached the target, however, as Sohtyr raised his free hand and sent a gush of flames toward them.

The blaze came flying at them with lightning speed. Aric halted, skidding through the floor and shrinking into himself. He covered his eyes and face, expecting the flames to engulf him at once, but the burning never came. He opened his eyes and saw a massive wall of fire hovering above him about an arm's length away.

Sohtyr chuckled. "You won't be able to protect them for much longer, sorceress," he said. "And they can't help you either." He extinguished the flames, then swung his arm flamboyantly above his head. Stone began to crackle everywhere.

Aric looked around and saw the army of statues coming to life. One foot after the other, the statues yanked themselves out of their stupor and stepped down from their pedestals, the indigo light from Eliran's relentless energy attack casting a ghostly hue over them.

"Oh, crap," Leth said as a statue carrying a lance twice as tall as him stepped closer. He parried a blow from the lance and thrust his sword into the statue's chest in one single, elegant move.

The statue fell to its knees with a loud thud.

"Good news," Leth said. "They can die." With the help of a foot, he pulled his sword from the statue's chest, and just as he did, the creature climbed back onto its feet. "No, spoke too soon!"

He staggered back and stopped just in time to avoid bumping into another living statue.

Finding himself surrounded, Leth deflected the blows coming from both sides, sweat breaking out on his forehead.

A few feet to his left, Clea unsheathed two daggers from the small of her back, raced toward Leth, and in a swift, scissor-like movement snapped the head off one of the statues. She then spun and snapped the head off the second one. Both of the statues fell awkwardly to the floor, and this time, they stayed there.

"Okay," Leth said with a sigh of relief. "I was right the first time. They *can* die."

Unfortunately, there wasn't much time to discuss it as another, far more numerous wave of statues fell upon them.

"Aric!" Clea yelled, deflecting an attack. "Decapitating them works. Just snap their heads off!"

You make it sound like it's easy, Aric thought, grinding his teeth and spinning as he parried the attacks from three different statues. He rolled to his left, then backward, trying to get enough room to launch an attack, but everywhere he went, more statues surrounded him.

Aric parried a sword and swung back to parry another attack, but this time from a massive battle-axe. The two weapons clanged loudly and Aric's hand went numb. His sword went flying beyond another cluster of living statues, and he was forced to roll backward to avoid another swing of the axe. He searched his arms, legs, and waist, trying to find some other weapon to fight with. He found only a dagger. It was long, but it was made of glowstone. It would have been perfect for killing a dragon, but it would certainly shatter against creatures made of stone or their steel weapons.

A pair of statues marched toward him on both sides, lances at the ready. Aric backtracked and found himself trapped against a wall, a third statue joining the other two. There was nowhere to go. This was it.

Then Eliran burst into existence with a flicker of light and shot a bolt of blue energy at each of the three statues, blowing them up. Without a word, she grabbed Aric's dagger by its blade, but did not pull it from his hands. The glowstone gleamed as brightly as one of Eliran's spells.

"What... What are you doing?" Aric heard himself ask.

"Saving you," Eliran replied. "Get into the vault. *Now!*"

She flickered back out of existence, turning into a bolting trail of light. Just as she disappeared, Sohtyr materialized right next to where she had been standing, turning into a similar trail of light and blazing after her.

Immediately, four more statues replaced the three fallen ones. There seemed to be no end to them. A sword thrust at Aric's chest, and he instinctively parried it. For a moment, he expected his blade to shatter as glowstone normally would, but instead, it shimmered and shrieked and the statue's sword disintegrated.

Wow!

Aric parried another attack, destroying a lance, and followed with a counter, slashing across a statue's chest. The creature staggered backward, and the gash across its chest spread out until the entire statue crumbled. Aric hacked at his other attackers, his blade singing as it broke the statues apart as if they were made of sand.

All over the hall, there were flashes every time Eliran and Sohtyr materialized in and out of existence. It was as if two shooting stars had found their way into the hall just to chase each other, statues exploding as they passed by.

Eliran's metallic voice rang inside Aric's head. *Get into the vault!*

Why? Aric asked.

Do it!

It was hardly the moment for debate. Aric darted toward the steel gate, carving a path through the living statues. He reached the huge metal doors and looked over his shoulders. The mages' lightning pursuit continued while Leth and Clea fought for their lives against a growing legion of statues.

I have to help them, he thought.

There's no time! Eliran replied. *The spell on your blade will wear off soon. You can either help us all or not at all. GET IN THE VAULT!*

Aric nearly went deaf, those four last words ringing like an echo inside his head. He cursed but stepped through the gates. On the other side, everything was blindingly bright, and Aric was forced to squint. It took him a moment to adapt, but when he did, his jaw dropped.

Everything was covered in white frost. The floor, the walls, the ceiling, and most importantly, the dragon god. The creature was as large as the Imperial Palace, probably bigger. It had been frozen in an awkward position that resembled a prancing horse, the lower half of its body buried beneath ground level. Its mouth was open in a silent roar, fangs the size of turrets gleaming inside. Several horns grew out from its head, some of them as long as the bridges that covered the Saffya, but even those weren't as creepy as its eyes.

Green lizard eyes shone beneath a layer of ice. They were wide open, staring down on Aric as if the creature were watching him.

This thing, Aric thought, speaking to Eliran. *What am I supposed to do with it?*

The sword, do you see it? Eliran asked.

He did. It was a large sword, but in the middle of that colossal chest, it looked like a needle.

I see it, Aric said.

That sword is storing a spell just like the one I stored in your dagger, except it freezes things and is much, much more powerful than mine.

What about it? Aric asked.

It's our only hope against Sohtyr. Pull it out. Now.

What?! Are you joking? That's what Sohtyr wants. We're supposed to stop *him, not* help.

That thing won't unfreeze all at once, Eliran explained. *You'll have some time. Not much, but enough.*

Aric looked over his shoulder. Beyond the gates, an army of statues was overwhelming Leth and Clea.

Your friends won't survive this much longer, Eliran said. *And neither will I. That sword is the only thing in here powerful enough to stop Sohtyr. We have no other option.*

"Merciful Ava," Aric muttered. He looked at the palace-sized creature rising above him.

If that thing were let loose upon the world…

He walked toward the sword. It was the most exquisite weapon he had ever seen. Its handle was made from a purple metal Aric didn't even know existed, wrapped with red and gold leather for grip. It had an extremely thin strip of the same purple metal serving as a guard, which looked to be merely decorative, as it would had been of little use as an actual guard. Beyond the hilt, the sword's glowstone blade pulsed as if it was alive.

Aric wrapped his hand around the exquisite hilt and caught a fright when the sword's guard magically extended out and around his hand, covering it in a weave of purple metal.

He closed his eyes.

"Goddess…"

Would he be fast enough? What if Sohtyr managed to put up too long of a fight?

Hurry, Eliran pleaded.

For the first time in their mental conversations, he didn't just hear her thoughts. He *felt* something. He felt…terror.

Please. Eliran's thoughts turned into a wave of pain as if a knife had been driven through his head.

Aric yelped and let the sword go, its magical guard shrinking back.

"Got you, little witch!" Aric heard Sohtyr's voice echo from outside.

Aric saw Eliran floating, paralyzed in the air, Sohtyr's hand magically holding her in place.

"I told you you couldn't get away," Sohtyr taunted her, chuckling.

A few feet from the mages, Clea was hit in the chest by a sword. Leth saved her by parrying what would have been a deadly blow to her neck, but coming to her help exposed him to a blow across his back from a second attacker.

Aric screamed and cursed, his eyes welling. He almost raced to their rescue, but one last, fading plead from Eliran stopped him.

The sword. Get the sword.

He looked at the magic weapon, hesitating.

I won't risk it, Aric thought, not sure if Eliran could still hear him.

Then he reared his leg and kicked the sword's handle as if he was trying to break down a door.

The glowstone blade shattered, splitting the sword in two, half of the blade remaining buried in the creature, the other half flying through the air.

Aric dashed away, picking up the broken sword, and raced out of the frozen crypt.

Sohtyr caught him from the corner of his eye and smirked. Then he realized what Aric was carrying in his hand.

"What do you think you're going to do with that?" the dark Mage mocked.

Aric, however, never replied. Two statues came at him and were instantly turned to ice. A green light flashed and Aric rolled, dodging the bolt of energy. The magical attack hit two of the statues pursuing Aric instead. The stone warriors lost their upper torsos, green fire melting and consuming them.

The Archon cursed, and Aric caught a glimpse of his furious eyes. Green sparks flew around the mage's hand as another of his energy attacks came. Aric tried to speed up even further. He swung the magic sword back, readying the final blow, but he wasn't fast enough.

A flare shot from the mage's hands. Aric barely even saw it, but he did feel it. It was like being hit in the chest with a log. He was knocked to the floor, all air abandoning his lungs.

Gasping, Aric tried to spring back up. He had to kill Sohtyr, even if it was the last thing he did. But there was no pain, so he looked at where he had been hit, and instead of a gaping, smoldering hole, he found the glowstone shards of his armor plate, intact and gleaming furiously. His cuirass had absorbed the energy attack.

"What the –" Sohtyr mumbled. He opened his mouth to say something else, but whatever it was would never be known as Aric buried the magical blade in his throat, turning the Archon into an ice sculpture.

Sohtyr's spell immediately broke, and Eliran fell to the floor at the same time that every statue stiffened again.

Aric stepped back from the frozen Sohtyr, looking down at his shimmering armor again.

"Thank you, Dad," he said to himself, gasping.

"You did it!" Eliran said, elated. "You killed the bastard!"

Leth poked at one of the statues surrounding him. The stone warrior lost its precarious balance and fell, smashing an arm.

"There was no need," Leth said. "We had it under control, you know?"

Aric chuckled while Clea shot Leth a stare.

"What? Still hate my cheekiness?" Leth asked her.

Instead of replying, she wrapped her arms around his neck and kissed him.

Aric expected to feel something akin to a punch in the gut. Surprisingly, though, he didn't. Instead, he remembered his cat.

"Geric!" he heard himself say out loud.

The great hall had turned into a mess of rubble, fallen weaponry, and severed body parts of the statues. Aric found the desert lynx curled in a shadowy corner and placed a soft hand on his warm fur.

"Hey, buddy," Aric said, scratching behind Geric's ear.

Blood was dripping from his flank and one of his paws looked burned, but he was alive.

"Is he all right?" Clea asked, stepping next to Aric.

"He'll live," Aric said, petting Geric's head.

"Saved our skins," Leth noted, joining them. "Wasn't he supposed to be a coward?"

"Nah!" Aric replied, hugging Geric. "Who's my brave cat?"

That was when a crowd broke into the hall, their steps echoing everywhere.

"What happened?" a voice called. "Are you guys all right?" It was Trissa. The rest of the company was behind her, looking thoroughly impressed by the chaos around them.

"Ava's mercy! What happened here?" Tharius asked.

"Is that the bad guy?" Dothea probed, pointing at the frozen mage.

"Why did you have to smash all the statues?" Orisius questioned.

Aric, Leth, and Clea exchanged a look. Where to begin?

"It's…a long story," Clea ended up saying.

"You're bleeding," Lyra said, rushing to her.

"It's fine," Clea assured her, but she still flinched when Lyra touched her clothes. "What about you guys?" Clea asked. "What happened to the dragon?"

"It just…went away," Tharius replied with a shrug.

"It was weird," Dothea added. "One moment it was on us like a famished dog after a lamb chop, then the next it just ignored us and left."

"I need to clean these wounds," Lyra said, taking her satchel off her shoulder.

"They're fine," Aric argued, standing up from where Geric was laying down. "Take care of my cat first."

"What?!" Clea and Leth asked in unison.

Aric failed to conceal a wicked smile. "I mean it, Lyra," he said. "Treat the cat." He turned and walked over to Eliran as Leth and Clea grudgingly gave Lyra permission to check on Geric.

The sorceress was still lying on the ground where she had fallen. She looked like she wanted to just fall asleep right then and there.

"Are you hurt?" Aric asked.

"I'm fine," Eliran replied, sitting up. "Just exhausted beyond words. You?"

Aric looked down on his cuirass. "Surprisingly, I'm fine," he said.

"That's not just a pretty thing you got there," Eliran told him. "That's for sure. It must be very old, too. It has been a very long time since non-magical soldiers had to worry about mages."

"Family heirloom," Aric explained. He looked at Sohtyr's ice statue beside them. "So, he kidnapped you at Lamash?"

Eliran sighed. "While you guys fought his dragon and I waited for him to strike, I had this brilliant idea. If I could destroy whatever it was he had come to take, his plan would be no more. So I tried to tear down the wall again. And again. And *again.* Took the beating of a lifetime. Even my combat tutor would have felt sorry for me. But I did it. I managed to blast that damned glowstone lock to pieces. Bruises aside, I felt really proud. So you can imagine how anticlimactic it was to find out what the fuss was all about."

Aric frowned, curious. "What *was* it all about?"

"A chant," Eliran replied. "Ten pages' worth of a stupid song in some weird, forgotten Akhami dialect. That's what the geniuses of the Academy decided to lock that place with." She waved a hand toward the great steel gates behind Aric. She sighed. "Then I got just as stupid and arrogant as them."

"You memorized it?" Aric guessed.

Eliran confirmed with a nod. "Before destroying the parchment, yes. There's this neat little spell, the favorite of every student of the Academy. The only way to pass fifth-level Visions and Prophecies, if you ask me. Anyway, I never thought Sohtyr would be able to get it from me. After all, mind spells are supposed to be my strong point." She shook her head in disapproval. "The pieces of parchment were still burning in my hands when he walked into the library, and he was pretty quick to realize what I had done. I still think I would have been able to resist him if I hadn't spent so much power cracking the glowstone lock, but under those circumstances, I was an idiot."

"Are all mages that arrogant?" Aric asked, smiling.

"You'd be surprised, but most of us are actually kind of wimpy."

Aric laughed. "I'm sure you're the exception," he said.

"'Exceptional' *does* suit me," Eliran said with a smile. "Thank you," she added after a small pause, "for trusting me. And also for being smarter than me. Breaking the sword in half was pretty damn genius."

Aric bowed his head, faking humility. "You can always count on me to wreck your rare, magical artifacts, my lady."

Eliran chuckled.

"So, what now?" Aric asked.

"Well, first we put mister snowman here with his buddy over there." She gestured toward the frozen god beyond the gates. "Then I'll close the gate and report to my bosses."

"Are they all as bad as Persea?" Aric asked.

"No," Eliran replied, "but that's not saying much." Aric chuckled and helped Eliran back to her feet. "What about you?" she asked.

"Me?" Aric looked across the hall. His Hunters were laughing at Tharius's impression of a dragon as he narrated their pursuit across the valley. "I'm going back home." He turned back to face Eliran. "I still need to finish my training."

CHAPTER 23

The Escape

Fadan had not been taken with the other prisoners to the lower decks. Instead, the Paladin commander, a tall man as thin as a needle, had ordered the prince be taken to his own quarters within the forecastle of the ship. It was a wide, almost luxurious cabin, with finely sculpted woodwork covering the furnishings and the ceiling.

Rain pattered ceaselessly on the cabin's large window. Through it Fadan could see the dark mass of water outside, shifting and rolling as if a god were playing with the world, creating mountains only to quickly turn them into bottomless chasms. Aboard this larger vessel, however, the ocean's turbulence felt somewhat less violent. It still forced the prince to hold on to something every once in a while, but that was only because he couldn't bring himself to sit down.

The Paladins had taken his sword but otherwise had not restrained him. Most importantly, they had not syphoned him. Which meant his father knew he was collaborating with the rebels, but not that he was a mage. It was beyond puzzling.

Whoever the mole was, he or she had known about both the rescue and Fadan's involvement, but not his abilities. That ruled out everyone he had travelled with, as well as his mother's spy. The problem was: that was it. No one else knew.

There was a knock on the door. The Paladin commander stepped in.

"Your Majesty," the man said with a small bow. "I believe we have not been introduced. I am Commander Therian. Third Inquisitor of the Augustan Paladin Cadre. I trust you are comfortable?"

Fadan nodded. "What about the men and women who came with me?"

"They've been taken below, to the cargo hold," Therian replied, pacing around Fadan as if inspecting a subordinate. "We were already carrying quite a few rebel prisoners. They'll fit right in."

"What is to happen to the prisoners?" Fadan demanded. "All of them?"

"That is for your father to decide, and for us to obey." Therian paused. "Your Majesty." The words seemed to have left a bitter taste in his mouth. He extended a hand. "I will require the glowstone device. *Now.*"

Fadan returned the Commander's cold stare but did not flinch.

He can't possibly mean the transmogaphon, he thought. *Otherwise, I would be wearing a syphon.*

Slowly, Fadan reached inside his shirt and removed his mother's pendant, taking care not to reveal his other glowstone necklace.

"Thank you," Therian said, collecting the pendant. He turned on his heels and marched to the door, then turned around. "One other thing. I have kept you unshackled, and even offered my own quarters out of respect for your father, but should you give me any trouble at all..." His eyes narrowed on Fadan. "Well, let's say my orders are quite clear. Your survival is *preferred,* but it is not mandatory."

The door slammed behind the commander, leaving behind a dumbstruck Fadan. What did that mean? Had his own father ordered his death?

Thunder drummed outside, and a flash of lightning illuminated the cabin for a moment. It was too late for such thoughts. He had made his decision, and now he had to stick with it. Even though everything seemed lost, he still had one spell card up his sleeve. His magic.

He stepped to the cabin door and peeked through the lock. There were guards standing outside, their shadows moving and their voices loud enough that he could almost understand what they said.

Carefully, Fadan picked up a chair from the commander's desk and fitted its back under the door handle. It felt like a somewhat useless precaution, but it couldn't hurt his chances, either. Then he took a deep breath.

I really hope there's an empty room down there, he thought.

He exhaled, reopening his eyes, and fell through the floor.

Something appeared in his way and Fadan reacted, rematerializing long before reaching the floor. He landed on top of a barrel and it swayed with the impact. The prince flailed at the ceiling, and his feet danced with the barrel until it stabilized.

His heart was pounding, and he tried to steady his breathing, fearing it was too loud. Fadan checked his surroundings. He was in some sort of storeroom. Shafts of light slithered in through the doorframe, revealing the contours of all kinds of containers. That had been phenomenally lucky. Not only was he alone, but he had also not lost his legs by rematerializing inside a barrel. How he had seen it despite the darkness was beyond him.

Carefully, Fadan got down from the barrel and went for the door. It would have helped if he knew the ship's exact layout, but he did know carracks tended to be triple-deckers, which meant there would be a third deck below him, where the prisoners would be held.

Fadan peered through the door lock, checking the other side. He had expected a silent corridor or a cargo hold. Instead, he found a wide, open area that resembled the attic where he'd practiced his magic in Citadel. The problem was, every single Paladin on the ship seemed to be right there. There were dozens of them, spread across the area as if it was their barracks.

Fire take me! Fadan thought.

The good news was that most of them looked to be asleep. The bad news, that plenty of them weren't, and there was no way he would be able to sneak past them.

What in the world was he supposed to do now? Falling through the floor once again was an obvious option if he wanted to go farther down, but he had already risked too much doing it once, and he had no intention of losing a limb or finding himself in the ocean below.

Fadan opened the door a tiny slit to get a better look at the other room. There were barrels, benches, and crates here and there, but they were too far apart from each other. He wouldn't be able to sneak behind them. Magic was his only option.

Then he saw it. A small pile of equipment tucked in a corner. Some of the sleeping Paladins had taken their armor and weapons off. There were swords, cuirasses, crimson Paladin waistbands, even helmets.

It wasn't exactly an invisibility spell, but it was better than the alternative. Maybe…

Of course, he still had to sneak out of the storeroom and get to the equipment.

Unless the equipment comes to me…

Fadan decided to experiment with the waistband. It was just cloth. If something went wrong and it fell to the floor, at least, it would be silent.

Tapping his power, the prince focused on one of the red stripes on top of the equipment pile and willed it to come to him. The waistband came alive, like a snake being charmed by a Cyrinian piper. It was gliding toward Fadan like an eel across a pond when –

CLANG!

The band had had its other end stuck beneath a sword. As Fadan pulled it toward himself, it had tilted the weapon sideways, sending it clattering to the floor.

Fadan shrank back behind the door, holding his breath.

A nearby group of Paladins played cards around an overturned crate. They turned at once, startled, shooting angry looks at the bundle of gear.

"Damn storm," one of them complained. "Who in their right mind sails this far into the Broken Sea, anyway?"

"Just play your card, Nor."

"I'm telling you," Nor said. "That commander is gonna get us all killed."

"Yeah, right. It's not the storm that's losing all your money."

"No. It's the lousy hands you've been dealing me all night."

The group chuckled and scolded as they returned to their game.

Exhaling heavily with relief, Fadan peeked outside again and focused on the crimson waistband lying on the floor. He tugged at it with his mind and it glided, drawing serpentine inches over the floor, until it finally reached the door. Fadan was so happy, he almost giggled.

He brought a sword to him next, followed by a helm, and finally one of the black cuirasses.

The Paladin uniform didn't exactly fit him perfectly, but it would have to do.

All right, Fadan thought. *Now for the hard part.*

He had no idea if those Paladins all knew each other well or not. If this was a single unit that had been together for a while, this was going to be a *very* short-lived plan.

Muttering a silent prayer, Fadan opened the door and strode out, brushing past the card players. One of them glanced at him, but everyone else was far more interested in their game.

Fadan's heart was hammering in his chest as he meandered through the crowd of Paladins. He made sure to keep his head low and avoid any eye contact. There was a staircase leading below, right in the middle of the deck. The prisoners would surely be down there. If Fadan could somehow find a way to release them, they would outnumber the Paladins. It would be a hard fight, but they could take the ship.

There was no one guarding the stairs. No one tried to stop him or asked any questions as he descended into the prisoners' hold. These Paladins had already decided they had won. They were about to have a very bitter surprise.

There was barely any light on the lower deck. A forest of silhouettes littered the floor. At least three hundred people piled on top of each other, their chains clinking with their every move. A couple of Paladins had been stationed down there as well. One of them slept over a wooden crate, snoring loudly. The other tilted his head when he saw Fadan.

The prince glanced over his shoulder, just to make sure no one had followed him, then returned his gaze to the guard.

Right, time to end this.

He saw a hammer hanging on a beam in the ceiling, right behind the Paladin who was staring at him.

"What is it?" the guard asked. "You lost?"

Fadan extended an arm forward and tapped his power. The Paladin must have found it very odd to see him waving his hand around, but before he had time to ask any questions, the hammer smacked across the back of his head and he fell flat on the floor.

There was a commotion among the prisoners, which Fadan quickly shushed before racing to the body of the fallen Paladin. He searched the man's belt and removed a thick bundle of keys held together with a metal ring.

"Your Majesty?" someone whispered.

Despite the darkness, Fadan recognized Lucilla's hairless features and rushed to her. He found the lock on her shackles, trying several keys until one of them finally clicked, and opened the metal bands.

"I knew you wouldn't just give up on us," Shayna whispered. She was sitting next to Lucilla, and Fadan released her next.

"Use your shackles to bind those Paladins," Fadan said lowly, proceeding to the next prisoner. "And find a way to gag them."

Whispers filled the hold as the crowd of prisoners realized what was happening.

"What took you so long?" Sabium asked when it came his time to be released. "Girls chasing you again?"

Fadan chuckled, then looked over at Lucilla and Shayna. "This time, I was the one chasing the girls, Master."

"I suppose my lessons weren't in vain after all," the old mage said, rubbing at his now-free wrists.

Alman was next. He took over for the prince, releasing the remaining prisoners while Fadan joined Lucilla and Shayna near the staircase.

"What now?" Shayna asked. The two guards were bound and gagged at her feet, struggling uselessly.

"Now we take the ship," Fadan replied.

"There's whole lot of Paladins up there, though."

"Most of them are asleep," the prince said. He indicated the Paladin cuirass he was wearing. "And not even armed."

More and more rebels stood, released from their chains, and a sense of excitement began to fill the hold. Then, among the faces, Fadan recognized someone.

The prince knelt and grabbed his arm. "Doric?"

"Let me go!" Doric begged, skidding backward.

Fadan did as requested, standing back up.

"Not everyone in here will be able to fight," Shayna told him.

The prince nodded, studying Doric's vacant eyes. "Will he ever recover?"

"He's stronger than he looks," Shayna replied.

"We should hurry," Lucilla intervened. "Before someone decides to come down here to check on things."

"Agreed," the prince said, stepping forward.

"Your Majesty." Lucilla cut in front of him. "If you don't mind, this is my part. You've certainly done yours."

Fadan smiled. "Of course," he said, taking a step back. "You take this from here."

"All right," Lucilla addressed the entire hold in a low voice. "Everyone ready?"

Nods and whispered yeses filled the deck. Lucilla double-checked the top of the stairs.

"Good. Now, there's more of us than there are of them, so let's give them the wrath of Ava. There may be weapons lying around. Get to them fast, and most importantly, don't linger at the top of the stairs. We can't get bottled up down here. Now" – she took one last look at the upper deck – "let's make these bastards pay. For the rebellion!"

"FOR THE REBELLION!"

Fadan didn't exactly climb the stairs. He was dragged as the crowd flooded upstairs. Lucilla and Shayna led the charge and singlehandedly took down a group of five Paladins, stealing their weapons.

At first, the Paladins were frozen, and those near the stairs fell quickly. Eventually, they overcame their stupor and began to put up a fight. Alarm bells tolled and the screams of battle filled the air.

Fadan saw a sword falling toward Shayna's head. Before he could even think about it, he pushed with his power. The attacker was sent flying away, knocking down two of his comrades with him.

"Clear the staircase!" Lucilla ordered, her sword moving in a blur. "Push to the edges of the deck!"

Fadan obeyed and rushed forward to aid Lucilla's vanguard, but a hand pulled him back.

"No." It was Sabium. "Stand back. Where they can't syphon you. You're not a frontline fighter. You're a spellcaster. Stand back and provide support."

A sort of battle line was starting to form as the Paladin officers managed to organize their defense. Some of the prisoners had found weapons and were giving their jailors the wrath of Ava, but most were forced to make do with whatever they could find – benches, crates, rope, hammers, whatever. It made for a poor fighting force. Luckily, they still had their numbers on their side.

"You wouldn't happen to have a bottle of runium, would you?" the old mage asked Fadan as he scanned the fight.

"No," Fadan replied. His head was whipping around, trying to keep track of what was happening.

"Well, couldn't hurt to ask," Sabium muttered.

The battle was quickly deteriorating into absolute chaos. Bodies were beginning to pile on both sides, and the bloodied and wounded tried to limp or drag themselves to safety, wailing in pain.

Fadan spotted a Paladin going for the kill on one of the rebels and lifted him into the air, smacking him against the ceiling. Not even the helmet kept the man from being knocked out.

"Well done," Sabium said. "There!"

Fadan saw it. A spear headed straight to a rebel's chest. He focused on the weapon, yanked it from the Paladin, and smacked him across the head so hard, the weapon cracked in two.

"Mage!" one of the Paladins yelled. "They got a mage."

The howl of a horn joined the chorus of alarm bells.

"Crap, they know," Fadan said.

"Never mind about that," Sabium told him. "Focus on the fight. There!"

Fadan lifted a barrel into the air and hurled it at a cluster of Paladins, pieces of wood flying everywhere as it smashed its targets.

"Remember," Sabium added, "we're on a floating torch, so no fire."

Fadan nodded in agreement and swung, looking for anyone else needing his assistance. He saw a rebel fighting with a wooden board. The poor man tried to parry a blow from an axe, the board splitting in two. As the attacking Paladin swung his axe back for another attack, Fadan noticed the glint of a blade and focused on it with his power. He hurled it through the air just in time to parry a blow to the rebel's head. Unfortunately, the man was outnumbered, and a dagger from a second Paladin struck him down before the prince could do anything about it.

The casualties were growing, and dozens of men and women now covered the floor, holding bleeding wounds. Their numerical advantage was steadily disappearing.

"Over there! The prince!" Fadan heard someone yell. "Syphon him!"

The prince turned toward the voice. It was Therian, the Paladin commander. He was coming down from the main deck with an entire squad of fresh troops.

Focusing a massive wave of power, Fadan pushed at the entire squad so hard, it would have rocked the ship itself, but none of them so much as flinched. They had syphons protecting them.

"Protect the prince!" Sabium shouted. "Protect your prince!"

Staggering back, Fadan searched for a weapon to defend himself with.

"Fall back!" Lucilla commanded. "Form a line around the prince!"

A couple of rebels managed to break free from their engagements but were immediately intercepted by the commander's men. Everyone else was too busy facing their own deaths to be of any help.

Therian's sword hissed as he unsheathed it. "There will be no more offers of surrender, young prince," he said. "I warned you."

Fadan stumbled over a bucket, scooping it up and hurling it at Therian's head, but the commander simply parried it away with a swing of his blade.

"I agree with you, commander," Lucilla snarled, her face twisted in a scowl. She had finally gotten away from the main fight and was marching toward Therian. "No surrender."

One of the commander's escorts charged at her. She quickly disarmed him with a swirl of her sword. She grabbed the now-unarmed soldier's collar, swung her head back, and head-butted the man in his temple. The Paladin collapsed, but a second one was quickly upon her, followed by a third, and then a fourth.

She was surrounded, her back completely exposed. The Paladins struck at once, and there was no way she could possibly defend all those attacks, when out of nowhere, Shayna was there.

Therian turned, fuming. "Sergeant," he snapped, "kill those two, immediately."

The sergeant barked a "Yes, sir," then signaled the four men still protecting Therian to follow him. The group piled around Lucilla and Shayna.

As they fought back to back, the women's swords looked like lightning, parrying the flood of attacks coming at them from every side. They needed help, and they needed it now. Fadan spun, trying to find anything heavy enough to knock down, at least, some of their attackers.

"Now us, young Prince," Therian said, his sword aiming high. "Your father will be very sad to learn of your tragic death, but at least this way, we can find ourselves a decent heir."

"No!" Sabium commanded, stepping in front of the prince, his head high, his chest thrust forward.

Fadan was going to push him away but never had the chance. Therian smacked the pommel of his sword over the old mage's head, and the poor man fell to the floor.

A stream of blood ran down Sabium's forehead as Fadan quickly kneeled beside him.

"Master?" he called, slapping the mage's cheeks.

Therian stepped forward, his narrowed eyes looming down on him like a hawk's. Fadan felt something turn in his stomach, and a cry of rage stuck in his throat.

There was a sharp scream of pain. Fadan turned to see a Paladin withdrawing his sword from Shayna's chest.

"NO!" he screamed.

Lucilla caught her friend with one arm and kept fighting with the other, but without someone to cover her back, she was hopeless. A Paladin shoved his sword through her back. Then another, and another.

Fadan watched Lucilla fall to her knees without letting go of Shayna or letting out a single yelp. A sea of tears flooded Fadan's eyes and he felt himself choke.

"You've brought your father nothing but shame," Therian said, swinging his sword back. "The throne deserves better."

Fadan did as he had been taught to. He didn't even think. Lunging forward, he grabbed the blade of Therian's sword with his bare hands and tried to yank it from his hands. But the commander was far too experienced for such a desperate maneuver. He stepped back and pulled the sword with him.

The blade slid between Fadan's hands as if they were a sheath. Pain shot up his arms, and he screamed as blood gushed out to cover his palms.

"Time to die, Your Majesty," Therian said. "For Arrel!"

Fadan back stepped until he collided with a wall. A scream stuck in his throat as Therian's sword swung back. But the blow never came.

Fadan realized the sword was frozen in midair and Therian's expression had changed to one of shock. Only then did Fadan see Doric standing behind the Paladin, his hand holding a dagger. The blade was buried deep in Therian's skull.

"This is my wife's son, you worm," Doric spat, then pulled the knife out and allowed the commander's body to fall lifelessly to the floor.

It hadn't taken long for the rest of the Paladins to surrender once their commander fell, not that Doric remembered much after killing the man. He had simply stood there, shaking and staring at the dead body. Even now, he still had a hard time believing he had *actually* killed him. He had barely done anything at all during the rest of the fight. It had taken him forever to even realize there had been a fight going on.

Hagon had been the real hero. He had rallied the rebels when Lucilla had fallen and forced the remaining Paladins to surrender. His actions hadn't just won the day for them; they had also spared even more bloodshed.

Doric knew Hagon despised him. It was no secret between them. Nevertheless, the two of them had shared a cell for the past three months. Had shared the rare scraps of food thrown at the floor of their cell. Had cleaned each other's wounds with dirty rags after their torture sessions.

Yes, Hagon despised him. Or at least he had, once. Doric was no longer sure. It didn't really matter now. They were free again, and Doric had helped. He had *helped*.

The remains of the battle were revolting. The deck, thick with blood, was dark and slippery. Bodies lay everywhere, fallen in impossible positions over the deck or the occasional container. Together with the other rebels, Doric had washed blood from the deck for what had felt like hours while others took care of the dead bodies, preparing them for a proper pyre once they reached the shore.

They had lost fifty-seven people, and almost one hundred others had been wounded. Among the dead were several people Doric knew, including Eirin and Lerica, childhood friends of his, and Alman Larsa, a man who would have been the Duke of Niveh if his parents hadn't refused the emperor's orders during the Purge. He had, apparently, been the one who had brought the prince into the rebellion.

When the cleaning was finally done and Doric had climbed up to the main deck, the storm was already behind them. An endless blue sky and a cold, salty breeze greeted him. It was the most beautiful thing he had ever seen. Well, after Cassia, of course.

He spotted the prince in the forecastle, staring into the distance with his arms folded over his chest, bandages wrapped around his hands.

"Your Majesty," Doric greeted.

Fadan seemed to pull himself from the depths of his thoughts and turned to face him. "Doric," he said. "I'm…happy that you're okay. And thankful, of course. You saved my life. All our lives, actually."

"I did very little."

Fadan nodded absently. "You did plenty, believe me."

"Are you all right?" Doric asked. "I heard you lost some friends today."

"Yes," the prince replied, turning back to face the ocean. "I'm fine."

"Please, forgive me the question but…does your mother know where you are?"

"She does. You may be pleased to know that, by now, she has probably left Augusta."

That caught Doric by surprise. "I'm sorry, what?"

Fadan smiled. "My mother has escaped the Citadel. Or at least, I hope she did. I can't be sure, but she has a very competent spy helping her."

Doric mumbled something unintelligible, and before he could actually formulate a sentence, Hagon stepped up to him.

"Doric," Hagon said. "Would you mind introducing us?"

"Uh… Yes, of course. Your Majesty, this is —"

"Lord Hagon Sefra, I know," Fadan interrupted. "Sabium has told me about you. You are my mother's cousin."

"That's right," Hagon said with a weak smile.

"How come we've never met?"

Hagon looked down, then back up. "Me and…my wife, Shayna…" He cleared his throat. "We, uh…have been with the rebellion for a very long time."

Fadan swallowed. "I'm so sorry for your loss."

Hagon nodded, and there was a small pause before he said, "I came to inform you. As the highest-ranking member of the rebellion here, I have assumed command of the ship."

"Very well," Fadan said.

"We are headed to Ragara," Hagon continued. "We can't risk taking you back to Augusta, but we can drop you near Capra if you so desire. I can spare a small escort, of course."

"That won't be necessary," Fadan replied. "I'm not going back to Augusta. Tell me something, Lord Hagon. Where would one find the rebellion's leadership?"

Hagon and Doric exchanged a look.

"Would you…like me to take you to them?" Hagon asked, excitement seeping into his voice. "Because I can tell you for a fact that they would be thrilled to have you join."

"I'm the prince, Lord Hagon," Fadan replied, turning his gaze back to the sea. "I'm not joining any rebellion. The rebellion, however, might be interested in joining me."

EPILOGUE

The Gathering Storm

Cassia had been slipping in and out of sleep, woken occasionally by the constant rattle of the carriage. When it stopped, she immediately sprang up in alarm. "What's wrong?" she asked.

Without a word, Venia stuck her head out the window. "Why are we stopping?" she called out.

"We need to rest the horses," the guard captain replied. "We're far enough from the capital."

Venia's head returned inside and gave Cassia a questioning look.

"He's right," Cassia said. "We can't just keep on going without rest."

"I'm pretty sure we could," Venia argued lightly, "but you're the boss."

The two of them stepped out of the carriage. Forest surrounded them, golden sunlight streaming between the swaying branches. They had been following an ancillary Imperial road, that much was obvious, but she wasn't entirely sure where they were, exactly.

With unsurprising efficiency, the Legionary escort dismounted, tied their horses, then pulled the carriage off the road.

It had been so long since Cassia had felt this way. So...*light.* There was an intoxicating, earthy smell coming from the damp forest floor, and it called to her in invitation. Cassia ambled around, her fingers running through the moss patches on the tree trunks. Venia followed.

"Your Majesty?" the captain called.

Cassia swung around. "Am I?" she asked. "Still the empress, I mean."

"Of course," the man replied. "An Imperial marriage is not easily broken."

"I suppose. Anyway, we haven't even been introduced. Might I know your name?"

The captain tapped a fist to his heart. "Darian, Your Majesty." He wasn't particularly well built for a Legionary, but his chiseled jaw would have made most of the statues in Augusta jealous.

"I like that name," Cassia said. "Tell me, Captain Darian, where are we headed?"

"I was coming to ask the same."

"You don't have a plan?" Venia asked. "So…what, we've been going in some random direction?"

"Easy, Venia," Cassia soothed. "The captain is on our side."

The spy wasn't so sure. "Is he? How much gold do you have? What happens when you can't afford his soldiers' wages?"

"Maintaining unit cohesion is my responsibility," Darian replied in Cassia's stead. "If the empress cannot afford the maniple's pay, I will procure it."

"*Procure it?*" Venia asked.

"I think he means steal it," Cassia explained.

Venia sent Cassia a bored look. "Yes, thanks for clarifying that to the closest thing to a thief here."

"Watch your tongue!" Darian warned, his hand going to the hilt of his sword.

Venia was going to bark something back, but Cassia stopped her with a gesture. "Will you both calm down!"

"This woman cannot speak to you this way, Your Majesty," Darian objected.

"She…" Cassia took a deep breath. "Just ignore the way she speaks to me, all right? Now, can we focus on the matter at hand, please?"

Venia and Darian shared a bitter glance, but both gave up on the argument.

"Our priority was to put as much distance as possible between us and the capital," Darian continued. "We can plan our next move calmly now."

"Which makes perfect sense," Cassia told Venia. The spy rolled her eyes.

"One possible destination could be the empress's home in Fausta, but that will likely be where the emperor will look for us first."

"Yes, that would be a bad idea," Cassia said. "What I want is to find the rebellion. They can keep us hidden, and they can lead me to Fadan."

Venia sent Darian a smile. "How would you like to join the rebellion, Captain?" she teased.

"The military does not hold political opinions," Darian replied coolly. "It's something spies could do well to learn."

Venia snorted but did not reply.

"So, how do we contact the rebellion?" Cassia asked. "Any ideas?"

"I infiltrated a rebellion cell years ago," Venia offered, "but those people were arrested shortly before I entered your service." She shrugged. "Does speak to my credit, though."

"Very helpful. What about you, Captain?"

"I'm afraid this sort of thing is not my field of expertise," Darian admitted. "I have nothing."

"Well," Cassia sighed, "there is one person… If she's not with the rebels, then no one is. The Archduchess of Pharyzah."

The others considered that for a moment.

"We can be in Pharyzah in a week at most," Darian offered.

Venia crossed her arms thoughtfully. "I suppose that's as good an idea as any. You know this woman well? Can we trust her?"

Cassia shrugged. "Not very well, no. But if she is with the rebellion, we should be fine."

There were no objections from any of the others.

"All right, then," Cassia said. "We have ourselves a plan."

Darian gave her a curt nod. "Very well. I will inform the men. Meanwhile, you should make yourselves comfortable. Unfortunately, we can't risk entering city centers, so finding inns will be hard. I expect we'll be sleeping by the side of the road most of the time."

He gave a salute, turned on his heel, and left under Venia's suspicious stare.

"Oh, relax, Venia," Cassia told her. "If Intila chose him, it's because he can be trusted. Besides, we're free." She opened her arms and took a deep breath. "When was the last you just enjoyed the wonderful forest air?"

"Yeah, yeah," Venia reluctantly unfurled her arms. "We'll see how wonderful you feel after sleeping in that carriage for a week."

This was three times as far south as Aric had ever been. The sun was so mercilessly hot that everyone had to keep their heads wrapped in white turbans at all time so it wouldn't cook their skins. Horses wouldn't have survived the journey, and walking this far south would have been torture, so the company and the other senior Hunters had ridden atop saddled camels. Everyone except for Prion, of course.

It hadn't taken long for the deserter to be caught, mostly because of his own stupidity. Paladins had arrested him trying to sell glowstone shards stolen from Lamash, in the streets of Radir. The Paladins hadn't had too much of a hard time figuring out he was a conscript on the run. The sentence, of course, had been the Pilgrimage.

Prion had begged for mercy for the entire first day and the better part of the second morning. But being dragged across the Mahar for miles and miles eventually took its toll, and he became quieter and quieter. Now he only mumbled from time to time, pleading to rest or for some water.

By order of Grand-Master Sylene, everyone ignored Prion's pleas, but every now and then, one of the senior Hunters gave him something to drink. Aric felt like it was a cruel joke.

"This is sadistic," Clea told Aric as they crossed a dune crest. "It's inhumane."

Aric agreed. No matter how much he disliked Prion, he surely didn't deserve this. No one did.

Without a word to Clea, Aric spurred his camel forward and galloped along the line of over fifty Hunters until he stopped next to Sylene.

"Grand-Master," he greeted. "A word, if I may?"

Sylene nodded.

"This…" Aric waved toward the back of the caravan, where Prion was being dragged on foot behind a camel. "Is this really necessary?"

"I think you already know the answer to that, Captain," Sylene replied.

"This is needless cruelty. It would be more humane to just kill him."

Sylene shot him a glare. "This isn't just an execution, Captain. That conscript abandoned his company, his fellow Guildsmen. Is that the kind of person you want by your side when you enter a dragon's cave? Someone willing to turn tail and leave you? The Pilgrimage is a *symbol*. You all belong to the desert now, and you do not turn your back on the Mahar."

Aric gritted his teeth in frustration. How could anyone agree with this? Even if Prion was well fed and hydrated, leaving him all by himself so far south in the desert was certain death. They weren't teaching Prion a lesson. They were needlessly prolonging a miserable death.

"Grand-Master, I must insist —"

"No, you will not," Sylene interrupted sharply. Aric obeyed and simply looked away. "Good. Now, there's something I would like to tell you. I received a visit from a mage."

Aric perked up. "Eliran?"

The Grand-Master shook her head. "It was a man. An old man."

"And you can be sure it wasn't an Archon?"

"It was a mage," Sylene replied flatly.

"What did he want?"

"To offer the Academy's gratitude. They are apparently in our debt."

"Are we sure that's a good thing?" Aric asked.

Sylene smiled. "He also informed me the Frostbound's security has been...*enhanced*. Whatever that means. I can't say I'm comfortable knowing that creature is sleeping beneath my desert, but..." She shook her head. "What can I do about it?"

"Keep the place under close watch?" Aric suggested.

"Yes, of course. Which reminds me. We will be starting a new class as soon as your Company graduates."

"You have new recruits?"

Sylene nodded. "Ten conscripts, and two Cyrinian Honor Guards. They couldn't have arrived at a better time. Every company in the roster needs reinforcements."

Aric looked over his shoulder at Prion. "Including mine. After today."

"And I will be sure you get first pick of the new batch," Sylene replied.

Aric sighed. "Thank you, Grand-Master," he said flatly. "By your leave."

Kicking his camel's haunches, Aric turned around and trotted back to the rear, settling his mount next to Dothea's. He glanced at Prion staggering at the end of the column. His lips were cracked in a dozen places, and gruesome blisters littered his face.

Aric checked around him, making sure no one was listening, then whispered to Dothea.

"Find a way to disappear without anyone noticing. When Prion is released, wait for the caravan to get far enough away from him, then kill the poor bastard."

Dothea nodded. "Yes, Captain."

What could possibly be so urgent that it couldn't wait until tomorrow? After spending months and months in that dreadful desert and nearly getting herself killed, Eliran was sure she deserved, at the very least, a bath. Sometimes, Eliran was sure Persea spent more time coming up with ways to make her life miserable than actually leading what was left of the Academy.

She knocked on the tall double door of her mistress's study and waited. From another door down the corridor, a mage left his own study, gave her a polite nod, and left toward the stairwell at the other end of the hall. Persea's door, however, remained closed.

Eliran fumed.

Now she's just making fun of me, she thought.

Not that it was surprising. Eliran and Persea's dance had begun years earlier, shortly after the Purge. For fear that the facility's secret underground location would fall into the wrong hands, only a few of the Purge's survivors had been directed to Ragara. Yet even among those few, only a handful ever caught Persea's attention. Eliran had been one of them.

Being handpicked by Arch-Mage Persea meant one became something of a legend. Nobody knew exactly why some students were chosen and others not, but everyone just assumed it was a sign of being somehow gifted.

The elite group couldn't have been more disparate. About the only thing they shared was their opinion of the woman. For the first few years, none of them had had any clue about the purpose of Persea's private little class. Most thought there was nothing more to it than Persea wanting to personally oversee the training of the best students of the Academy. Eliran had always known better, but nothing could have prepared her for the day when she found out. They were to become Persea's assassination squad. "Archon Hunters," as the Arch-Mage herself called them.

For some inscrutable reason, no one had tried to quit the group after finding out their purpose. Eliran suspected the chance to be taught by Persea was simply considered too valuable for any of them to pass up. Her power was, after all, awe-inspiring.

Sometimes it was hard for Eliran to believe her mistress could actually do those things. Not to mention how effortless she always made everything look. No matter how much Eliran resented her mistress, there was no doubt in her mind that she wouldn't have become half the mage she was without those private lessons.

For Persea, failure was always on purpose. She never cared how hard you were trying. Never gave you any credit for it. If you failed, it was because you wanted to, and that meant you were worthless. She never used physical pain. She didn't need to. Her method focused on torturing the spirit. A gruesome approach that had broken a handful of Eliran's fellow apprentices, and something Persea had always been all too comfortable with.

The hairs on the back of Eliran's head prickled and the double door swung silently open. On the other side, framed by two statues of Ava, each holding a torch, Persea sat at her desk, scribbling. She didn't even look up. She simply commanded, "Come in."

With a sigh, Eliran walked inside and sat across from her mistress, the study's door magically closing behind her.

The Arch-Mage continued scribbling, saying nothing. The study was packed full of books and parchment rolls, some carefully lining book cases, others piled on top of each other on the floor. The pungent smell of mist-flower tea floated about the air, a smell Eliran had learned to associate with her mistress.

When was the last time you slept, old woman? she wondered.

Eliran tapped her fingers anxiously on the arm of her chair. "You misspelled a word there," she eventually said.

"Don't be childish," Persea replied without stopping. "I need to finish this."

Eliran rolled her eyes. "Then it was a good thing that you called me right away. It's not like I just returned from the other end of the Empire and really needed to rest."

"I will be even busier later," Persea explained, finally finishing her writing and setting her quill down. "Besides, you can rest when we're finished."

"I'll believe it when it happens."

Persea shook her head in disapproval. "When will you grow up, Eliran?"

"That's a great question, mistress," Eliran replied. "But I have a better one. Try this instead. 'I'm so sorry I nearly got you killed, Eliran. How are you? I hope you at least had a pleasant journey north.'"

"Oh, please. You think I wouldn't know by now if you weren't fine? You had a rough mission. So what? You think you're the only one?"

"Why did call me here, mistress? I look like a scarecrow, and I feel like a herd of cows just trampled all over me. Will you do me the courtesy of getting this over with?"

"Gladly," Persea replied, reaching into one of her desk's drawers. She picked up a heavy-looking object and set it on the table.

Eliran leaned forward. It was wrapped in purple silk, and Persea delicately peeled the cloth away, revealing an exquisite dagger. It was as beautiful as it was menacing. The golden handle was shaped like a dragon, with its wings serving as the guard. Instead of one, it had two parallel blades. Glowstone shards sparkled along its entire length.

"What is it?" Eliran asked, unable to mask her curiosity.

"Your next job."

"Oh, goddess!" Eliran threw her arms in the air. "You are unbelievable!"

Persea raised a hand, begging for silence. "If — and only if — you want it," she said. "This one is optional."

Eliran frowned suspiciously.

"Whoever is going to do this is going to need to be extremely motivated," Persea continued. "If you don't want to do it, then *I* don't want you to do it either."

This definitely did not sound right. Since when did what *she* wanted matter to Persea?

"You still haven't told me what it is," Eliran reminded her.

"A Fyrian ceremonial dagger."

"Well, it definitely looks like one. What's so special about it?"

The Arch-Mage extended an arm toward the dagger. "Touch it."

Something in the way Persea said that made Eliran think this would be a bad idea, but she reached out anyway, albeit hesitantly. Her fingers brushed against the handle, and she immediately snatched them back as a jolt of pain shot through her arm.

"Fire take this!" Eliran cursed.

Persea chuckled. "Quite a kick, isn't it?"

"Quite," Eliran echoed bitterly.

"Well, go on. Grab it properly."

Eliran was pretty sure this was going to hurt like crazy, but now she really wanted to find out what that thing was. Trying not to think too much about it, she grabbed the dagger firmly in her hand.

The pain instantly snapped through her whole body, as if she were being bathed in molten lava. The world went black, then bright explosions flashed all around her.

A large hall. A circle of hooded figures chanting incoherently. A dragon roaring. A woman screaming. The dagger in her hand. She prayed something in a foreign language. She stabbed something or someone. Blood ran everywhere.

The pain became too much to bear, and with a jump backward, she forced herself to drop the dagger. Persea's study reappeared. She was breathing heavily, and her heart was pounding. She realized she was standing, her chair having tumbled to the floor beside her.

"What in the mother's name just happened?" Eliran asked.

"Take a guess," Persea prompted.

"It felt like...a memory?"

The Arch-Mage smiled widely. "Exactly! Her name is Astoreth, and she is a Head Archon, just like Sohtyr."

"A Head Archon? How good of a memory are we talking about?"

"It's fragmented," Persea replied, "but surprisingly long. This Astoreth must have used the dagger extensively and performed some intense magic with it for her to imprint this strongly on it."

"How did you get it?"

Persea turned sideways, looking away from Eliran. "Apodyon and Ursula were following a lead near Aparanta. I knew it was someone big, but just like with you, I couldn't know it was a Head Archon. This Astoreth killed Apodyon, but Ursula made it out alive." She stepped over to the dagger and picked it up from the floor using the purple silk cloth. "And not empty-handed."

"Apodyon is dead?"

"Yes, but we shall make it count," Persea replied. "Eliran, this memory has dozens of names, locations, everything."

"And what exactly do you want me to do with it?"

"I want you to take it," the Arch-Mage replied, "and I want you to hunt down every last one of these Head Archons."

"You're kidding me?" Eliran said. "You want *me* to single-handedly defeat the entire Circle?"

"You're the only one who's ever killed a Head Archon. You know their magic, what they're capable of."

"I told you, the *Hunter* killed Sohtyr, not me. This is a job for someone like you, an Arch-Mage."

"And I would do it if I wasn't certain both the Academy and the rebellion would unravel if I left them for a single moment. This is too much of an opportunity to ignore. We can take this war to them, Eliran." Persea laid the dagger on the desk and held Eliran's arms. "You are much more powerful than you imagine. If only you allowed yourself to reach your full potential —"

"There she is," Eliran said, yanking her arms from Persea's grasp. "The old tutor, back for some more derision."

The Arch-Mage rolled her eyes, sighing in disappointment. She turned away from her student and walked back to her seat. "Anyway, I told you it was your decision. Do you want the mission or not?"

Eliran gave her mistress a cold stare. "I will not be leaving immediately. I want some days to rest."

"Obviously."

"I want to do this my way. *And* I'll need a bigger stipend."

"You'll have it."

Eliran stared at the Fyrian dagger. "Very well, then," she said, grabbing the weapon.

The two of them exchanged a silent look, and Eliran turned away, opening the study's door with a wave of her arm.

"Be careful," Persea said to her back, then called, "Eliran!"

The young sorceress stopped at the study's threshold and looked back.

"I want regular reports," Persea said. "Don't you dare disappear for weeks like you did in the desert."

⌣⌐

Vigild's steps echoed through the marble corridor. Golden streams of light fell obliquely from the tall windows. As he reached the end of the hall, two Legionaries standing outside the emperor's study saluted him with closed fists on their chests.

"His Majesty has sent for me?" Vigild asked.

"He has, Your Excellency," one of the soldiers replied. "Grave news, it seems."

The chancellor frowned. "The nature of the news His Majesty receives is none of your concern, soldier."

The Legionary's eyes glared back at him, and he straightened up even more. "A thousand apologies, Excellency."

"Open up."

Averting his gaze from the chancellor's eyes, the Legionary obeyed, and Vigild stepped inside.

Tarsus was alone at his dragon-bone desk, a piece of parchment trembling in his hands. Red-rimmed eyes met Vigild's, and the chancellor knew immediately what had happened.

"They... They left me," Tarsus mumbled. "Vigild, my son and my wife...left me."

Vigild sighed inwardly. "Now, Your Majesty, we mustn't jump to any conclusions."

"Fadan has joined the rebellion, Vigild!" Tarsus snapped, the parchment shaking in his hand. "Our agents swear it." His eyes wandered. "My own son wishes to overthrow me. And my wife has fled our home." He dropped the report and wrapped his hands around his head. "Oh, goddess... What have I done?"

Vigild perked up. "Your Majesty," he said softly. "You have done nothing."

"I drove them away." Tarsus's pale features twisted in despair, and his eyes seemed to sink even deeper into their sockets. "I made them hate me."

Oh, fire keep us! Vigild thought. He didn't have time for this silliness.

The chancellor strode to the emperor and struck a finger on the man's forehead, pushing and pinning him to the back of his chair. Tarsus's body jerked and his mouth opened wide, a scream trapped in his throat.

"The rebels have brainwashed your son," Vigild said.

The emperor's expression became one of rage, and he clenched his fists. "The lying scum!"

"The nobility is full of traitors." Vigild pressed his finger even harder against Tarsus's forehead. "They have corrupted your son and wife with treachery."

"How dare they?" Tarsus slammed a fist against the table, the corners of his mouth twitching in anger.

"They seek to take the throne from you." The chancellor released the emperor, panting from the effort.

There was a moment of silence as Tarsus seemed to reacquaint himself with where he was. "Vigild?" he said, noticing his chancellor beside him. "Vigild, I must fight these rebels with all I have. No matter the cost. They cannot get the throne!"

"You have sacrificed much, Your Majesty," the chancellor replied, laying a sympathetic hand on the emperor's shoulder. "But I shall do my best to alleviate your burdens."

"Thank you, Vigild," Tarsus said, slumping forward. "I am so...so tired."

Behind the emperor, Vigild smiled. *That's better,* he thought, walking toward a window. Outside, Augusta sprawled toward the horizon.

"Do not worry, Your Majesty. It will all be over soon."

Find out more about the world of Arkhemia at
www.vrcardoso.com

Made in the USA
Las Vegas, NV
29 May 2023

72654176R00282